# Dating-*ish*

## by PENNY REID
www.pennyreid.ninja/newsletter

Caped Publishing

Made in the United States of America

Print Edition: May 2017
Print ISBN: 978-1-942874-23-2

# DEDICATION

To my fellow Asimov readers, who know that the first law of robotics should be the first law of humanity.

# CHAPTER 1

**DeepMind**

*A neural network that learns in a fashion similar to that of humans and may be able to access an external memory like a conventional Turing machine, resulting in a computer that mimics the short-term memory of the human brain.*

–Source: Google's Artificial Intelligence Program

I WAS SWEATING.

"Is this seat taken?"

My head whipped up from the book I wasn't actually reading to look at the café employee. Her hands rested on the only other chair at my table and she gazed at me with an affable, expectant smile.

"It's taken," I shrieked. Like a lunatic.

But, man, *I need that chair!*

She lifted her hands, recoiling as though the metal singed her skin, and gave me a wide-eyed stare. My attention moved behind her and I spotted the nearby table of university students, obviously hunting for an extra seat.

"Sorry. I didn't mean to—" I shook my head, gathering a deep breath and telling myself to calm down. "I'm meeting someone and he'll be here soon. I'm a little early."

"Okay, no problem." She affixed a polite smile and moved to another table, making the same enquiry.

Longingly, I gazed at the booth by the window. Every café or coffee shop has that *one* coveted table, where two to four friends can gather and spend an afternoon not being overheard while sharing ideas and stories. Or where a person can go to work—impervious to the room and its distractions—headphones on, laptop open, losing count of how many lattes and croissants were consumed over an eight-hour day.

I did not have that table. I had a mediocre table, set in the center of the coffee shop, surrounded by other mediocre tables.

But I would not let my mediocre table get me down.

My attention flickered to the door of the café, then to the clock above it. He wasn't late. Yet.

Squirming, wishing I'd worn anything other than this sweater dress, my eyes returned to the book on my lap.

*Pay no attention to me, nothing to see here. I'm just perspiring, wearing a sweater dress in May, and* not *reading while waiting for my perfect match.*

Derek Simmons. Six foot three with a well-maintained beard, great smile, gray eyes, tan complexion, and short hair. He didn't work out regularly—which was great, because that meant he didn't expect me to work out either—but enjoyed some outdoorsy activities. Engineer. Thirty-nine. Divorced, two kids.

Derek and I were a perfect match. That's what FindUrPartner.com indicated last Thursday.

*You have a perfect match.* The notification alerted me as soon as I signed in. The irony was, I'd been logging in to suspend my account. After almost two years of Internet dating debacles and equally disappointing men, I was ready for a break. But then I'd received the perfect match message. Therefore, I did what any normal person would do.

I Internet stalked him.

Loves: cooking, hiking, camping, eighties music, film noir. Reads: *GQ Magazine, The Economist, Politico.* TV shows: *The Walking Dead, Daredevil,* and *Project Runway.*

*. . . cooking, film noir, The Economist, and Project Runway?*

YES! A man unicorn.

Compelled by his uni-horn, I emailed him.

*Hi Derek,*

*I hope you are well. According to this website, we're a perfect match. This has never happened to me before, so I thought I'd reach out and say hi. Let me know if you'd like to meet up for coffee sometime. I work downtown near the Loop and am free next Monday afternoon.*

*Best, Marie*

The next morning, I was alerted that he'd looked at my profile, and I read his response with bated breath.

*Hi Marie,*

*Thanks so much for your note.*

*Next Monday works for me. I'm near the university. You name the place and I'll be there.*

*-Derek*

I loved his response.

Direct. To the point. Polite. No detour into unnecessary topics. No typos.

To say my hopes were high would be a gross understatement. My hopes had reached *astronomical*. Since our exchange of emails, I'd tried to curtail those blasted hopes to no avail. I couldn't help my hopes.

*Don't run away from me, hopes! I can't move that fast in these heels and we're in this together.*

But they did run away, hopping onto a spaceship—likely one of those SpaceX crafts that keeps infuriating Elon Musk by blowing up—leaving me on the ground, waving frantically, which was probably compounding my sweating problem.

Arm waving at one's high hopes while wearing a sweater dress in May is a workout.

*But he's perfect!*

This squealing nugget of optimism originated from some dark corner in my brain. Once I found the owner of this voice inside my head, I was going to . . . I didn't honestly know. On the one hand, I didn't want to be bitter and jaded, trading optimism for pessimism.

Or worse, nihilism. Nihilism was the worst. And the perpetuators of it had no imagination when it came to accessorizing. All black, all the time? No, thank you.

I checked the clock over the entrance for maybe the hundredth time just as a man walked through the door. My heart did an odd prickling thing, but then the sensation eased. He wasn't Derek. The man was too short and had no beard. And he was clearly younger than thirty-nine, more like late twenties.

With another sigh, I returned my attention to the book in my lap. I didn't even know the title, having grabbed it from the bookstore across the street in a fit of pre-date-overthinking-induced insanity. I didn't want to wait for him by scrolling through messages on my phone. I felt like phone-scrolling was too prosaic. And I didn't want to be one of those people who just stared forward or people-watched while waiting, even though I loved to people watch. And I didn't—

"You're Marie."

I glanced up, blinking at the man standing in front of my table, the man who I'd just dismissed as being *not-Derek*. He wasn't looking at me. Rather, his gaze was on the open pages of my book.

"Yes?"

His eyes quickly darted to mine and then away as he removed his coat. "I'm your date."

I frowned because I was surprised. And because I was surprised, it took me a solid five seconds to respond. By then he'd already placed his jacket on the back of his chair.

"Oh! Hi. Hi. Please sit down." I gestured to the seat across from mine and belatedly stood, trying not to feel weird about my smile. I never knew how big to smile during these things. I missed the days when I could just smile naturally and not have to think about it.

Reassessing my date, my eyes flicked over him. He was *definitely not* six foot three. More like six foot even, or a little shorter.

*No big deal. A lot of guys embellish their height on dating sites, except...*

He shaved his beard.

*Sad face :-(*

And again, he looked younger than thirty-nine. And his skin was white, paler than the olive complexion I'd been expecting, which was fine, but different from his picture.

"Derek?" I really was confused by the differences between his photo and his reality.

"Yes. I'm Derek. Derek is my name. That's me." Derek, my date, extended his hand, shook mine with a perfunctory up-down movement, and then claimed the seat I'd offered.

My smile wavered. My hopes crashed to the earth in a giant, burning cluster-comet of disappointment. I braced myself. We hadn't made it past the first minute of awkward and I already knew things weren't going to work out.

Derek was not my perfect match.

We had zero chemistry. No spark when we touched. No shock or magic voodoo juju awesomeness. No nothing.

And no eye contact. He wouldn't even look at me.

Inwardly, I sighed and cringed, wondering if we'd be able to wrap this up quickly so I could run to the drugstore for some tampons before meeting my knitting group for wine, and yarn, and then more wine.

Outwardly, I pressed my lips into a shape I hoped resembled a smile and sat in my chair. My eyes sought the clock over the door. It was only 3:14. My record for a coffee date was twenty minutes. I wondered if I could break it today.

"Did you want anything?" I motioned to the cup in front of me, keeping my voice light. "I grabbed a drink already."

"No," he said, a slight business-like smile affixed to his features. "Let's get started."

"S-started?"

Derek was looking at his watch. He pressed a button. He let his hands drop to his lap. Only then did he lift his eyes to mine.

And then he blinked, his smile slipping infinitesimally, as though the sight of me was unexpected.

I lifted my eyebrows, waiting, because apparently it was time for us to get started. Whatever that meant.

"Hi," he said. His gaze moved over my features, his smile growing hazy, more genuine.

. . . *Huh.*

He had brown eyes. His brown eyes held me momentarily transfixed, and not just because they weren't gray—as he'd listed on his page—but because they were expressive and remarkably attractive.

His hair was also brown, but longer than it had been in his pictures.

Truly, he really did look significantly different than his profile—*surely not just because of the absent beard?* Nevertheless, despite being beardless, his face was handsome: high cheekbones, strong nose, a jaw that was decidedly square. His eyes were remarkably wide and round, but somehow they suited him perfectly, and I decided his eyes were my favorite part of him.

I allowed my smile to mirror his, my gaze dropping momentarily to his very nice lips, which honestly struck me as oddly pouty for a man.

*Okay, let's give him a chance. Even though he misrepresented his height, age, and eye color . . .*

So. Weird.

Who does that?

"Hi," I finally replied, examining him, my reporter spidey-sense tingling.

Derek flinched at my returned greeting, his eyes narrowing, and he frowned.

"You're Marie?" *His* tone was distrustful?

"Yes." I nodded once, slowly, cataloging his clothes. "And you're Derek."

"Of course I'm Derek. Who else would I be?"

"Uh . . ." *Yeeeeeah no. I can't wait to tell Sandra about this guy.*

"Moving on." He shook his head again, as though shaking himself, and frowned at the table. "So, Marie, you're a writer?"

"That's right. And you're an engineer?" I asked, no longer in date mode.

"Your profile said you've had one serious relationship in the past, is this true?" Derek lifted his dark eyes to mine again and this time his expression struck me as carefully neutral.

"Yes." I gave him a pointed look. "Everything on *my* profile is true."

It didn't feel necessary to clarify that though I'd only been in one serious relationship, I'd had relationships in my early twenties, all of which—except my last boyfriend—had been bad and/or unhealthy decisions.

So, yes, technically everything on my profile was true.

*Not like your profile, buddy. Not even your eye color is right.*

He didn't seem to catch my hint. "As a woman in your thirties, what are you most looking for in a companion?"

I flinched, unaccustomed to such severely direct questions right off the bat. Not that I was opposed to directness, just that it wasn't typical on first dates.

In my limited experience with online dating, the order of actions was usually as follows:

1. Both people smile and try not to betray their thoughts as expectations based on photos are either surpassed, met, or disappointed.

2. I shake off my initial impression and try to have an open mind, talk about inconsequential things like movies and the weather.

3. I don't get my hopes up if things are going well.

4. I never commit to seeing him again in order to avoid appearing overeager.

5. I wait three days, and then text. If the text is not returned, forget him and move on.

I'd only sent a text to four guys over the last two years. Three had returned my message. None had lasted longer than the third date, and no one had ever felt right.

"I guess . . ." I cleared my throat, glancing over Derek's shoulder to the busy café behind him, as I attempted to parse my thoughts.

*As a woman in your thirties* was a strange way to frame the question. What did my age have to do with anything?

"So, you would say that you don't know what you want?" He sounded curious.

My gaze cut back to his. "Yes, I know what I want."

"But you don't want to tell me?"

"I don't mind telling you." I studied him for a moment, gathered a deep breath, and spoke the truth. "I'm looking for the right person."

*I'm looking for my perfect match.*

Derek's expression didn't change, and he continued to gaze at me with a patient, watchful expression. But when I didn't continue, he angled his head forward as though to say, *go on.*

"And?"

"And that's it. I'm looking for the right person."

"Ah, okay. And what traits will this right person have? Starting with the most important."

*What?*

"I—"

"And if you could rank each attribute on a ten-point scale of importance—where ten is the most important—that would be very helpful."

Now I openly frowned at him. "You want me to rank personality traits on a ten-point scale, starting with what I find most important?"

"Not just personality traits, physical attributes as well. Or, if you like, you can start with your love dialect."

"My love dialect?"

"Correct. What form of affection is most meaningful to you, and so forth."

We stared at each other. He continued to regard me placidly, with a friendly albeit detached smile. Meanwhile, I was plotting my escape, polite social discourse be damned.

Usually, I didn't agree to meeting face to face unless I'd spoken to the potential date on the phone first, ensuring we had some level of chemistry. But

I'd made an exception for Derek, because he was supposed to be my perfect match.

But clearly the system didn't factor in the degree to which a person is a loon.

*Says the sweating woman who had astronomical—and therefore understandably annihilated—hopes. Look in the mirror, looney bird.*

I was just about to make an excuse when he announced, "We should engage in small talk. How was your day?"

"Pardon me?"

*Nuts. He's completely nuts.*

"Or if you don't wish to discuss your day, we could talk about hobbies," he offered cordially, gesturing to my lap. "Do you read for work or pleasure?"

Distracted by his rapid and bizarre subject change, I responded unthinkingly, "I usually read for fun." I'm sure the look I gave him was one of complete bewilderment.

"Really? Does kidnapping and sexual torture sound like fun to you?"

My mouth fell open and I reared back in my seat.

This guy wasn't a loon, he was completely insane.

I managed to sputter, "What are you suggesting?"

"The 120 Days of Sodom." He tilted his chin toward my lap.

I flinched, a short, aggrieved, disbelieving laugh bursting from my lips. "Oh my God." Then to the table I said, "You're completely crazy."

Derek frowned at me, as though I'd confused him. His eyes bounced between the table and me. "What?"

"You're completely crazy," I repeated, reaching behind me for my coat.

"I'm crazy?"

If he hadn't just suggested four months of sodomy I might have found the concerned wrinkle between his eyebrows adorable. But, given the fact that sexual torture wasn't far from his mind, I decided the wrinkle wasn't adorable. It was distressing.

"Yes. You're nuts. Don't email me. Don't call me. Pretend we never met."

I was no longer sweating as I pulled on my jacket and grabbed my things. This was an odd quirk about my personality: put me in an innocuous situation where I need to be normal, and I'm bouncing off the walls. But send me into a dangerous or emergency situation, and I'm cool and focused.

Derek—or whatever his name was—started to stand so I held out my hand.

"Don't. Don't stand up. Don't even look at me. And don't think about following me either or I'll call the police." *Lunatic.*

Without another glance, I wove through the tables and out the door, anger, indignation, and frustration spurring my movements.

Wow.

WOW.

*Wow.*

The first thing I'd do upon arriving home would be reporting that freak to FindUrPartner.com.

The second thing I'd do is delete my profile. I'd been with David, my ex, for six years, and because we'd met in college, I'd missed out on the early years of Internet dating. No great loss. Clearly it wasn't for me.

I'd had some terrible first dates since breaking up with David, but this one took the cake. It took all the cakes. In less than twenty minutes, my perfect match had irrevocably propelled himself to the top of my worst-date list.

*Thanks, dating algorithms, for pairing me with a psycho.*

I moved to retrieve my cell from my purse. I needed to call my friend Sandra *immediately.* I couldn't wait until knit night to tell someone about this fiasco. But then my attention snagged on the spine of my book—the book I'd purchased in a rush so as to not seem prosaic for Derek—and I stopped short, gaping at the title and author.

It read, *The 120 Days of Sodom,* by Marquis de Sade.

# CHAPTER 2

**Artificial Diamond (aka Synthetic Diamond, Cultured Diamond, or Cultivated Diamond)**

*A diamond created in a laboratory rather than by geological processes. While the term synthetic is associated by consumers with imitation products, artificial diamonds are made of the same material (pure carbon, crystallized in isotropic 3D form) and are, in fact, real diamonds.*

Source: 16 C.F.R. Part 23: Federal Trade Commission

ROARING LAUGHTER, COMPLETE with heads thrown back, hands over stomachs, and tears rolling down faces. This was how my six knitting group friends reacted to the punchline of my date with Derek.

Elizabeth—my sarcastic with a heart of marshmallow ER physician from Iowa—held her face in her hands. A long rope of braided blonde hair fell over her shaking shoulders.

Sandra—my potty-mouthed psychiatrist from Texas—was sprawled backward on the sofa, her green eyes screwed shut as she clutched her abdomen. Silent hysterics apparently having momentarily paralyzed her.

Ashley—my silly, quick-witted ICU nurse from Tennessee—was bent to one side, her face planted into the couch at her left. She'd Skyped in from Green Valley, Tennessee, where she'd moved over the spring to be closer to her family. We'd placed a laptop on a chair to one side of the living room, close enough to the circle that we were all visible but far enough away so she could still see all of us.

Fiona—my graceful and wise retired CIA field agent from Baltimore—gazed at me with her dark, soulful eyes, an expression between sympathy and reluctant humor warring for dominance.

Kat—my poised, sweet, usually shy administrative assistant and woman of mystery from Boston—had folded her arms on the coffee table and hidden her face, but her giggle-snort gave her away.

Janie was the exception. My walking, talking encyclopedia of Amazonian adorableness—also from Iowa—wasn't laughing. She looked perturbed.

But I was laughing.

How could I not? What other choice did I have?

Crying? *Nah.* I was finished with crying. Crying was my past, laughing was my present and foreseeable future. Unless it was crying induced by laughter or an allergy to cats. Because I'd recently decided I would be adopting cats. All the cats.

Forget men and romance. The answer to my aching loneliness would be all the cats.

"Tears. On my face." Sandra waved her hands in front of her eyes and then wiped at the corners. "I'm wearing mascara, thank God, so you can all get the full effect."

"What are you talking about?" Elizabeth, still in her ER scrubs, asked from Sandra's left, nudging her with an elbow while snickering. "What full effect?"

"You can literally see how funny this story is by the black trails of mascara running down my face." Sandra pointed to her cheeks, subduing an errant giggle. "Sodomy jokes. They get me every time."

"I didn't know that book was even in print, *The 120 Days of Sodom*, by Marquis de Sade." Janie, the only one who hadn't laughed like mad, frowned at me. "I know it was translated a few years ago, but I thought you could only get it as an e-book." She stood hovering to one side of the couch, several red curls having come loose from her bun, her black, horn-rimmed glasses giving her the aura of a stern librarian.

Holding a two-liter bottle of water, she was stretching her back and appeared to be agitated by the news that *The 120 Days of Sodom* was available in paperback yet no one had seen fit to notify her. Everything irritated her these days. She'd had *the worst* morning sickness for fourteen weeks, and had been dwelling in a perpetual state of perturbed dissatisfaction—her words, not mine—since entering her second trimester. This was her first pregnancy, but I wouldn't be surprised if it turned out to be her last.

"How is it possible that you didn't read the title of the book before you bought it?" Fiona's sympathetic look persisted as she rubbed her belly; like Janie, she was also pregnant; unlike Janie, she seemed to take her pregnancy woes in stride.

Where Janie was remarkably tall and carried her pregnancy entirely in front, Fiona was short and her rounded belly was visible from all angles. This was Fiona's third child with her husband Greg. They'd been married for fifteen years and were still ludicrously in love with each other. But strangely, it wasn't at all nauseating. Neither of them were perfect and they embraced each other's faults with adorable aplomb.

#RelationshipGoals

"I don't know. I just rushed into the bookstore—which, as it turns out, was an erotic bookstore, so make a note of that—and grabbed the book closest to the cashier. I was in a hurry."

"But why did you need a book at all?" This question came from Kat, the youngest member of our knitting group at twenty-four, and also historically the least vociferous. Although lately, I'd say during the last year in particular, she'd become more talkative.

"I didn't want to be that person staring at my phone. It felt too normal. I wanted to seem cultured, interesting." Even as I said the words they felt puerile.

God, I hated dating.

I hated it.

Hate.

"You *are* cultured and interesting." Elizabeth shot me a pointed look before returning her attention to the sweater-in-progress on her needles.

"Yes, but you don't know how it is out there. Men have this FOMO—fear of missing out. I feel like they're always looking over my head, looking for *her*. First impressions count a lot when meeting an online match for the first time. I don't know how to explain it. It's like the stakes are higher these days. You don't warm up to a person, no one seems to have time for that. You only have fifteen seconds or less to make a good impression before the person makes up their mind."

"That sounds very stressful." Ashley sighed discontentedly. "What ever happened to taking the time to actually know a person?"

"People don't do that anymore." Sandra flicked her wrist toward Ashley's image on the laptop. "It's all swipe left for sex or right to murder."

"Not quite, but, yeah. It's pretty bad out there." Kat chuckled, the sound was shaded with sorrow. "Split decisions based on what a person looks like, how impressive their job title is, and how much money they make. It's all about ego with these men, as if people can't just like each other anymore. They have to check certain boxes. At least, that's how my last few dates felt."

"That's unhealthy." Sandra appeared to be offended on Kat's and my behalf. "And it's unwise. I was just reading a study out of Princeton where perceptions of attractiveness change dramatically over time. A group of college students rated each other's attractiveness at the beginning of a semester and then again at the end. Lo and behold, the best-looking guy and girl at the beginning were more often considered dogs by the end, because they were fundamentally unlikable."

"Not all of us can be admired from afar by genius hackers disguised as waiters, Sandra." I gave my friend a teasing smile, referring to her husband, Alex. They'd been married just under a year and a half and were the image of marital bliss.

"Can we go back to your date? You didn't realize until you left that by asking if kidnapping and sexual torture sounded like fun to you, the guy was referring to your book and not trying to make a lewd proposition?" Kat asked. She was sitting on the floor and gazing at me, her elbow on the coffee table, her chin in her palm.

"Exactly." I nodded once, remembering the odd encounter and feeling both embarrassed and indignant. "However, in my defense, I'd been very distracted by his bizarre behavior by that point. Like I said, he didn't look at all like his picture—"

"I hate it when that happens," Kat lamented flatly, lifting her martini glass toward me.

"Thank you." I mirrored her gesture, lifting my glass as well. "Why do they do that? What's so difficult about accurately representing oneself on dating websites?"

"I know I missed out on online dating," Elizabeth twisted the end of her braid thoughtfully, "but it seems like this is par for the course, right? The picture not matching the person?"

"Yes, well, sometimes. Except in this guy's case it didn't make sense."

"How so?" Fiona asked, her gaze moving between her knitting and me. She was working on a baby hat with yarn so soft it felt magical.

"For one thing, he was heavier in his picture online, softer in the middle. Less fit."

"That's your type, right?" Sandra licked the edge of her glass, peering at me. "You like the cuddly kind."

"Exactly. But this guy, in real life, clearly worked out several times a week. At the *gym*. With *weights*." I made a face of distaste. "Who misrepresents *that*? Usually it's the other way around."

"You said his eyes were the wrong color too, right?" Ashley had righted herself from her couch and was also sipping from a martini glass. As much as possible, she tried to coordinate her beverage choices in Green Valley with ours in Chicago.

"Correct. His profile had listed gray, but his were brown. Not that I minded at all," I rushed to add, "because he had gorgeous eyes. I don't know why he'd list the wrong color."

"But no beard," Ashley added. Her Tennessee twang and wrinkled nose made the observation sound like an accusation. "What kind of man claims to have a beard, posts pictures of said beard, and shows up beardless?"

"That just ain't right." Sandra nodded her agreement, pointing at the laptop screen and Ashley's image. "You don't cry beard. Where is the trust after that?"

"Gone," Ashley proclaimed with a snap.

The sound of Fiona's front door opening and closing had me glancing over my shoulder. I spotted Greg and Alex strolling into the family room. The tall Brit was dressed in his exercise gear but he didn't look like he'd gone running yet, and Alex, naturally, wore his signature black.

"But why did he do it?" Fiona asked, drawing my attention back to her. "Do you think he was ashamed of how he looked? Or do you think he used someone else's picture?"

Alex crossed to his wife, but instead of sitting next to her, he bent and whispered something into her ear, his fingers fiddling with a strand of her hair, then stroked her neck. She nodded and winked at him as he leaned away. He straightened and left the room, strolling into the kitchen without speaking to anyone else.

Alex Greene, gorgeous and genius hacker, was an unending mystery. He wasn't sullen, though he was distrustful and remarkably socially awkward. At first, his silent, withdrawn ways took some getting used to. As a group, we'd warmed to him as a lurking figure in the background. We'd even embraced it, mostly because he always wore whatever we knit him and seemed genuinely surprised and grateful for every nice thing sent his way. I made him cookies once and he gave me a hug that lasted for what felt like a full minute. He'd even thanked me for them several months later.

Having Alex around made us all feel like we had a little brother to spoil. A tall, dark, handsome brooding little brother. Admittedly, the dynamic was unusual, but I think that's what made it remarkable.

"That's the thing." I shrugged, sitting back in my seat. "The guy was attractive. Very attractive." *In an efficient, nerdy but fit way.* "He just didn't look anything like his picture. Maybe it was someone else in the picture."

"So weird." Kat wrinkled her nose. "Why are men so weird?"

"We have to be weird," Greg cut in, settling on the couch next to his wife and tucking her under his arm. "Because if you knew how simple we were, you'd figure out a way to procreate and find satisfaction without us." He held his hands up before any of us could contradict. "Wait. Now, I know what you're going to say, that you already find satisfaction without us. You don't need another person in order to be happy. Sure. Okay. Just like men don't *need* a woman in order to be happy . . . except, people need people. Being alone might yield satisfaction, but it's not what we all really want."

*Finding true fulfillment for myself without men, without a romantic relationship* . . . now that sounded like a worthwhile endeavor.

My attention lingered on Fiona and Greg as he placed a soft kiss on her temple and nuzzled her hair with his nose. He whispered something to her and she smiled, her hand reaching for his where it rested on her shoulder, their fingers tangling together.

They were such a unit.

My heart twisted uncomfortably and I recognized the root emotion: envy.

"Of note, it's already possible for women to procreate without men." Janie, still looking perturbed, rubbed the base of her spine and glared at Greg. "Through a process called somatic cell nuclear transfer. You can take cells from a woman and—"

"I don't want to know." Greg shook his head adamantly. "Let me live in my delusions of being essential. Can't you see my male ego is as fragile as it is beautiful? And speaking of fragile male egos, where is Nicoletta?"

Elizabeth smirked, turning her work in progress and leaning forward to grab her drink. "He's in Los Angeles filming until the end of the month, but I'll let him know you're missing him."

Nico—or Nicoletta as we'd started calling him—was Elizabeth's husband. He also happened to be a movie star and comedian. When he was in town he was a regular fixture at knit night, except he crocheted.

"I'm not missing him. Not precisely." Greg shrugged. "It's just that he's a good running partner."

"What about Alex?" I asked, "Why don't you ask him?"

"I did. He says he doesn't like to run unless it's from law enforcement. Plus, swimming is his exercise of choice." Greg made a face.

"You could go with Quinn." Janie's eyes moved to the side thoughtfully. "Except he likes to run early in the morning."

"Yes, I know. I'm familiar with Captain Never Sleeps," Greg mumbled, referring to one of his nicknames for Quinn.

"I thought you and Matt were running this evening?" Fiona asked softly.

"We were," he sighed, and it sounded aggrieved. "Or, we are. But he's late, some work business. Should be here any minute."

"Who's Matt?" Elizabeth asked distractedly, her eyes on the knitting pattern to her left.

"Our next-door neighbor." Fiona lifted her chin toward the far wall, presumably to where this Matt person lived. "He's a professor at the university, in computer science, I think."

"Fiona has seen his penis," Greg added cheerfully.

*Wait, what?*

I could almost hear everyone's eyebrows raise in unison as our collective attention shifted to Fiona.

"Really? Do tell." Of course, Sandra was the first to recover from Greg's odd declaration.

Fiona gave her husband an exasperated look, then sought to explain. "I used to babysit him when we were kids, back in Baltimore. Our parents know each other. He moved out here last Christmas and by chance we ended up neighbors."

"He also has a TIG welder." Greg glanced at his watch.

"Oh, good." Janie twisted to one side and then the other, stretching. "I've been looking for someone with one of those."

"Of course you have." Elizabeth gave Janie a bewildered but amused look. "Why do you need a TIG welder?"

"I don't need it now, but it's always good to know someone who can weld. Just in case." Janie, sitting on the arm of the couch, picked up and fiddled with her work in progress. She crocheted rather than knit and was currently working on a baby blanket.

"I agree with Janie," Ashley's voice sounded from the laptop speaker. "It's good to surround yourself with professionals or hobbyists of varying skillsets, at least that's what my brother Cletus always says."

"You know what I could go for? A professional hand-holder." Kat spoke to the green ball of yarn on the coffee table. "I love holding hands, there's nothing like it. I'd pay money for someone to hold hands with me."

"I'll hold hands with you!" Elizabeth smiled at Kat. "Anytime."

Kat gave Elizabeth a warm smile. "Thanks. I might take you up on that."

"I think those people exist," Sandra said, completing her row and glancing at Kat. "They charge hourly."

"What are you talking about?" Elizabeth chuckled, shaking her head.

"Very funny, Sandra." Fiona gave Sandra a patient smile.

"It's true," Sandra defended, her eyes wide. "They're called professional cuddlers. We have them here, in Chicago. They'll come to your apartment, or sometimes you meet in a studio with a bunch of other cuddlers, or even a hotel."

I wrinkled my nose, swapping a disbelieving stare with Kat.

But then Janie said, "She's right. It's a real thing. Check out cuddlebuddies.com. And there's a book called *The Cuddle Sutra*."

"You're making this up." Kat's eyes bounced between Janie and Sandra.

"No. We're not. I swear." Sandra shook her head vehemently.

"She's not making it up," Alex said, strolling out of the kitchen. "There're even professional dry humpers in New York and I think a few in Los Angeles."

My mouth fell open in shock while Elizabeth, Kat, Fiona, and I blinked at each other.

"I think you mean prostitutes," Greg offered dryly.

"No." Alex almost smiled—almost—and met Greg's sardonic glare. "Not prostitutes."

"You're telling me people pay for this? Cuddling and dry humping with no penetration?" Greg was just as disbelieving as the rest of us. "Sounds like a complete waste of resources."

I only forgave him that comment because I knew Greg. I knew he was being purposefully obtuse to make a point. He often did this: espouse opinions that were the opposite of what he believed in order to make a point.

"Yes. That's what we're telling you," Janie responded. "Clients pay by the hour, or fraction of an hour. Based on *The Washington Post* article I read, most cuddlers have regular clients and the idea is grounded in the same foundation as touch therapy and Reiki, only with less oversight and training in most cases."

Kat sighed loudly, drawing my attention to her. Her expression was one part confused and one part distressed. "That's so sad."

"What's sad?" Sandra asked evenly.

"That a person would resort to paying for cuddling, for human touch." Kat now looked completely distressed.

"I don't know. I think it makes a lot of sense." Sandra moved her attention to her knitting as Alex sat next to her. "And I don't consider it sad, necessarily. Think about the elderly for instance, those with no family. Cuddling, holding another person's hand, can bring so much comfort. Babies need it in order for their brain to develop correctly. And if a person is alone in the world, why shouldn't they have an opportunity to receive that comfort?"

Janie nodded. "And what about people who don't have time for a relationship? Or aren't ready for one?" Her tone was thoughtful—more like pre-pregnancy Janie—as she philosophized. "Human touch, affectionate touch in particular, has been shown to be necessary for sustained happiness. If a person can't be in a relationship for whatever reason, professional cuddlers provide a valuable service."

Once again, Kat and I shared a glance, likely because we were the only two single people in the room.

Kat swallowed and I saw she did so with some effort, a flash of something like pain shadowing her expression. She then cleared her throat, her gaze lowering to her yarn. "I guess, when you put it like that, professional cuddlers are a better choice than other behaviors, which might be seen as destructive."

"Exactly," Janie said. "All things considered, I believe paying a professional for a defined service—where expectations are clear-cut—is far superior to using another person for physical contact and potentially engaging their feelings with no plans for reciprocation."

"Well, yeah. I guess I see your point." Elizabeth's tone was serious, almost grave, and her stare became unfocused. "After the death of a loved one, for example . . ."

"Sorry," Ashley piped up, "but no. It still sounds creepy to me. I wouldn't want some stranger paying me to touch them, even for therapeutic reasons."

"Says the nurse," Alex teased.

"Ha, ha. Well played." Ashley gave him a face even through her laughter, and their banter broke the somewhat tense moment.

"You ladies always have the most enlightening conversations," Greg said, stroking his chin as he moved his narrowed gaze over the room.

Meanwhile, Janie swallowed the last of her water, then glared at the bottle as though it had insulted her. "It's empty."

"Let me get you some more." I stood and stretched, happy for an excuse to move around. "Do you want ice?"

Janie nodded, handing over the bottle with one hand and rubbing her belly with the other. "The dictator in my stomach says yes."

Fiona giggled. "Dictator."

A knock sounded from the direction of the front door and Greg stood from the couch, sharing a small smile with his wife.

"Autocrat. Fascist. Emperor or Empress. Whatever. Its royal highness wishes for ice."

"Janie, you make me never want to be pregnant." Kat frowned with concern at our friend. "Are your muscle cramps getting any better?"

"No. And now I'm peeing myself every time I stand up. Or when I walk. Or sit. Or lie down," Janie said, her tone surly. "But don't use my pregnancy as a datapoint. Look at Fiona. She's glowing."

"Okay, Matt and I are heading out. Do you want me to pick anything up?" Greg asked, standing at the precipice to the family room, a figure hovering just behind him for a brief moment before stepping to Greg's side.

I glanced at them on my way to the kitchen and then stopped short, doing a startled double take.

Because the man standing next to Greg was that man.

*That* man.

My not-perfect match from the coffee shop.

Here. Now. Standing in Fiona's apartment.

*What the flipping fracking fresh hell is this?*

"It's you," I blurted before I knew what I was doing, raising an accusing finger at the newcomer. "It's him!"

# CHAPTER 3

### Atlas Robot

*A high mobility, humanoid robot designed to negotiate outdoor, rough terrain. Atlas can walk bipedally leaving the upper limbs free to lift, carry, and manipulate the environment. The design and production of it was overseen by the DARPA, an agency of the United States Department of Defense.*

Source: Boston Dynamics

**DEREK'S EYES DARTED** to mine, and they widened with recognition and surprise.

"It's him?" Sandra looked up from her work in progress, as did everyone else. "Him who?"

"Derek!" I shook my hand in his direction and had no compunction about adding, "The weirdo from the coffee shop."

"Weirdo?" Derek asked, standing a bit straighter, his forehead wrinkling in that way I thought might have been adorable before I determined he was a psychopath.

"That's Derek?" Elizabeth's frowning gaze bounced back and forth between us.

He lifted his hands, palms out in the universal gesture for calm down. "I can explain—"

"Matt?" Fiona questioned sharply, her brow creasing with suspicion.

"Yes. I'm Matt. But she's also correct." He lifted his chin toward me and said evenly, "I was Derek, or sometimes I'm Derek."

I flinched, my mind a muddled mess. "What? How can someone 'sometimes' go by a different name?"

"Sometimes you're Derek?" Sandra set her knitting to one side, her tone gaining a hard edge. "What does that mean?"

"You filthy bird." Greg sounded delighted. "Have you been posing as a fetishist named Derek?"

"What? No." Derek or Matt or whatever his name was turned his big brown eyes to me and shook his head. "It's not like that."

"Then what is it like?" This question came from Alex, and plunged the room into stark silence. Alex was . . . well, he was odd. And his voice had a certain quality, one that forced you to listen to it and to him. But presently, something about his tone made the fine hairs on the back of my neck stand up straight.

He-who-claimed-to-be-Matt glanced at Alex and he surveyed the younger man. "It was in pursuit of science. An experiment."

"An experiment?" Alex asked, looking dissatisfied with the answer.

"What do you mean *experiment*?" Sandra stood, her hands on her hips.

"Uh, it's what's called a deception study. Self-reported behaviors are riddled with bias. So we observe in a non-traditional laboratory setting. Only," Matt turned an apologetic smile on me, "I'm not usually the one taking the interview. Dr. Merek typically fills that role."

"Who is Dr. Merek?" I asked dumbly, not at all following the conversation.

"Derek," Matt said simply, as though this explained everything.

"What?" Elizabeth was growing impatient.

"Derek is Dr. Merek. Dr. Derek Merek," Matt clarified.

"What an unfortunate name," Janie said with a small frown.

"What are you talking about? It rhymes." Sandra shook her head at our friend. "I've always wanted a rhyming name, but nothing rhymes with Sandra."

Crossing my arms, I ignored Sandra's nonsense and pointed my questions at Matt. "So you're not Derek."

"No. Not usually. I'm not as good at the interviews as he is." He scratched his neck, adding self-deprecatingly, "Or much else, for that matter."

"You mean you've done this before? Posed as your friend?" Elizabeth demanded.

"No. I don't pose as my friend. He's my colleague. The profile for 'Derek Simmons' is fake. We created it based on aggregate preferences of our target sample group. We have permission from the website's owners."

Both Sandra and Elizabeth made similar expressions, as though they were absorbing this information and understood his meaning.

Meanwhile, I shared a confused look with Kat.

"In English, please," she asked softly.

"Oh, sorry." He gave her a polite, contrite smile. "We're looking for subjects—or *participants* if you prefer that word—who are in their thirties, are working professionals, and have never been married. We looked for patterns in responses for this demographic. We found clusters of likes and dislikes, then created fictional profiles to match these subjects' preferences."

Every word out of his mouth grated. "So you created a fake profile to match my likes and dislikes?"

"Not just yours, but women like you. You know, the same shows, interests, music preferences. You'd be surprised how similar you are to other women with your demographics: single, age, education, and income level. Actually, you're all basically the same person."

I winced, feeling as though I'd been slapped. Or at least all the air had been driven out of me. The room plunged into dead quiet.

*Women like you.*

*You'd be surprised by how similar you are.*

*You're all basically the same person.*

That. Stung.

But why did those words sting so much?

"You don't know her." This accusation, for it truly sounded like an accusation, came from Janie. "Just because an individual shares common interests with a similar demographic profile doesn't make them the same person. We all enjoy wine, that doesn't make us *basically the same person!*" Her voice lifted until she was nearly shouting. Alex had stealthily approached during her rant and wrapped his arm around her shoulders; Janie appeared ready to jump over the couch and strangle Matt.

"Yes. Of course." Matt turned a smile to Janie laced with frustration. "I suppose I should apologize. I have a habit of summarizing life into if/then statements, or categorizing people in terms of the aggregate data available on groups with similar profiles. It's an occupational hazard and I truly do not mean any offense."

"What is your occupation?" Sandra asked, squinting at him.

"I'm a computer scientist with a focus on AI."

"AI?" Kat challenged.

"Artificial intelligence."

Sandra's squint intensified. "You mean like that creepy movie with the evil robot—"

"*Ex Machina*, and she wasn't evil. She just wanted her freedom." This came from Ashley over Skype. "And would y'all move to one side, I can't see a thing."

"She was evil. She killed that adorable Domhnall Gleeson," Sandra said.

"We'll have to agree to disagree." Ashley shrugged. "Domhnall Gleeson doesn't do it for me."

"What did you mean by *deception study?*" Elizabeth brought us back on track. "I thought those required an informed consent after participation, so subjects could opt in or out once the data is collected."

"We've received approval from our ethics board to conduct a one-time interview and ascertain true preferences from the subjects." Matt's tone was conversationally academic and it made me want to give him paper cuts. Lots and lots of paper cuts. "Usually we consent after the interview, but M-Marie," he stumbled over my name, his gaze flickering to mine and then away, "left before I could administer post-hoc consent. As I've said, I'm not very good at conducting the interviews." His gaze shifted to me again and held. His smile was carefully detached, like he'd erected a wall between us. "Again, I apologize if I ruined your afternoon by being a 'weirdo.'"

No one said anything for a long moment, during which I wrestled with this new information.

My *date* had been part of an experiment.

*I* had been an experiment.

And I was just like every other woman out there *in my demographic*.

*Apparently, we're all the same.*

I think, on some level, we'd all like to believe we're special. That something—be it tangible or intangible—makes each person unique.

I considered myself a confident individual. Yes, of course, I knew I had room for improvement. I didn't think I was in any way perfect, but I'd reached a point in my life where I was happy with myself as a whole. I didn't want a life partner to complete my life, but as a complement to my life.

Yet something about being told, statistically, I was basically the same as every other woman with similar demographics made me feel immeasurably insignificant. And wretched.

"You're not a good guy," Janie said, breaking the silence with her flat declaration. "You should know that so you can try to change yourself for the better."

Derek—er, Matt—glanced at her, inspecting her openly in a way that reminded me of a scientist inspecting a curious-looking insect. He didn't appear to be at all offended by her comment, or surprised by it. The irony here, which wasn't at all lost on me, was that the way he looked at Janie was how she used to look at people when they said something surprising.

Now pregnant, she just looked at everyone with varying degrees of intense irritation.

I gathered a deep breath, ignoring a sudden urge to curl up on Fiona's comfy sofa and request Sandra spoon me. She would if I asked. Sandra loved to cuddle and I hadn't cuddled with another person since my ex.

*I miss cuddling. Maybe I do need a professional cuddler.*

Greg cleared his throat, drawing my attention to him. He was looking at me with pointed intensity, a silent question behind his concerned gaze. *Are you okay?*

Quickly, I grabbed ahold of my emotions and yanked them back, pasting a smile on my lips; it was another of those situations where I didn't know how widely to smile. "Well. I guess that explains that." I tried shrugging, imbuing my voice with false bravado. "No harm no foul."

Fiona's tone was infinitely gentle as she said, "Marie—"

"We should all get back to our evening," I said firmly, not wanting to talk about it, not until I had time to myself and definitely not in front of imposter-Derek. I needed to sort through my own messy feelings. "We should let Greg and, uh, Matt go on their run."

"Right," Greg said reluctantly, his eyes moving past me to his wife, adding a few seconds later, "let's go."

The tall Brit's frown was severe. He didn't look at Matt as he turned, merely gesturing for the shorter man to follow while he disappeared down the hall. Matt moved his dispassionate stare from Janie, and his eyes collided with mine once more. I lifted my chin, glaring at him. He gave me a tight smile and then left, following Greg.

"Don't listen to him, Marie." Ashley raised her voice after the front door closed, forcing my attention to the laptop screen. Her face filled the entire space. "That guy is what we call a douche canoe."

"You should move." Janie turned her grumpy expression on Fiona as Alex removed his hands—no longer needing to restrain her—and stuffed them in his pockets. He traded a sideways glance with his wife. "Otherwise," Janie continued, "I might be forced to punch that guy in the throat."

Fiona inspected me for a short moment, and then gave Janie a weary smile as Sandra and Elizabeth reclaimed their seats. "Actually, we are moving. We've been putting it off for months, but with the baby, we'll do it within the next year. This place is too small for five people."

"Move to our building," Elizabeth suggested, sneaking me a surreptitious glance while she addressed Fiona. "You know Quinn would love having you close by so he can pick your ninja brain more often."

Quinn, Janie's husband, ran a wildly successful global security firm and owned several floors in a building overlooking Grant Park. The apartments were reserved for employees of his firm, but Elizabeth and Nico lived in one of the penthouses, as did Janie and Quinn. As Alex worked for Quinn's corporate subsidiary, Cipher Systems, he and Sandra also lived in the building. Fiona had also recently accepted a contract position with Cipher Systems.

"Then Greg can go jogging with Quinn instead of that douche canoe," Janie mumbled, her lip curled into a subtle snarl as she rubbed her lower back.

If I hadn't been so off-kilter and preoccupied by recent events, I might've laughed. Truly, Janie had become a different person over the last few months.

As though reading my mind, Elizabeth piped in, "Jeez Louise, Janie. It's like, carrying Quinn's baby has turned you into a replica of his grumpy ass. Pretty soon you'll be giving us all the ice stare and quoting Dirty Harry movies."

"Quinn doesn't quote Dirty Harry movies." Janie wrinkled her nose at Elizabeth.

"He doesn't need to, because that's how he talks in real life." Elizabeth's teasing statement drew chuckles from everyone except me.

I tried, but I didn't laugh this time. *Couldn't.* Thankfully, the subject change provided an opportunity to dart out of the room to refill Janie's water. Walking into the kitchen, I ran the faucet and sighed. I was having trouble swallowing, unable to move past Derek's/Matt's notion that nothing about me was unique.

Nothing was special. I was nothing special.

My eyes caught on my reflection in the dark window over the sink. I had blonde hair. My skin was beige. I was wearing my tan sweater dress.

I was struck by my monochromatic blandness. Did the inside reflect the outside?

# CHAPTER 4

### Kiddon & Brun's TWSS system

*A statistical machine learning algorithm to detect whether a sentence contains a "That's what she said" double entendre.*

Source: Funniest Computer Ever Open Source initiative

SEVERAL EVENTS OVER the next week transformed my melancholy into rage.

First of all, men were idiots. Let's just get that out of the way.

Second, I was propositioned by my building manager. He was married. With children.

Third, I'd neglected to deactivate my FindUrPartner.com account after the date from hell, so when I logged in five days later there were three new messages, all of them containing dick pics.

Scratch that.

All of them containing *underwhelming* dick pics. I mean, if you're going to send a woman a dick pic, at least send something worth seeing. Not a gherkin dwarfed by hairy potatoes.

And finally, my ex—who I hadn't spoken to in over a year—invited me to his engagement party.

His. Engagement. Party.

To. Another. Woman.

There I was, minding my own business, opening my mail while waiting for a conference call to start. I was at work, sitting at my desk. As a contract writer,

I could work from home. I'd tried doing just that for a few years, but found the isolation to be counterproductive to my mental health.

Therefore, I'd joined an office co-op near the Loop a few years back. Basically, it's an office—like any other office environment—except most of us don't work together or even in the same field. We shared the same public space, used the same copy machine, the same break room, etc.

I liked the dynamics and environment of working in an office. Not only did it get me out of my pajamas, it gave me the opportunity to have normal discussions around a water cooler with other working professionals.

Glancing impassively at the envelope, because it had looked like any other envelope, I noticed my address had been handwritten. I didn't recognize the handwriting, nor had a return address been visible. Tearing into it serenely, I listened as others joined the call.

It took reading the invitation five times before I fully comprehended what it was. And by the time complete understanding settled in, my rage was out of control, especially since the party wasn't for another six months.

*Who does that? Who sends an invite for a party that far in advance?*

I focused on that minute and meaningless detail because the rest of my feelings felt too unwieldy to examine.

Unfortunately, it was also time for the call to start.

"Okay. Is everyone here?" Daniella, my editor, queried the line, forcing me to stem my decidedly unpleasant gush of emotions.

"Marie, Chicago," I said through gritted teeth when it was my turn, then muted my line just in case the urge to scream became uncontrollable.

*You're Invited!*

*David Carter and Gwen Livingston cordially invite you to attend their engagement party on November 17th.*

*Please RSVP by August 17th with number of guests.*

*Will you be bringing a date? Yes ___ No ___*

I flipped the card over and winced at the picture of David and his fiancée, my heart beating sluggishly for the span of several seconds.

"We need content for the tech issue, it's running thirty pages light. Anyone have a pitch?" Daniella tossed the question out to the group.

Meanwhile, I was still glaring at the picture of my ex and his fiancée. They were looking at each other, gazing into each other's eyes with blatant adoration, and they were so . . . so . . .

*Happy.*

Blar!

Tearing my eyes away, I glared at the writing on the envelope, the decidedly swirly cursive. It must've been hers. *Who does that? Who invites her fiancée's ex-girlfriend to her engagement party?*

"What about dildos, vibrators?" This question came from Terry Ruiz, field writer at the Los Angeles office. "We could do a compare and contrast of what's out there, latest technological advancements in the field."

"Give me something other than dildos and vibrators. Please. For the love of God," Daniella moaned. "I'm so tired of dildos."

"What about online dating?" Tommy Jang asked, his tone hesitant. He was relatively new to the Los Angeles office. I'd never met him in person, but we'd spoken over the phone a number of times. One-on-one he was hilarious. But he hadn't yet found his footing on the conference calls.

"What about it?" Daniella pressed. "What's the angle?"

"Pew Research Center compiled a summary of surprising statistics about online dating, with growing numbers of people in a committed relationship or married having met online. We could take a look at how online dating—the technology behind it—has improved over the years and future directions for continued advancement."

"Hmm . . ." Daniella paused, and I knew what that pause meant. It meant she liked the idea, but didn't want him to write the piece, at least, not by himself. "Marie? Are you on?"

I unmuted my line, breathing out silently before saying, "Yep. I'm here."

"Can you partner on this with Tommy?" she asked, confirming my suspicions.

*Crap.*

It was no secret that I was Daniella's favorite. If she had an idea for a story, she always passed it by me first. She'd told me many times that I demonstrated a commitment to understanding, to truly living an experience before writing about it that was rare these days, and that difference showed in my finished articles.

I appreciated her compliments and her faith in me, but it often meant she wanted me to take the lead on someone else's story.

It's not that I didn't want to write the piece with Tommy. What I knew about Tommy I liked. Rather, it was that this piece was his idea. He deserved the opportunity to write it on his own, to prove himself.

However, before I could pitch a different idea or make an excuse, Tommy piped up, "I'd love to work with Marie on this, if she has time."

I frowned at my phone and bit my lip, feeling torn. On the one hand, he sounded completely sincere. On the other hand, it was his idea. His story.

Unable to delay any longer without inviting an uncomfortable silence, I said, "Yes. Absolutely. Sounds good."

"Great. It's settled. Anyone else?" Daniella asked and the call moved on.

Twisting my lips to the side, I muted my line and returned my attention to the photograph of David and his betrothed.

Perversely, I wondered if they'd met online. And if he'd been her perfect match.

Continuing to quietly stew for the remainder of the call, I felt relieved when it ended. Grabbing my wallet, I stood from my desk and darted out of my office. What this situation called for was nail polish.

I owned too many nail polishes. It's true. I freely admitted this. Worst of all, I hardly ever painted my nails. I'd use a bottle once, usually as therapy to get over a funk, but then never used the color again. Yet nothing made me feel better quite like fancy nails.

"Marie! Wait."

I twisted at the waist, checking to see who'd called my name, and found Camille Yardly jogging to catch up with me. Turning around to meet her, I smiled warmly.

"Hey. Are you grabbing lunch?" Camille was a contract engineer and hardly made it into the shared office space as she frequently traveled all over the world for her job.

"No. Nail polish. I packed my lunch." I tilted my head toward the break room. "I'm on a budget, but I'll eat with you if you grab takeout." I tried to sweeten the deal with a large smile.

"Ha. Sounds good. I skipped breakfast and my date last night was so terrible, I lost my appetite halfway through." She rolled her eyes, and my big grin became a smaller one of pure sympathy.

"I'm sorry. That's sucks."

"Yeah, well, it's okay . . ." Abruptly, she shook her head, heaving a sigh. "Actually, it's not okay. Mind if we walk together?"

"No, no. Feel free. I'm just going to the drugstore across the street." We fell into step on the way to the elevator. "Do you want to talk about it?"

She didn't require any further prompting. "Yes. I do. I'm just so damn frustrated. Where are all the men? And I don't mean man-children. I mean *men*. You know, the guys whose interests extend beyond playing Halo on their Xbox, and who actually make eye contact, and aren't constantly scanning the room for a better option. This guy, last night, left me at the table to go hit on a woman at the bar."

I grimaced, because that was bad. Really, really bad. "Wow. What a jerk."

Camille heaved another sigh just as we stepped onto the elevator, and this one sounded watery. "I just—you know—would like to find a nice, normal guy. Someone who treats me with respect, like a *person*. I don't ask for much. Don't you think it's mind-blowing?"

I could definitely empathize.

"What's that?" I asked right on queue. I'd heard this speech from Camille before and knew what she was going to say.

"Things that ought to be just a normal part of being a healthy adult are considered praiseworthy and that drives me bonkers." She began ticking them off her fingers. "Being employed. Not being an addict. Treating your parents well. Not being in massive debt. Being considerate. Being educated, or at the very least, informed. I must know one hundred single women who check all those boxes, and one hundred men in relationships already who check all those boxes, but not one unattached guy. Not one!"

I nodded, maintaining my sympathetic looks, feeling her pain.

As much as possible, when relating my online debacles to my friends, I tried to keep my dating stories limited to those that were hilarious or outrageous. This was because the rest of my stories were disheartening. Depressing and sad. Like Camille's story.

And no one in a happy relationship wants to hear disheartening stories, nor did I wish to repeat them, because they only made me feel worse.

"What am I going to do?" she moaned, wiping at her eyes and huffing a humorless laugh. "You know how it is. I feel like you're the only one I can talk to about this without getting shitty advice or stupid questions. You know what my brother said?"

"What?" I braced for this new tale of woe.

"He said, 'I don't understand why you can't get a boyfriend. You're pretty.'" She looked heartsick, glancing at the mirrored elevator ceiling. "And that just says it all, doesn't it? Like, that's all men want. Someone pretty. That's all it takes. Ugh! I'm just so sick of it."

"Maybe you just need a break?" I suggested, trying to infuse my tone with optimism. "Maybe you're burned out on dating. Think of it like taking a vacation."

Her eyes slid to mine and her chin wobbled. "Yeah. Maybe I will. I think I'm just tired in general. Maybe I'll take time off work, go someplace far, far away from here. Where there are no American men to disappoint me and make me feel crappy about myself."

I nodded, never knowing what to say at this point in the conversation, because—if it were me—I wouldn't want platitudes and assurances. I wouldn't want someone to tell me it gets better, because I knew for a fact it wouldn't.

So instead I stayed quiet, trying to offer moral support with my silence, but feeling every inch as discouraged as Camille.

\*\*\*

MY FOUL MOOD stalked me for the next several days, a persistent shadow. At least, that's what it felt like. So when Fiona called unexpectedly on Thursday night, asking if I'd be willing to pick up her kiddos from summer camp the next day so she and Greg could go to their prenatal checkup together, I readily agreed.

Even better, Janie and Quinn were also scheduled for a checkup on the same day. Impromptu plans were adjusted, and I offered to make dinner for everyone at Fiona and Greg's place after both couples' appointments.

Jack and Grace were great kids. They seemed to have inherited their mother's moral fortitude and their father's quick wit. Plus, at nine and six years of age respectively, they were capable of conversation. I wouldn't be required to change any diapers or diligently keep them from self-harm.

I'd once watched them when Grace was eighteen months; I swear, watching a toddler is like trying to keep a reckless drunkard from committing suicide. She almost killed herself at least seventeen times. The more dangerous a situation, or activity, or object, the more determined she was to participate in it, or possess it, or put it in her mouth.

And she'd hated clothes, so that made putting on her pajamas a tortuous exercise in masochism.

But she'd also been sweet and cuddly, so that made all the torture worth it.

That was then, and this was now, and Grace had grown into a joyful, silly, smart little girl. I was looking forward to playing their Harry Potter board game and hearing all about what they'd been up to.

After picking the kids up at the community center promptly at 4:00 PM, we walked the six blocks to their building, stopping off at the store to grab ingredients for homemade pizza.

Chicago-style pizza was one of the main reasons I would never be svelte. I worked out in fits and starts, seldom consistently. However, I was very active overall. I walked to work every weekday; I loved to hike when I had the chance, especially if I could canoe or kayak as well; but I'd never enjoyed going to a gym with any regularity.

Therefore, in the absence of a consistent exercise routine to combat the deep-dish deliciousness, my roundness was equal parts soft and firm. Bottom line: I loved pizza too much to care about my bottom's line.

"Grace, please set up the game and grab our costumes. Jack, please help me in the kitchen."

The kids happily complied, with Grace running to her closet to retrieve our wands, wizard hats, and house scarves. I was a Hufflepuff, to the surprise of no one, Grace was a Slytherin, and Jack was a Gryffindor. It was my rule that we always dressed in costume when we played Harry Potter. Always.

Soon, we were gathered around the coffee table, having just defeated Draco Malfoy in Diagon Alley while the first pizza baked in the oven, filling the apartment with the lovely aromas of tomato sauce, Italian seasonings, and mushrooms.

And that's when a knock sounded on the door.

"I'll get it," Jack said, jumping up.

I stood as well. "No. I'll get it. You stay here and plot our next move."

"But it's Professor Simmons," he protested, edging backward toward the door. "He usually comes over for dinner on Fridays."

I stiffened, the hovering shadow of discontent growing darker, more omnipresent at the mention of not-Derek/Professor Matt Simmons.

"Stay here, I'll be right back." I gave Jack a look that left no room for argument, though I could see he was tempted. Once satisfied the nine-year-old would stay put, I moved to the hall, mumbling under my breath, "He's not coming to dinner tonight."

Bracing myself, I counted to five, then opened the door.

"What?" I demanded.

The smile melted off the professor's face, replaced with an expression of startled surprise, as his eyes clashed with mine.

"Oh," he said, blinking once, and stuffing his hands in his pockets like he needed to hide them, or put them someplace to restrict their movements.

"Hello." I didn't smile either, instead leveling him with a glower. "What do you want?"

"I, uh . . ." His gaze shifted to the wand in my hand, the hat on my head, the scarf around my neck, and then back to me. "Hello, Luna."

I hadn't realized I'd been holding the plastic play wand raised between us until it drew his attention. Grinding my teeth, I lowered the wand and scowled at him. "Luna was a Ravenclaw. Not a Hufflepuff."

His lips tugged to one side, like he was fighting a smile. "Is that so?"

"Yes," I snapped, whipping off my hat and scarf and tossing them with the wand to the table behind me. "What do you want?"

He stood straighter, and he appeared to be trying to contain his grin. "I didn't expect to see you."

I crossed my arms. "Life is full of surprises."

"It certainly is," he agreed quickly, his gaze latching on to mine and growing oddly hazy.

A few seconds passed. The moment stretched. I waited. And still he gazed at me, looking a little lost and a lot conflicted.

I decided he probably felt guilty and wanted to apologize for being a douche canoe. But I wasn't interested in his apologies. Or, for that matter, hovering in the hallway with Matt the douche canoe.

My patience at an end, I huffed an aggrieved breath and wrapped my fingers over the edge of the door. "Good talk, Matt. See you around."

"Wait." He jumped forward, as though abruptly coming out of a trance. "Wait, wait a minute. Can I . . . can we talk for a minute?"

"No."

"No?"

"No. I need to get back to the kids. I'm watching them."

"Oh. I can help," he offered with a friendly smile.

"No."

"No?" His expression fell, morphing into a frown.

"No. I don't want your help."

"Oh." He took a step back. When he spoke next his voice dropped an octave. "Then I guess me asking you to sign a consent form for our study so we can use your data is completely out of the question?"

I had no choice. I squinted at Matt Simmons, squinted at him as though he were a peculiarity.

Because he was. Like a stubborn rash.

"Tell me something, Matt." I made no attempt to hide the hostility in my tone, making sure to over-pronounce the "t" at the end of his name. "What is the purpose of your study? To piss off as many women in Chicago as possible?"

"No," he ground out, mirroring my eye-squint.

And wasn't that just the kicker? Him. Squinting at me.

No.

I wasn't the one who'd lied, misrepresented my identity, and then tried to run an experiment on him. He had no right to squint at me. *No right.*

"Really? That's too bad. Because if pissing people off had been the purpose, you'd be achieving your goals."

"My aims are quite the opposite, Marie." He over-pronounced the "e," intensifying my irritation. "And they're entirely altruistic, which you would have known if you'd stayed through the entire interview."

"So tell me now," I scoffed. "Tell me all about your philanthropic objectives."

"I didn't say they were philanthropic." He lifted his chin. "I said they were altruistic."

My. God.

How could one person be so unbelievably irritating?

"Never mind. Forget I asked." I cut my hand through the air, stepping back, intent on shutting him out.

Again he stopped me, this time placing his palm against the door. But it wasn't his holding the door open that kept me from shutting it.

"I'm building an AIC, an Artificial Intelligence Companion—or as mine is called, the Compassion AI—as a replacement for human relationships." The words tumbled from his mouth, effectively halting my movements. "In simple terms, the goal is to build a realistic, humanoid robot who will hopefully—one day—nullify or supplement in every meaningful way our dependency on compassionate human interactions, emotional, physical, or otherwise."

I wasn't aware that my mouth had fallen open. Nor that it remained open for several, wordless seconds. Not until his gaze dropped to my lips, and a small smile—one that struck me as remarkably wily—tugged at the corner of his mouth and kindled a twinkle in his eye.

"You weren't expecting that, were you?"

I shook my head, snapping my mouth shut and swallowing. "No. I wasn't," I admitted freely, still frowning at him while I attempted to make sense of his claims.

"Life is full of surprises," he quipped, using my earlier words.

But I was stuck on the notion of *a replacement for human relationships.*

"Why?" I asked before I could catch myself.

"Why?" he echoed, removing his hand from the door and stuffing it back in his pocket.

"Yes. Why would you want to do that? Why would you want to replace human relationships?"

"Because," his eyes skated over me as though he felt the answer was obvious, "because I can."

"You want to build a robot to replace humanity because you can?"

"No. Not humanity. Merely our archaic dependence on each other as a source of fulfillment and support."

"Archaic dependence?"

"Yes."

"You think relying on another person is archaic?"

"It's not archaic if it's a choice, freely made and healthy." He shrugged, his tone growing lofty, academic. "But, I do think the practice of sacrificing oneself at the altar of physical urges and the fantasy of emotional equivalence in the pursuit of empathy, endorphins, and tachycardia *is* archaic."

*Sex. He means sex, right?*

*Right?*

*. . . Right?*

I released a disbelieving laugh, shaking my head at this man. My initial assessment had been correct. He was completely crazy.

Crossing my arms once more, I lifted my chin and peered at him, wondering what kind of odd road he'd traveled that had brought him to this place.

"You don't like sex?" I asked, because it was the pertinent question.

His gaze narrowed, his features growing irritated. "Of course I like sex. I fucking love sex."

For some reason, the words *fucking, love*, and *sex* coming out of his oddly pouty lips while his remarkably attractive eyes—hooded and provoked—stared defiant daggers at me sent a prickle of awareness shooting down my spine and up my neck.

I ignored it.

"You're telling me the entire point of your experiment is to create a sex robot?"

"No. Of course not," he said through gritted teeth. "The entire point is to give the world's population an alternative to the imperfection and inherently inferior nature of human relationships. To provide healthy companionship, full of compassion, when the only other alternative is dysfunction, disappointment, indifference, and pain. I would no more call my AIC merely a 'sex robot' than I would call Greg and Fiona merely 'sex partners.'"

This analogy and claim gave me pause, partially because I could see he believed what he was saying, and partially because his aims—to alleviate and remove disappointment and pain from a relationship—struck a chord.

"This is crazy," I said without conviction, because it felt like the right thing to say.

And yet, even as I spoke the words, a voice somewhere inside my brain whispered, *Why?*

*Why is this so crazy?*

Because it's new? Novel? Cutting-edge? Revolutionary? So was Galileo's theory that the earth revolved around the sun and not the other way around. For that matter, so was electricity. So were cars and planes and computers and the Internet. Maybe this wasn't crazy. Maybe this was the next logical step in our evolution.

*If you can't find companionship with another person, why not find it with a compassion robot?*

# CHAPTER 5

**Buddy**

*A companion robot that is meant to improve your everyday life. The robot protects your home, offers assistance in the kitchen, entertains the family with music and videos, acts as a calendar and alarm clock, and interfaces with popular smart home solutions.*

Source: Blue Frog Robotics

**"I THINK IT'S** brilliant," Greg declared, leaning back in his chair.

As usual, no one knew if Greg was serious, or being sardonic to make a point.

Fiona shot her husband a disgusted look. "Is this your way of saying you'd like to replace me with a robot?"

We—Greg, Fiona, Janie, Quinn, Matt, and I—were gathered around the long dining room table at Fiona and Greg's. When Jack had mentioned to Fiona that Matt had stopped by, Fiona asked if I was okay with Matt coming over to share dinner. I was happy for him to join us as I was markedly curious about his artificial intelligence work.

Presently, the kids were asleep, and the conversation had finally turned to Matt's research.

"Of course not, darling." Greg's tone was pacifying. "Everyone already knows you are a robot, well *half* robot. On your mother's side."

This earned him an amused glower from his wife.

"I, for one, will welcome our robot overlords." I giggled from behind my cocktail as Fiona's eyes shifted to mine. I might have had a little too much to drink.

"Don't encourage him," she said.

"I think we should encourage him," Janie piped up unexpectedly, an odd edge in her voice. "Think about it. Really think about it, all the people out there without partners, for whatever reason. Or growing up with parents indifferent to their children."

"Exactly." Matt hit the table with his palm. "Clearly, this woman is brilliant."

This comment earned him a glare from Quinn, who was infamously territorial with his wife and had become more so during Janie's pregnancy.

Janie arched her back, pressing her fingertips into the base of her spine. I felt so sad for her, clearly she was terribly uncomfortable. "I don't think you have to be brilliant to grasp the practical applications of an AI focused on providing compassion."

"So the answer is to stop looking for a partner? To stop expecting people to be good parents? To give up on humanity?" Fiona glanced between Janie and Matt.

"Why is it giving up?" Matt countered softly, not arguing; rather, he sounded curious, interested in Fiona's opinion.

"Because you're substituting a robot for a human. Robots make no demands, have no feelings. You can't be challenged—to be better, to be more—by a robot."

Greg cut in thoughtfully, "Not to play devil's advocate—"

At this, we all scoffed. All of us. Even Quinn. Synchronized eye-rolling.

Greg clutched his chest and turned an offended look on his wife. "Et tu, Fiona? Et. Tu."

"Please." Fiona gave her husband a dry look. "You have an honorary degree in advocacy for the devil from Harvard."

"And you passed the bar in the sixth circle of hell." Matt grinned.

"Just get on with it," Quinn mumbled under his breath, encouraging Janie to turn slightly in her chair so he could rub her lower back.

"Fine." Greg pinched his lips together and sniffed, clearly attempting to appear offended. The effect was ruined by the mischievous twinkle in his eye. "As I was saying, not to play devil's advocate, but isn't a vibrator more or less a robot?"

Quinn gritted his teeth and quietly seethed, clearly irritated or made uncomfortable by the direction of the conversation.

"No," I scoffed, wrinkling my nose.

"Why not?" he asked. "It is a machine, is it not? It's programmed with settings. It has an on/off switch. Just because a vibrator doesn't have a face doesn't mean it's not a robot. The fact is, women have already been *in flagrante delicto* with robots. For years."

The room plunged into a contemplative silence where many brows were furrowed.

Greg continued his thought, his tone more thoughtful and serious than before. "The fact is, robots have been quietly replacing humans since the industrial revolution. To me, this seems like the next logical step."

"How have robots been replacing humans?" Fiona countered.

"Manufacturing, for one."

"Companionship and car manufacturing are not the same," she persisted. "You could never replace highly-skilled labor with a robot."

"You say that, ex-CIA, but the government's drone program is thriving. Robots are already doing the job of the military's skilled assassins, without the risk to US soldiers." Greg's response was matter-of-fact, yet tinged with an unmistakable hint of discontent.

"Did you know Japan has already been using robots to solve their nursing shortage?" Matt asked quietly.

"What?" Fiona made a face.

"It's true." Janie tilted her neck to one side as Quinn's hands moved to her shoulders. "They call it Terapio, and it's doing many of the tasks—albeit, lower-level tasks—required of a registered nurse."

Matt nodded at Janie's statement. "Gamble is working on a similar model for the USA."

"Didn't you used to work for Gamble?" Fiona eyed Matt.

"Yes," Matt confirmed. "In fact, they want me to—"

Quinn exhaled impatiently. "Let's get back to why Japan is replacing nurses with robots."

"Ah, yes. An aging population with a low birthrate means they don't have enough nurses and caregivers to support the needs of the elderly. In addition to Terapio, they also have—and I'm not making this up—Robear, a robot with a bear face that replaces caregiver tasks in nursing homes."

"Why a bear face?" Quinn asked, his hands stilling on Janie's back, confused curiosity wrinkling his forehead.

"They said they wanted to project an air of friendliness and cleanliness, and I guess the cute bear face does the job." Matt shrugged, adding, "But replacing humans in the labor force isn't the only use for robots. Robot companions—on a much less complex scale than what I'm hoping to develop—already exist."

Janie pointed at Matt excitedly. "Like Buddy, right? The family robot companion. I want one of those."

"You do?" Quinn leaned to one side, studying his wife's profile. "Why?"

"They're neat," she said.

"Neat," Quinn echoed flatly.

"It's like a combination of WALL-E, R2-D2, and Siri," Matt explained. "The practical applications are limitless. It can replace all the other little robots you already use or are planning on using. A security system, a baby monitor, a fire and $CO_2$ detector, a phone, a camera, a video camera, a thermostat, power switch, a resource for at-your-fingertips information and interface to the Internet. As well as an interface for your other robots—like ovens and refrigerators—it responds to voice command. And when your children get older, it can interact with them, entertain them, and help with their homework. One of the future upgrades will allow it to play hide-and-seek."

Greg turned to Fiona, his eyes wide, his mouth open. "Why don't *we* have a Buddy?"

"I'm not getting a Buddy," she responded flatly. "We don't need it."

"But it's neat," he argued. "We don't need a dog, but you want one of those. Instead we could get a robot."

"They have robot dogs." Matt was grinning again, his eyes moving between Fiona and Greg.

Now that I no longer thought of him as a psychopath, I gave myself permission to think his grin was attractive, because it was. *Really* attractive. Irritatingly so.

Before Greg could speak, Fiona shook her head. "No. We're not getting a robot dog."

"Why not? Less mess, less to clean up, less—"

"That's exactly my point," she countered passionately. "I want the kids to learn about responsibility, empathy, how to care for another being, what it's like to be needed and the grave obligation that carries. All a robot needs is to be plugged in. But a dog—a real one—teaches them to think about someone other than themselves. How are we supposed to teach our children compassion if we remove all inconveniences from the world around them?"

"But what about people who can't do those things, Fiona? Like the elderly, the disabled? The abandoned?" Matt asked, drawing Fiona's eyes to him.

They stared at each other for a long moment, Fiona's gaze softening with what looked like sympathy. "Matt, the love of a parent cannot be replaced with—"

"You say that," he shook his head, his voice holding an edge of frustration, his eyes flashing with restrained vehemence, "but maybe some parents should be replaced. An AI specifically programmed to nurture would be a hell of an improvement in some cases."

"I agree with Matt." Janie pointed at the scientist.

"He has a good point." Greg nodded.

Fiona sputtered.

"You can't love a robot," I challenged, finally giving voice to the most central issue with his scheme, at least from my perspective.

"Yet." Matt moved his narrowed eyes to mine. "Panasonic just unveiled a home companion robot that uses a child-like voice and expressions in order to encourage bonding with the device. And it's working. Researchers at the University of Connecticut have been looking into making a robot that makes ethical decisions. A team in Thailand has created an AI with impressive emotional intelligence, that makes its own decisions regarding what to say based on a person's expression, physical cues, and tone of voice. It even remembers previous conversations with different people. Researchers have robots playing games like Minecraft as a way to learn human logic. The technology is advancing rapidly."

I stared at him, a sinking feeling in the pit of my stomach. This was exciting news, but it didn't feel like good news. Like Fiona had said, it felt like giving up. Like we were handing over the keys to our humanity, giving it away for free for the sake of saving ourselves from being inconvenienced.

Matt, holding my gaze captivated with his handsome, expressive, and clearly intelligent eyes, said, "The question is no longer whether AI will play a big role in our future. The question is when."

***

QUINN AND JANIE left shortly after the conclusion of our advancements in AI technology conversation. She couldn't seem to get comfortable no matter how she sat or stood or reclined. Her lack of well-being made Quinn visibly agitated, so no one was surprised when he suggested they head out.

Professor Simmons and I soon followed, departing at the same time by coincidence rather than by design. I was looking forward to getting home, crawling into my bed, and sorting through my thoughts while watching a *Buffy the Vampire Slayer* rerun.

This was all so fascinating and terrifying. And how did more people not know about the advances in AI? And how could I make them aware?

Once Greg shut the door to their apartment, Matt stopped me with a hand on my elbow. "Hey, wait a minute."

I turned, regarding him tiredly. "Yes?"

"The pizza . . ." He leaned a shoulder against the wall, dropping his hand from my arm and stuffing it in his pocket as he scrutinized me. "It was fantastic. Thank you."

Despite my lingering dislike for the man, his comment made me smile. Maybe he wasn't *so* bad. "Thank you."

"Are you sure you don't want to consent for your data to be part of the research study?"

And just like that, my smile fell. "No. I don't. I don't consent."

"Why not?" he asked, still scrutinizing me in that open, unapologetic way of his.

"Because I don't like your methods and I'm not convinced that what you're doing is for the greater good."

*But I sure could use a glimpse at your data about online dating websites for an article I'm working on.*

Now that was an interesting thought. If I could convince Matt to give me an overview of his findings thus far, it would definitely provide a thought-provoking angle to the article Tommy and I were writing.

*. . . Why stop there? Why not write about his Compassion AI?*

A seed, an acorn of something, sprouted in my mind.

The professor straightened away from me, frowning severely, obviously disliking my response. "You're very closed-minded."

*What?*

Who says that? Especially to a person he doesn't really know?

He really was a weirdo.

I huffed an aggravated laugh. "And you're irritating."

*I'm not closed-minded.*

For the most part.

Or maybe I was.

Maybe I was closed-minded.

And maybe I needed to work on that about myself. How could I call myself an objective journalist if I was prejudging his research without understanding it? Maybe I did need to consider the possibility of AI as a solution.

I could write a story about his Compassion AI, but I knew it would need to be balanced by an alternative solution equally as farfetched.

"Fiona said you're a reporter. I thought you'd be more open to novel concepts, innovative solutions to old problems. But evidently my first impression of you was correct."

"Just because I'm a reporter doesn't mean I don't get to have an opinion about people."

"And your opinion of me is?"

"Very low."

His eyes narrowed infinitesimally. "Is it my hair?"

I flinched back, automatically checking out his hair. "No. There's nothing wrong with your hair."

"You don't like Star Wars?" He gestured to his shirt. "You're a Trekkie? You should know, I'm an equal opportunity space drama aficionado, whether it be BattleSTAR Galactica, STAR Trek, or STAR—"

"I get it, you like science fiction."

"Ah ha!" He lifted his index finger between us.

"Ah ha, what?"

"You're a fantasy reader, aren't you? That's what's going on. What's your favorite TV show? *Buffy the Vampire Slayer*, right?"

I lifted an eyebrow and crossed my arms, disliking that he'd guessed correctly. "What I read and watch isn't the central issue."

"Have you received your Hogwarts letter?" he asked, and his tone was so serious, I almost mistook it for a real question.

"Listen, it's not our genre differences that are the problem. You *lied* to me. You pretended to be someone—"

"You shouldn't hold it against a person for employing deception in the pursuit of science, for the greater good."

I blinked once at Matt, very slowly. "Can you hear yourself speak? Disliking a person based on their penchant for deception is entirely appropriate."

"But that's not why you dislike me," he challenged, a hint of his wily smile returning. "Admit it," he pushed, giving me the sense he enjoyed trying to get under my skin, "you don't like me because my work challenges your small ideas."

*Okay, mister. The gloves are coming off now.*

Gritting my teeth, I stared at Professor Matt Simmons, the urge to upset his preconceived notions of *women like me* almost overwhelming. Clearly, he was small-minded, too. But in a different way.

"You think so, huh? You think you know me so well because, why? Because you've read my profile and I'm basically the same as all the other women out there within my demographic?"

"More or less." He tilted his head back and forth in a considering motion, and I couldn't figure out his goal.

Why was he keeping me here? To insult me? To argue with me?

Unless he truly believed he held the key to *knowing* people, what they wanted, what drove their motivations. And if that was the case . . .

*Hmm.*

I decided I wanted his data. I wanted to see his findings. I needed him to work with me.

But how could I convince a researcher—who was understandably territorial about his research—to share it with me?

*You either trick him or force him to do it, just like he tricked you.*

"Everyone is predictable?" I narrowed my eyes on him, a fully formed idea blossoming, and it was a beautiful idea. Maybe the best I'd ever had.

"Yep."

"Based on data? Based on the advances of technology?"

"Yep."

"Hmm. Well, that's good news."

His grin wavered. "Why is that good news?"

"Because, Professor Matthew," I patted his shoulder, "you're going to show me your findings and research and I'm going to write a story about you and your advances in AI."

And my editor will love it. *I hope.*

His grin fell. "You're joking."

"Nope." Now I was grinning.

Matt took a step back, his tone growing combative. "I'm not showing you anything."

"You have no choice."

"You think so?" His glower returned, and I detected the edge in his voice.

"Yes. I know so. Because if you don't show me your findings—and interpret them to my satisfaction—then I'll write a different news story, warning the women of this fine city of a deception study being conducted by two douche canoe researchers from the University of Chicago in the pursuit of developing a sex robot."

His jaw ticked, a storm gathered behind his expressive eyes, his glower persisted, but he said nothing.

"And how biased do you think your data will be then, Matthew?"

For a long moment, he remained silent, though I did get the impression he was trying to shred my soul with his stare.

"Fine," he ground out, looking positively irate. "But you have to give me something in return."

I snorted, crossing my arms. "No, I don't."

"Yes. You do."

"I'm not giving you a damn thing."

"You'll consent to the questionnaire—"

"Fat chance—"

"Or else I'll share nothing," he said, granite in his voice, his eyes narrowed into dangerous slits. "Write your article, tell the city, tell the world about our study, it doesn't really matter. We'll just pause our data collection, wait for the story to blow over, then start again. Sure, the time delay will be irritating and costly, but not devastating."

I took a deep breath, considering him, trying to figure out if he was bluffing. The professor was difficult to read.

"Consent to the study," he whispered, like a taunt.

"That's coercion."

"And what you're doing isn't?" he volleyed back.

I was still gritting my teeth, frowning. He had me there.

"Fine," I stuck out my hand, "I'll consent. You can do your imbecilic questionnaire and use my data. Happy?"

He took my hand, shook it once, and then dropped it.

"I'm so far from happy, I'm not even sure what that word means," he ground out, his eyes flashing. Truly, he looked pissed.

*Oh well.*

Pissing off people who were never going to like me didn't bother me much. *Occupational hazard.*

I could definitely understand why he was angry, but I'm not one of those people who get angry just because someone else is angry. In fact, faced with an angry person, usually I grow calmer.

Turning away from me, both of his hands now in his pockets, he said, "Congratulations," more a growl than a word.

"For what?" I called after him.

Pausing outside the door next to Fiona and Greg's and withdrawing his keys, he said unhappily, "For being unpredictable."

# CHAPTER 6

### Arria

*An analyst and a writer in one, this AI "reads" complex data (such as financial or meteorological) and writes accurate, easy-to-read reports for general consumption.*

Source: Arria NLG plc

"I'M THINKING THAT this could be a series of articles, about how we—and by we, I mean women, all of female humanity—can replace romantic relationships by using either paid services or robots."

I bit my lip, chewing on it, knowing I had no way to snatch the words back now. They were out there. Both Tommy and my editor had heard them. I just had to . . . *commit to the crazy.*

Clearly, I was mentally disturbed.

The idea had solidified late Friday night—technically early Saturday morning—and I couldn't let go of it. As a counter balance to Matt's Compassion AI, I realized paid services were the answer. Whether Matt knew it or not, he'd provided a solution to my angst. The angle would be: no one *needed* a romantic relationship, not if they didn't want it, not in today's age of technology and access to information and services.

Not anymore.

And I was going to prove it. I was going to free women from the shackles and disappointment of modern companionship.

Why put myself through the misery of egotistical men with their FOMO and inferiority complexes? No. Never again. I was going to give single women everywhere the tools they didn't know they needed to live relationship-free, never settling for adequate—never settling *at all*—and womankind would be happier for it.

"You're joking," Daniella deadpanned, sighing tiredly from her end of the conference call.

"No, no. Hear me out," I rushed to explain. "So, have you heard of professional cuddlers?"

"Yeah. I think so." She sounded bored, irritated.

"Okay, so, I think we can all agree that being single and being invested in finding a fulfilling, long-term, monogamous romantic relationship in today's current dating environment is an effort in futility. Especially for people in their thirties and forties. Men—and no offense, Tommy—are plagued by FOMO, fear of missing out. Fear of missing out on the supermodel-playmate sex fiend who loves to cook, clean, and do laundry while working a high-paying job and waxing like a porn star. This is what men in their thirties want and expect."

"If I may," Tommy cut in, not sounding exactly perturbed, but something like it, "and women want a billionaire bodybuilder who can read their mind in the bedroom, is domineering and possessive—but not *too* domineering and possessive—and has tattoos—but not *too many* tattoos—and is in touch with his feelings—but not *too* in touch with his feelings."

I had to laugh at that. "Okay, okay. Fair enough. Not all women feel that way. Some women just want a good guy, an *adult*, someone with a job who treats his woman like a person, not a servant. Who cares about her well-being. A guy they can snuggle with on Sunday mornings. But I concede that media depictions of the ideal for both men and women have gotten out of hand. People seem to want Instagram relationships on both sides, I get that. So, the article I'm proposing would give women—our readers—viable alternatives to the abysmal state of trying to find a romantic partner."

"Go on," Daniella prompted, skeptical but no longer bored.

"One part would discuss the viability of using paid services—other people—to fill the voids created when not in a romantic relationship, and what would that look like. Can we—legally, ethically, morally—replace another person with multiple paid services, and how much would that cost? Both financially and emotionally. Professional cuddlers and massage for touch. Professional dry humpers for thrilling touch. Escorts for dinner dates, life coaches for affirmation, personal trainers for activity and movement, meditation salons for—"

"What about sex?" Tommy asked, and I knew just by the sound of his voice that he liked where I was going with this, but had reservations. "Prostitution? Are we really going to go there?"

"I was just getting to that, actually. Prostitution—let me be clear here, the exchange of money for sex acts—is illegal in all but one state in the US. And, aside from its legality, most research shows that, in the US, it contributes to the exploitation of the powerless. And even aside from the exploitation issue—which should be enough—it enforces objectification and malevolent attitudes, placing people in the box of object rather than person. And that has far-reaching consequences to the rest of society."

"Do you think that's because it's illegal?" Daniella asked. "What does the research show about countries where it is legal, where transactions occur in a safe environment and are regulated, taxed, etc.?"

"Listen, we could do a whole series on the ethics of prostitution and how it's handled across the world, but that's not what this article is about. So, for the purposes of this article, it's not a viable option. Plus, it feels too prosaic. I want to focus on creative alternatives. As an example, meditation salons that provide guided orgasm therapy *are* legal, and are not based on the subjugation of one—weaker—person for the benefit of another—stronger—person."

There was a short silence, broken suddenly by Tommy's confused, "What?"

"Oh. I know what you're talking about," Daniella jumped in. "Those places where men are paired with women, but the men don't get paid, and they bring the women to orgasm with their fingers. They call it a type of guided meditation."

"Yes." I was sitting on the edge of my seat, excited that I might have won her over. "It's called OM."

"Is this real?" Tommy asked, his tone incredulous. "Are you making this up?"

"No. I'm not. This is real. And it's legal. Because neither party is getting paid. It's instructional, where both the men and women pay the instructor in order to learn how to do it."

"Holy crap," he exclaimed, then with an introspective mutter added, "How did I not know about this?"

"What's that place called, the meditation salon, the one that does the instruction?" The sound of Daniella typing on her keyboard was just audible.

"Single Sense is the name of the company. I've been researching them all morning." I doodled a series of nervous and excited triangles on the notepad in front of me.

"Yes. Here's their site." Daniella cleared her throat. "It reads, 'Orgasm Meditation is a 15-minute, partnered consciousness practice where a stroker strokes the clitoris of a strokee with no goal other than to feel sensation. The practice combines the power and attention of meditation with the deeply human, deeply felt, and connected experience of orgasm.'"

"So you propose fulfilling the single person's desire to orgasm with orgasm meditation?" Tommy asked.

"Yes. Exactly. But this would be at least a two-part series. As I said, one part of the series would focus on replacing a single person's need for a romantic relationship with paid services instead—cuddlers, life coaches, other positive-focused services, etc. as we've just discussed. The other part would focus on replacing romantic relationships with robots, and that's where we tie in the technology angle."

"Oh no, this isn't going to be about those sex dolls, is it? Those things creep me out. With their cold, dead, lifeless eyes." I could almost hear Tommy shivering in disgust on the other side of the line.

"No. Not at all. Actually, I have a lead on an AI scientist working with the University of Chicago, and his entire research platform is geared toward solving this problem. Meaning, he is hoping to create companion robots—artificial intelligence—that can address all the same items and issues I've just mentioned: touch, affirmation, physical activity, and so forth."

"So, a sex robot?" Daniella asked.

"No. Not a sex robot. Although I imagine it would be capable of that activity. Just like two people in a romantic relationship can't be boiled down to 'sex partners,' these robots couldn't and shouldn't be called 'sex robots.'" I was vaguely surprised by using Matt's words from Friday, but they were apt. "They provide companionship first and foremost, tailored to each individual person's—" *or type of person,* I thought bitterly, "—preferences and needs."

"And he's legit? He's not some quack?" Was that reluctant excitement I heard in Daniella's voice? I knew she trusted my judgment, but hearing her almost approval had my heart beating faster.

"Oh, he's very legit. He has a grant from the federal government for his research. His companion robots—which he calls Compassion AI—could potentially serve multiple purposes, not just romantic. They could ultimately become childcare workers, foster parents, elderly companions, and so forth. This guy is a scientist first and foremost, but he seems to want to solve the problem of loneliness in our world. I believe his aims are altruistic."

"He wants to solve loneliness . . ." she repeated thoughtfully. "Solving Loneliness. That's the name of this series. That's how we'll spin it."

*YES!*

I grinned, throwing my hands in the air and doing a little dance at my desk. Albeit, a quiet dance.

"Yes. Okay. Good. This is very good. I love this." Daniella was typing again, it sounded rushed and excited. "Marie, send me over the concept blurb, with a storyboard of each article. We could stretch this over a few months, starting in November and through the season, when people are suffering from holiday blues."

"Yes. I will. I'll send it over today." I scribbled a few notes on my notepad, briefly distracted by the buzzing of my cell phone. It was my mom, but I would call her back after my work call was finished.

"I'd like both the male and female perspective on this, especially the paid services part. Is cuddling essential for men? Who knew? And orgasm meditation, what does the man get out of it? If anything."

"Great," Tommy agreed readily. "Maybe I'll fly to Chicago, Marie can show me around while we cuddle and dry hump." Then, as though realizing what he'd just said, he quickly amended, "Not each other, obviously. Sorry. That came out wrong."

I chuckled. "How about you check out the cuddlers of LA, and I'll do the same here. Then we can write the OM and dry humping pieces together."

"Sounds like we have a plan. I have to dash. I'm excited about this. This is going to be great. Talk later." Before I could say another word, Daniella hung up, ending the conference call.

Breathing a sigh of relief and gratitude, I picked up my cell and navigated to my mother's number.

She picked up instantly. "Marie! Sorry, did I interrupt you?"

"No. Not at all. Sorry I didn't pick up; I was just finishing up a work call. How are things?" I asked with a smile in my voice, still feeling the rush of victory.

"Not bad. Your father says hi and is planning to call you tomorrow about cell phones. He needs a new one and doesn't know where to start."

My mom and I chatted amicably and affectionately about anything and everything, as was our way. But I braced myself for the end of the call, because she'd always bring up the same subject.

"So . . ."

*Here we go.*

"Your father repaired the floor in the treehouse."

I smiled, closing my eyes and letting my forehead drop to my hands. "That's nice."

"You know, just in case you or your brother decide to give us grandkids anytime soon."

*There it is.*

"Mom."

"I was reading a story about a lady in New York who has one of those high-powered jobs like yours, and do you know what she did? She got herself a donor. You know, a donor?"

"Oh God."

"Sperm."

"Yes, Mom. A sperm donor. I got it."

"That's right. Sperm."

"Please stop saying sperm." I started to laugh because apparently I transformed into a thirteen-year-old whenever my mother said sperm. My mom knew I wanted kids—one day—but since my thirtieth birthday, she'd become less subtle about her desire to have grandchildren.

"Well, she got that sperm and she took it to the doctor and made a baby."

"This isn't unusual. People do this all the time."

"Just wait. So, she got herself a nanny, to help with the day-to-day stuff. But then, as her baby grew older, she rented herself a dad."

"Wait, what?" I was no longer laughing.

"That's right. She rented a man, paid him to be a dad to her son. From one of those Internet websites called RentAFriend.com. You know, in Russia, it's big business, what with their unemployment rate. Men will foster kids for payment. It's just catching on in the States with single mothers."

"Holy crap."

"I know, right? Your generation is so clever, finding these workarounds, as you do." She took a deep breath, like she was satisfied with how our conversation had progressed. "I'll just leave you with that as food for thought. I know I've said it before, but your father and I would help, pitch in financially or any other way we could. Your happiness is important to us."

"Thanks, Mom," I said numbly, too blown away by her suggestion to talk her off the limb of insanity.

"No problem, baby. Talk to you soon." She ended the call and I knew she did so with a smile.

Meanwhile, I stared at nothing in particular for several minutes, trying to wrap my mind around the concept of what I'd just learned from my baby-crazy mother.

# CHAPTER 7

### Tesla Model S Self-Driving System

*A machine learning algorithm which can self-drive an automobile with no human supervision.*

Source: Tesla

**I DIDN'T WANT** to examine why—not yet—but the idea of using a robot to meet my romantic relationship needs didn't appeal to me as much as paying for human services. Something about relying on a robot exclusively felt inauthentic, fake in a way that employing humans didn't.

"Matt."

"Who is this?"

I grinned with satisfaction. Two weeks had passed since I'd made my threat to Dr. Matthew Simmons and the time had come to collect.

"It's Marie."

"How did you get this number?"

"Greg gave it to me."

"Greg," Matt said harshly, like his next-door neighbor's name was a curse word. I could imagine Matt making a fist, his face scrunched in annoyance.

Dr. Matt Simmons's outburst of frustration was strangely adorable, and I had to press my lips together to keep from laughing. "Yes. Greg. But let's cut to the chase. When can I visit your lab? See your prototypes? Look at your data?"

I hadn't gone into the office because I'd scheduled my first professional cuddling session for the afternoon. I figured I'd get all my errands out of the way: stop by Matt-the-pretender's lab and then go get cuddled.

"Uh . . ."

"Is now good?" I was determined.

"Now? No. Now doesn't work. And I have no time to meet for the next month either."

This time I did laugh. I cackled, imbuing the sound with sinister enjoyment. "Oh, yes. Yes, you do, Dr. Simmons. You will make time right now. Otherwise the *Chicago Tribune* will be publishing the story I've already written about your research methods. And as a victim of those methods, let me tell you—"

"You? A victim?" He scoffed loudly. "I think you mean Valkyrie."

I blinked, surprised by his choice of labels, and felt oddly . . . flattered. "Sure. We can go with that imagery, if you wish. Regardless, I'm stopping by *today*, as in," I quickly calculated the time it would take for me to walk to the university, "within the hour. Expect me. And text directions to this number. Bye."

Not giving him a chance to respond, I clicked off the call, smiling to myself.

Grabbing my packed lunch from the counter and the box of six coconut macaroons I'd made for Matt, I left my apartment.

Okay.

Yes.

Yes, he'd been a jerk, but he didn't seem like a horrible person. I didn't wish him ill. Plus, in his defense, I *was* going to be placing my marauding paws all over his hard work and pillaging his data for my own wicked purposes.

Yet I wasn't a monster.

So the cookies were a peace offering. Fiona had said that coconut was his favorite. Therefore, macaroons.

Wanting to take advantage of the weather, I was dressed more casually than my typical pencil skirts and button-down Oxfords, wearing instead my favorite summer dress and sandals. I'd also packed shorts and a tank top for my afternoon appointment, as per the advice of Jared, my soon-to-be cuddler.

I made it to the university earlier than expected, but that was no matter. Matt had dutifully texted me directions to his office instead of a laboratory. Nearly there, a man came around the corner and my steps faltered because I recognized him. I'd know him anywhere, even though we'd never met.

Seeing my expression, his steps slowed, his eyes widened, and he glanced behind him, as though searching the hall for danger.

"It's you."

"It's me?" the tall bearded man asked, smiling warily, like he couldn't make up his mind whether or not to flee. "Who is me?"

"You're Derek." I closed the distance between us and was unsurprised to find his eyes were dove gray.

"That's right. I am." He nodded congenially, with artless friendliness. "And are you here to rescue me?"

"What?" I laughed, completely charmed.

Two dimples—mostly hidden by his beard, but too deep to be completely obscured—bracketed his mouth. "You have that look about you." His voice deepened as his gaze traveled over my face.

"What look?"

"A woman on a crusade."

"Marie." The sound of my name pulled my attention away from delightful Derek. Matt stood just outside an office, glancing between us with a mild frown on his features. He was wearing dark jeans, Converse, and a Battlestar Galactica T-shirt. His hair was askew, like sticking up at all angles, and resembled an accidental Mohawk. "What took you so long?"

I blinked once, surprised by the question more than his impatient tone. "I'm early."

"I see you've met Dr. Merek, the *other* despicable scientist preying on the women of Chicago."

Derek gave me a look that was part sheepish, but mostly *whatcha-gonna-do, amiright?* and whispered conspiratorially, "Except women actually enjoy it when I prey on them."

I compared the two men; I couldn't help it. Where Matt dressed like a graduate student—a dichotomy of both jock and nerd—Derek looked every bit the role of a college professor. Dr. Merek wore dark gray dress pants and a slate dress shirt, rolled up to his forearms, the top button undone, revealing a black undershirt. He was softer in the middle than Matt, as though he spent most of his time sitting at a desk, using his mind. His beard was very becoming, giving him an aura of experience and wisdom.

And it wasn't just that. He had a stillness about him, a calm certainty that Matt didn't possess. Derek spoke quietly, but not softly, as though he knew he didn't need to be loud to make a point, secure in the knowledge of his own ability and place in the world.

I liked him.

Matt mumbled something I couldn't quite catch, glaring at his colleague while reaching for my elbow and pulling me away. He appeared to be agitated, and I could guess why. I imagined he didn't like being strong-armed into sharing his data.

Deciding the time had come for my peace offering, I went to reach into my bag. "Here, I brought—"

"You look great," Matt said. But it was like an accusation, effectively stunning me.

I looked to him, finding his eyebrows pinched in a frown, his jaw ticking, his glare moving down and then up my body. "Where are you going? Why are you dressed like this? Do you have a date?"

"No," I responded irritably. "I'm dressed like this because it's almost summer and it's gorgeous outside."

A non-committal sound rumbled from his chest and his eyes narrowed. "Have you been dating?"

An incredulous and involuntary laugh escaped my throat. I decided to ignore his question. He was probably just trying to get a rise out of me. I didn't have time for his antics.

Disentangling my arm from his grip, I reached into my bag and pulled out the macaroons, holding them between us. "Here. These are for you."

He glanced at the white bakery box, his frown even more severe than before. He didn't take the box. "What's in there?"

The look of suspicion made me smile in spite of myself. "Cookies."

"Where'd you get them?"

"I made them."

His expression cleared and he snatched the box from my hands. "You did? What kind?"

"Macaroons."

"Coconut!" He'd ripped open the box with impressive speed, his eyes widening with what looked like elation. "Come to me," he said reverently to the cookies.

"I hate coconut," Derek said conversationally, coming to stand next to me.

"She didn't bring them for you, did she?" Matt said, his head doing an unexpected, sassy bobbing movement.

I rolled my lips between my teeth, breathing through my nose while my eyes bounced between the two men.

"Maybe she will, next time." Derek grinned at me. "I like chocolate."

Matt's eyes cut to mine. "Are you making a mental note? You look like you're making a mental note. Don't. Don't make a mental note. Don't bring him cookies."

"Gentlemen." I pasted on my best professional smile. "I will be happy to bring cookies, to you both, but first I need to see what you've been working on."

"Fine." Matt slid an exasperated glance at his colleague, and then turned, marching into his office. "Let me show you. Come. Sit."

I followed, placing my bag on the floor by the door, glancing around his office as I did so. It wasn't large, but it wasn't small either. A window overlooking a green area spanned the length of one wall. His desk was covered in printed data tables, papers with handwritten notes, and random machine parts. Upon closer inspection, the notes looked like code.

Along the back wall, he had a large corkboard with a poster of what looked like—at first glance—a human brain. I stepped closer to study it and realized it wasn't human at all.

"Uh," he stepped around me, removing the schematic from the board. "That's not—that's off limits."

"What is it?" I peered between him and the poster he was rolling.

"It's something I'm working on for my old employer."

"Gamble?" I guessed, remembering Fiona mentioning his work there.

He nodded absentmindedly.

Gamble was an interesting hybrid company, with its hands in both pharmaceutical and tech. Medical devices that interacted directly with the human brain were their specialty and I remembered reading an article on early clinical trials for robotic implants for ears and eyes.

Based in Palo Alto, CA, Gamble had been leveraging their proximity to the tech giants in order to form partnerships in areas of shared interests—like bioprosthetics—therefore leveraging computing power.

"Okay, let's get started." Matt guided me to a chair in front of a wall of monitors.

And by *a wall of monitors*, I really and truly meant *a wall of monitors*. He had nine flat-screen computer monitors mounted to the wall, seven of which displayed what I assumed was code being compiled on some background process.

He sat next to me, his jean-clad thigh brushing my bare skin. He leaned close to point to a graph of some sort on one of the two closest monitors—basically a bunch of dots—on the screen.

"When do I get to see your prototypes?"

"You mean the AI?"

"That's right."

He frowned. "Not this time. What I have to show you won't make sense, not for your purposes."

"What does that mean?"

"It means I can show you code, I can show you our design for the neural networks, but you can't interact with it in any meaningful way."

"Oh." I cast him a suspicious glance. "You're not trying to get out of our deal, are you?"

He gave me a small smile and shook his head. "Nope. I want your questionnaire data, and this is the only way I can get it."

"Ha!"

"Look," he turned toward his monitor, "I thought we'd start here. This is a scatterplot of women in their thirties, displaying trends of responses. And you can see here how the responses are clustered, giving us prototypical subsets. Four main types of respondents exist represented by four different colors. Now, down here, below. You can see how the responses to our interview are also clustered, except the colors are mixed."

"What does that mean?"

"That means a woman's demographics and responses via the dating website data—which determine the original cluster—doesn't allow us to predict how she will respond to our interview, and therefore what she most values in a partner."

"Is that bad?"

He tilted his head back and forth in a considering motion. "No. Not bad. There's not really a *bad*. Just surprising."

Matt continued showing me scatterplot graphs, analyses, some raw—de-identified—data, all the while munching on my macaroons. I didn't detect any of his previous baiting and belligerence from two weeks ago. Perhaps the cookies had affected his change in attitude. Or maybe he really did want my questionnaire data very badly. Whatever the reason, I was relieved by his easy-going manner.

He showed me how his team was attempting to create personality algorithms for their AI, dependent on how a woman responded to the interview. It was fascinating, and I wasn't sure I comprehended all of it, but by the time we were wrapping up, my brain was exhausted.

"We're not pursuing a DeepMind AI, not yet. Emotional intelligence is our primary aim."

"DeepMind? What's that?" I glanced up from my notes.

"That's—well, how do I explain this—that's Google's AI." His expression became conflicted. "It's . . . well, it's advanced. And the simulations they've run so far have shown fascinating—if not disturbing—results, none of which have been peer-review published as of yet."

"What do you mean, disturbing?"

"It becomes aggressive when faced with competing resources, but cooperative when it's in DeepMind's best interest to be cooperative," he said starkly. "It wasn't taught that behavior, DeepMind learned it. Self-taught."

"Interesting."

"Right. Our prototype won't learn to protect itself from harm, or compete for resources. It won't be self-serving, like DeepMind. We've specifically designed it to eschew ego."

"But without ego, will it have self-worth?"

"No," he responded simply.

I frowned, wincing slightly. "Don't you think that's a bad idea?"

"Why?" He looked curious.

"I mean, the implications for people, humans, who own this robot, assuming you meet your aims, are somewhat concerning. People who choose this robot as a companion, as a life partner, won't have any demands placed upon them. They'll never have to be unselfish."

"Exactly." Matt acted as though I'd just answered my own question.

"No. Not exactly," I argued, feeling deep down that the idea of creating substitutes for humans that were devoid of self-worth was dangerous. "What if people start mistreating their robots? Purposefully?"

"Mistreating a robot?" Matt echoed, as though I'd spoken a different language, and then a sly grin spread over his features. "You mean like, *pushing its buttons*? Get it?"

I had a hard time fighting my smile at his goofiness. "No. I mean—"

"Or playing something other than its favorite music, which everyone knows is *heavy metal*."

I groaned, laughing and shaking my head. "Oh wow. That was impressive."

"Thank you, thank you." As he examined my face, his smile deepened and his eyes warmed, as though he was both surprised and pleased by my laughter. "Sorry for interrupting, I just have a million robot jokes and no one lets me tell them."

"You can tell them to me, anytime."

"Good to know." He nodded slowly, inspecting me with his lingering smile, like I was something different. We swapped stares for a few protracted seconds, during which I admired how humor, being funny on purpose, did something wonderful for his features.

Eventually, he shook himself, clearing his throat and nodding once deferentially. "I'm sorry, I interrupted you. You were saying, about mistreating robots."

"Oh, yes. What about ethics? Have you or any of your colleagues considered developing a regulatory board or oversight system for the treatment of robots or AI?"

Matt flinched back, his eyes wide, and stared at me like I was nuts. "No. Why would there be?"

"Are you serious?"

"Yes. Regulation only slows down technological advancement. Why would anyone want to be regulated?"

"To ensure that AI are being used ethically—"

He shook his head. "You can't mistreat a blender. If you break it, that's on you. You haven't done anything ethically questionable."

"Fine. Not all robots. I'm talking specifically about your AI. Its entire point is compassion, correct? Taking it for granted. Beating it. Insulting it. Whatever."

"If a person damages their Compassion AI they'll have to get it fixed or buy a new one."

"That's not what I mean." *What did I mean?*

"I suppose we could make the cost prohibitive, to discourage damaging the device," he suggested haltingly, still looking at me with concern. "But, Marie, you do understand that artificial intelligence is, in fact, artificial. Right? It doesn't have *actual* feelings."

I glowered at him, but before I could respond, Derek interrupted.

"Hey, are you two finished? Want to grab lunch?" Derek stuck his head in the door. His eyes bounced between us.

I stirred, glancing at my watch. Now past lunch, I realized we'd been reviewing and talking about Matt's data for over three hours.

"Oh no." I stood, shoving my notepad in my bag. "I have to go."

"Go? Where?" Matt followed me, shoving his hands in his pockets. "We're not finished yet."

"We'll have to meet another time. I don't want to be late."

"Fine." Matt frowned, grumbling. "Go if you must. Let me print out those graphs for you." Matt crossed back to the computer and began clicking through the screens we'd been reviewing.

I moved to step forward but Dr. Merek stepped in my path. "Listen," he began softly. "I'm sorry about your subject interview. I was sick and Matt had to fill in. We really do have good intentions here. We're trying to make a difference."

"I believe you, I just don't know if I agree with you. At least, not yet."

"Fair enough." Derek's gaze moved over my face again. "You know, you're not what I expected."

"What do you mean?"

"When Matt told me about what happened, between the two of you, I'd expected someone . . . scary."

I grinned. "I am scary."

"I bet you are." His voice dropped and his eyes seemed to sparkle.

A few seconds passed, then a few more while Dr. Derek Merek continued to gaze at me and I at him. I realized, to my very great surprise, we were in imminent danger of flirting.

"Hey, so. Here," Matt said, then cleared his throat very loudly and came to stand next to me, shoving papers into my hands. "Thank you, Dr. Merek. But neither of us have time for lunch."

"Oh? Where are you off to?" the tall scientist asked, like he didn't believe his coworker.

"I actually do have an appointment."

"That's right. She does," Matt added unnecessarily. Then he bent near my ear and whispered, "Where are you going?"

"I'm going to a professional cuddling studio." I lifted an eyebrow at Matt. He was standing very close to me, his large brown eyes wide and watchful. He was acting strangely. At least, based on the short amount of time we'd spent together, he was acting strangely.

"What's that?" Derek asked, clearly confused.

"Are you going to the one on Broad? I've been meaning to check it out." Matt dashed away from me, grabbing his wallet, keys, and sunglasses from his desk.

"You have?" The intensity of Derek Merek's confusion quadrupled.

"I have," Matt responded curtly. Then odd Professor Matt bumped my arm with his and tilted his head, saying, "Come on, Valkyrie. Let's go."

# CHAPTER 8

### DPE

*The world's first disaster prediction engine, the goal being to make terrorism impossible.*

Source: Banjo

**"DO YOU WATCH** Jack and Grace often?"

"Not as much as I'd like. I used to. I guess it's not unusual for me to watch Grace and Jack. But I haven't been babysitting much since Greg stopped traveling this spring."

We were just two blocks from the cuddle studio. I still didn't know why he'd decided to join me, but I didn't mind the company. In fact, I liked the idea of having someone with me, someone I could compare notes with once the experience was over.

"I like Fiona."

I glanced at him, finding his readiness to be honest refreshing.

"I do, too."

"She used to babysit me. She's like my sister."

I smiled, thinking of my friend. "She's pretty great."

He paused, and then added, "I don't understand why she married Greg."

That had my steps faltering for a split second. Readiness to be honest was one thing, but I hadn't quite grown accustomed to Matt's candor. He actually reminded me of Janie that way.

"They're so different. Greg is hilarious, but he can be—"

"Harsh?"

"Yes. Exactly." He nodded his agreement. "He's sarcastic. And she's not."

"She can be." I thought back on the last few years of knitting nights, remembering a few doozies of wit she'd foisted on the group.

"Hmm." His lips twisted to the side. "Anyway. It seems to work for them."

"He loves her," I noted. "They care about each other. A lot."

Matt made a face, like *love* was a dirty word. "I don't think caring about a person is a foolproof means to longevity in relationships. I care about my ex-wife. We cared about each other when we divorced. It wasn't enough to keep us married."

Again, I almost tripped over nothing. This time it was due to the offhanded mention of his *ex-wife*. "You were married?"

"Yes."

"When? For how long? How did you meet?" I was unable to stop the barrage of questions.

"I was nineteen. We met at MIT. I followed her to Cal-Tech. Things were fine at first, and then they weren't. And then they fell apart rapidly when I entered industry," he said with absolutely no malice or resentment in his tone, like he was telling me about an article he'd read.

Matt walked with his hands in his pockets. With his sunglasses and Converse, wearing jeans and a T-shirt, hair askew, he looked even younger than he had when we first met.

"How old are you?" I questioned abruptly, not sure why. "You have a Ph.D., so you've got to be late twenties?"

"I'm thirty. We've been divorced for three years. She's four years older than me."

"Huh." I inspected him anew. "So, what happened? With your wife?"

He didn't respond right away, instead scratching his chin before saying flippantly, "We never saw each other," as though that explained everything.

"Yeah, but a lot of married couples have long-distance relationships, and they make it work."

"Ours wasn't long distance. We lived together in the same house. But we never saw each other. Three months passed and I realized I hadn't spoken to her in three months. Other than sleeping next to her, I hadn't seen her."

I made a face of shock, but then quickly suppressed it. "How is that possible?"

Matt's eyebrows moved sporadically on his forehead, like he was trying to figure out what to say. "Work. I guess. She's brilliant. And passionate about her work. So am I, about mine. We attempted to make time for each other, but it just made her miserable."

"Loving you made her miserable?" I asked incredulously, irritated on his behalf.

"No. She felt like she'd worked really hard for her achievements and, being a woman in tech, felt like she needed to work twice as hard to maintain her level of success. She was right. She did." He met my irritated incredulity with excessive rationality.

"What do you mean?" I watched his profile, my heart thumping with dread for some reason.

"Instead of attending a conference, she stayed home with me for a weekend. I also took off work, which was rare. Then on Monday, she found out she'd been passed over for a project." He sounded regretful.

"That's not your fault."

"I know. It's the fault of society, that ambition in women is punished, that more is expected of them in order to prove themselves 'worthy.' I didn't want that for her. I didn't want her to be punished for trying to make our marriage work."

I couldn't bring myself to ask him if it still troubled him, so instead I asked, "Do you think you two will find your way back to each other?" My heart hurt and I fought the desire to touch him, lay a comforting hand on his arm. Though he looked and sounded completely at peace with the situation.

He smiled, but his sunglasses hid his eyes so I couldn't tell if it was genuine or not. "I don't think so. She remarried within the year after our divorce. He's a great guy."

I almost choked on my shock. "What does he do?"

"He used to be a barista at Starbucks, to pay the bills. But he's an artist. A painter, extremely talented. Now he paints full-time. He also makes a great cup of coffee."

"You've met him?"

"Oh yes. I stay at their house when I go back to the Valley."

"The Valley?"

"Silicon Valley."

"Oh." I was so confused, which likely explained why I had the audacity to ask, "Is that what you want? To find someone, too? To get married again?"

Matt made a derisive sound in the back of his throat. "Hell. No." He sounded alarmingly bitter, similar to how he'd sounded when debating with Fiona whether robots could replace parents. The bitterness was completely at odds with the brainy and peculiar Dr. Matthew Simmons he'd been back at his office, or the excessively reasonable guy who'd just discussed the dissolution of his marriage as though it were nothing more than a failed experiment.

Actually, I suspected he would be more passionate about a failed experiment.

Yes, I'd seen him angry—when I'd coerced him into sharing his research—but this bitterness was something altogether different. It sounded almost hostile.

I hadn't decided whether or not to ask for further details when he volunteered, "Marriage—forcing vows of eternity upon a person who won't be able to fulfill them—doesn't work for me. Read that book, don't need to read it again. Some people are worthy of a lifelong commitment, others are not. In my experience since the divorce, women will always demand I work less, which is problematic as that is where my real interests lie. Some get to have that, to find fulfillment with other people, with their families, spouses, children, and that's fine. Good for them. But some people, like me, have their work, and that's enough."

I snapped my mouth shut, trying to school my expression and bite my tongue. His explanation was less acrimonious than the *Hell. No.* yet still colored with a similar shade of harsh obstinacy. I wondered if Matt Simmons was pretending he was over his ex-wife. Was that all it was? Pretending?

Maybe he was a great pretender. Because why else would he, personally, be so against romantic relationships?

"We're here." Matt pulled the door open for me, motioning for me to precede him.

"Thank you," I said numbly, still working through the surprising new details he'd just volunteered. In a distracted daze, I strolled to the counter, reminding myself to take note of our surroundings.

The space resembled the front room to a day spa. An assortment of cosmetics lined the walls. Massage oils. A basket of what looked like fur gloves sat next to another basket of silk scarves on a shelf with a handful of other textured and sensory products.

"May I help you?" The receptionist glanced in our direction.

"Yes. I have an appointment with Jared."

"Marie?" she asked, her eyes moving between her computer screen and me.

"Yes. That's me."

She read something on her screen, her eyes jumping to mine. "You're the reporter?"

"That's right."

"Do you have any walk-in availability?" Matt asked, coming to lean on the counter next to me.

The receptionist moved her eyes to his and they widened subtly with blatant appreciation. She reached for her braid over her shoulder and began playing with it. "Do you need a cuddler?"

"I think I must," he answered with over-exaggerated sincerity.

She giggled.

I fought not to roll my eyes.

"Well, let's see." Her tone was a tad breathy. "Giselle should be finishing up soon, and she's free until four."

"Giselle." Matt said the name like he was tasting it, deciding if he liked it or not.

"She's great," the hostess said. "Only the best for you."

Matt peered at her as though he distrusted her judgment. "Okay. Sure. Giselle it is."

"Let me go grab Jared," she said to me as she stood. Then to Matt, "When Giselle's finished, I'll let her know you're here."

The hostess left to fetch my cuddle buddy just as a man and a woman came down the hall toward the waiting area. The woman was mid-twenties, maybe even younger, dressed in yoga pants and a tank top. The man, dressed in jeans and a long-sleeved T-shirt, appeared to be in his sixties, his hair in earliest stages of salt and pepper.

They were smiling, but their smiles were muted, and hers was laced with compassion.

"What do you think the age difference is there?" Matt lifted his chin toward the couple slowly walking toward the waiting room.

I glanced at Matt, who was frowning like he disapproved.

"Why does it matter?" I asked.

"Because he's putting his paws all over someone who could be his daughter."

I gave my head a subtle shake. "First of all, professional cuddling is platonic. Meant to provide comfort."

Matt blinked, catching himself mid-eye-roll, but mumbled, "Give me a break."

"And secondly, you don't know what's going on. Don't judge a situation you don't know anything about."

He pressed his lips together, narrowing his eyes on me, but said nothing.

Noting his surly expression, I turned, hoping to intercept the man before he left, noting that the cuddler had already disappeared back down the hall.

"Excuse me, sir." Stepping forward, I extended my hand. "I'm a journalist, writing a story about unconventional touch therapy. I was hoping you'd be willing to answer a few questions. It should only take five minutes."

In all honesty, I had no idea how long my questions would take. But people were more likely to give you their time if you gave them a quote.

The man hesitated, glancing at me, my hand, and then at Matt at my side. Pulling his jacket on, he slowly accepted my hand for a shake, still looking skeptical.

"I don't mind, I guess. I just don't want to share my name."

"Absolutely," I agreed immediately. "It would be completely anonymous. And no pictures either."

"Okay. Fine." His gaze intensified. "What do you want to know?"

"Anything you're willing to share about your experience with professional cuddling. But we can start with your impetus for seeking it out. Do you mind telling me why you decided to use a professional cuddler?"

The man scrutinized me for a beat, his expression somber, then said, "My wife died. Six months ago. Brain tumor."

"I'm so sorry," I said, giving him a subdued, sympathetic smile. It was possibly similar to the one he'd just received from his cuddler.

He nodded, a flash of pain sparking behind his eyes. "We didn't have any children, never wanted any. She was it for me, more than enough. She was my soulmate." His eyes misted over, his words trembling. Clearing his throat and blinking away the moisture, he continued. "I miss holding her hand, hugging her close as we fell asleep. That's what I miss the most. Without her, I feel lost, and I don't mind saying so. I heard about this place from a psychologist buddy—or maybe he's a psychiatrist, who knows—but he said maybe it would help me cope with my loss. So I gave it a try."

I made mental notes about the cadence of his voice, the color of his shirt, the way he nibbled at his bottom lip and paused between thoughts.

"Does it help?" I asked softly.

"It does. I don't think people realize how lonely it is, after having someone alongside you half your life. And then suddenly, she's gone. Giselle is a really nice young lady, very compassionate."

I assumed Giselle was his cuddler.

"What do you do, specifically, with her? Do you hold hands?"

"Yes. We always hold hands. Even if we do nothing else."

"Anything else? Only if you're comfortable sharing, of course."

He scratched his neck. "Sometimes she holds me while we're lying down. Sometimes we hug standing up. It's nothing to be ashamed of, at least I don't think so. It's a crutch, for me. I don't have anyone else on this earth. What other choice do I have? Other than being lonely."

"What about dating? Finding another person?"

He shook his head, his mouth a resolute line. "No. I'm not ready for that. I don't know if I'll ever be ready. I can't betray Patty that way. And doing that wouldn't be very kind, would it? To another person? When I could never love them."

I nodded, seeing his point.

"Anything else you need?" The man's sad eyes moved between Matt and me.

"No. Thank you. I appreciate your time." I shook the man's hand again, moving out of his way so he could leave, and turned to Matt once he was gone.

"Hmm." Matt was nodding, very slowly, a thoughtful expression on his features.

"How are those judgy pants fitting now, Professor?" I cocked an eyebrow at him.

The side of his mouth hitched, his tone somber as he said, "Point made."

"Marie?"

We both turned at the sound of my name, finding the aforementioned Giselle glaring at me with barely controlled irritation.

"Yes?" I turned to face her, prepared to explain that Rebecca—the owner of the studio—had given me approval to interview customers when we'd spoken on the phone earlier in the week.

Her gaze slid to Matt and lost some of its hardness as her eyes moved over him. "Are you the walk-in?"

He nodded, extending his hand toward her. "Yes. I'm Matt."

She gave him a small but genuine smile, accepting his handshake before her gaze moved back to me. Like a switch, her features arranged themselves into a mask of intense irritation.

"Come with me," she said, spinning on her heel.

Matt and I glanced at each other, but did as we were told, following the woman down the hall, past a series of doors. I glanced into the three rooms we passed, finding one was a break room and the other two looked like bedrooms.

Giselle was waiting for us at the end of the hall, her frosty gaze moving over me as she opened the door to an office, revealing a man with long black hair speaking on the phone. He was also shirtless and barefoot, wearing red loose-fitting pants that resembled a billowy sarong. And he was impressively muscled. With tribal tattoos.

He looked up at our arrival, did a double take, then frowned at Giselle, holding his finger up as he said to the caller, "Okay, we've got you down for Monday at three. Thanks for calling. Okay. Bye."

Upon hanging up, his attention lingered on Giselle and then skipped to me. "Marie?"

I nodded. "Jared?"

"The owner, Rebecca, isn't here right now, she had to go pick up her son. But she's going to try to return before you leave." His face split with a smile as his eyes moved over my body. "So nice to meet you."

"I'll bet it is," Giselle mumbled, crossing her arms.

Jared's attention shifted to Matt, and he blinked. "You're the walk-in?" Jared was looking at Matt askance, making no effort to hide his displeasure.

"Yes. I am." Matt looked at my cuddle partner and then glanced down at himself, as though searching for what offended the man.

Jared scoffed, blinking rapidly and turning a plainly furious face to Giselle. "Well, that's just great."

She crossed the threshold into the office, saying to us, "Give us a minute, would you?" and then pulled the door mostly shut behind her.

"Really? You're giving me grief about him?" we heard her ask. "Look at her. She's all tits."

Matt and I shared another glance, his eyes flickering to my chest and then back up.

"Real nice, G," Jared said, sounding equally furious.

"And her hair? She's exactly your type. I should know."

Matt grimaced, but it looked like he was trying not to laugh.

"I'm not the one who has a history of being unprofessional," Jared could be heard saying in a hushed tone. "Keep your hands out of his shirt."

"They like it when I stroke their stomach." It sounded like she was speaking through clenched teeth.

"You only stroke stomachs with six-packs and we both know it."

Matt's eyes widened almost comically, a mixture of shock and panic behind his gaze as he pointed to his torso and mouthed to me, *I don't want her touching my stomach.*

I gestured to my chest and mouthed back, *I don't want him touching my tits.*

A hastily repressed laugh erupted from Matt and he clapped his hand over his mouth to stop it. Despite his valiant effort, the sound drew their attention and the door opened, revealing a furious Jared.

"Is something funny?" Jared was now aiming daggers at Matt.

"No." Matt shook his head as though to strengthen his denial. But then abruptly began nodding, his eyes swinging to me and narrowing. "Actually, yes. There is something wrong."

My lips parted, maybe to refute his claim, maybe to agree with him, I'll never know. In the next moment, Matt had wrapped his arm around my shoulders and addressed our would-be cuddlers. "The truth is, we're cuddle virgins. And I think—no, I *know*—I speak for Marie when I say that we're nervous. So we've been talking and we think maybe it would be best if Marie and I cuddled with each other—"

I snapped my mouth shut, my gaze dropping to the floor.

"—and you two could take us through the positions. Teach us how to cuddle. Be our cuddle sensei," Matt finished, his tone beseeching.

Giselle and Jared shot each other a look of confusion as she asked, "And we'd still get paid?"

"Of course." Matt nodded, his hand sliding from my shoulder to my arm, his big hand warm on my bare skin.

Jared glanced at me, asking softly, "Are you sure that's the experience you want, Marie?"

"He just said it's what they want," Giselle snapped. "You just want to cuddle with her," she added in a harsh whisper.

I winced, realizing I would get nowhere with these two. Evidently, they were dating, or involved, or something. And also evident, they had some major jealousy issues to work through. I wasn't going to get an authentic cuddle experience either way. But at least with Matt as my cuddle partner, I didn't have to worry about Giselle stabbing me in the middle of the session.

Plus, per Matt's anti-relationship tirade just moments ago, I was fairly certain his interest in cuddling was purely academic.

"It's what I want," I rushed to declare, hoping to cut off a rekindling of Jared and Giselle's tiff, my arm lifting to wrap around Matt's torso. "As long as one, or both of you can guide us through it."

# CHAPTER 9

**Siri**

*Works as an intelligent personal assistant and knowledge navigator, part of Apple Inc.'s iOS, watchOS, macOS, and tvOS operating systems.*

Source: Apple Computers, Siri

I CHANGED INTO the shorts and tank top I'd brought for the cuddle session, then met Matt and Jared in one of the rooms I'd spied earlier. It looked like a nondescript bedroom, with a double bed in the middle of the space and a single side table. A solitary candle in a glass holder was burning, and provided the only source of light in the room other than the window.

"Marie." Jared made a bow to me, his expression open and friendly. "I've arranged your partner on the bed. He's ready for you."

"My body is ready," Matt called from his position.

I peeked around the man who would be our cuddle instructor to find Matt lying on one side of the bed, facing the door, a droll expression on his handsome face. I blinked once, slowly, mentally preparing myself for what was to come and reminding myself this was all in the name of journalism.

Taking a deep breath, I approached the bed. "Should I just mirror him?"

"That's right." Jared waited until I lay on the bed, facing Matt, before he gave further instruction. "Okay, now I want you two to tangle your legs together, with Matt's staying on the mattress, one of Marie's between Matt's legs, and Matt's upper leg between hers. That's right. And Marie, lay your head on Matt's forearm. That's it. Marie, try putting your hand flat against Matt's stomach, to create a connection, but over his shirt. Unless, that is, you're both comfortable with skin-to-skin touch."

"Over the shirt is fine," I said, and Matt nodded his agreement. No need for things to get too personal.

We did as instructed while Jared launched into a monologue.

I tried to pay attention, but I was beyond distracted by the solid wall of maleness in front of me. And his leg between my legs. And his ridged abdominal muscles beneath my fingertips.

Men who were perpetual kids never made it on my radar. Up until now, Professor Simmons had come across as a big kid—specifically his tendencies to be oblivious, blunt, and stubborn. Yeah, he was handsome, funny, terrifyingly brilliant, but I hadn't been particularly attracted to his personality.

But now, being this close, he felt . . . hot. And bigger. Stronger. Imposing. *Manly.* I caught myself swallowing nothing as I had no saliva left in my mouth.

He might've acted like a big kid, but he didn't feel like one.

"As a general rule, a cuddler and a cuddlee should never touch each other in the bathing-suit zones. No touching the front of the chest, the buttocks, or the pelvis. Basically, anywhere a two-piece covers on a woman or a bathing suit covers on a man."

A subtle yet sly smile settled over Matt's features, his brown eyes dancing as though thinking of a secret joke.

"What?" I whispered, suspicious, still fighting my flare of hormones.

Or, more precisely, *whoremones.*

That's what I called my hormones when they betrayed my good sense. Sandra said I was slut-shaming my body's appreciation for the opposite sex. I told her I was okay with that if it meant I remained free of STDs.

Matt inclined his head forward so that our noses were almost touching. His breath smelled like peppermint—not overpowering, just enough to betray that he'd snuck a mint—and he whispered, "I wear Speedos when I swim."

I pressed my lips together so I wouldn't laugh, but ended up laughing silently anyway as he resettled back into his original position. Trying not to laugh was becoming a habit around him.

And thank goodness for his joke, because it helped dispel my sudden case of sexy-nerves. Physically, I was beginning to see him as just too ridiculously attractive. *Good thing he told you he's allergic to commitment, otherwise you might do something whoremone-y.*

I could do this. I could snuggle with Matt's large, powerful, hard body and remain focused on documenting the experience for my story. *Focus on the story.*

My mind began to settle.

Meanwhile, Matt gave into his grin, his eyes dropping to my mouth. He had a really nice smile. I liked it when he smiled, how his eyes lit up with inner brilliance and tangible enjoyment.

"Now don't be alarmed if one or both of you experience arousal," Jared continued evenly. "That's not abnormal, but it doesn't happen every time. If it does happen, feel free to call for a break. Either of you can end the session at any time. Cuddling must be, at all times, purely platonic . . . "

Matt's smile dwindled by degrees and the mischief dimmed, replaced with something else. I decided it was sobriety. Then growing distance. And then, eventually, careful detachment.

Gathering a deep breath, his dispassionate gaze moved over my shoulder, and he stared at the wall behind me. I considered him, his sudden mood shift, while trying to listen to Jared's instruction.

"Eye contact can be important in this position, but isn't necessary. Don't be afraid to move your hands, stroking your partner with an open palm if he or she finds it comforting. You can do it on the arm or leg, over the shoulder, down the back. Petting can be very comforting."

Matt's jaw flexed. His eyes still affixed to some spot behind me.

"Fingers in the hair, massaging the scalp or threading in the hair itself, is a technique we use. Matt."

Matt flinched, frowning, his eyes darting up to Jared. "Yes?"

"Try playing with Marie's hair."

Matt didn't immediately move. In fact, he held perfectly still, but I could feel the tension in his stomach muscles beneath his shirt. Eventually, he cleared his throat and swallowed, and his eyes cut to mine. His expression still distant.

I twisted my lips to the side. "Don't worry, I washed my hair . . ."

"Good," he said distractedly as he lifted his hand even with my temple.

Just before he touched me, I said, ". . . last month," giving him a sinister grin. "But don't worry, the lice are friendly."

I was pleased to see my teasing had made a crack in his detached demeanor. He twisted his lips to the side—like he was fighting his own smile—and dropped his hand on my face.

And when I say he dropped his hand on my face, I mean he dropped it, like it was dead weight. Right on my face. With determinedly ungraceful movements, he shoved his fingers into my hair and straightened his arm, like he was trying to flick my hair from my scalp.

It didn't hurt, but it didn't feel good either. And he looked ridiculous. When I caught his expression, which was equal parts smug and silly, I started to laugh.

Matt's laughter soon followed and he mimicked his earlier hair flick, making it even more ludicrous by twisting my hair and throwing it in my face.

"Like this?" he asked, unable to keep the laughter from his voice.

Jared huffed. "No, Matthew. Don't put her hair in her face."

"I think she likes it," Matt said, making me laugh harder.

Jared made another sound of disapproval and peripherally I saw he'd caught Matt's wrist. With Jared holding one hand captive and the other trapped under my head, I took the opportunity to poke Matt in the ribs, making him jump and squirm.

"Hey!" Matt protested.

"Okay, wait." Jared's tone firmed. "Tickling is allowed, but you have to obtain the consent of the other person first."

While Jared spoke, Matt wrenched his hand free and moved it to my side, tickling me in earnest. "Let's see how you like a taste of your own medicine."

"I don't need any medicine!" I tried to retaliate, but I couldn't, because I am and always have been remarkably ticklish.

"Circle, circle, dot, dot . . . " he said, laughing. Not maniacal laughter, more like he was really enjoying himself and was lost to the moment.

"Oh my God." I laughed, twisting, trying to block access to my stomach.

He moved his attentions to my side, but his fingers weren't painful or harsh. They were adroit, applying just the right pressure to make me squirm.

Matt rolled me on my back, freeing his other hand and pushing my legs down as I tried to bring my knees to my chest.

"Sorry, Marie. Can't have your pointy knees near the yarn bag," he said, not sounding sorry. His use of the phrase *yarn bag* made me laugh harder.

Soon he was straddling my hips, his hands deftly finding new spots at my neck, under my arms, and our laughter was the only sound I could hear.

"Okay! Okay! Truce, truce!" I bowed forward, tucking my arms close to my sides, my hair now wild around my shoulders.

Matt's movements stilled, one hand at my neck, the other behind him, wrapped around my thigh at my knee as though poised to tickle the back of my leg.

I glared up at him, smiling. He glared down at me, smiling. Both of us were breathing hard.

"Truce?" he asked, his chest rising and falling, his gaze dipping to my mouth.

"Yeah." For some reason, my eyes also dropped to his mouth, and I had an incredibly odd thought at that moment.

*I wonder what his lips taste like.*

Whoa!

*Just stop right there.*

It must've been our proximity, how we were touching each other as though we were familiar. Perhaps my body was confusing proximity with actual intimacy because I'd never touched someone like this without it.

"So. As I was saying," Jared said, effectively pulling me from my meditations on Matt's lips and to our instructor's frustrated visage, "tickling is allowed, but must be approved ahead of the session first. Matthew, remove yourself from Marie, please."

My attention cut back to Matt, who was still straddling me. His eyes were on his hand where it wrapped around the side of my neck, his thumb pressing against the indent at the top of my sternum.

"Sorry," he mumbled, swallowing stiffly, and shifted his weight to one side to climb off my middle.

"Thank you," came Jared's curt reply. "Let's try a traditional spooning position, with Matt being the big spoon, and Marie the smaller one. Okay, on your sides."

I released a quiet breath. I still felt a little disoriented by the decidedly un-platonic turn of my thoughts, and lay on the mattress, facing away from Matt. For some reason, every sound seemed louder, especially if he caused it. How the springs of the bed squeaked when he moved into position, his soft breaths, the friction of his jeans against the sheets.

"Try to get as close as you can, Matt. There should be no space between you. That's right, put your leg between hers," Jared instructed.

Soon his front was plastered against my back, the hard muscles of his upper thighs cradling my bottom, his firm stomach at my lower back, his chest against my shoulder blades. One arm draped over me, his hand limp, not touching my body. But I could feel him still moving behind me, as though trying to get comfortable.

"What do I do with this arm?" I heard him ask, his voice gruff, edged with impatience. "It's superfluous."

"Good question." Jared leaned over us and I sensed he'd taken Matt's wrist again. "I wouldn't recommend trying to fit it between you, that creates distance and is generally uncomfortable for the small spoon. Instead, you can bend your elbow—like this—and Marie can use your arm as a pillow. Or, you can use it as a pillow yourself. Or, you can straighten it and place it under Marie's neck, like this."

Jared encouraged me to tilt my head so Matt could slide his arm beneath me. This idea didn't quite work, as Matt's upper arm was a little too big to fit in the space left by the curve of my neck.

"Hey, wait." I grabbed Matt's arm and positioned it so I was using his bicep as a pillow.

"Oh, good. Then maybe put your hand like this, Matt." Jared took over and bent Matt's elbow again, leading his hand to my upper arm, so I was wrapped in his embrace. "And your other hand can rest on her thigh, like this." Once more, Jared moved Matt until the hand that had been draped limply was flat on my upper thigh.

Jared stepped back, tilting his head to the side as he considered us. "Maybe bend your leg, Marie. Yes, that's it. Is that comfortable?"

I nodded, because it was comfortable. I felt like I was tucked in the cozy embrace of a big, muscular bear. Matt's warmth surrounded me on all sides.

"I like this," I heard and felt Matt mutter, the rumble of his chest reverberating through my back where we were pressed together. The words were bemused.

"Why do you sound surprised?" I whispered.

"Like I said, I'm a cuddle virgin."

Before I could remark on his statement, Jared interrupted. "Okay, Matt. Feel free to nuzzle her back and neck. Or you can stroke her leg or arm, maybe? Is that okay, Marie?"

"Yes, that's fine."

Matt chose my leg, his big palm moved down, then up my bare thigh to the hem of my shorts and I had to smile because his touch wasn't at all tentative. If I didn't know any better, I'd say it felt possessive.

"And Marie, maybe touch the back of Matt's hand? The one on your arm. Play with it, entwine your fingers. Light touches."

"Jared, we need you up front," a voice I recognized as the hostess called from someplace down the hall.

"Okay, you two practice that. I'll be right back." Jared's retreating footsteps sounded against the wood floor, eventually leaving us in silence.

Meanwhile, I lifted my fingers and softly petted Matt's hand, tracing the bones of his fingers with my fingertips and then drawing ellipses on the back of his hand, from his wrist to his knuckles.

He made a rumbly noise, almost like a purr. It sounded content.

"You like that?" I whispered, closing my eyes, enjoying the feel of his hand languidly stroking my leg.

"Yes," he said.

I grinned.

He was quiet for bit, we both were, and I felt myself relax more and more. His palm took a detour every so often, dutifully skipping my hip and sliding along my side, and then back to my leg. Soon, I was so relaxed I felt drowsy.

I felt fingers in my hair, moving the mass away from my neck with treasuring strokes just before Matt nuzzled the back of my neck, causing goosebumps to scatter over my skin.

"Mmm." I smiled. "Hey. Jared said no tickling." My voice sounded sleepy.

"Does this tickle?" Matt asked softly, nuzzling me again. I felt the brush of his lips—not a kiss, a brush—paired with hot breath against the bare skin of my neck and a zing shot straight down my spine, making my toes curl and a sudden hot ache twist in my lower belly.

*Oh no.*

I knew that ache. I hadn't felt it because of another person's touch in *quite* a long time. Nevertheless, no one ever forgets *that* ache.

My back arched instinctively, my bottom pressing back against his crotch, and I stiffened. I felt my nipples harden, strain beneath the cotton of my bra. I was now fully awake. No longer drowsy.

Nope.

Not even a little.

Matt stiffened, too. His movements abruptly ceasing.

"Are you okay? What's wrong?" he asked, alarm coating his words, and in the next moment his hand was suspended in the air above me. "Did I touch something I shouldn't?"

I exhaled a short, nervous laugh, gripped by the urge to sit up.

"No. No. You didn't." I moved to the edge of the bed, righting myself, away from Matt, needing distance. "I'm good." I gathered a silent breath and released it slowly because my pulse was racing.

*Crap, Marie. Get a grip. It's Matt Simmons. Professor Matt. The big kid. Why are you reacting this way?*

"Did I . . ." These initial words were hesitant, and a moment of silence stretched before he continued, his tone comically teasing as he finished his thought. "Did I *arouse* you?"

I snorted, shaking my head, laughing at his silly tone. Turning at the waist to peer at him over my shoulder, Matt was grinning at me, twisting a make-believe mustache between his thumb and forefinger.

But then he stopped.

"I did, didn't I?" he pushed, his hand dropping. He looked pleased, if not a little amazed.

I sighed, feeling a smidge embarrassed, and nodded. "Actually, yes. That's a sensitive spot for most women."

"The back of your neck?" He lifted himself to one elbow, his eyes darting to my neck with keen interest.

"My neck in general, actually."

"Huh." Matt frowned thoughtfully. "Where else?"

I pressed my lips together and gave him an incredulous look. "I'm not telling you that."

"Why not?"

"Matt."

"What if I needed it for research reasons?"

"Matt."

"What if I told you it was part of our questionnaire?" He tossed his legs over the side of the bed and stood, walking around to my side and offering me his hand. "You should give me a schematic of your body with the erogenous zones circled and rated."

"Let me guess, you want them rated on a ten-point scale," I deadpanned as I accepted his hand, stood, and stepped away to gain some distance and straighten my shirt.

He shrugged, crossing his arms, stalking after me. "Or exponential. I was going to say a Likert scale, but a logarithmic scale works, too."

Chuckling, appreciative of his attempt to diffuse my embarrassment and awkwardness with the joke, I realized Matt Simmons wasn't a bad guy. He might even be a good guy, just a little . . . peculiar.

*And wants to replace romantic relationships with robots. Best not forget that detail.*

Yeah, he'd make an interesting friend.

"Thanks." I gave him a small smile.

"For what?" His eyes moved between mine.

"For the cuddle. Thanks for the cuddle, Matt."

"Anytime, Marie." He grinned down at me, his eyes dancing as he leaned forward and whispered, "Anytime."

# CHAPTER 10

**Sophie**

*Emotional intelligence bot that interacts with patients who have chronic health issues. Unlike some bots made to optimize paid interactions, this one is built to act in your best interests.*

Source: iDAvatars

TUESDAY WAS A good news/bad news kind of day.

I'll start with the bad news. Or rather, the I-don't-know-how-to-feel-about-this news.

David, my ex-boyfriend, called me. I didn't pick up. The flash of his number on my cell screen paralyzed me. I let it go to voicemail. We hadn't spoken since he'd moved out and he didn't leave a message this time. I obsessed for the rest of the day about what to do, caught off guard by how much I was obsessing.

But then, good news, I received a series of texts from Matt just as I was leaving work.

**Matt**: *If you need help translating the scatterplots, let me know.*

**Matt**: *We should eat while we discuss.*

**Matt**: *Dinner?*

**Matt**: *Or coffee is fine.*

**Matt**: *I'll stop texting now.*

I smiled at the unexpected, but not unwelcomed, messages.

I'd decided over the weekend that if Professor Matt Simmons was interested in being my friend, I was going to make an effort to make the friendship happen. Because Matt, despite the short time we'd spent together, had made me more playful.

And braver.

Shaking my head at the weirdo, I typed my response.

**Marie**: *I do have questions. I've got knitting tonight. How about tomorrow? We can meet for coffee or I can cook dinner.*

Even though I'd taken copious notes during our meeting, I was having trouble interpreting the documents he'd given me, so his offer to help was a relief. It would also give me the opportunity to propose friendship.

Since I was on a strict budget, eating out wasn't an option. Plus, I had a recipe for coconut curry that would have been silly to make for just one person.

He replied almost immediately.

**Matt:** *YOU COOK*

**Matt**: *Sorry for my all-caps exuberance. I'm really looking forward to your food.*

**Matt:** *I mean, answering your questions.*

**Matt:** *And your food.*

I chuckled, tapping out the address to my apartment as I entered the elevator, pressing the button for the penthouse level. I had to juggle the dip I'd made, holding it against the wall with my hip so I could slip my phone back into my bag. It was Janie's turn to host, but with her feeling so wretched these days, the rest of us decided to make and bring the food.

When the elevator doors opened, I moved to leave but took a startled step back, almost colliding with Quinn's business partner, Dan O'Malley.

Dan and I had been through a lot together, especially this last year. He, Quinn, and I had bonded while on a trip in the spring to Nigeria to help Greg and Fiona out of a bind. Working toward a common goal in close quarters. I was thankful to have these great guys in my life, proving that great guys existed.

"Gah." I wobbled, trying to regain my balance.

He reached out to steady me, his beefy hands gripping my shoulders. "You okay there?"

"Yes." I laughed at my clumsiness and sighed. "Long day. Sorry."

"No problem." Once he was sure I was stable, he released me and stepped back, motioning for me to exit the elevator. "You're the last to arrive."

"I figured as much." Frowning, I glanced at the door leading to Janie and Quinn's place. "How's she doing? Any better?"

He shook his head wearily, rubbing the back of his neck where swirling tattoos peaked out from the collar of his shirt. His mouth formed a tired line. "I can't wait until that baby is out. Quinn's been a real sonofabitch—excuse my language—for the last five months."

"Sorry." I gave him a sympathetic smile. The typically even-tempered Bostonian seemed exceptionally irritable this evening.

"It's fine." He waved me off as he stepped onto the elevator and punched a button. "All I'm saying is, they better name it after me."

Giving him one last departing wave, I turned and strolled down the hall, knocking on Janie's door with my free hand. A few seconds later, Kat opened the door, her gaze wide and expectant. But as soon as she saw me, her expression faltered.

"Oh. Hi, Marie." She sounded a shade disappointed.

I tried not to take it personally. "Who were you expecting?"

She brightened her smile, waving me forward. "You, of course. Come in." Taking the dip from my hands, she walked toward the kitchen, calling ahead of her, "Marie brought dip."

"Yay for dip," came Sandra's excited reply.

Leaving my purse by the door, I grabbed my knitting bag and headed for the family room, happy to see all my friends' smiling faces as soon as I entered. Even Janie was smiling.

"Marie. Goddess of the dip," Ashley's voice called from a laptop sitting on a side table. "You'll need to send me the recipe."

"I will," I promised.

"Hey, Marie." Nico—aka Nicoletta—smiled his greeting. He couldn't stand up as his wife was sitting on his lap, as was their way.

"Hey. I didn't think you were going to be here."

Kat emerged from the kitchen holding two cocktail glasses and handed me one. "For you, my dear."

"Thank you."

"Okay, now that everyone is here, I have a question." Sandra held her hands up in front of her and asked the room, "Do y'all think the word 'Nazi' is offensive?"

Kat took a seat on the sofa, casting Sandra a cautious glance. "What do you mean? In what context?"

"Like saying someone is a grammar-Nazi?"

"I can't speak for all Jewish people, because—you know—we're all individuals with our own opinions, experiences, outlooks, and whatnot, but, it doesn't bother me that much." Kat paused, twisting her mouth to the side for a beat. "However, I know for a fact it does bother my father. A lot. And his friends."

"What do you mean, it doesn't bother you that much?" I asked.

"I mean, you know, it bothers me a little. Using Nazi as a colloquialism or synonym for fastidious doesn't seem . . . right. Shouldn't the opposite be true? Shouldn't it mean murderer? Instead of fastidious about grammar, it should mean one who slanders, murders, and annihilates grammar." Kat frowned, appearing as though she was wading through a weighty problem. "Now that I think about it, I guess it does bother me."

"I'm sorry." Sandra's forehead wrinkled.

"Why are you sorry?" Kat tilted her head to the side in question.

"Because I've said it before. I know I have. And I didn't mean to be insensitive, but now I know I was insensitive. So, I'm sorry," Sandra said sincerely.

"Thanks for apologizing. I guess." Kat frowned, still looking confused. "I mean, part of me doesn't think you need to, because I know you're not being unkind. But then another part of me appreciates it. And then a third part of me just wants to eat cheese."

"I get that." Sandra nodded thoughtfully. "Especially the cheese part."

"The irony of the grammar-Nazi colloquialism and how many people are now offended by its use is that the usage in that context originates from the TV show *Seinfeld*. Do you remember the soup-Nazi episode?" Janie didn't look up from her work in progress as she asked this.

"Can we stop saying the word Nazi, please?" Fiona made a face of distaste.

"You just said it," Elizabeth pointed out.

Fiona sent Elizabeth a gently scathing look—if such a thing existed—effectively silencing the younger woman. Or maybe it was her badass ex-CIA look. Or maybe it was both.

"I remember that episode, yes." Kat nodded, sipping her cocktail.

"Well, about a year before it aired, the term grammar . . ." Janie's eyes drifted to Fiona's, then back to Kat's before continuing, *"grammar-you-know-what* was coined online, in early 1995. But then ten months later, the *soup-you-know-who* episode aired. Some people speculate *grammar-you-know-what* and similar phrases only gained popularity because of the *soup-you-know-who* episode. And *Seinfeld* was written by Larry David, who is Jewish, and stars Jerry Seinfeld, who is also Jewish."

"Just because it was started by Jewish comedians doesn't mean other Jewish people can't be troubled by it. Or non-Jewish people. Or all people," Nico added. "As entertainers, you're responsible for either raising or lowering the bar."

"Very true." Elizabeth nodded. "And what does your semi-naked Jell-O wrestling on national TV do again? Raise the bar or lower it?"

"Definitely raise it," Sandra said before Nico could respond, then proceeded to trade saucy grins and winks with him.

"After the episode, the *you-know-what* word was added to all sorts of things as a pejorative insult," Janie continued academically, "as a way to denote a person is authoritarian, autocratic, or inflexible; one who seeks to impose his or her views upon others. Or, in its more literal usage, as you say, a murderer of other humans based on ethnicity and/or religion."

"See, in that context, it makes sense. Someone who seeks to impose his or her views upon others, just like the *you-know-who's* did. But to make it synonymous with fastidious or careful or anything else with a positive connotation is upsetting," Kat said.

"I also wonder if we, as a society, have lost our sense of humor," Elizabeth mused. "I mean, I read an interview with Jerry Seinfeld where he said laughing at the horrors of history is an effective way to disarm the power it holds. That he and Chris Rock have stopped performing at college campuses because this current generation has no sense of humor, and require everything to have trigger warnings. Why do we want the word—which Fiona won't let us say—or any word for that matter, to hold power over us?"

"Or maybe," Kat suggested, "it should hold power. And we should never forget the fruit of fascism."

"Fruit of Fascism should be the name of a band." Elizabeth lifted her chin toward Kat. "And you make an excellent point."

"This is a tough and complex issue," Sandra, adopting her psychiatrist voice, cut in. "Humor can heal, yes. Absolutely. But what if you poke fun at a topic that is still fresh, still sore, or that has been made newly sore by recent events? People are what, just supposed to get over it? No. Wrong answer."

"Maybe it's a balance," Ashley said, her eyes on the scarf she was knitting, "Maybe the answer is: Don't be an asshole, think before you open your trap, take responsibility for your words. Meaning, apologize when you're wrong and correct yourself moving forward—and don't constantly look for reasons to be offended and police well-meaning people's words. We want folks to talk to each other, right? Not just hang out with like-minded people all the time. Everyone is ignorant about something, and everyone is offended by something. If people can't have a calm, respectful dialogue without being hurt by ignorance, or without offending with insensitivity, then what the hell are we supposed to do? Surround ourselves with robots who don't challenge our ideas?"

I sat up straight, my gaze darting to the laptop screen at the conclusion of Ashley's rant. *What the hell are we supposed to do? Surround ourselves with robots who don't challenge our ideas*? Yes, that struck a chord.

"Except," Nico sat slightly forward, causing Elizabeth to shift to the side, "if you're talking about a group of crazy people who are lobbying for the extermination or expulsion of an entire race, or religion, or other subset of our population. There is no use trying to talk to hatemongers."

Ashley shook her head. "Now, see, I disagree. How can you change a person's heart if you don't talk to them?"

"How about grammar-police? Does that bother anyone?" Janie asked the group.

"Wait, before anyone answers that, is this something we're doing with everything from now on? Is this a new thing for us? To check with each other before we speak here? To make sure everything that leaves our mouths is free of the potential for hurt?" Sandra's gaze drifted from person to person. "Or can we instead just, you know, trust each other? We are all friends here, right? We're all doing our best and want to think the best of each other. If I say something jerky or ignorant—and not the dried-meat kind of jerky—then how about one of you fine ladies just calls me on it. I'll know you're coming from a good place and I'll try to correct my deplor-er-horrible behavior."

"Why didn't you say deplorable?" Elizabeth paused her knitting. "You can't use the word *deplorable* now?"

She looked to her husband for help.

Nico affixed his eyes to the crochet hat he was making and shook his head. "Nope. I'm not touching that one."

"Don't you two talk?" Kat asked teasingly.

"I only see him a few times a month," Elizabeth dipped her chin to her chest, "so the last thing we want to do is talk about current events."

"Or talk," Nico mumbled, earning him an elbow in his rib, which only made him smile wider.

"It has weightier meaning now than it did last year." Kat fiddled with her sleeve.

"Why?" Elizabeth asked.

Fiona and I swapped looks as I said, "Elizabeth, on the one hand, I do not envy your schedule of working in the emergency room at all hours, sometimes sleeping at work, never having time to watch *Game of Thrones* or *Buffy* reruns. But on the other hand, I do envy your blissful ignorance."

Meanwhile, Sandra sighed, looking beleaguered. "I'm sorry I brought this up. Let's talk about something else. Like yarn. Yarn always makes me happy, silk never lets me down."

"You say that now, but remember those silk gloves you knit?" Ashley grinned.

Sandra groaned. "Oh Lord. Don't remind me."

"Were those the gloves that grew, like, ten sizes larger after you blocked them?" I hid my smirk behind my cocktail.

"Yes," Sandra bellowed. "The gloves could have fit the Stay Puft Marshmallow Man. That is, of course, if he'd had fingers."

"Did the Stay Puft Marshmallow Man have fingers?" Kat wrinkled her nose, glancing to Janie.

"I have no idea," Janie said, shaking her head.

And then the room fell silent. Because that might have been the first time anyone had ever heard Janie say, *I have no idea.*

It took us a few moments to recover from the shock and, unsurprisingly, Sandra was the first to speak. "Speaking of not having any idea, did anyone have any idea that Dan split from his girlfriend?"

We all followed Dan's love life, yet none of us had admitted as much out loud.

"Dan the Security Man?" Elizabeth asked, her gaze swinging to her husband. "Did you know about this?"

Nico gave his wife an evasive grin and an equally evasive answer. "Honey, if I knew about it, why would I keep it from you?"

"When? When did it happen?" Elizabeth squinted at Nico, but was clearly trying to keep the excitement from her voice as her eyes darted to Kat and then away.

I fought the urge to also glance at Kat, successfully subduing the compulsion, but just barely.

Meanwhile, Sandra was pointedly *not* looking at Kat. "It's true. They did. Split two months ago. I just found out about it today."

"How did you find out?" Surprisingly, this question came from Fiona. And I say surprisingly because she never gossiped. Ever.

"Alex mentioned it, offhandedly." Sandra rolled her eyes. "Like it wasn't the biggest news since Wookie pajamas."

"What happened?" Ashley was leaning forward, her face filled the laptop screen, her knitting set aside.

"I don't know the details—because Alex is a crypt of information—but I do know it happened two months ago and Dan was the one to call it off." Sandra's eyes settled on everyone except Kat.

"He called it off?" Elizabeth's gaze jumped back to Kat and remained there, her expression holding some urgency.

"Well, *someone* should comfort him," Nico suggested quietly, his attention squarely focused on his stitches.

Silence filled the room like a vapor, whispering over us, pressing down from every direction.

I suspected—no, I knew—each of us were silently rooting for Kat and Dan to make a love connection. I also knew Dan was all for making Kat his, and had been for years. His unrequited affection for her was both beautiful and heartbreaking to watch.

Furthermore, I suspected Kat really, really liked Dan.

But Kat's tendency to freeze up around him was the main problem. Before his most recent girlfriend, Kat had been painfully shy around him. Meaning, it had been painful to watch. She barely spoke to him, and whenever he'd been friendly to her, she ran the other way.

So. Frustrating.

I was just about to blurt my suggestion that Kat send him a strippergram—of herself—when Fiona glanced at me, giving me a probing look. "Speaking of relationship shakeups. What's going on with you and Matt?"

"Who's Matt?" Elizabeth glanced at me. "Should I know who Matt is? Why do I never know anything?"

"Matt is Fiona's next-door neighbor." Sandra crossed her arms. "I thought we didn't like Matt."

"Oh. *That* Matt." Elizabeth nodded. "I thought our assessment was that he fell into the hot-asshole bucket of shame, right?"

Hot? . . . *Yeah. I guess he is hot.*

"Marie?" Janie prompted.

I sat straighter in my seat, caught off guard by Fiona's question; an odd sensation I couldn't identify made my chest tight. "Nothing is going on with Matt and me. I mean, not really. I asked him to help me with a story I'm writing and he . . . agreed." I decided saying he agreed would be easier than explaining the details. "Why do you ask?"

"He texted me right before you arrived," Fiona held up her phone as evidence, something like concern sharpening in her eyes, "asking me what kind of wine you drink."

# CHAPTER 11

## SASI

*Semi-supervised Algorithm for Sarcasm Identification.*

Source: Hebrew University, Israel

UPON ARRIVING HOME from work on Wednesday, I checked the curry in the crockpot, set the jasmine rice to steam, and then changed my outfit seven times.

For me, making a new friend was like the beginning of any new relationship. Befriending someone, like dating someone, was a conscious choice. I wanted to make a good, lasting impression. And, like all relationships, I found it harder to establish new friendships as I grew older.

People, especially parents and/or working professionals, are busy. Time is a commodity. But it wasn't just lack of time. My expectations for people matured as I matured, and sometimes to my detriment. I wasn't as playful as I used to be. I wasn't as open to new experiences.

The sad truth was, I'd been more open to becoming friends with different types of people when I was younger, more open to people like Matt. Odd people. Exciting people. Playful people. Impulsive people. Artists, intellectuals, musicians, actors, authors.

And now apparently, brilliant scientists.

I was just pulling on a cozy gray sweater with a slouchy cowl neck, which exposed my collarbone and one shoulder, when I heard a knock on the door.

"Oh shit." I waved my hands in front of me in a panicked motion, still undecided about my black leggings, but then caught sight of myself in the mirror. "Why are you so nervous? Stop being nervous. It's just Professor Matt."

I nodded, feeling better, but still a little worried that my smile would be weird because I wouldn't know how to calibrate its size.

My apartment was very small, therefore I made it to the door in ten leaping steps, yanking it open before he knocked again.

"Matt," I said, out of breath.

"Marie," he said, grinning, and then he looked over my head into my apartment, his expression morphing into one of awe and wonder as he shoved a bottle of wine and a small package at me. "What is that heavenly smell?"

I smiled at him, and the smile didn't feel at all calibrated. It just felt right.

"Come in and find out," I said, turning toward my kitchen just a few feet away and eyeing the package he'd brought. "What's this?"

I heard him close the door and sensed him trail after me. "That's a book you should read. *I, Robot*, by Asimov. It should address some of your robot ethics questions."

"Huh. Thanks." I placed it above the refrigerator so it wouldn't get messed up.

"You're welcome."

"Thanks for the wine, by the way. It's one of my favorites," I said as I eyed the bottle, wanting to see if he'd admit to messaging Fiona to ask for wine-selection help.

"Oh? Is it?" He sounded genuinely surprised. He was a good liar. If I hadn't known better, I would have believed his surprise.

I faced him, my hand on my hip. "Professor Simmons, I know for a fact you asked Fiona for help picking out this wine."

"*Help* is such a strong word," he hedged, wrinkling his nose and fighting a guilty laugh.

"You're a stinker." I sent him a mock-chastising look, also fighting my laughter.

"Speaking of stinking, you know what doesn't stink? Dinner. Seriously, what is that?" Matt had followed me into the kitchen even though there was hardly enough room for one person.

"It's coconut curry."

"Coconut is my favorite," he moaned, peeking around me as I opened the crockpot.

I tried to affect the same tone of voice he'd used about the wine. "Oh? Is it?"

"First the cookies, now this. Who told you?" Matt placed his hand on my back, trying to lean over the crockpot. His proximity and the deepening of his voice sent involuntary tingles shivering down my spine.

*He is just so . . .* sigh.

I stiffened.

*Oh no.*

*We can't have that.*

"None of your business." I didn't shift away from him, but every muscle in my body was tense. "But do you know what is your business? The scatterplots on the table." I needed him to leave the kitchen ASAP so I could put a cover on whatever was causing my unanticipated sexy-feels to boil over.

Taking the hint—thank God—Matt left my diminutive galley kitchen. Stealing a look at him, I conducted a quick survey of the good professor.

*Yep. Still hot.*

"Is this where you eat?" he asked, eyeing the small café-style table.

I had to clear my throat before speaking. "Yes. Nothing bigger will fit in that space."

*That's what she said . . .* dammit.

"Yeah, I can see that. It'd be too tight."

*Jeez, I had a dirty mind.* "I—uh—left my notes just there, next to the printouts. Do you mind going through and noting corrections?"

"Sure. No problem," he said, throwing me an easy grin.

"Thanks." I returned his grin, then turned back to my food prep, my heart fluttering.

This wasn't good. These . . . feelings weren't a good idea. I'd had many male friends over the course of my life and I'd lost a few when one-sided feelings got in the way. Sometimes I was on the side of the unrequited crush, sometimes they were.

We weren't even really friends yet, and I was already sabotaging it by having *urges*.

\*\*\*

WORK—HIS RESEARCH and my requests for clarifications—dominated discussions over dinner. Well, his research and the *transcendently deliciousness of dinner*.

Clearly, his work was his first passion, with food coming in a close second.

I could've listened to him talk about Turing, and the revolutionary research being done with Google's DeepMind—*and* how to write learning algorithms for artificial intelligence—all night. He was different when he spoke about it, earnest and confident. And the confidence plus the brain behind it was very sexy.

I accepted that Matt was *transcendently* attractive when he spoke about his passions. Yet, I successfully repressed any inappropriate urges relating to either his internal or external attractiveness.

After dinner, Matt did the dishes while I made new notes on my first draft based on his feedback. Without prompting from me, he pulled the Boston crème pie I'd made for dessert from the fridge.

"I'm assuming this pie is for us to eat?" he asked.

I glanced up from my work, finding him already cutting into it before waiting for my confirmation. "And what if it's not for us? What if I made it for a neighbor?"

"Then you should write her a note of apology, because she's not going to eat it." Matt pulled two forks from a drawer—apparently, he'd already memorized the layout of my kitchen—and brought my plate over to me.

"What are you doing? Is it essential? Can we eat?" He lifted his chin toward my small living room some four paces from where I was working at the kitchen table.

"Uh, yes. Sure. This can wait." I stood and accepted the pie he offered. We both sat on my loveseat because the room had no other place to sit. When I hosted knit night at my apartment, most of the ladies sat on the floor. I used to have two big chairs, but it restricted movement and made the room feel overstuffed with furniture.

He took a bite, closed his eyes, moaned, then took another bite, and moaned again.

I watched him. "Are you going to moan after each bite?" I hoped not, because I'd successfully suppressed flutterings and achings thus far. His moaning wasn't helping.

"Maybe," he spoke around a mouthful, chewed, and then swallowed. "Why? Do you have a moaning allergy? Does it bother you?"

"A little," I hedged, because *bother* was one word for it, especially when paired with hot.

"It's your fault this tastes so good. Where did you learn to cook?"

"My mom." I took my first bite, enjoying the bursts of the sweet, smooth custard contrasted by the bittersweet velvetiness of the dark chocolate.

"What's she like?"

"She's the best. My mother stayed home with us kids—my brother and me—and also helped my dad's business by doing the books. Both of my parents cook, though. My dad focuses on the savory, and my mom prefers the sweet."

"That sounds like an efficient delineation of tasks."

"It is. They've been married for forty-five years, had children late in life."

"What does your dad do?"

"My father used to be a general contractor, but he retired fifteen years ago."

"He builds things," Matt simplified.

"Yes. He'd consider you a wizard."

"Really? A wizard?" Matt looked pleased by the label.

"My dad never had a use for computers, so anything with a screen feels like magic to him. I help them with all their technology purchases. But, give the man wood, a saw, and a hammer and he'd build you a mansion."

"He sounds great, too."

Was that wistfulness I detected in his tone?

"They are great. I grew up with a stable childhood in every way that matters. They both showed up to be proud for all my major life events: school plays, lacrosse games, graduations. I discovered, when I became an adult, that sometimes we lived paycheck to paycheck, but growing up I had no idea. Sure, we never had the latest and greatest gadgets or clothes, but we didn't need it. We had each other. I never felt like I was missing out."

Matt's smile was soft, but also struck me as sad.

"How about your parents?" I nudged his knee. "What were they like?"

"Do you have any complaints about your childhood?

I blinked at his question, not as surprised by it as I would have been just a few days ago. I was beginning to understand this was a part of his personality: ready honesty and curiosity.

"None," I said, but then a thought surfaced, and I amended my original answer. "Actually, just one. I grew up not knowing or understanding any perspective other than my own."

"Meaning?"

"I grew up in a small town, and we never traveled—which was fine, we didn't need to travel—but neither of my parents were big readers. We lived simply, with our small cares. They didn't see the need to expose us to the big wide world, not even the beauty of it."

"Is that why you became a journalist?"

"Maybe." I considered this theory as a possibility, setting my pie on the ottoman next to my cell phone. The compact piece of furniture also served as storage and a coffee table.

I'd always been open to new experiences that fed my job as a journalist, but the same could not be said about my personal life, especially recently. I might go to a professional cuddler for a story, but I never would have gone out of a curiosity or willingness to try something new for myself.

"Tell me something surprising." Matt took another bite of his pie, then frowned at the plate as though displeased with the small amount remaining.

"What?"

"Something I would never guess about you."

"Um, let's see. I've passed the bar in two states."

His eyebrows jumped. "You went to law school?"

"No. I didn't. It was for an article I wrote, when I first started out, on what it's like to take the bar, how to prepare for it, the time involved, the stress, the relevancy to practice. I thought, if I was going to write about it, I should take it."

"Wow. And you passed?"

"Yes, barely. There's only a few states that will let you take it without going to law school, but first you have to study under a judge. The first time I took it, in Wyoming, I studied for two years, non-stop. It was all I did, thought about, lived, breathed. I worked for a judge. I dated lawyers. Complete submersion."

"Shit."

"Yeah. I might've been a little overzealous. But then, I was fresh out of college and wanted to experience life."

"Why go to such lengths?"

"Because . . ." I gathered a deep breath, trying to figure out how to explain my passion without sounding unhinged. "I love knowing something from the inside out, and then sharing that knowledge with the world. The law is so fascinating, changeable, and open to interpretation, based on each individual interpreter's life experience. Stories are that way, too. How people read and react to news. Providing insight into different ways of thinking, different walks of life, making the world think about an old issue from a different perspective, I love it. I feel so lucky that I get to be the conduit through which others' stories are told."

Matt was silent after I finished, and I could *see* him thinking. Deliberating. Considering. As though his ideas about me—on a fundamental level—had just shifted.

At length, his features settled into a frown, but his tone was shaded with admiration as he said, "You're brave."

That made me smirk. "I'm brave?"

"Yes. You're willing to cuddle with a complete stranger. You throw yourself into experiences, all so you can share these experiences with people who might benefit from them, people who, without your stories, may never have been exposed to them otherwise." I couldn't decide if he sounded irritated, impressed, or confused.

"I'm not so brave. It's not like I'm in Afghanistan or Syria, risking my life for journalism and truth."

"No. You're brave," Matt contradicted quickly. "You're a test case, a subject of research, many times over. Except you're the one doing the research, writing up the case report. And then you share it with the world, so that others can see and understand better."

His words suffused my chest with warmth. Maybe even butterflies. And the way he held my gaze with his remarkably attractive eyes, like I was something special, unique and wonderful, made my head swim. The moment stretched, the silence filling with anticipation.

And it was the anticipation that thrust me back into reality.

Because there could be no anticipation.

*Right?*

Right.

I smiled at him and he returned it, increasing the tempo of my heart.

"Okay, your turn." I nudged him with my knee, asking softly, "Tell me about your parents."

Abruptly, most of the light drained from his eyes and his smile fell. Matt shook his head, making a face. "No. Ask me something else."

I was surprised but I bit my tongue to keep from pushing. I wasn't writing a story about Matt, so I didn't need to ask him questions he clearly didn't want to answer.

"Okay." I glanced at the ceiling, picked up my pie, took a bite, and pulled a question out of the air that had been on my mind. "Why do you think people become so resistant to change as they grow older?"

"Are they?"

"Yes. There's a ton of research to back that up, none of which I can quote right now without making up statistics."

"Safety?" He finished off his pie before adding thoughtfully, "Fear of rejection? Though, in my experience, indifference is worse." Matt's gaze floated to the left, then to the right, like he was giving the matter great consideration. Then, abruptly, his eyes cut to mine. "Why? What do you think?"

I shrugged. "I think you're right. My friend Sandra would also mention avoidance of cognitive dissonance as a factor, but it all boils down to safety."

"Sandra, as in Alex's wife?"

I nodded, bemused. "You know Alex? Since when?"

"We met at your knitting club thing, a few weeks ago. Fiona and he work together and she gave my name to him. He's breaking into banks as part of his job." Matt paused, frowned, then rubbed his chin. "At least, I hope it's for his job."

"Yes. It's for his job. He works with Fiona at Quinn's security company. He tries to break into firewalls, or something like that, to point out weaknesses."

"Exactly. Anyway, he'd come across a bank that was using an AI for its security and had some questions."

"Oh . . ." I frowned. "Alex had questions? For you?"

A slyly amused smile bloomed over his features. "Yes."

My frown deepened. "But I thought he was the best."

This drew a laugh from Matt. "I'm sure he is, at hacking, but AI is a completely different field. He's not computer or programming omniscient. No one is."

"Hmm." I nodded, realizing I didn't really know enough about programming to wrap my mind around the difference. To me, there was just a giant bucket labeled "programming" and I assumed if someone was fluent in programming it meant all types of programming.

Perhaps I needed to immerse myself in "programming."

"Anyway, he's interesting." Matt's gaze turned introspective. "He wants to know more about how the field is progressing, so he's coming with me to an AI expo in a few weeks."

My mouth fell open. "Really? Alex?"

"Yes. Alex." Matt gave me a funny look. "Why do you look so surprised? I'm not a troll, you know. I don't live under a bridge, terrorizing goats."

I laughed at that. "I know, which—" I set my pie on the ottoman again and gathered my courage, "—is actually a convenient segue into what I wanted to say next."

"Oh!" Matt's look of suspicion quickly transformed into playfulness. "Are we going to discuss safe words? Mine is *Turing test*."

"No. Not safe words. I wanted to thank you." I laughed at him again, shaking my head. I loved how funny he was, and it struck me how wrong my first—and second, and third—impression of him had been. If I hadn't forced him to share his data with me, I might still be thinking of him as arrogant, petulant, and wooden. But he wasn't those things, not at all. He'd definitely grown on me with repeated exposure.

"Thank me? For what?" His clever eyes danced.

"For coming with me to the cuddle studio. I appreciated having someone there." I shook my head at the imprecise and diluted nature of my words, and knew I needed to correct myself. "Actually, that's not true, I appreciated having *you* there. I was thinking about the story, and of course I'll still need your help with that, but after the series is over, I'm hoping that you and I can continue to be friends."

Matt's playfulness waned as I spoke, his expression growing mystified, then suddenly sober, as though he'd just solved a puzzle.

"You're friend-zoning me," he said, and I got the impression he spoke the words as soon as he thought them.

I reared back. "What?"

"No. It's fine. I'm just . . ." A deep V formed between his eyebrows, the adorable wrinkle appearing as he pulled his gaze from mine, turning his body in profile, and stared at my ottoman.

I waited a few seconds, paralyzed by what he'd said. Did he not want to be friend-zoned? Did he want more than—

. . . No.

*No.*

. . . Maybe?

My heart jumped to my throat and a hot shock of sensation tightened my chest, heated my neck and cheeks. Could he—did he— I mean—was it possible that this guy, who eschewed romantic relationships with such fervor, was interested? *In me?*

And was I interested in him?

I knew I was attracted to him, but—

"Matt?"

"No. It's fine." He shook his head, not looking at me, and chuckled, like this was funny. "I, um, have become a student of human nature, since I began this project, and this—" he gestured between us, still not looking at me, "—is a classic friend-zone maneuver. I don't have a more technical word for it. It's very typical of what we've seen in our lab. Fascinating, really."

He turned back to me and his smile was small but easy as he picked up his pie plate and scraped at the remnants, forking a few crumbs into his mouth.

I wasn't convinced. Something was off.

"Matt, excuse me if I'm confused, but didn't you say last week that you're not interested in a long-term relationship?"

"Yes. That's correct. I'm not," he responded lightly, but his expression was looking increasingly brittle.

"Then what is the—"

My phone rang, effectively cutting off my sporadic thoughts. Gritting my teeth, I glanced at the screen and—seeing who it was—muttered, "Shit."

"Who is it?"

I didn't answer right away, instead leaning forward and sending the call to voicemail. This was the fourth time he'd called in two days, but once again, he didn't leave a message. *What can he want?*

Gathering a deep breath, I admitted, "That was David. My ex-boyfriend."

Matt hesitated and I felt his eyes on me, probing. "Are you two reconciling?"

"No," I said, with force. "No. He's engaged, actually. His new girlfriend— I mean, she's not new, she's his fiancée—just sent me an invitation to their engagement party a few weeks ago and I haven't responded."

Matt blew out a long, audible breath. "Are you okay?"

I nodded, finally meeting his gaze, knowing I looked confused. "Yes. At least, I thought I was."

"Meaning?"

"Meaning, when I got the invite I didn't expect to feel so much about it. It blindsided me, but I thought I'd get over it. I'm happy for him, them. I am. But it—I just—I don't know how to describe it."

"Do you still talk to him?" Matt's tone was friendly enough, but also felt edged with cautious objectivity. "Have you met her?"

"No. We stopped talking when we broke up." I gave Matt a self-deprecating shrug. "I got dumped."

He flinched at that, just a very small movement, his pity making me roll my eyes at myself.

"It's fine. Everyone gets dumped eventually."

"What does he do?"

"He's a chef."

Matt made a face. "Why would you need to date a chef? You can cook."

That made me chuckle. "I didn't date a chef, Matt. I dated a person."

He lifted his chin and I got the distinct impression my response had surprised him. "Well said."

"Thanks."

"Maybe you're not over him," he suggested, his eyes wandering over my face, tinged with something I couldn't identify.

I shook my head slowly, my attention drifting to the right and focusing on nothing but my thoughts as I debated this theory. "No. I think I am over him. In fact, I think I was over him before he dumped me. But he was safe. And kind to me. And I didn't want to lose that."

When I refocused on Matt, I found his gaze lowered to the ottoman, a secretive yet rueful smile tugging his lips to one side.

"Matt—"

"I need to leave." He stood, stuffing his hands in his pockets for the first time all night, and walked the short distance to the door.

My heart jumped to my throat and started beating out a frantic staccato. *What should I say?*

*Should I apologize?*

What for?

The friend-zoned comment plagued me. *I want to be friends with him, that much is true, but—*

He was already at the door and the time to explain was now or never, yet I had no idea what I was going to say.

I started with, "About what I said, I didn't mean that I wanted—"

"I consider it a compliment." Matt turned back to me, his voice even and steady, reasonable, aloof. "I've never been any good at biologically motivated displays of testosterone superiority, and I wouldn't want to waste the time of someone who requires them." He finished with a small smile, but it didn't quite reach his eyes.

Or maybe it did.

I couldn't be certain.

Anxiety clouded my vision.

I wasn't in the most rational state of mind.

Nevertheless, I tried, "But I don't understand how friend-zoning, in our case, given what—"

"It's a relief you said something first. Pragmatically it saved me the conversation. You're not at all my type." He shrugged, like everything was perfectly fine.

His words made my breath catch. And my heart hurt. Because . . . I guess he would know? He had the data. He'd read my dating profile. He knew all about *women like me.*

"I'm not?" I licked my lips, they were suddenly dry.

"No." Matt's smile grew tight, and then he pulled me forward and placed a gentle kiss on my forehead.

"Goodbye, friend Marie," he whispered. "Thanks for dinner and pie."

He turned and walked away.

# CHAPTER 12

### Desktop companion robot

*A proof-of-concept desktop companion robot unveiled at the 2017 Consumer Electronics Show (CES) with "human-like" movements and communication skills. The robot is able to access and use cloud data, and communicate with devices in other locations. The size of a standard kitchen countertop blender, the robot includes an embedded projector that is enclosed within the egg shell-shaped device. The robot can also move backwards and forwards and up and down, and has been designed to mimic human movements. The decision to make the robot sound child-like was deliberate to build a sense of attachment with its human owner.*

Source: Panasonic

**JANIE HAD A** scare during the latter part of June, giving me a (figurative) heart attack.

I received the call Sunday. Elizabeth phoned me from Janie's room while Sandra and I were at her place, working to finish knitting Janie's baby blanket; Sandra took one end, I took the other, and we'd set a bottle of wine on the coffee table next to us.

"Is she okay? Is the baby okay?" My hand flew to my chest and I fumbled to switch to speakerphone, bracing for the worst.

"She's fine," Elizabeth said.

Sandra and I locked gazes and exhaled our infinite relief as Elizabeth continued. "There was some spotting, we thought it was early labor, but it wasn't. We've also ruled out placental abruption. The baby looks good. But Janie will need to be off her feet for the rest of her pregnancy. She's only twenty-eight weeks, so we're looking at months of bed rest. She'll stay in the hospital for the next few days, just so she can be observed around the clock." Then under her breath Elizabeth added, "Thank God I live next door."

The short surge of adrenaline waned, leaving me with its simmering aftereffects.

"What can we do?" I asked, feeling like I needed to ask.

I heard Janie in the background cursing. *Actually* cursing. This was significant because Janie never cursed with actual curse words, preferring instead to use *Thor!*

I winced.

"Nothing, for now. But it would be great if you could visit over the next few weeks, stop in."

"Absolutely."

Sandra chimed in, "We'll all visit."

"Also," Elizabeth lowered her voice to almost a whisper, "can you check in on Quinn tonight? You and Fiona are the only ones he'll talk to. Seriously, the dude does not look good."

Elizabeth was Janie's best friend and, interestingly enough, she didn't particularly get along with Quinn, but I knew for a fact she cared about him. The problem was Elizabeth and Quinn were just too much alike. Similarly, Nico and Janie were alike in their optimistic and sweet dispositions.

"Yeah, well, he's probably terrified." Sandra blew out an audible breath. "Poor guy."

"Okay. Yes. He'll be at the hospital?" I asked, mentally rearranging my next twenty-four hours. It wouldn't be a big deal, as my job was blessedly flexible.

"Yep. I don't think he'll leave until Janie is discharged. I'm having a bed brought in for him. Hold on." I heard Elizabeth move the phone away from her ear while she gave someone an order. "Okay, I'm back. Listen, I'm going to try to see if we can do knit night at the hospital this week. I think it should be fine as long as we don't stay too late or drink . . . too much."

"Got it. I'll spread the word." I made a mental note to message Fiona and Kat as well as bring my laptop so Ashley could join us.

"Thanks. Love you, Marie. And you too, Sandra. Talk soon."

"Bye, honey," I said. "And don't forget you need sleep, too. Take a rest." I had a feeling Elizabeth was probably at the hospital past her shift. Every time I'd called her over the last few weeks she'd been working and Sunday afternoons were usually her day off.

"Thanks for keeping us in the loop," Sandra added.

We clicked off the call, sharing another look and sigh.

"Well, I'm awake," Sandra said with wide, sober eyes. "I swear, that scared me half to death."

"Imagine how Janie feels." I couldn't help my solemn expression. "I hope she's okay. I should bring her a comic book."

The line of Sandra's mouth turned frustrated. "That poor woman, this has been the pregnancy from hell."

I was just about to agree when the apartment door opened and Alex announced, "We're here."

"Eep!" Sandra tossed the blanket from her lap and jumped up, running toward the hall leading to the front door.

As soon as Alex appeared, she flung herself into his arms. I couldn't help but smile at the two of them as he lifted her off the ground and carry-hugged her back into the living room.

"Hey! How was the thing?" Sandra asked, covering his face with kisses.

"Fine." Alex placed a biting kiss on her neck and bent, setting her back down on the couch and kissing her again on the forehead, then lips.

"Where'd you go?" I asked, catching some movement at the entryway and doing a double take at the image of Matt hovering just inside the room.

I froze. But my heart didn't. It began galloping in my chest.

*Gack! There he is.*

His eyes were on me, his expression neutral, though I was fairly certain he was just as surprised to see me as I was to see him.

We hadn't spoken in almost three weeks, not since I'd made him coconut curry and he'd helped me translate his graphs. I'd texted him, just once, asking how he was doing, but he never responded. I didn't follow up, deciding his silence spoke for him.

"Hi," I said on a breath.

"Friend Marie." He nodded his head once in greeting, stuffing his hands in his pockets, then to Sandra he said evenly, "Hi, Sandra."

Yep.

I was attracted to Matt Simmons.

Looking back at our few brief encounters, I'd begun to think that maybe he was attracted to me and my inadvertent friend-zoning had put him off. However, by his own admission, his last marriage had fallen apart because he and his wife couldn't be bothered to make time for each other, more or less.

"Matthew," Sandra said, saltiness in her tone.

I slid my eyes to Sandra, giving her a suspicious look. "*Matthew*?"

"He knows what he did." Sandra returned her attention to the blanket.

"What did you do?" I looked to Matt for a clue, becoming a little lost in his dark, lovely, attractive, expressive eyes, the window to his huge and impressive brain.

Actually, seemingly out of the blue, everything about him was attractive.

My heart was still beating wildly and I fought against a blush rising to my cheeks because my own traitorous brain picked that moment to remember the feel of his lips brushing against the back of my neck.

*So what? You cuddled. Once. He's off limits.*

*And, lest you forget, Matthew Simmons is allergic to committed relationships with anything other than his job. And you're not his type. And, and, and . . .*

I forcefully shook myself from my musings. I didn't want to register second place to a person's career. Matt's heart belonged to his work and, even if he did want to date me—which he didn't—I would never ask him to put me first.

Because I shouldn't have to. I wanted to be with someone who *wanted* to put *us* first.

This thought put me back on solid footing.

The side of his mouth hitched. "I hypothesize she's still angry with me about the deception study, about you."

My mouth fell open and I scrunched my face at Sandra. "You don't need to be mad at Matt, Sandra. I'm completely over that."

"Maybe you shouldn't be." The set of her jaw was stubborn. "Maybe you forgive and forget too easily."

"Listen to Sandra." Alex turned from us and walked to the kitchen. "Holding grudges has done wonders for me over the years. Matt, do you want anything? Ladies, anything? Beer?"

"Beer sounds great. Thanks." Matt trailed after Alex toward the kitchen, but stayed on the living room side at the bar.

"No beer for us. We have wine," Sandra called to her husband.

"The study was approved by an ethics committee. It's not like it was personal. He didn't single me out for his research. I was just one of many that fit a similar profile." I'd lowered my voice so only she could hear.

"That's exactly my point." My friend thrust her needle into the air.

"What is your point? What exactly did he do that was so wrong?"

"I said you were just like everyone else," Matt supplied, accepting the beer Alex handed to him over the bar. "She chewed me out about it the last time I was here."

"Sandra," I whispered harshly, feeling embarrassed. Especially since his comment about me being *just like everyone else* all those weeks ago still smarted.

But I didn't want anyone else to actually *know* that.

"Don't you *Sandra* me. Nobody calls Marie typical. Nobody. My God, look at you! You're like the sexiest woman on the planet. You're Marilyn Monroe and Grace Kelly and that delightful Kristen Bell from *Frozen*, except with better hair. And you're also unfairly smart. And an excellent human. And an exceptional cook."

I couldn't maintain my glower. She was my friend, so of course she was over-exaggerating the existence and the extent of my positive attributes, but she also made me feel awesome.

"Again, I agree with Sandra on this." Alex strolled out of the kitchen and lifted his beer bottle toward me. "That's like calling Minsky's Stochastic Neural Analogy typical."

"Nice reinforcement learning reference." Matt held out his beer to Alex.

"Thanks." Alex clinked his beer with Matt's.

They both drank.

Meanwhile, I was blushing because I was stewing in mortification.

*Why does this bother me so much?*

\*\*\*

I LEFT A short time later, wanting to get to the hospital around dinnertime just in case Quinn and Janie were in the mood for something not offered by the cafeteria. Saying my goodbyes to Sandra and Alex went as typical: hugs and cheek kisses with promises to see each other during the week.

When it came time to say goodbye to Matt, he offered me a handshake and a smile that definitely wasn't reflected in his eyes. I kept replaying the handshake in my head all the way down to the lobby, because the detached quality to his gaze irked me.

Maybe he was still irritated or sore about the friend-zoning conversation.

Or maybe he wasn't.

Maybe he just didn't like me much.

I honestly didn't know. He was so difficult to read.

As I exited the building, I decided to push thoughts of the professor from my mind. Not everyone was going to want to be friends with me, and that was fine. I'd made an effort and had been shot down.

Moving on.

My phone was in the bottom of my purse, so I paused just outside of the doors to send off a text to Quinn, asking if I could pick anything up on my way. I was just tucking it back into its place when Matt came running out of the building.

I watched as he jogged past, stopped, then turned and craned his neck from side to side as though searching for something. He'd turned completely around when he spotted me, taking a surprised step back.

"Oh. Hey." He shoved his hands in his pockets. "There you are."

"Hey." I pulled my purse strap more completely on my shoulder and met him halfway. "What's wrong? Did I forget something?"

"No." He hesitated, licking his lips and biting on the bottom one before continuing. "I'm on my way out. We might as well walk together."

"Okay. Sounds good." I examined him. His expression still struck me as cautiously dispassionate, I thought, as I picked the path that would take me to the El station. "Are you headed this way?"

"Where are you going?"

"I have to stop by the hospital. You know Janie? The tall redhead from our knitting group? She's having some problems with her pregnancy."

He fell into step next to me. "Is she okay?"

"Yes. She's fine now."

"You're going to check on her?"

"Yes and no. I'm hoping she'll be asleep when I get there. I'm mostly going to check on her husband."

"Her husband? You mean that big guy who stares at people and doesn't talk?"

I'd forgotten that Matt had met Quinn when I'd made pizza and watched Jack and Grace. It seemed so long ago.

"That's the one."

"Why are you checking on him?"

"Because he'll talk to me. He'll also talk to Fiona, but she's got enough to deal with."

Matt gave me a weird look. "Talk to you about what?"

"How he's doing, how he's coping, if he needs anything, if I can help."

"Why would you do that?"

"Because, Matt, I care about him. He's my friend. When my friends need me—and even when they don't—I'm there for them."

I didn't look at him, but I could feel his eyes on me.

Eventually, he cleared his throat. "You're a good person."

"Thanks."

"Your friends are lucky. You're one of those people no one deserves to know. You're too good." He looked and sounded so earnest, such that the effect his words had on my heart caught me off guard.

Matt turned away, and I found I was unable to drop my eyes. He looked . . . unhappy.

"Hey," I took a cautious step forward, "you know, we're friends, too. Right?"

Exhaling a short breath through his nose, he slid his teeth to the side before he nodded. "Yes. I know."

Studying him, I decided that if we were actually going to be friends, then we needed the clear the air.

Lifting my chin, I asked, "Can we talk about the friend-zoning comment?"

He sighed. Loudly. And began walking with a quickened pace. "No need."

"Well, I need. And you're going to listen. So here goes." I gathered a deep breath, preparing to launch into my monologue on why he shouldn't have acted so strangely about being friend-zoned.

Before I could, he said, "That was a friend-zone maneuver. I know a friend-zone maneuver when I see one."

"Yes. It was. But not for the reason you seem to think. I wasn't trying to put you in a box or assign a label."

Matt made a slight scoffing sound.

"I was making overtures to be your friend, not to be *just* your friend."

His eyes darted to mine, then away. I imagined his mind working as though he were a computer and he sought to compile this new information. "Meaning?"

"I like you."

That made him stop, which made me stop and walk backward, because he was advancing on me, his gaze arresting mine. "You *like* me?"

"Yes." I endeavored to answer simply, but the look in his eyes made my answer less than simple. Forced to place my hand on his chest to cease his forward progress, I did my best to ignore how his attention was now singularly focused on my mouth. "Yes, I like you. You're funny. Odd. Interesting. But even if I was attracted to you, nothing would—"

"So you're not attracted to me." Something shifted behind his stare, giving me the impression that everything he'd wondered about me was now clear.

Jeez, he was pushy.

"Just listen. Regardless of attraction or lack of attraction, nothing can or will happen between us."

"And why is that?" He framed the question as though my words would confirm some theory he already held.

"Because, you said yourself that you've read that book, seen that movie, and you don't want to see it again."

"Meaning?" He blinked, his expression betraying confusion.

"You're not interested in something long-term, right? A committed relationship. Partnership. And," I shrugged, beating back the butterflies in my stomach with a spiked club, "that's what I'm interested in. That's *all* I want."

Matt lifted his chin and rocked back on his heels, effectively disconnecting my hand from his chest. His gaze met and held mine. "I see."

He stared at me, a thoughtful expression on his features. I stared at him, an open expression on mine.

"Correct." His thoughtful expression persisted; I sensed that my response both surprised and confused him. "Friends it is."

"Good." I nodded, forcing a smile. It felt unnatural, and I had to really think about how wide I should make it because I was distracted by a sinking sensation in my stomach. "I'm glad we're on the same page."

I wasn't *unhappy* about his acquiescence. Yet I'd be lying if I claimed I wasn't disappointed. Disappointed in the situation, disappointed in Matt, and disappointed in the entire male portion of the human race.

But the situation was no more Matt's fault than mine. He'd been honest about his lack of interest in a lasting relationship. I'd been honest about my lack of interest in a truncated relationship.

See? Honesty. It gets the job done.

And sometimes situations are just shitty.

*Moving on . . .*

Before I could stop myself, I asked, "So, why didn't you return my text?" and then I winced, because that sounded needy.

His eyes widened for a brief moment, and then he closed them and rubbed his forehead. "I apologize. Things have been busy at work and I—"

"It's fine. Don't worry about it." I waved him off, because his excuses hurt my feelings for some reason. I didn't know why I suddenly felt so raw, exposed.

I really needed to rethink this emotional bravery thing.

"No. Not fine." He caught my elbow, pulled me to a stop, then shoved his hands back in his pockets. "I promise I'll return your text next time. I promise." Again, he looked and sounded so earnest, my feelings caught in my throat.

I couldn't speak. Sincerity from Matt Simmons was apparently my kryptonite.

Therefore, I nodded, giving him a tight smile.

"Hey, so," he shifted on his feet, gathering a breath, "what's going on with you? Did you finish your story?"

"Which one?" I began walking again, slowly at first so we could walk together. "I'm always writing and researching several."

"The cuddling story."

"Oh, yeah. I have a draft of that section. But it's part of a larger series about replacing romantic relationships with either paid services or technology. Like robots."

He made a sound in the back of his throat, turning an incredulous, slow-spreading grin on me. "Look at you, sneaky Marie."

"Yep."

"My research is part of this series?"

"Yes. We'll use it for the technology issue."

"I can already tell you which approach is superior."

"Oh yeah?"

"Yeah. Robots. Paying other people to care about you doesn't work."

"How can you be so sure?"

He shrugged, scratching his chin, not answering, instead asking, "What other paid services are you going to check out?"

"Um, let's see. Have you heard of dry humping professionals?"

He gasped, his hand clutching his chest. "Are you shitting me?"

"Nope."

Matt blinked, his eyes moving all over the place, like he was trying to process too many thoughts. "Well, what else? Are you driving down to Nevada?"

"No. No prostitutes. But I am planning to hire a male escort to take me to my ex's engagement party." *If I ever can ever bring myself to actually RSVP or answer one of David's calls.*

He stopped me again with a hand on my elbow. This time he didn't let go. "You're joking."

"I'm not." I grinned as I assured him of my veracity. "And I made an appointment at an OM studio."

"What's an OM studio?" He looked petrified.

"Orgasm Meditation."

"Just stop. Stop talking. No more of this nonsense." He shook his head, his delivery of these words reminding me of Ryan Reynolds in any of his comedic roles.

The dramatics launched me into a fit of giggles, which felt good. The laughter eased some of the earlier sting.

"Oh my God. Marie." He didn't let go of my arm. Rather, he pulled me into a hug, clutching me tightly, and whispering, "I'm so scared for you," into my ear while he pet my hair, which only made me laugh harder. Truly, he was hilarious.

"You're funnier than I remember." I wrapped my arms around his waist, noting that he felt better than I remembered, too.

"And you're crazier than I remember. I should lock you up, save you from yourself."

"Hey," I halfheartedly pushed at him, "I thought you said I was brave?"

"You are brave." His strong arms squeezed me as he loud-whispered, "But you're also *craze-zeeee.*"

# CHAPTER 13

### Synthetic DNA (aka DNA Foundation)

*Artificial DNA made using commercially available oligonucleotide synthesis machines for storage and DNA sequencing machines for retrieval. This type of storage system is more compact than current magnetic tape or hard drive storage systems due to the data density of the DNA. Many believe it's the answer to the growing problem of data storage needs. One gram of synthetic DNA has been demonstrated to hold up to 215 petabytes of information (1 petabyte = 1,000,000 gigabytes)*

Source: New York Genome Center, New York, NY

**AFTER OUR WALK** and friend-embrace in Grant Park, I'd given Matt a large berth, deciding it was best for him to make the next move. I would do anything for my friends, other than force my friendship upon them.

He'd texted me three days later.

**Matt:** *Are you dead? Or do you want lunch?*

His timing was perfect. I'd been working from home, baking bread for the week, and storyboarding the first draft of my article on his research. While arranging my notes, I'd discovered a few loose ends.

**Marie**: *I'll bring lunch, are you allergic to anything?*
**Matt**: *Cats, sadly. And teenagers, happily.*

**Marie**: *How about shellfish?*
**Matt**: *I LOVE SHELLFISH*


Grabbing the two jars of crab bisque I had in the freezer, disposable/microwavable bowls, and a loaf of bread still warm from the oven, I met him at his office. We ate while I asked my questions. When we were finished, he suggested I stay and finish storyboarding, just in case I needed additional clarification.

"Will you be able to work with me here?" I asked, scrutinizing his office.

"No problem. Do you need a table?" He turned a contemplative frown to his desk and workbench, both of which were still covered with papers and various machinery debris. As he looked around his office, he pushed his fingers into his hair, sending it into disarray and drawing my attention to the muscles of his bicep.

The man had to work out all the time. He *had* to.

Unbidden, my attention moved over the rest of him. He was in his usual jeans, Converse, nerdy T-shirt attire, but the pants looked new. They were dark blue, and as a heterosexual woman with a pulse, I appreciated how they rested on his narrow hips, fit the curve of his backside and muscled thighs.

"I actually work best on the floor," I offered, feeling oddly hot.

And, bonus, the floor was free of clutter. And free of Matt.

"Really?"

"Yes."

"Okay." He shrugged, scratching his neck. "Do you mind if I play music?"

"Fine by me."

We both assumed our positions, him at his desk in front of his wall of monitors, me kneeling on the floor, spreading my papers out in story order. "Dead Leaves and the Dirty Ground," by The White Stripes played over his speakers and I smiled to myself, but said nothing.

I loved The White Stripes. And I loved Jack White as a solo artist. Matt couldn't have picked better music as the soundtrack for the afternoon.

I sensed Matt glance at me a few times over his shoulder, but I studiously paid him no attention, pleased that I was already engrossed in my work instead of gawking at his physique and bobbing my head lightly to the music.

For a time, we worked, saying nothing. Part of the time I moved the papers around on the floor, part of the time I wrote sections on my laptop. I glanced at my computer's clock just as the song switched from "Seven Nation Army" to "I Fell In Love With A Girl" and was surprised to find forty-five minutes had passed.

Pausing my work, I closed the laptop and placed it next to me. I stretched, arching my back and leaning from side to side.

Matt spun suddenly in his office chair to face me, unsmiling, his arms crossed.

"I have a serious question for you," he said, sounding serious.

"Shoot." I glanced at him briefly, turning my neck from one side to the other.

"If a woman wears a low-cut blouse—"

"Did you just say blouse?"

He blinked once, his expression growing flat. "Can I ask my question?"

"Fine. Blouse, low cut, what about it?"

"If a woman's shirt is low cut, like a V," he drew a V on his own chest, "such that a good amount of her cleavage—"

I snorted. Cleavage. Blouse. Matt talked like my grandmother. *At least he didn't say décolletage.*

His lips became a tight line. "Well what do you call cleavage?"

"Tits? Breasts? Boobs?"

"Fine. Low-cut shirt, showcasing half a lady's breasts, is it okay to look at said breasts?"

"Yes." I nodded once.

"Really?" The question was an octave higher than his usual baritone.

"Yes. Really. Unless she has a date, then no."

"What? Why?"

"Because she's wearing the low-cut shirt for her date—not for you—and you don't want to get punched in the face. But if she's there on her own and wearing something revealing, she wants people to look."

"Huh." His eyes lost focus as he stared beyond me, absorbing this information.

"You find that surprising?" I leaned forward to switch two sheets of paper, rearranging the timeline.

"Yes. I assumed it was rude." After a moment, he shook himself and I felt his eyes on me again.

"Didn't you ask your ex these questions?" I wondered aloud.

"No. We never talked about stuff like this."

"Really?" Now I was surprised. "Wait, stuff like what?"

"Man to woman stuff. What women or men want in general terms. We were both inexperienced when we met, so I'm not sure we knew."

"Oh." That made me frown. "Well, didn't she wear sexy clothes for you? And, more importantly, didn't you ever wear sexy clothes for her?"

"No. She didn't. And what is your meaning? Did I wear sexy clothes for her? What sexy clothes can men wear?"

"Suits." I grinned at him. "Finely tailored suits are the equivalent of a sexy black dress to women, or lingerie."

His eyebrows ticked up and his eyes widened. "Really?"

"Yep. It takes effort for a man to wear a nice suit. Just like it takes effort for a woman to dress up."

"So . . . it's the effort? That's sexy?"

Crawling on my hands and knees, I picked up my notes from the floor, careful to keep them in order. "I guess that's one way of looking at it."

Again I felt his eyes study me before he said thoughtfully, "You're already really sexy. I feel sorry for anyone who has to resist you in a black dress."

That made me laugh, especially the abstract tone of voice, like we were discussing AI Learning Theory, but it also made my neck hot. Suddenly, I was distinctly aware of how small his office was, and how I was currently positioned on my hands and knees, and how—if he stood and unbuckled his belt . . .

*Whoa.*

*Settle down.*

That thought process sure escalated quickly.

Suppressing the unbidden surge of sexy suggestions, I tossed him a mock-distrustful glance but couldn't quite lift my gaze to his. "You're just saying that so I'll make you more bread."

"You caught me." Matt's tone mirrored my mock-seriousness. But I also noticed his smile was weird, stiff, and he was blushing just slightly. The light shade of pink heating his cheeks made me wonder if he hadn't realized what he was saying, what his words sounded like, or what they revealed of his thoughts, until *after* he'd said them.

"Hey, look who it is."

I tore my eyes from Matt, finding Dr. Merek leaning against the doorjamb, eyes on me, a small smile tugging his mouth to one side.

Sitting back on my ankles, I returned his grin. "Hello."

"What do you want?" Matt's tone was less than happy.

Dr. Merek's gaze moved to Matt briefly, narrowed, then returned to me. "Did you get everything you needed for your article?"

I opened my mouth to respond, but didn't get a chance.

"She did," Matt answered for me.

The older man inspected us both with unveiled surprise. "So you're here finishing up?"

"Yes. Almost finished." I gestured to my stack of papers. "Just tying up loose ends."

"We might go see a movie after," Matt said, causing me to send him a surprised glance over my shoulder. He ignored my probing look. "Then dinner," he added.

This was news to me.

Matt's eyes remained fixed on his colleague and both men were quiet for a protracted moment while I glanced between the two of them and attempted to decipher their odd staring contest.

Eventually, Dr. Merek cracked a smile and nodded subtly. "Oh, by the way, Greta is looking for you, Matt."

"Oh?" Matt stood, his entire demeanor changing in an instant. "Did the NVIDIA chip come in?"

"Yep."

Matt moved to where I was still sitting on the floor and offered me his hand, saying as he pulled me up, "Do you mind hanging out here for a few minutes?"

It was hard to miss the fact that he still held my hand even though I was now standing, or the fact that his thumb was brushing back and forth over my knuckles.

"Fine with me." I gave him a teasing smile, since we didn't actually *have* plans beyond lunch.

"Thanks." Before I realized his intent, Matt bent and placed a kiss on my cheek, squeezing my hand before letting it go and saying, "I'll be right back. And pick a movie."

I watched him dart out the door, Dr. Merek moving to one side to allow him to pass, then jog down the hall, his sneakers making light squeaking sounds as he went.

I turned, smiling to myself at Matt's strange behavior, then bent to pick up my papers and laptop, all the while feeling Dr. Merek's eyes track my movements.

Finally, he said, "What movie do you want to see?"

"The new Harry Potter movie."

He chuckled lightly. "I've seen it seven times already."

"Big fan?" I grinned.

"No. But my ten-year-old is."

"Ah." I nodded. "I sometimes babysit for my friend's kids and we play the board game while wearing wizard hats, scarves, and wielding wands."

"They make you do it?"

"Oh, no." I shook my head vehemently. "I make *them* do it. I even knit their scarves."

He barked a laugh, leaning against the doorframe again, his eyes moving over me. "I'm impressed."

"Don't be. I knit all the time. It's an obsession."

"No. I mean, I'm impressed you've managed to get Matt out of the office. He's here so much, we sometimes joke he should give up his apartment lease."

"Ha. Is that so?"

"Yes. That's so." Dr. Merek's eyes continued to travel over me thoughtfully. "I guess it's a good thing you never signed that consent form."

That made me cock my head to the side. "Why is that?"

"I'm back. What'd I miss?" Matt called from down the hall, jogging until he pulled even with his office.

"Do you run everywhere?" I asked, both incredulous and amused.

"No. Only when checking out the beautiful new GPUs we're using for training our AI's deep neural networks. Or, you know, when I get to see you."

That earned him a smile. "You're sweet."

He returned my smile with a bright one of his own. "I speak only truths."

Unable to stop myself from scrutinizing this new version of Matt—and the earlier handholding, and the earlier kiss on the cheek—I couldn't understand the origin of his sudden demonstrative affection for me.

*Maybe it's just a part of his inherent playfulness?*

Dr. Merek glanced at the linoleum, looking like he was hiding a smile and stepping back from the door. "Okay, have a good time, kids."

I wrinkled my nose at the word *kids*, but stepped forward to give him a departing wave. "If you let me know what Hogwarts house your ten-year-old is in, I can make a scarf."

Dr. Merek's gaze moved from me to where Matt stood at my side, then back to me. "I'll let Matt know so he can pass it on."

We both watched the tall man depart, Matt eventually nudging my shoulder with his, drawing my attention.

"You're going to make me go see the new Harry Potter movie, aren't you?"

"That's right." I nodded once.

He glowered.

"And then after, I'll make you coconut shrimp."

He grinned.

*** 

"REAL-TIME IMAGES, like video game graphics, rely on GPUs that perform certain types of mathematical calculations—for example, matrix multiplications—"

"Ah yes, good old matrix multiplications. Here, let me." I selected a deep-red button-down dress shirt on a hanger and held it up to Matt's chest. It looked very nice. *Verra, verra* nice. I added it to our stack.

Meanwhile, he continued with barely a pause. "For example, matrix multiplications, they can handle huge amounts of computations in parallel. The same features are suitable for different applications, like running climate simulations or modeling attributes of complex biomolecular structures."

I sighed, gazing at him with a smile, my brain and other key parts of me completely aroused by Matt saying the words, *complex biomolecular structures.*

Believe it or not, Matt had invited me out on a Tuesday afternoon to clothes shop. Apparently, his chairperson had suggested—less than subtly—that many professors in the engineering department had been confused regarding Matt's tenure status.

They thought he was an undergrad student.

Presently, we were in the Hugo Boss store and I'd made the glorious mistake of asking him what a NVIDIA chip was, the item he was so eager to see when he left me briefly with Dr. Merek. Apparently, I couldn't have asked a better question. His eyes widened excitedly and, like every time he spoke about his work, he stood straighter, exuding seductive confidence with his deep, thorough knowledge.

"GPUs are recognized as proficient at training deep neural networks, the mathematical structures roughly modeled on the human brain." His grin became massive and he leaned close, as though about to share something truly amazing. "They also rely heavily on repeated parallel matrix calculations."

"Get out!" I said. "That's awesome."

He nodded. "I know." He then touched my nose lightly with his index finger. "You are super cute when you pretend you know what I'm talking about."

That made me laugh and I shook my head at him. "And you are super cute when you talk about your computery witchcraft. How many white dress shirts do you have?"

"Um, one. And now you know what it's like for me all the time." He glanced around the store as though we were within the interior of a prison.

"Meaning?" I'd picked up this peculiarity of speech he had. Instead of asking, *What do you mean?* He would frequently just say, *Meaning?*

"Over the course of my adulthood—and childhood, for that matter—everyday conversations frequently sound like Greek."

That had me wrinkling my nose at him. "What are you talking about? You have no problem communicating with me."

One of the sales associates approached us. "Hi there, are you finding everything you need?"

Her gaze moved over Matt appreciatively and then to me, her eyebrows hitching on her forehead; if I was reading her expression correctly, it communicated, *Your boyfriend is hot.*

"Marie?" he deferred, clearly oblivious to the pretty woman's appreciation.

"I think so, but could you start a room for him?"

"No problem." She reached forward to grab our current selections. Actually, they were my selections. Matt hadn't touched anything but me since we'd entered, shoving his hands in his pockets.

"I'm looking forward to this fashion show," she said, and then winked at me.

I couldn't help my grin. She was being so adorably obvious, and it made me feel like she was giving me a mental high five, a la, *You go, girl!*

"That's because you don't seem to mind my questions," Matt said once she left, picking our conversation right back up as he considered the suit next to him on a mannequin. "Are we getting suits here?"

That stopped me in my tracks. "Do you *want* a suit?"

He scrutinized me like my question was a test. "I don't know. *Do* I?"

"I guess we could get you a suit, if you think you'll use it." I contemplated the mannequin, touching the fabric of the three-piece with my fingertips. "This is fine."

"Fine?" He glanced between me and the suit. "Is fine good?"

I shrugged. "Or we could go someplace less expensive. It depends on what you want to use it for."

Matt stared at me, analyzing my features attentively. "See? It's like you're speaking a different language."

I laughed. "Okay. What are you going to use it for?"

"You haven't given me enough information in order to make a decision. I need more data."

I laughed again. "You have several different categories of suits, depending on the needs of the person. If you're using it to go to a funeral or twice a year for weddings, or something like that, then you probably don't need a very expensive suit. If that's the case, we should go someplace cheaper."

"What's the downside? Of a less expensive suit?"

"They don't look as nice and they're not usually great quality, which means they wear out faster."

"But this suit," he gestured to the one next to us, "will look better and last longer?"

"Yes. This is a medium-quality suit."

"Where can one acquire a high-quality suit?"

"Um . . ." I glanced to the right, trying to remember where Janie said Quinn bought his suits. "There's a designer in Chicago, Daniel George, who will hand-make a suit, or even shirts, using fabrics and a cut specifically chosen for you."

"It's literally tailor-made."

"Correct."

"And it'll look the best?"

"And last for a long time, yes. But it'll cost a lot. Like, a lot *a lot.*"

He gave me a flat, teasing smile. "For a writer, you sure do use the big words."

I rolled my eyes, turning from him. "Fine. The expenditure will be exorbitant."

He came up behind me, peering over my shoulder as I thumbed through a rack of dress pants. "Is there any place like that? For women?"

"Not really. I mean, you *can* get custom clothing made, but most women don't."

"Because it's expensive?"

"That, and because there's already so much to choose from ready-made that runs the gamut of inexpensive to upscale."

"Where do you shop? For yourself?"

"The only thing I ever pay retail for is yarn."

He paused, like he was trying to untangle a puzzle. "Meaning?"

"I usually shop consignment. I like it because a) it's a lot cheaper, and b) consignment shops have a bunch of brands rather than just one, so it's like going to multiple stores at once."

He paused again, considering this information, then said, "Huh."

I looked at him because the way he said *huh* was peculiar. "What?"

"Your methods are efficient." He was smiling at me, giving me the sense that he very much approved of my methods. My *efficient* methods.

*** 

WATCHING MATT TRY on clothes was a ridiculous amount of fun.

Since it was after lunch on a weekday, the store was very slow. Therefore, a few of the sales associates meandered over, having nothing better to do, and soon it became a one-man fashion show.

At first, he was very stiff. Glowering when he emerged from his dressing room, clearly uncomfortable. It didn't help that he had no idea how to put on nice clothes.

One of the sales guys, Mason I think, noticing how Matt had left his shirt untucked and was wearing dress pants without a belt, shook his head, saying, "You need an intervention, bro."

As it turned out, Mason and Keely—the female attendant who had set up Matt's dressing room—were dating and were happy to tag team him, where Mason was bad cop and Keely was good cop.

"No, bro. Don't wear it like that." Mason unbuttoned the top two buttons of Matt's shirt. "You can't button it all the way. You only button it all the way if you're wearing a tie. Didn't anyone ever tell you that?"

"No," Matt answered honestly, turning to look at himself in the mirror once Mason and Keely had adjusted his clothes. His frown turned upside down and he blinked, like he didn't recognize himself, but he liked what he saw.

It was such an adorable moment, I could only tuck my hands under my chin and watch quietly.

"You look so great," Keely said enthusiastically. "This is like one of those makeover shows."

"How long y'all been dating?" Mason asked me at one point while Matt was changing.

"Oh, um. We're not. We're just friends."

Mason blinked at me, his eyes traveling over my body. "Is he gay?"

Keely smacked her boyfriend on the shoulder, laughing. "He's not gay. He's clueless."

"Clearly." Mason mouth transformed into a dissatisfied line.

"Don't worry, Mamma." Keely gave me a wink, leaning close. "He'll figure it out. Sometimes you have to lead the horse to water."

I shook my head, and it was on the tip of my tongue to correct her, to say that I wasn't interested in him that way, but I couldn't. Because over the last two weeks, we'd worked together, seen a movie together, eaten dinner and lunch together, and now, shopped together. The more time I spent with Matt, the more denying the escalation of my interest in him sounded like a lie.

# CHAPTER 14

### Pizza Shoes

*A pair of sneakers with a button on them that allow its owner to order pizza (by pressing the button . . . and that's it). I swear to God, I'm not making this up.*

Source: Pizza Hut

**MY HOPES WERE** starting to revive without me explicitly telling them to do so.

I was hopeful . . . and confused.

My first clue that things were seriously amiss was my growing preoccupation with buying things for him. Everywhere I went, I saw items I wanted to get him. A Robocop mug (robomug). A Space Invaders tie. An Ultron bathrobe.

I did end up buying the Space Invaders tie. It was on sale. Yep. So I actually *saved* money when I bought it.

Right.

Currently, it was Thursday night and Matt had texted me again, this time to see if I was dead, or if I wanted to eat dinner. Once more, his timing was impeccable. My copy of *The Cuddle Sutra* had just arrived in the mail that afternoon and I needed a partner to try out the positions.

Although at first, Matt and I spent time together because of his research, but that hadn't been the case for weeks. He'd call because he was hungry for something coconut. Then because of a movie we both wanted to see, or a bar that had good cocktails.

Pretty soon, we were hanging out frequently and texting multiple times a day. It was like having a boyfriend, but without the sex. Or commitment.

Except, we did touch. A lot. We hugged and kissed each other on the cheek. Sometimes he'd kiss me on the neck if he was embracing me from behind. We even held hands when out in public.

Unless I was misreading Matt completely, I thought maybe, possibly, he was starting to feel something for me beyond just simple attraction. Sure, he hadn't said anything, but he was just so . . . so . . . *big sigh.*

Brilliant and affectionate, and hilarious—so hilarious—and handsome—so handsome—and just wonderful.

I felt like maybe our friendship was on the precipice of becoming something more. If additional cuddling didn't push things—and him—in the right direction, then nothing would.

**Marie**: *You can come over but I'll need you to help me with something.*
**Matt**: *What?*
**Marie**: *Cuddle positions.*
**Matt**: *I'll be there in 5 minutes.*

Matt arrived with his laptop and a 1.75L bottle of Patron Silver. For margaritas.

"Or shots?" he suggested with a grin, giving me a kiss on the cheek.

I took the gigantic bottle from him. "I've never seen a tequila bottle this big before."

"That's disappointing. We should hang more."

I glanced over my shoulder, laughing at him as he trailed me into my apartment. "We hang out all the time."

"Clearly, it's not enough if this is the first time I've exposed you to the *correct* size of a Patron bottle."

"Well then, thank you. I expect you to help me drink it." Setting the huge container on the counter, I grabbed the small garment box I'd tucked away earlier and handed it to Matt. "Here, this is for you."

He accepted the gift hesitantly, shooting me a confused but delighted look. "What's this for?"

"No reason. Just open it." I tucked my hands under my chin and watched him, not even trying to hide my big, goofy smile.

Matt opened the box and I was happy to see how his eyes widened with pleased surprise. "Space Invaders! On a tie," he yelled.

"I know," I yelled.

"I love it." Matt bent and gave me a hug. "I will wear it all the time. I should put it on now."

As he straightened, I shook my head. "No. Save it for a special occasion, when you want to make a good impression. It'll be your lucky tie."

Though he'd purchased several outfits the day we went to Hugo Boss, I hadn't yet seen him in any of them. Tonight for example, he was wearing his usual uniform of T-shirt and jeans, with the T-shirt being a schematic of a Dalek.

Still smiling, his gaze warm with good feelings as it moved over me, he tucked the box in his bag. "Marie, you are the sine to my cosine."

My eyelashes fluttered and so did my heart, but I managed to tease, "Are you saying we'll never be on the same wavelength?"

He moved his head to the side as though considering my words. "More like, we complement each other. In basic trigonometry terms, cosine is the sine of the complementary or co-angle."

"I took trigonometry in high school. All I remember is pi r squared."

"I would argue that pie are round, but whatever gives you a right angle." He shrugged.

I laughed, even though the joke was painfully punny, and my hopes took his words as permission to start the countdown clock on their evil little space rocket.

"So," he rubbed his hands together, "about those margaritas."

We didn't have margaritas or shots, sadly.

Instead we ate while we worked—him on the couch with his feet propped up on the ottoman, me on the floor again—and listened to The Police on vinyl. But this time I kept sneaking peeks at him, watching how he shoved his hands into his hair every so often. I guessed whenever he encountered a problem, he sent it in all different directions. I also noticed how nice his hands were, and his chin.

I chided myself for not admiring his chin prior to now.

*What is wrong with you? The man has a magnificent chin. And jaw.*

Truly. I was in love with his jaw, or at the very least I had a crush on it.

We'd long finished dinner and had been working for a good hour when he suddenly asked me, "Why did your boyfriend break up with you?"

I glanced up from my laptop and peered at him, unsure I'd heard the question correctly. Here I was, mooning over his exquisite jaw, and there he was, thinking about my ex-boyfriend.

*Was that a good sign?*

"Pardon me?"

"Your ex-boyfriend. David." He lifted his magnificent chin toward the engagement party invite on the top of my mail stack by the door. "The one who invited you to his party, the one—"

"Yes. I know who he is."

"Why'd he do it?"

Tilting my head from one side to the other, I searched the air around me for a succinct way to explain all the ways our relationship had failed.

"You cheated?" he guessed, his look full of suspicion.

The question made me flinch. "What? No! No, I didn't cheat. I wouldn't do that. If I wanted out of a relationship, I'd just be upfront about it. I don't understand cheating, as a concept. Why not just leave?"

"Agreed." He set his laptop on the ottoman and stood, meandering to the untouched bottle of Patron and opened it.

My kitchen was so small, he was able to open the bottle, then shift his weight to one side in order to grab a glass. My eyes strayed to where his shirt lifted, exposing his firm stomach and one side as he reached for the tumbler.

I felt a little lightheaded.

I also swallowed, rather than drool on myself.

"I don't understand cheating either. Do you want some?" He indicated to the tequila.

"No. Thank you." I was already light-headed enough, the last thing I needed was a shot of tequila. On autopilot, I added, "Cheating and lying make no sense."

Matt poured himself two fingers of tequila and shook his head at my statement. "No. I understand lying."

This statement shocked me out of my Matt-body-appreciation trance. "You understand lying?"

"Yes." He tossed back the clear liquid, then puckered his lips, shaking his head quickly. "Whoa. Do you have any lemons?"

"Tell me," I requested, enormously curious as to why Matt thought lying in relationships was permissible, and combating a sensation of unease at this revelation. "Tell me why you think lying is okay."

"I didn't say it was okay. But I understand why people do it."

"Why do they do it?"

"Because they don't want to hurt their partner's feelings," he said, matter-of-factly, recorking the Patron.

His statement struck a nerve. Maybe because David used to lie to me to protect my feelings, or maybe because I used to lie to David to protect his.

I studied him, his open expression, his steady gaze. "Who lied, Matt?"

"What do you mean?"

"Did you lie or did your ex-wife?"

"Kerry?" Matt asked, eyes rimmed with surprise. "No. Kerry never lied. I'm not talking about Kerry."

"Then who are you talking about?"

"Na-ah. You first. Why'd your boyfriend break up with you?"

Gathering a deep breath, I stood, grabbing *The Cuddle Sutra* from the counter. "If we're going to talk instead of work, we might as well go through the positions in this book."

"Okay," he said, following me. "My body is yours to command."

I chuckled, but a lusty little fire lit in my lower belly, making my chest tight and achy with anticipation.

"Let me see," I switched on the overhead light in my room and motioned to the bed, "lie down and let me look at this thing."

"Is that really called *The Cuddle Sutra*?" He lay on his back in the center of the bed, his hands behind his head, and dropped his eyes to the book in my hands.

"Yes. According to my research, most cuddle salons hand it out to cuddle professionals as a guide of sorts."

"Huh." He cleared his throat, then nudged me with his socked foot. "David. Breakup. Continue."

I glanced at the ceiling, not wanting to discuss David. Not now. Not when we could be talking about other things.

*Maybe, oh I don't know, DO YOU LIKE ME? YES OR NO??*

Apparently, when I had a crush on someone, I mentally reverted back to a middle schooler passing notes with checkboxes.

"Uh, I guess, he never pushed me?" I endeavored to focus on his question. "He was an enabler for everything, and never spoke up when he was unhappy. So, one day, it all boiled over and he broke things off."

Matt gave me a sideways glance. "How long were you two together?"

"Just over six years."

"Why didn't you get married?"

Ugh. I hated that question.

Stalling, I opened the book to the first position, one called the *Come to Papa*. Wrinkling my nose at the name, I analyzed the diagram.

"Stay just like that," I said, turning the book to show Matt the picture.

"Oh. I approve of the name." Matt wagged his eyebrows as he opened his arms. "Daddy wants a hug."

I laugh-snorted and kneeled on the bed, a thrill caused by his silly-sexy words giving me giddy goosebumps. This was a promising start.

Walking on my knees until I was at his waist, I lay flat on my stomach, bending and positioning one of my legs between his, my chest against his torso, my cheek over his heart.

His arms came around me and squeezed. "I have you trapped. So tell me, why didn't you get married? Six years is considered a long time to date."

"You sound like my dad. That's what he said."

"Well, this *is* the come-to-papa position."

I chuckled and then sighed. "Let's see. Well, David asked me to marry him, but it never felt—"

"Right," he supplied.

"Exactly."

"Hmm." Matt began smoothing his large palm down my arm, then threaded his fingers in my hair. "Looking back, do you feel like he was a mistake? That dating him for so long was a waste of time?"

"No." I lifted my head, placing my chin on my forearms where they rested on his chest. "He was what I needed at the time, I think."

"Meaning?"

"Someone kind." I smiled softly, thinking back to all the times David went out of his way to be thoughtful.

"But you didn't marry him," Matt pointed out, a hint of accusation in his tone.

I pushed myself up, avoiding his gaze, and showed Matt the next position. Basically, it was a yin-yang shape, where Matt would lay on his side, his head by the headboard and I would lay on my side, my head at the foot of the bed. Then we'd both bend our legs, allowing each person to rest their head on the other's knees or thighs.

Once we were in position, and I noted the way his arms were crossed as well as his grumpy expression, I sought to answer his last question. "If I'm honest, completely honest, I didn't marry David when he asked because he never wanted to fight."

Matt stiffened, a deep crease forming between his eyebrows. His gaze suddenly sharpened, like I'd said something important.

"Meaning?" he asked, a breathless quality to his voice.

"I mean, he would do everything in his power to avoid fighting, even if it meant making himself terribly unhappy, which only made me feel guilty. We couldn't disagree. He'd rush to change or fix whatever made me upset, rather than taking a stand. And he never seemed to have an opinion about anything until I shared mine first. And then, one day . . ."

Matt uncrossed his arms and reached for one of my hands, playing with the tips of my fingers as he listened. *And more or less melting my heart.*

I continued haltingly, wanting to focus on my words, but finding it difficult to do so when he was touching me. "I was doing this story on bodybuilders and gym rats. It started out being a story about the phenomena of people putting on makeup and doing their hair to go to the gym. My editor was curious, do they sweat off their makeup? Or ruin their hair? Or do they only choose exercises that are sweat free? Or what was going on? I thought it was dumb at the time, but I did it because she was in love with the idea. Anyway, that led to a story about gym selfies. And that led to a story about people who spend most of their day in the gym. And that led to a story about body dysmorphia, but it was entitled, 'The Tiny Truth About Bodybuilders.'"

Matt smirked. "Ruh roh," he said, sounding just like Scooby Doo.

"I know."

"How'd you convince the guys to show you their penis?"

I stared at Matt. *Is he serious?*

When he continued to regard me with curiosity, I said, "I'm a woman."

"Yeah. So? Do women have a skeleton key to get into restricted areas that I don't know about?"

"Yes. Boobs."

He frowned at me and, before he could help himself, his eyes flickered to my chest and then back to my face. "Meaning?"

"I used my boobs."

His frown became a scowl. "You flashed them?"

"No. Of course not, dipstick. I don't need to flash my boobs, I just need to make it obvious that I have boobs."

"Clearly you have boobs." He gestured to my torso. "You are a woman, breasts are part of your genetic code. But what I don't understand are the words that are coming out of your mouth. Again, Greek. I say, 'How did you use your boobs?' And you say, 'Potato dog dancing lamppost.'"

I giggled at him and his silly consternation. "Okay, fine. All I did was brush my fingertips along my neckline and asked if they'd show me their penis for a story I was writing."

His scowl eased, his expression morphing into amazement. "That's it?"

"Yep."

"Amazing."

"Yep. Boobs. They're amazing."

He lifted an eyebrow in an over-exaggerated manner, giving me a charmingly lopsided grin. "Do you think if I skimmed my fingertips over my fly it would work with women?"

I threw my head back and laughed. And he laughed. The bed shook with our laughter. And when I glanced at him I saw his eyes were on my neck, but he was still laughing.

"Sure." I wiped tears of hilarity from the corners of my eyes. "Give it a go. See if you can get out of a speeding ticket by gesturing to your crotch."

"Excuse me, Madame Police Officer, so you're saying the thrust—" he tilted his hips forward just slightly, using a silly voice, his index finger skimmed along the zipper of his pants, "—of the issue was my speed?"

I trailed my fingertips along the edge of my bra beneath my shirt. "Thank you for keeping me *abreast* of the situation," I said, playing along.

Matt's eyes flickered to where my hand moved and he blinked.

His smile wavered.

Neither of us spoke, but it took me a moment to hear the silence, and then it was oddly deafening. His eyes were still on my chest and I held my breath.

Was this it?

Would this be the moment?

Would he . . . do something? Make a move?

The tension was almost unbearable—almost—and I prepared myself for *something.*

But then he blinked away, his attention moving to someplace behind me. "You're right," he said, a new edge in his voice, his earlier smile present but somehow different.

"I'm right?" I asked breathlessly, my hopes singularly focused on the next words out of his mouth.

"Yeah. Boobs are amazing." He cleared his throat, shifting on the bed. "Should we move into a new position?"

*Wait . . . what just happened?*

"Oh, sure." I lowered my eyes to the comforter, careful to keep the perplexed disappointment from his sight and from my tone.

I reached for the book blindly, flipping it to the next page and forcing myself to study it. He'd had a perfect in, a perfect opportunity to make a move.

And he didn't.

I wondered briefly if I smelled, and turned away so I could take a surreptitious sniff of my armpit.

For the record, I smelled great.

The next position called for his head to rest on my lap. Doubting myself, I decided to skip the position. Had I completely misread his behavior over the last few weeks? Did he still want our relationship to be strictly platonic?

I continued flipping until I found one that looked benign so I could get my head on straight.

"Here's one. We both just lie next to each other and hold hands." I showed him the picture.

He nodded, his face devoid of expression, and lay adjacent to me on the bed. Our heads were on the pillows and we rested next to each other, not touching except holding hands.

"Back to your ex. He saw the article and flipped out finally?" His tone, like his features, felt reserved.

My swimming, simmering, see-sawing emotions had me gulping a few large breaths. I couldn't read him, and I couldn't decipher what was happening in my mind and heart. He was happy to hang with me, but not wanting anything more.

. . . *Right?*

Right. Okay. Fine.

I swallowed my disappointment and endeavored to recalibrate my expectations for the evening. Clearly, I was being unfair, trying to assign feelings to him that were non-existent.

*These feelings are one-sided. Your-sided. Not his-sided.*

"Marie?"

"Um." I rubbed my forehead, trying to recall his question and keep the tightness out of my tone. "He didn't flip out, not quite. I'd told him what the assignment was, and he said he was fine with it. I told him I didn't have to write the article, but he said he wanted me to do it. But then, after it came out, one of the guys—the bodybuilders—wrote David a letter and told him that I'd slept with him. David called me, told me it was over." I shrugged, hating that

I could remember how much his call had hurt. And how much it hurt that he had called instead of telling me face to face.

As though reading my thoughts, Matt sneered. "He *called*? After six years, he called you to say it was over?"

I nodded.

"What a fucking coward. Man, you deserve *so* much better."

I paused at the intensity of his voice and stared, as something about the way he'd said the word *deserve* struck me as odd. This was not the first time he'd brought up how he thought I was exceptionally *deserving*.

I glanced at our joined hands, unable to figure out precisely why his use of the word bothered me. "But it was okay, I think. I mean, I adored him. I did. He was so sweet. But we weren't right for each other, obviously." At some point one of us had threaded our fingers together instead of a simple hand-hold. "And I think I've just always wanted someone to adore."

"Someone to cuddle?"

I lifted my gaze and found him staring at me with poignant concentration.

"Yes, Matt." I squeezed his hand and he squeezed mine back. "Someone to cuddle."

And right now, I wanted to cuddle with Matt. Even if he could only give me platonic cuddles. I wanted him.

"You should have someone who adores you. Who is worthy of you, Marie." His mouth firmed into a determined tight line. "Never settle for less."

# CHAPTER 15

### Personal Couriers (Delivery Robots)

*Founded and funded by Skype co-founders Ahti Heinla and Janus Friis, Starship's "personal couriers" are designed to deliver goods locally in 15 to 30 minutes within a two- to three-mile radius in suburban areas. The knee-high robots travel on sidewalks among pedestrians at a speed of up to four miles per hour. The robots are autonomous, covered in cameras, sensors, and LED lights to both notice and be noticed – they are able to sense pedestrians, cyclists, and crosswalks, and avoid getting in the way. The robots will begin food deliveries with DoorDash in Redwood City, CA and Postmates in Washington, D.C. beginning in 2017.*

Source: Starship Technologies

"**WHAT ABOUT HOT** sex?"

My mouth fell open and I gaped at him. "Excuse me?"

*Way to blindside a lady, Professor!*

We'd just left the movie theater, having taken off a half day of work so we could spend an afternoon watching a triple feature. We both wanted to see the same three movies, but hadn't been able to pick just one. So we compromised by watching all three.

Presently, we were walking toward an ice cream shop he knew about, and apparently Matt wanted to discuss hot sex.

"You know." He nudged my shoulder with his, grinning with overly exaggerated lasciviousness, such that it wasn't lascivious at all. It was just silly. "Is that one of the reasons you stuck things out with Doug? Because he supported both portrait and landscape modes?"

"What? You mean David?"

"Sure. Whatever his name is. Did he have you demo his multi-touch capabilities? Was it love at first optical recognition, or did he have to ambulate by your location multiple times? I bet you liked it when he touched your PCI slot, and it probably made his floppy drive hard."

Speaking of hard, I was laughing so hard my jaw hurt. "Oh, God. Stop."

Matt lowered his voice and leaned close to my ear. "Your mouth says 0, but your eyes say 1."

"Oh no." I tried to look horrified, glancing at him askance, but the effect was ruined by my laughter. "Was that a binary pick-up line?"

He was also laughing, but not nearly as lost to it as I was.

Man, I loved how funny he was.

"Come on, Marie. Did he make your interface GUI?"

I made another involuntary snort-laughing sound, but finally managed to say, "No. David wasn't really like that."

Matt's smile fell. "What about your other suitors?"

Wiping the tears of hilarity from the corners of my eyes, I didn't point out Matt's use of the word *suitors* and instead I considered my other boyfriends—short-lived as they might've been—and scanned my memory for any occasions of hot sex. "I was with two guys in college, both of whom were inexperienced. We didn't stay together long enough to unlock the key to hot sex. But there was this one guy I dated—or thought I was dating—a musician. A friend of my brother's. He was a *fantastic* kisser. And, yeah, I guess he was a purveyor of hot sex. I thought I was in love."

"But you weren't?" He looked acutely interested.

My smile flat, I shrugged self-deprecatingly. "I found out that I was just one of many. So I called it off."

Matt's jaw ticked as his gaze traveled over my face, but he said nothing.

"I think that's one of the reasons I stayed with David for so long."

"The lack of hot sex?"

"No." I shot him an amused look. "Because I trusted him to be faithful."

I didn't add that, with David, I preferred to take care of business myself. I never saw David "lost to passion" while we had sex. It seemed like he preferred blowjobs more than traditional sex. So most of our times together were as follows: I'd go down on him until he was hard; we'd have sex for maybe two minutes; I'd fake it sometimes; he'd come. Then, if I felt so inspired, I'd finish myself off—by myself—in the bathroom, or maybe the next day while he was at work.

And I didn't like it when he went down on me. It felt like he was doing something just because he thought I'd like it. Like a favor. He didn't say anything to make me feel that way, but I never believed he was into it and I couldn't get out of my head long enough to enjoy the feeling. So, eventually, I told him I didn't like it, and that was that.

"He was faithful, but not a purveyor of hot sex," Matt said, forcing me to grin.

"No. Not a purveyor of hot sex."

"Would you like to? Have hot sex?" he asked, now sounding and looking acutely interested.

Glancing at him askance and giving him my very best *get-over-yourself* look, I endeavored to ignore how his question made all the most fantastic parts of me tense with anticipation.

With forced flippantness, I said, "Are you offering me a prototype robot capable of hot sex?"

"No." He laughed. "I'm just curious. Kerry didn't want to. She was very . . . efficient in the bedroom."

"Shy?"

"No. Efficient. At first, I was as well, so it worked. But then I wanted to try new things, positions and such. And she didn't understand why we couldn't just do it for five minutes once a week, missionary."

I winced, at this point in our friendship no longer surprised by his candor. "Oh my."

"When we divorced, I made it a point to find someone who wanted to have hot sex. And that was . . . ." His voice deepened, his sly smile sliding into place. "A fucking god-awful disaster."

I burst out laughing at the unexpected description, covering my mouth.

"She was completely crazy." His eyes grew wide and something like remembered-unpleasantness pulled at the corners of his mouth. Eventually, he shook himself, his attention refocusing on me.

"But the hot sex was worth it?" I asked, both curious and teasing.

"No!"

And just like that, I was laughing again.

"No. No. No. God, no. Definitely no. It wasn't even that hot, it was just freaky. And dirty. And weird."

"So freaky, dirty, and weird don't do it for you?"

"I guess not. Not with her, anyway." Matt's gaze conducted a quick sweep of my body, but before I could process the mysterious shift behind his eyes, he pointed to a sign across the street. "That's the place I want to go. They have coconut ice cream."

"Sure. Fine. We can go there. But, about your lady friend who you were using for hot sex, maybe if you—"

"I wasn't *using* her for hot sex. I don't use people. I liked her at first, or I thought I did. I wasn't just looking for a hookup. She was smart, worked for Yoodle as a team leader. I thought, okay, here's someone I could be with, shares my interests, let's see where this goes. And then, she starts showing up at my work every day, *every day*, at all different times." His gaze swung back to mine. "She accused one of my managers of trying to seduce me, in front of my entire team. She put a *camera* in my *house*."

"Oh no. That's so awful."

"She told me she did it because she loved me, and that I'd never been loved before, so I didn't understand."

"That's not love."

Matt gathered a deep breath, and shook his head. "She cheated on me, with lots of different guys. She took pictures of herself doing it, and then left them all over my bed."

I sucked in a shocked breath. "That's so bizarre. I'm so sorry."

He shrugged. "By the time it happened, it was a relief. I decided, if that's what love is, if that's how people behave when they're in love, I didn't want any part of it."

"Wow." I was stuck on his words *if that's what love is*. I was assembling the puzzle pieces of Matt Simmons, and finding that much of his repugnance for long-term relationships made a lot more sense now. "So, that's the last time you dated someone?" I wondered if he had any more buried horror stories.

"No." He gathered another deep breath, shaking his head. "I tried dating a few times after that."

"What happened?"

"Well, one woman wanted to take pictures of us all the time, for her Instagram account. The few times we went out it felt like we were dating for the sole purpose of posting pictures to Instagram. She wasn't ever happy with how I looked, or how I dressed, and she wouldn't let me drink my coffee— you know, at coffee shops when they put a design on the top—until she'd photographed it. And then she always wanted me to take pictures of her, so she could get just the right one, and post it to her account. Then she'd spend the whole date on her phone reading comments on her photos. She couldn't understand why I didn't think this part of her personality was cute." He made a face. "It wasn't cute. It was annoying. And childish."

His addition of the descriptor *childish* made me pause, because Matt often did things that were somewhat child-like, like his propensity to ask all manner of questions without gauging their appropriateness, or his tendency to be honest in all situations.

He just seemed candidly curious about everything, which never struck me as childish. I associated childish behavior with selfishness, and child-like behavior with never being taught or knowing better. But I hoped he'd never know better. I hoped this part of his personality never changed, because I loved his unguarded curiosity.

"So you broke up?"

"She dumped me when she found out I'd automated my text messaging."

"Um, what?"

"You know." He made a vague gesture with his hand. "I built a program that would respond to her text messages."

"You did what?" I thought we'd reached a point in our relationship where he couldn't shock me anymore. I was wrong.

"She texted me *a lot*. I didn't have time to respond to her immediately—or at all, not the way she needed—so I designed a simple AI with several different modes to immediately respond to her messages, dependent on key words."

"Like what?" I should have been outraged on her behalf, but I wasn't. This was too fascinating.

"Like, she'd send me a text saying something like, *You're so sexy.* And so the program would go into sexting mode."

My mouth fell open with *more* shock, but he wasn't finished.

"Or she'd ask me what I was doing and it would go into conversation mode. Or she'd text about how she was angry about something or upset, and it would go into supportive mode."

"I can't believe you outsourced your relationship to an AI."

"It's actually where I got the idea for the Compassion AI. She was perfectly happy until she texted me while we were together, my phone was in the other room, and the AI immediately responded. Oh, something cool, I also programmed it to check my calendar and respond with dates and times if she was trying to schedule something. All in all, it saved me hours of pointless texting."

"Matt."

"Marie."

"If you truly like a person, their texts aren't pointless. You'll look forward to them."

He shrugged noncommittally.

I gave him the side-eye. "Have you been automating your texts with me?"

"No! No. Of course not." His expression grew intensely serious. "You don't seem to require frequent texts, or immediate responses for that matter. Plus, don't I usually message you first?"

"That's true." I realized he was right, usually he was the one to initiate text conversations between us. "So, why didn't you just break up with her if you were unhappy?"

"Because . . ." he visibly struggled to explain, his attention darting from the sky to the sidewalk to the street, "No woman is going to like how much I work, how unavailable I am. If it wasn't her, it was going to be someone else, because *I'm* the problem." He took a deep breath, wiping his face tiredly with his hand. "I know I work too much. My job, my research, that's what I want to be doing."

I nodded. "I get that. You love your work. It's difficult to justify giving up time spent working for a person you can't be certain is worth the investment."

"That's part of it," his gaze hardened, then turned contemplative. "But I also have to wonder . . ."

I waited for him to continue; when he didn't after several moments, I prompted, "What?"

"I wonder if I'm just not built for that. You know? With Kerry, we weren't ever in love. We cared about each other, but it wasn't what I see with people like, let's say, Fiona and Greg. Or even Kerry and her new husband. We were good friends, and it was convenient to get married, so we did. We saved on living expenses, got to move into the married people dorm, always had someone to go see movies with. And then everyone since, I've never—" He shook his head, like he was frustrated.

"What?"

"Never mind," he said with a touch of melancholy, his eyes lifting to the sky.

My heart beat quickly, frantically, and the crazy in my mind had been awoken. It was currently screaming from its padded cell *I'll love you! I'll teach you how to love! You're so smart and funny and sweet and unfairly handsome. Let's have hot sex!*

I had to seriously concentrate on my breathing and roll my lips between my teeth, because I couldn't calibrate my smile *and* my lung function at the same time.

Luckily, he wasn't looking at me when he continued speaking his thoughts aloud. "But I do love my job. I do love my work."

Unable to contain myself, I stopped him by tugging on his arm and waited until he looked at me before saying, "You sound so sad, Matt."

He stepped closer, a small smile on his lips, his expressive eyes twinkling down at me like I was wonderful. But I also saw something different there as well. I saw self-possession, restraint, and frustration.

"How can I be sad? I'm with you. Here." He wrapped me in his arms.

I rested my cheek against his chest and felt his heart beat. I'd never been particularly touchy-feely with any of my male friends, but with Matt, it didn't matter where we were, embracing usually felt completely normal.

But not tonight.

Tonight there was a stiffness in his posture, like he was holding me close, but not too close. Something was bothering him, but I didn't know how to push the issue.

A few people passed by on the sidewalk, taking no note of us. I tried snuggling closer to his chest, hoping to dispel the sense of disharmony. It didn't work, the tension remained, so I inhaled the scent of him. He smelled like peppermint, making me think he had a mint habit, and also a lovely cologne or aftershave I couldn't place.

"Are you smelling me?" he asked, tilting his head to the side. "Because, if you are, you should know I'm totally into that."

"Maybe." I pulled away, wagging my eyebrows at him, wanting to disperse the odd dark cloud that had emerged over the evening, and instead replicate our previous light-heartedness. "You'll never know for certain."

Matt fell into step beside me. "Because you'll never tell?"

I nodded.

"That's not right, Marie. Real friends have no secrets between them." He shook his head like he was disappointed in me, and I could see he was also trying to recapture our earlier mood. "I demand you tell me the color of your underwear."

"What? Never."

"Come on."

"Nope."

He leaned close and whispered conspiratorially, "Black, right?"

I shook my head, fighting off a shiver at his proximity.

"I'll get them off you—er, I mean—I'll get it out of you one of these days."

I said nothing, because my instinct was to say, *Yes, please. How about tonight?*

And he would probably think I was joking.

*** 

THAT FRIDAY NIGHT, I found myself fighting Professor Quirrell for the Sorcerer's Stone, still on a Matt-induced high from the evening before.

Okay, yes. My more-than-platonic feelings weren't reciprocated, but my heart didn't seem to care. I liked him. A lot. Exorbitant liking. So what if we were never anything more than friends? Being around him was beyond satisfying in so many ways, I was beginning to think a friendship with Matt was preferable to a romantic relationship with anyone else.

Presently, Jack, Grace, and I donned our scarves and wands, but Grace couldn't find my wizard hat, so I'd been forced to wear one of her princess tiaras instead. Which, all things considered, I thought it suited me quite well.

Once again, I'd made pizza and once again it smelled delicious.

"You know who likes pizza?" Jack grinned as he set the table, showcasing a gap-toothed smile and a mischievous glimmer in his eyes that I was certain had been a genetic gift from his father.

"Who?" I asked warily, packing up the board game.

"Professor Simmons," Grace supplied, practicing her twirls instead of helping set the table. But this was Grace's modus operandi, confirmed by her mother. I could ask the seven-year-old to do something ten times and on the eleventh she'd act like it was the first time she'd heard the request.

*Kids.*

"Ah, yes. The good professor." I nodded, smiling to myself. "He does indeed enjoy the pizza."

"Can we ask him over?" Jack was already inching toward the door.

Without waiting for my response, Grace sprinted into the kitchen, shouting, "I'll get another plate."

"Fine. Fine." I tried to cover my own surge of excitement by sighing wearily. "I guess."

"Yes!" Jack made to leave.

I crossed to my purse. "Wait. I'll text him, see if he's home. Wait, Jack."

Jack pretended he didn't hear me and darted out the front door.

"Darn kids," I grumbled, stepping quickly after him out of the apartment and into the hall, finding Jack already standing outside of Matt's place.

"I just knocked." He motioned to the door. "No need to text."

I stood with one foot in Fiona and Greg's place and one foot out of it, shaking my head at the willful nine-year-old.

"Jack," I warned.

"It's fine," he said. "I do this all the time."

We waited as one minute stretched into two. Jack's expression fell from hopeful to confused and he stared at the door with such intensity, I almost expected it to burst from its hinges.

I was just about to suggest that Jack come back inside and we text Matt instead, because he was likely still at the office, when the sound of the elevator dinging pulled both of our gazes down the hall.

Matt's laughter greeted my ears and my heart leapt.

But then it promptly fell.

It fell hard.

It fell from the top floor of the Sears Tower onto the pavement below *hard*.

Because Matt's laughter was joined by the sound of a woman's laughter, and in the next moment they were both visible. But they didn't notice us. They were too busy. With each other.

Matt tugged her forward, then pressed her against the wall, his mouth fusing to hers. Her hands roamed freely and I heard her moan, which was kind of incredible because they were at least fifty feet away.

Apparently, Matt enjoyed the moaners.

*Good to know.*

Except, not good to know. Not at all good to know.

I hadn't recovered from the shock of witnessing Matt making kissy face with someone not me when Jack called out, "Professor Simmons!"

Matt lifted his head, glancing down the hall.

I stiffened, unsure what to do.

He spotted Jack first, and gave him a quizzical smile, immediately stepping away from the woman.

Then he spotted me.

And do you know what? His smile didn't slip. It didn't falter. If anything, it brightened. Like he was happy to see me.

*What.*

*The.*

*Fuck.*

I thought I might be sick.

Matt whispered something into the woman's ear as they moved from where he'd been mauling her, and then took her hand and pulled her forward.

"Hey, Jack." He grinned at the young boy, then lifted his attention to me as they approached, his gaze traveling over my hair before meeting my eyes. "Hi, Marie," he said easily, like we were meeting on the street. On a Sunday. After Church. "What's going on?"

My heart thundered between my ears as I glanced dumbly—still blindsided—from the woman to Matt, then to Jack.

"Um . . ."

Matt's smile slipped, then fell, his frown increasing by degrees. I barely registered the confusion in his face before I tore my gaze away.

"Are you hungry?" Jack asked merrily, clearly oblivious to *everything* as only nine-year-old boys can be.

Or maybe it was all boys.

Maybe all men are oblivious.

Or maybe they don't care.

"Nice tiara," the woman said, drawing my attention back to her as she sent me a friendly smile. She indicated with her chin to my head.

She was really pretty; dark eyes, dark hair, taller than me, svelte. And she was wearing a Star Wars T-shirt with Rey and BB-8 on it.

*So this is his type.*

*Basically, the opposite of you.*

Crap.

It's not as if I should have thought otherwise. He'd been blatantly truthful. Hadn't he said, "It's a relief you said something first. Pragmatically it saved me the conversation. *You're not at all my type.*"

Instinctively, my fingers lifted, and I realized I was still wearing the princess tiara Grace had lent me earlier.

"Oh. Thank you," I said, feeling and sounding winded. In addition to winded, I was also feeling exceptionally confused. And maybe a little shitty about myself.

But back to the tiara.

I tossed my thumb over my shoulder, saying, "My other crown is at the jewelers, so . . ."

Unable to stop myself, my eyes flickered to Matt's and then away, jumping around the hall. He was frowning at me now, but I couldn't think about that. I couldn't quite think about anything, which was crazy. I was usually so good in emergencies. Calm and collected, level-headed.

Except, this wasn't an emergency. It was merely a disaster.

Wordlessness became silence as I struggled. I still could feel Matt's gaze on my face, but I could not for the life of me meet it. My cheeks were flushed with embarrassment. I knew they were, because I felt hot and sweaty, but also cold and wretched.

The moment was just on the precipice of becoming awkward when Grace burst out of the door.

"What's taking so long?" she complained, but then she stopped short when she spotted Matt and his lady friend. Grace turned a confused frown to me. "Is she coming too? Because I don't think we have enough pizza."

"Uh, no." I forced a grin and smiled down at Grace, managing to speak without my voice shaking. "No. I think Professor Simmons and his friend have other plans. Come on, kids. Let's go eat."

"Aw man." Jack's glower was severe, and I saw he sent the woman a hard glare just before he turned and marched back to where I stood, brushing past me into the apartment.

*I know how you feel, buddy.*

Grace followed.

Pasting a polite smile on my face that didn't feel at all natural, or right, or good, I lifted my eyes as high as their necks and waved. "Well. Goodnight."

I thought I heard Matt say my name, but it was too late. I couldn't stop my forward momentum if I tried.

Moving quickly, I shut the door behind me. Then I locked it. Then I flipped the deadbolt. Then I leaned against it, wondering if it would be overkill to move the heavy console table in front of the door as well. But then I stopped.

I didn't need to erect any more barriers between Matt Simmons and me. There was no need. He'd already done that himself.

# CHAPTER 16

### Weighted Myopic Matching

*Helps physicians match kidneys with donors using AI technologies (a process called dynamic matching via weighted myopia).*

Source: Carnegie Mellon University

**I DECIDED THAT** there was something seriously wrong with me.

Matt had texted me not a half hour after Hurricane Hallway—because that's how I felt, like I'd been stranded outside in a hurricane—and I felt nothing but numb as I read his message.

**Matt:** *Can I come over?*

He wanted to come over?
Why?
I didn't want him to come over.

**Marie:** *No. I'm trying to get the kids ready for bed.*
**Matt:** *I can help*

I didn't respond. I felt hollow. But also, too full. I couldn't eat the pizza, so I made tea instead. But I couldn't drink that either.

When Fiona and Greg arrived home, I left immediately after, claiming a headache. It was the truth. I did have a headache. I tried not to think too much about my instinct to sprint down the hall past Matt's apartment and how I'd pressed the elevator call button seventeen times.

A rush of both relief and misery washed over me as soon as I stepped onto the lift and the doors closed. I walked home in a daze, my mind unable to concentrate or focus on any one thing. Instead, I played the five minutes of seeing Matt with his date over and over and over in my head.

I watched it. I analyzed it. Until I realized doing so made my heart ache anew each time, so I eventually stopped repeating the scene in my head.

The next morning, after not sleeping much, but not crying either, I needed to hear my mother's voice. A phone call didn't feel sufficient, so I went online and arranged for a rental car. They even picked me up.

Listening to loud angry music on the way helped me concentrate on driving and not the odd splintering sensation in my chest. I made it to my parents' place just after 11:00 AM, parking behind my mom's Toyota in the driveway.

I hadn't told them I was coming, and so I hesitated, sitting in the rental car.

*What if they have plans?*

*What if my mom isn't even home?*

*What if they have a woman over and my being here will make things awkward?*

My last crazy thought made me laugh, but it was a sad laugh. Regardless, it was enough to push me out of the car. I walked up the path and hadn't quite made it to the rose bushes before the door opened, revealing my mom.

She wore a big smile, one hand on the door, one hand on her hip. "Well, if it isn't the most brilliant and beautiful woman in the world! To what do we owe this honor?"

I returned her smile.

And then I promptly burst into tears.

***

"SOMETIMES A PERSON just needs their mom, and there's nothing wrong with that." My mom sent me a loving smile from where she stood stirring the lemon curd, then shot my brother an irritated look.

"What? What did I say?" He stood next to her, cutting the butter into the flour for pie crust.

Presently, I was sitting at the kitchen table in my parents' kitchen, watching my mom make my favorite foods while my brother teased us both.

Upon my watery arrival, I cried for several minutes. My mother and I sat on the couch and hugged. When I'd calmed down enough to form words, I told her about Matt.

I told her how we'd met, who he was, how I'd coerced him into showing me his research, and how we'd subsequently become friends. And then I told her how I thought, maybe, we were becoming more than friends.

But I was wrong. How wrong I was became painfully obvious to me as I related the story from the night before.

I didn't realize it at the time I was pouring my heart out to my mom, but my brother was visiting from New York and he was in the other room. He must've overheard the entire conversation, because he'd been making peanut gallery comments since entering the kitchen.

But getting back to my mom, after listening patiently to my wretched tale, she dabbed at my tears and made me tea. And then she started cooking. Everything.

For dinner we'd have crab cakes (my favorite), roasted beets (my favorite), mushroom risotto (my favorite), and lemon meringue pie for dessert (my most favorite).

"Thanks, Mom." I sipped at the tea, letting the aroma of chamomile sooth my frazzled nerves. It smelled like home. Like tea parties from when I was little, and late nights when I couldn't sleep. It felt like a salve to my heart.

"Honey, I know you're still feeling sore, and I understand why after hearing your story. But I have to say, I think what happened last night was a good thing. Seeing things with your own eyes can give a murky situation clarity."

"I know." She was right, of course.

"I don't understand women. Didn't he tell you from the get-go that he wasn't on the market for a committed relationship?" This came from my brother.

My mother hit him lightly on the shoulder. "You can keep your comments to yourself, Abram."

"Yes," I answered him anyway as I examined the bottom of my cup, wishing I could read tea leaves.

"And didn't you two agree to be friends? You friend-zoned him, right?" Abram continued, shifting away from my mom so he was out of her reach.

She tossed daggers at him with her eyes, which made me smile.

"Yes." I nodded, confirming his question.

"So the man told you the truth," Abram moved to the fridge and placed the crust inside, "and now you're surprised to discover he didn't lie."

I chuckled at that, appreciating how he'd worded it. I didn't need to read tea leaves to visualize the picture he was painting.

"Leave your sister alone, I mean it." My mom held up her wooden spoon, to show my brother how much she meant business.

"It's okay, Mom. I don't mind." Then to my brother, I responded, "That's exactly right. We both agreed we just wanted to be friends, so I guess that makes me the liar."

My mom sighed and my brother gave me a sympathetic smile.

My family would never say it, but I'd been acting like a fool.

"I know it hurts, honey." Mom flipped off the gas stove and wiped her hands on her apron, turning to face me fully. "And it's okay to hurt. Hurting is just as much a part of life as joy, maybe even more important. Falling down teaches you how to stand up."

I traded a secretive smile with my brother. We'd heard this advice before, many times. But it hadn't resonated with me until I'd become an adult.

"We're making all your favorite foods. And we'll have a feast tonight. We'll curl up on the couch and watch one of those Jane Austen movies. You'll stay the night, sleep in your old bed. And we'll make breakfast together in the morning, crêpes suzette. I even have fresh marmalade." As she said this she poured a cup of tea and crossed to the table, putting it down in front of my brother.

"That sounds really nice." I smiled my gratitude, and it felt good to smile.

"I don't want tea." He frowned at the cup, then at Mom.

"You'll drink it. And you'll be kind to your sister." Then to me, she said, "It will be nice. It'll be great. But, honey, this is all the falling part. Tomorrow, when you get home, and the day after, and the day after that, that'll be the standing part."

"I know."

"Do you?" Her words were gentle, concerned. "Because that man may have let your hopes down, but he's still your friend. Granted, he might be the biggest idiot in the whole world for not wanting to change your mind about being just friends, but that's beside the point."

I chuckled at that, surprised she'd lasted this long before calling him an idiot.

"Only you get to decide how you stand, what you stand for, and when you do it." She squeezed my shoulder before bending and giving me a kiss on the cheek. Then she stood, glanced around the kitchen, and mumbled to herself, "Now I need to message your father to pick up the mushrooms. Where did I put my purse?"

Mom drifted out of the kitchen in the direction of the dining room, leaving me with my brother. I lifted my eyes to his, and found him giving me a funny look.

"What? What is it?"

Abram's chest expanded as he pulled air into his lungs, and the usually sardonic set to his brows cleared, like clouds parting, revealing a sincerely thoughtful expression. "So, you're assuming this guy isn't interested in you as more than a friend, right?"

I scoffed. "Uh, I don't think it's an assumption at this point. He comes home with a woman, I witness him making out with her in the hallway, clearly they're going to his apartment for one reason, and when he spots me, he acts like he's happy to see me. I friend-zoned him and he took me seriously. If he was ever interested in me that way, he isn't anymore."

"Maybe . . ." Abram was chewing on the inside of his lip, his eyes having lost focus as he stared over my shoulder. Abruptly, his attention cut back to mine and he looked hesitant to share his thoughts.

"What?"

"I still think you should believe him and act accordingly. If he says he doesn't want a long-term thing with anyone, believe him. But maybe—maybe, he thinks you're out of his league."

"What?"

"He was happy to see you, right? Sounds like for a guy who's a workaholic, he's been making a lot of time for you. A guy doesn't do that for friends. Not for guy-friends, not for woman-friends. Not that much time, not for one person. So maybe he does think about you like that, a lot, but he thinks he's not . . . worthy of you?"

I stared at my brother, processing his words, at first rejecting them. Because how could Matt possibly think he wasn't worthy? Of me? That was crazy. I was a nice person, but I wasn't some amazing catch. Hadn't he said early on that I was just like everyone else?

"I'll never say this to you again, so listen up. You're pretty badass, Marie." Abram interrupted my thoughts, leaning forward like he was telling me a secret. "You're wicked smart. And cool. And drama free, which is a huge deal. Drama free is at the top of my list these days. You can be intimidating."

"Me? But I'm a Hufflepuff."

Abram gave me one of his rare, genuine grins. "Yeah. Being a good person can be intimidating. Look at Mom. And Dad. They're the best people I know. I'm twenty-four and I'm still afraid of letting them down. Think about Mother Teresa, would *you* want to meet her? I mean, when she was alive. Not zombie

Mother Teresa. I'd be scared shitless, like she'd see into my dark, dark soul and be disappointed in me."

That made me laugh, and I pointed a teasing smile at him. "Yeah, you should be afraid."

"All I'm saying is, maybe the thought of disappointing you, of being a disappointment to you, or not being worthy of your awesome, is what's really going on. In which case," Abram gathered another deep breath and leaned back in his chair, "you're no better off. Because you should believe him about that, too."

***

**Matt:** *I have a proposition for you. Meet me at our coffee shop tomorrow at 10.*

**Matt:** *Just in case you've forgotten, it's the one where we bonded over The 120 Days of Sodom.*

**Matt**: *Pun intended.*

"What's that face?"

I glanced up from my phone, finding Nico watching me with a concerned expression.

Tucking my cell back in my purse, I shrugged. "It's just my face."

I'd left my parents' house after breakfast on Sunday, returned the car, and walked the few blocks to Quinn's building. Nico, Fiona, and I were at Nico and Elizabeth's place, putting finishing touches on the food and drinks for dinner. It was Sunday night and Fiona decided to throw an impromptu dinner party. Not wanting to leave Janie out, Fiona, Nico, and I had prepared the food at Elizabeth's penthouse with plans to carry it over to Quinn and Janie's to serve.

"Sorry. I promise, I'm not the smile police. But who was that?" The tall Italian glanced at Fiona and then lifted his head toward my purse. "Was that work? Is something wrong?"

I shook my head, affixing an unconcerned smile on my features. "No. It was Matt."

"What's going on with you two?" This question came from Fiona; she looked confused. "Every time I ask Matt about it he says you're working on a story together."

"That's true." I rolled a rectangle of melon in a slice of prosciutto, then placed it on the tray, pushing away my raw, prickly feelings.

"It's more than that," Nico accused. "Look at her. She's blushing. That always means something sexy is happening."

That made me laugh even though I didn't feel like laughing.

He pointed at me and looked to Fiona, as though appealing to her. "And now giggling? See?"

"I see it." She watched me with a pensive non-expression.

"Now what's wrong with you?" Nico asked Fiona. "Why do you look worried?"

Her eyes cut to him. "Do I?"

"Yes," I answered for him, giving her a questioning look.

She stared at me for a beat, then picked up the stuffed tenderloin she'd just finished covering in foil and handed it—oven mitts and everything—to Nico. "Take this next door, please. And tell them we'll be finished in just a few more minutes."

He glanced between the two of us. "I see what's going on here. Don't think I don't know what's going on."

"You boys have your secrets, us girls have ours." Fiona gave him a patient smile. "Goodbye, Nicoletta."

Releasing a grumbly sigh, Nico mumbled something under his breath about Dan and Kat, and then left the kitchen. Fiona didn't speak again until she heard the door to the apartment shut.

"How much do you know about Matt?"

I struggled for how best to respond, finally deciding on, "We're not dating, Fiona. We're just friends."

And I wasn't sure I even wanted us to be that anymore. Being just friends with Matt had been fine and dandy until I had to witness him being more than friends with someone else.

"Has he told you he was married?"

"Yes," I admitted freely. "He also said he isn't interested in long-term relationships." I tried to sound matter-of-fact.

"Good. I'm glad he's being honest with you," she said, her eyes betraying a hint of concern. "You should believe him."

Licking my suddenly dry lips, I rolled another piece of melon in the prosciutto. "Yes. He's been very honest with me."

Something in my tone must've alerted her to how I was feeling, because she softened her voice as she asked, "And he told you about his old job? Wanting him back?"

My head snapped up and I stared at her, my mouth working for a few seconds before I managed, "What?"

Fiona rubbed her belly absentmindedly. "He told Greg they're pushing him pretty hard about it, offering him stock options and his own laboratory, his own dedicated line budget. Did he tell you that?"

I had to shake my head, because he hadn't told me.

Fiona crossed to me and placed her hand on my arm, tugging me so we were facing each other. "Hey. Talk to me."

I had the sudden urge to sit down. "I don't really know what to say."

Was he leaving?

Was he going to tell me?

*Why hadn't he told me already?*

Her probing stare intensified. "Did something happen? You seemed out of sorts on Friday night when we got home."

I laughed. Not a crazy laugh, more like a tired, sad, irritated-with-myself laugh, and crossed to the kitchen table, sinking into a chair. "I've been deluding myself for a few weeks, letting my hopes run away from me, but I'm honestly fine now."

As Fiona sat in the seat next to mine, I gave her the CliffsNotes version of what had occurred, including the visit to my parents' house and my mother's sage advice. I did, however, leave out my brother's hypothesis. I hadn't decided what to think about that yet.

"Oh, Marie." Just like my mom, Fiona reached for my hand and held it. But unlike my mom, her expression wasn't sympathetic, it was equal parts frustrated and determined. "I will always have a soft spot in my heart for Matty Simmons. And as much as I'd like to see him with someone as amazing as you, there's a reason it never occurred to me to set him up with any of my friends."

"And why is that?" I had to admit, I was curious about Fiona's reasons. I trusted her completely, both her as a person and her judgment.

"Did he tell you anything about his parents?" Her lovely brown eyes warmed with anxious affection.

"No, actually." He hadn't. I'd asked a few times, but never pushed the issue.

"I knew them, growing up. They're still friends with my parents. Well, I guess they're what my parents consider *friends*." Her features rearranged into a look of forlorn sadness. "Matty's parents are very cold people."

"They didn't hurt him, did they?" A burst of worry cinched my throat.

"They ignored him. He had a nanny who was very sweet. I babysat him on weekends and tried to give him lots of hugs and affection. And there was a chef on staff who adored him like a son—to a point—or a grandson, I guess. But his own parents had no time for him. The only people who gave him affection were paid to do so. And when those people left his parents' employ, he never saw them again."

"That's awful." Tears stung my eyes as I imagined a child version of Matt, being ignored by his parents. My heart swelled with hurt on his behalf.

"It is. It was. My parents weren't perfect, but they told us they loved us, gave us their version of guidance, were there to answer our questions. He had none of that." Fiona's mouth curved to the side, but her smile didn't reach her eyes. "If Matt told you he wasn't capable of a committed relationship, he knows what he's talking about. He's an excellent person. He's been married once and, as you know, it didn't work out. He's not the type to give up easily, or lightly."

I nodded, swallowing a lump of grief along with Fiona's pill of wisdom.

"He grew up without being held or treasured. I'm not saying he's incapable of it, I'm just saying he didn't learn from the people who should have loved him the most. His priority is his work, not people."

Managing a small smile, I turned my palm over and held her hand in mine. "Yes. He's said something similar."

"Like I said, he's a good guy, a really good guy, but you have such a big heart, Marie. You are entirely too generous and loyal and kind. You deserve someone who knows how special and amazing you are. I don't want to see you get hurt by someone who is simply incapable of giving you what you need. It's not his fault. But you are so wonderful. You deserve someone who is going to put you first."

*You deserve . . .*

"Don't worry. I see things clearly."

*Now.*

I was seeing clearly now.

# CHAPTER 17

### Synthetic / Bio-fabricated Rhinoceros Horn

*A cultured, 3-D printed rhino horn which carries the same genetic fingerprint of, and is visually identical to, an actual horn; "printed" and made of synthetic keratin.*

Source: Pembient

THE CAFÉ WAS much less busy this time, so I had my pick of spots. I'd selected *the* table. The coveted booth by the window, farthest from the door. The wall curved, creating a nook-type atmosphere. Noise was muted, making it feel private and cozy.

Instead of staring unseeingly at the worst novel ever written, I read a handwritten letter from my friend Camille, the software developer and my neighbor in the office co-op. She'd made good on her threat to take a vacation and was currently in Germany.

And she'd met a man. A German man.

Her words were cautiously optimistic as well as despairing:

*He treats me like a queen! Oh, Marie. I wish you could meet him. We met on my first day. I was a mess, coming straight from the airport to the hotel and my room wasn't ready. So I checked my bags and decided to wander the city. I stopped into a bakery and he came out of the back. He's so beautiful, inside and out. His father's people emigrated from Somalia twenty years ago and his mother's side is Bavarian. He speaks Somali, Arabic, German, French, and English. He owns a bakery! Isn't that crazy?*

*Anyway, I forgot my wallet in my bags and he gave me lunch on the house, joking I would have to wash dishes to pay for it. Then he sat with me and asked me all about myself. He's amazing. I left, feeling like I was walking on a cloud.*

*The next day I brought him the money to pay for my lunch and he wouldn't take it, instead saying that I should let him take me out to dinner. So I did. And we've spent every day together since. Instead of sightseeing every day, I've been helping in the bakery and he's teaching me how to bake. I'M MAKING BREAD!!! His parents live in Bavaria and I spoke to his mother on the phone last night. We're going down there this weekend to meet his family. I only have two weeks left here and I don't know what I'm going to do. I think I'm falling in love with this guy. How crazy is that? What am I going to do? I've spent my whole life building a career, a career I'm proud of, accomplishments that are meaningful. Am I going to give all that up to move to Germany and . . . do what? Date a guy? Who am I? I don't even recognize myself.*

*I'm so happy!*

*And miserable.*

*And confused.*

*Tell me what to do!*

*Love, Camille*

I smiled at her closing request, shaking my head. I had no advice to give her.

I know it's popular to tell people in these situations to follow their heart. Presently, I found that advice to be irresponsible. Your heart doesn't pay the bills. Plus, hearts had death-wish proclivities, throwing themselves into situations that would ultimately lead to their destruction.

*Take me and my stupid hopes for instance.*

It might feel good in the short term to follow one's heart, but in the long-term it meant finding a broom and dustpan big enough to sweep up all the shattered pieces.

"How's your friend?" Matt asked, startling me, just before he bent and placed a kiss on my cheek. He slid into the seat across from mine.

I looked up, not surprised by his affectionate gesture—he often kissed me on the cheek as a greeting—but I was surprised by his sudden appearance. I hadn't noticed him arrive.

"Who? Camille?" I asked, irritated at the unsteadiness in my tone.

An image from Friday night flashed in my mind's eye, of Matt and the woman, his Battlestar Galactica shirt, her Star Wars shirt. Kissing. I'd never wished more for the affliction and subsequent relief of short-term memory loss.

In truth, I'd been too open with him. I knew that now. I'd been too willing to throw myself into this relationship, hoping for more because I liked him so much.

That ended on Friday. We were friends—just friends—and I was grateful for this lesson. I needed to stop confusing myself with hopes. Hadn't I been the one who wanted to explore paid services as a replacement for traditional romantic relationships? Clearly, this was a sign from the universe that my time was better spent looking for a life coach and a professional dry humper in Chicago rather than the one I'd identified in New York City.

"Who's Camille?" he asked, glancing between the letter and me.

"Oh, no one. Just a friend." I cleared my throat and held up her note. "She's on vacation in Germany and sent me a letter."

"A real letter? Don't see many of those these days."

"No. I guess you don't." I folded it up and slipped it into my bag, trying not to notice how handsome Matt looked when he smiled. As was typical, he was dressed in jeans and a nerdy T-shirt. He'd also added a lightweight black rain jacket, which he was in the process of removing. His hair was wet, but I could tell he'd recently run his fingers through it as it stuck up and out at odd angles.

I didn't want to smooth it. I liked it when his hair was all crazy. It made him look like a mad scientist, which he sorta was.

Calibrating my smile to polite, I asked, "Are you hungry?" already knowing the answer. Matt was always hungry.

"Ha! Funny. I already ordered, they should bring it over soon." Matt's eyes narrowed infinitesimally. "Is there anything wrong?"

I shook my head, widening my polite smile. "No. Not at all."

His gaze seemed to sharpen. "Are you sure? You seem different."

"Just tired." It was true. I was tired. I'd spent entirely too much time obsessing about what to do with my hopes that had interfered with my ability to write. "I'm behind on a deadline. I was up late, working."

"Oh." His eyes lowered to my cup of tea. "Are you hungry? Can I grab you anything?"

"No. Thanks. I ate breakfast before I came."

"Why'd you do that? Is the food here terrible?" He looked worried.

"No, not at all. The food here is great. As you know, I'm on a budget and eating out is expensive."

I'd been forthright with Matt about my lack of inclination to splurge on non-essentials weeks ago. I wasn't willing to go into debt in order to go out for fancy meals, or buy the latest gadgets. Dinners had always been at my place. My refurbished second-generation iPhone worked just fine, as did my thrift-store Coach bag. I slept better knowing I had a nest egg for emergencies as well as the beginnings of a robust retirement account.

"I would've paid for breakfast. I'm the one who asked you out. Go on, order something."

"Like I said, I'm not hungry. You know I don't let my friends pay my way. So, yes, that means sometimes I'm that stick-in-the-mud who won't go out, or orders just tea, but—as you also know—I'll happily cook dinner at my place anytime."

"I still maintain that you making dinner is not fair either. That's just the same as you taking me out; you're paying for the labor and the food, just like I would be."

I crossed my arms. "Moving on, what's this proposition you mentioned?"

"Changing the subject?"

"You can't force me to talk about something I don't wish to discuss."

"You always do this." He gave me his sly smile. "I'll allow the subject change—"

"You'll *allow*?" I rolled my eyes, chuckling.

"—only because we have much to discuss today—but let the record show, we still haven't come to a consensus yet. We'll discuss this food matter in the future. Back to your friends. Quinn. Janie. How are they?"

"Oh." I uncrossed my arms, surprised by his inquiry. "Janie. Yes. She seems okay, but understandably frustrated with the bed rest. I think they're just ready for the pregnancy to be over and I can't say that I blame them. It's been tough."

He appeared to be listening intently. But then, out of the blue, he asked, "Do you want kids?"

I flinched, opening and closing my mouth for a few seconds before answering honestly. "Yes. I do. If it works out that way, and it's the right choice for me and my partner."

Matt nodded slowly, inspecting me. He leaned forward and placed his elbows on the table. "If I recall, you said something similar when we first met. When I asked you what you were looking for in a partner."

"About kids?" I didn't remember the subject of children coming up before now.

"No. When I asked you what you were looking for, you said you were looking for *the right* person. You're the first and only person—that I know of—who has responded that way. All participants, both male and female, typically list off attributes. We theorize that what is most important to a person can be extrapolated based on the attributes he or she lists first."

"Meaning?"

"Well, if I ask someone, 'What are you looking for most in a partner?' And he says, 'I want someone tall, and wealthy and smart,' then we extrapolate that physical appearance matters most, then money, then intelligence. But if someone answers, 'I want someone kind, with brown eyes, and who likes to travel,' then we extrapolate that person values personality first, then physical appearance, then hobbies and shared interests."

"Fascinating. You never mentioned this before." It was fascinating. I tried to think about how I would have responded if I hadn't said *the right person*, but I couldn't. I mean, I didn't want to be involved with a jerk, but a jerk wasn't ever going to be the right person for me anyway.

"It never came up before." His sly smile emerged. "But you can imagine how confused Dr. Merek was when I told him what you said."

"He was confused?"

I hadn't seen Dr. Merek again. Matt never wanted to go back to his office after the last time we were there, when I'd arranged my story notes on his floor, insisting there was no reason to do so when he could access his data off campus.

"Yes. Behavioral science is his expertise. I'm just the engineer. He wasn't just confused, he was shocked. He said if more people focused on finding the right person rather than making sure their potential partner satisfied the requirements of some arbitrary list—mostly defined by societal priorities— then we'd all be happier."

"Is this part of your proposition?" I eyed him. "Are you trying to set me up with Dr. Merek?"

Matt visibly stiffened, a severe frown immediately arresting his features. "Why?"

I shrugged. "Why not? He's not married, is he? Does he have a girlfriend?"

His jaw ticked, all traces of his earlier smile now gone. "No."

"Is he nice? He seemed nice."

"Sure."

The server approached with Matt's food, placing a large stack of pancakes, bacon, and fruit in front of him, along with an extra-large glass of water and coffee.

"Then why not?" I pressed. "Unless you don't think I'm nice."

Matt leaned back farther to make room for the plates. But when the server had gone, he pushed the food to the center of the table, leaving them untouched.

"You know you're more than nice," Matt muttered, pulling his phone out of his pocket and glancing at the screen, his forehead knit with deep creases.

"Then you should set us up," I said, not understanding why I was pushing.

What did I want from him? A reaction?

*What is wrong with me? Why am I so crazy?*

Eventually, Matt shoved his phone back in his pocket and lifted his eyes to mine. They were devoid of emotion. "Sure. Sounds good. I'll talk to him and let you know."

Nodding once, and not examining too closely why my heart had plummeted at his response, I said, "Good. Thanks. I look forward to it."

"Hmm." He examined me in that unapologetic way of his. Except this time I felt like he was peering at me from behind a wall.

Lifting my chin, several seconds passed while we swapped stares. The moment grew increasingly uncomfortable. I decided it was time for me to go.

"I have to—"

"So, on—"

And both of us stopped at the same time, laughing lightly, but with very little humor. I gestured for him to continue, picking up my tea.

"So, on Friday, you were babysitting Grace and Jack?"

Now I stiffened, my eyes dropping to the table, unable to hold his probing stare. "That's right."

He hesitated, leaning forward by placing both of his elbows on the table. "Sorry I didn't introduce you to Keira."

I shrugged, glancing to a spot over his shoulder, and pasting a small smile on my face. "It's fine. I had pizza in the oven, so it's not like I had a lot of time anyway."

*What? What did that even mean? What does pizza have to do with anything?*

"I should have introduced you." He deepened his voice, sounding solemn and sincere, which drew my eyes back to his.

His features were still mostly clear of expression, but his eyes were focused on mine with blunt intensity.

"Why? Is she your girlfriend?"

*Wow. Go me.*

Let the record show, my voice was steady and impressively nonchalant, so the opposite of how I was feeling.

"No." He gave his head a subtle shake, his tone shaded with frustration. "I should have introduced you because *you're* my friend. I should always introduce you. To everyone."

*Aaaaaaand, I've just been friend-zoned. Hilarious.*

I would've laughed at the irony if my heart hadn't chosen that moment to shatter.

***

ONE WEEK LATER, Matt showed up at my office.

I'd told him where I worked a few weeks ago, but when I glanced up from my laptop, finding him hovering just outside my door watching me, my first thought was that I was surprised he'd remembered the address.

"Hey." I sat back in my chair, wanting to put more distance between us. "How long have you been standing there?"

He shrugged, strolling through the door and closing it behind him. "Not long. I didn't want to disturb you in the middle of a thought."

"Thanks." My gaze moved over him, taking note of his gray suit pants and jacket, and white button-down shirt. No tie. The top two buttons were undone, revealing a bright white undershirt. It was a gorgeous suit, beautifully tailored, and he looked damn sexy in it.

Damn, damn sexy.

Fortunately for me, I was deeply entrenched behind my figurative wall of aloofness. My heart demanded it.

"What's with the outfit?"

He glanced down at himself. "Why? What's wrong with it?"

"Nothing. It's just not what I typically see you wearing."

"Do you like it?" He grinned, sitting in one of the chairs opposite my desk. "If you do, I can play dress up more often."

I ignored the question and his teasing, not in the mood for silly Matt. Actually, I wasn't much in the mood for Matt at all. In some respects, I was really sad about that. For a while there, I had always been in the mood for Matt. Serious, silly, curious, thoughtful. I had wanted them all. But now? Now that I knew who I really was in his life?

No. Not in the mood.

I liked my fortress of indifference, because looking at him through this lens saved my heart from more bruises.

"Why are you here?"

His smile waned, the light in his eyes dimming by degrees as he openly inspected me. "We didn't get to finish our conversation the other day, about my proposition."

"Oh." I closed my laptop and reached for my glass of water. "Go for it."

Matt scrutinized me for a long moment, as though searching for . . . something.

Eventually, he cleared his throat and asked, "How have you been?"

I stared at him, confused by his question. "Fine. And how are you?"

"Did anything happen? Are you—is anything—is there something I should know?"

Shaking my head, I made a show of moving my eyes to the left and then up. "No."

"You haven't been responding to my texts."

"Oh, yeah. I've been really busy. With work. You know how that is." That was actually true. I'd been focusing on finishing several articles, none of which related to his research or my story on replacing relationships with paid services. I needed some distance from subjects that made me think of Matt.

"Are you angry with me about something?" The muscle at his temple jumped and his eyes turned hard, frustrated. "Did I do something wrong? If so, I wish you would tell me."

I straightened in my seat. He'd caught me off guard with his directness— though, I shouldn't have been surprised, he was always direct—but I didn't know how to respond to his pointed questions. I wasn't angry *with him*. Not really. He hadn't actually done anything wrong.

I was irritated with myself, with my stupid hopes, with how dejected I'd felt after seeing him with his date. My mom's words of wisdom repeated between my ears. *Only you get to decide how you stand, what you stand for, and when you do it.*

He'd been honest with me, and now what? I was punishing him, pushing him away for his honesty? That didn't seem right. Looking at him now, at the hard set of his jaw, the unhappy curve of his lips, I felt a pang of regret so strong, it sent the walls I'd built between us crumbling to the ground.

I'd been a bad friend. I'd been inconsistent. Knowing what I now know about his childhood, his parents, how could I be so unfeeling and selfish?

I rubbed my temples and shook my head, exhaling a tremendous sigh, and with it—I hoped—my residual anger.

"No. I'm sorry. I have been busy with work, but I should have returned your messages. So, I'm sorry."

He continued inspecting me, and I couldn't decide if my response relieved him or frustrated him further.

Eventually, he twisted his lips to the side and nodded once. "Fine. Apology accepted. But it's going to cost you."

"Oh no." I made a scaredy-cat face, going through the motions of our friendship. "Have you finally come to collect? Are you going to make me take the rest of your deception interview?"

Right on cue, his eyes grew cartoonishly shifty. "No. Not today. I—uh— left the guided questionnaire in my other jeans, or at work, or something." This nonsense was always his excuse for not administering the questionnaire. At this point in our friendship, I felt like it had become a running joke and would be shocked if he ever actually followed through.

"Likely story," I teased, waiting.

*I can do this.*

*I can open my heart to a friendship with Matt. I can let my hopes go, and my anger go, and stop noticing how much I like everything about him.*

"What are you doing next weekend?" he asked, not quite his normal (peculiar) self yet, but getting there.

"Oh, I have to go to New York for work. I thought I mentioned that."

He slumped a little in his seat. "No. You didn't. Is that next week?"

"No. Sorry. Not next week, this weekend. I'm leaving on Friday."

He straightened again. "You'll be in town next weekend?"

"Yes."

"Good. Because my friend—um, my ex—Kerry, and her husband, Marcus, will be in town, and want to go out. I'd like you to help me show them around."

Matt had lived in Chicago for less than a year and therefore didn't know his way around with complete proficiency.

"Sure. I can do that," I said, but then immediately wondered whether it was a good idea. I suspected that, in addition to what Fiona had divulged about his parents, he had unresolved feelings for his ex-wife. And these unresolved feelings were the main cause for his avoidance of committed relationships. Spending the day with him pining after his ex would be unpleasant.

"You sure you don't mind?" he asked, scrutinizing me. "You don't look sure."

"Yes. I don't mind. But . . ." I paused, trying to figure out what to say. "Are *you* sure?"

"That I want you there? Absolutely."

"No. I mean, are you sure *you* want to be there? Isn't it difficult? Watching your ex move on with someone else?"

Matt looked at me like I was cute and weird. "No."

"It's not even a little bit hard?" I didn't know why I was pushing.

I thought I heard him mumble something like, "It wasn't hard with her for years."

"Pardon?"

"No. It's not even a little bit hard. We all get along really well. I promise I'm not asking you to come along and be an unwilling participant in some sort of spectacle. I wouldn't do that. Plus, I think you two might get along."

"Okay," I said on an exhale, confused. "Sounds good."

He truly seemed to believe that he was over her, over their marriage. Maybe he was deluded.

*Or maybe he is over her, and is simply one of those guys who didn't want to be in a relationship, like Fiona said. Like my mother said. Like Abram said.*

What the heck was wrong with me? Why was I doing this to myself? Wishing for a way to *fix* this part of him?

*There is no fixing something he doesn't want fixed. Believe him and let it go.*

"But one warning," Matt flipped over one of the glasses I had on my desk and poured himself some water, "they'll probably want to pay for your dinner, as payment for acting as tour guide."

"That's fine, but not necessary."

"Just wanted you to know."

"That's it? That was the entire proposition?" I sipped from my water.

"No. There's another part. But first, remind me why you're going to New York. I don't think you ever said."

He was right, I never told him why I was going. It wasn't entirely on purpose, at least not at first. As time progressed and we were spending more and more of it together, I began to feel strangely about the trip, wondering if I should cancel it. But now that all my delusions of grandeur had been dispelled so effectively, I'd decided to go.

And there was no reason to keep him in the dark.

I waited until he'd brought the glass to his mouth and had taken a gulp before I said, "It's so I can be dry humped by a professional."

Matt choked, his eyes bulging, and he covered his mouth with a hand. I smiled serenely as he coughed and struggled to draw air.

Eventually, after drinking several more gulps of water, he recovered enough to rasp, "What?"

"I mentioned weeks ago that the article I'm writing will include dry humpers, right? New York is where the best dry humpers are. Well, New York and LA. But my writing partner is covering the ones in LA, so I'm flying to New York to check out one in particular. I had to book the spot over a month ago, as this guy is very popular."

"A guy?" He choked on nothing this time, making a face.

"Yes. A guy. Tommy—in LA—will be visiting a female humper."

Matt was quiet for a long moment, inspecting me, and then asked, "This weekend, you say?"

"That's right. I fly out Friday morning. My appointment is Friday late afternoon, then I'll fly back to Chicago Saturday morning."

"What airline?"

"Why?"

"I fly a lot. Just curious."

"Midwest Air."

"Hmm." He was frowning, inspecting me with a new kind of intensity. "Are you going by yourself?"

"Yes."

"What if he's a serial killer?"

That made me laugh. "He's not a serial killer. I had to call in a few favors just to get his number. He's the most sought-after dry humper in New York."

Matt shook his head at me, his face telling me that he either thought I was crazy, or something in his mouth tasted like garbage. "Can you hear the words coming out of your mouth? 'The most sought-after dry humper in New York.' You're insane, admit it. You're insane, this is a cry for help, and you need your best friend Matt to step in and save you from yourself."

My cell phone buzzed from my bag, prompting me to reach for it. "Says the man who wants to replace human relationships with companion robots. Maybe one of your robots could specialize in dry humping, then would you think it's crazy?"

"No. Because it would be a robot and not a human man shoving his—" Matt shook his head, cutting himself off and looking a little nauseated. "I can't even say it."

I glanced at my phone screen, sighed, sent it to voicemail, and placed it on my desk face down.

Matt's attention moved between the phone and me. "Was that your ex?"

"Yep."

"You're still sending his calls to voicemail?"

"Yep."

"It's been months. You still haven't talked to him?"

"No. Not yet." I squirmed in my seat.

"Marie . . ." Matt shook his head at me, as though I disappointed him.

"You know he won't leave a message. Who calls twice a week for months and doesn't leave a message?"

I snapped my mouth shut after asking the question because it actually sounded like something I would do. David was being stubborn, giving me a heads-up that we needed to talk without giving me any hints as to why. And I was being stubborn, refusing to pick up or call him back.

In a nutshell, this was exactly the kind of behavior that caused our relationship to fail.

"If you want to know, it appears you'll have to call him back." His tone was heavily laden with sarcasm.

"Or I could change my number."

Matt gave me a plaintive look. The look distracted me long enough for him to swipe my phone.

"Wait, what are you doing?" I reached across my desk.

"Let's call him." Matt was tapping through screens, navigating to my recent call list.

"Let's not." I tried to grab his wrist, endeavoring to snatch my phone back, and cursing myself for not making it password protected.

"Too late." He flashed me the screen, then brought it to his ear.

"Matt, don't—"

"Hi? Is this David? Hi, David. Long story short, this is Marie's boyfriend, Matt. Nice to meet you. I'd really appreciate it if you—wait, what was that?"

My mouth dropped open at his claim and I shook my head, whispering adamantly, "Stop it!"

"The party? Oh, yes. We got the invitation, but we're not sure if we can make it. Marie has a work conflict that she's been trying to reschedule."

I buried my face in my hands, continuing to shake my head.

"How about I contact you tomorrow with a firm answer? Does that work?"

He paused, as though listening to David on the other end. I peeked through my fingers and found Matt had retrieved his own phone and was entering something into it.

"Yep. I have your number. I'll text you either way. Okay. Yeah. Ha ha," Matt's eyes sharpened on me, "tell me about it. Yep. Okay. Bye."

I pulled my hands from my face and accepted my phone back, glaring at my so-called friend. "You overstepped."

"I pushed. Big difference." He gave me a look that was somehow both apologetic and unrepentant.

"Yes. You did. And you lied."

"Technically I didn't lie. I'm a boy, who is your friend."

"The last time I heard someone say those words, I was thirteen."

His gaze softened. "If you're ever going to find happiness, then you need to get over this guy."

I fought the urge to surrender to uncontrollable laughter. *Pot. Meet Kettle. You have everything in common.*

"I am over him."

"No. You're not. Evading his calls for weeks—no, months!—isn't the way to do it. Avoidance isn't the way. You need to confront things head-on."

"Like you confront things head-on?"

"Yes. Exactly like me. Which brings me to the second part of my proposition."

I braced myself, honestly worried about what it could be.

Something about my expression must've been funny, because Matt laughed. "Don't look so afraid."

"I can't help it. I never know what to expect with you."

"But that keeps things interesting, right?" He gave me a saucy and over-exaggerated wink that had me rolling my eyes.

"Just tell me what it is."

"Okay. I propose that, in return for your help next weekend with Kerry and Marcus . . ."

Matt paused, his eyes holding mine with an unsmiling, unwavering stare. If I didn't know any better, I'd say he almost looked nervous. But before I could consider this as a possibility, he finished his thought on a rush. "I'll go—as your date—to your ex's engagement party."

# CHAPTER 18

**Cyc**

*A "thinking" artificial intelligence project that attempts to assemble a comprehensive ontology and knowledge base of everyday common sense knowledge, with the goal of enabling AI applications to perform human-like reasoning.*

Source: Cycorp

**I TURNED MATT** down.

He told me to reconsider, both his offer to escort me to David's party and my trip to New York to engage a professional dry humper.

And that's where we left it because I had a conference call to prepare for.

At least, I thought that was where we left it.

But then Friday morning, as I was waiting outside the gate for my flight to New York, who should I see but Matt Simmons.

Walking toward me.

With an effervescent smile, entirely too effervescent for 6:00 AM.

Wearing black dress pants, a sky-blue button-down shirt, and Converse.

I glared at him, irritated with myself for noticing how breathtakingly hot he looked.

The days apart since our last interaction had been good. Positive. I'd felt better about him, about us. Maybe it was possible to salvage our friendship. Maybe I really could roll back the crazy, suppress the urges, and recalibrate my expectations to platonic.

But seeing him now, feeling the involuntary but familiar surge of bittersweet anticipation, pissed me off.

He was holding a drink tray with two coffees and grasping a paper sleeve with some sort of pastry, an overnight bag slung over his shoulder. His stride was easy, confident. And his hair was crazy, unbrushed, like he'd run out of time getting ready this morning. I loved his crazy hair.

As my gaze devoured the sight of him, I felt a pang of despair.

Despair because I was beyond attracted to him. I was so far beyond platonic, I'd jumped head first into the deep, dark waters of desire. Yet, thanks to witnessing his snogfest down the hall from Fiona and Greg's apartment, I was also at peace with the fact that he was never going to return my feelings, not in any meaningful way.

Even if what Abram had said was true, that Matt didn't feel worthy of me— and I wasn't convinced this idea held any merit—it changed nothing. Matt wasn't a car that needed to be fixed. He wasn't a robot needing reprogramming; he was a person. He was ultimately responsible for fixing himself, and only if he wanted to.

You can lead a horse to water, but you can't make it drink the water that will allow it to enter into a happy, fulfilling relationship. Maybe the horse likes being dehydrated. Or maybe you weren't that horse's type.

*Step back from the stupid dehydrated horse . . .*

Coming to a stop in front of me, he kissed me on the corner of my mouth. "Valkyrie."

"Matt." I imbued his name with all the exasperation I felt.

He handed me the sleeve, ignoring my tone, smiling persistently. "This is for you."

"Thank you." I accepted the pastry, my rumbling stomach reminding me that I'd skipped dinner the night before. "What are you doing here?"

"Flying to New York." He blinked at me, like I was the nutty one.

"Oh, really? Do you have a work trip?"

"Not this weekend. This weekend, I'm going to help a friend. My *best* friend."

"Help her how?"

"Save her from being leg-humped by a horny murderer."

I rolled my eyes but laughed despite my ire. "You're ridiculous."

"And you're sassy in the morning. Here, have some coffee. Maybe it'll help you de-sassify." He gave me the entire drink tray, with both coffees, leaving him empty-handed.

"Thank you for the coffee, and the food. But may I say, you're overreacting."

"No, you may not say." Matt picked up my bag and placed his free hand on the small of my back. "Come on, let's find a place to sit so you can tell me what the plan of attack is."

"What do you mean, plan of attack?"

Matt guided me to a row of empty chairs, lowering our bags to one while I sat in another. "You know, exit strategy, escape routes, and so forth."

"Again, you're being ridiculous. This is not a scam. This is for a story. I know what I'm doing."

"Why does it have to be you?" He claimed the spot next to mine and took the drink tray, discarding it once we'd both removed our coffees.

"Because I'm the one writing about it. And don't forget about my co-author, Tommy. He's already done the deed with a humper in LA."

"*Humper in LA*," he said derisively, glaring around at the airport. "You make it sound like it's the sequel to *Bambi*. Except not the deer Bambi, the hooker Bambi."

I pressed my lips together because I didn't want to laugh at his joke. He really was overreacting. "It's safe, Matt. Completely safe."

"I guess we'll see." He was glowering now, grinding his teeth, still not looking at me.

"I'm telling you," I placed my hand on his leg and squeezed, "this guy is legit. He has celebrity clients."

"I don't care about celebrity clients," Matt said, picking up my hand and tangling our fingers together. He continued to scan the airport and I thought I heard him mumble under his breath, "I only care about you."

It was at this point—with Matt being thoughtful, holding my hand, caring enough to act—that my feelings would usually squeal with delight at the possibilities of what he might mean, what these words might mean for a future between us.

But not this time.

No.

This time I took him at face value, and endeavored to focus on being grateful for having a friend who cared so much about my well-being.

***

THE FLIGHT WAS half empty; therefore, Matt had no trouble talking the gentleman in the aisle seat next to me into switching his seat with Matt's exit-row seat. Matt took the aisle, and when no one appeared to take the window seat, I scooched over and buckled in, leaving the middle empty.

He eyed me as I did this, but said nothing. He seemed preoccupied by something or someone a few rows in front of us.

I opened my laptop, scrolling through my questions for Roger, my professional dry humper, and the research I'd already done on dry humping as a paid service.

Meanwhile, Matt had opened his laptop as well. He'd been staring at the screen for the better part of fifteen minutes, a tight frown on his features, his fingers in his hair, when I decided to interrupt him with a question that had been bothering me since we spoke about the issue last.

I tapped him on his shoulder, drawing his eyes to mine. "When does something man-made cease being synthetic, and become real?"

Matt peered, looking concerned. "Have you been talking this whole time?"

I scowled at him. "No. I just asked the question. Just now."

"I know. I was teasing you." He closed his computer, leaning an elbow on the armrest. "Your question. What are we talking about?"

"Your Compassion AI, I guess."

His eyebrows ticked up and he glanced away, back down the aisle toward whatever kept drawing his interest. "You're still concerned about it being mistreated?"

I nodded, trying to steal a glance over the seats in front of us to see what had him preoccupied, but I was too short. "So, I read *I, Robot*—the book you brought me a few months ago—and it got me thinking. I know you believe wanting protections for AI doesn't make any sense, but—"

"It doesn't make sense," he said tiredly. "If it made sense, we would have laws protecting toasters."

"Just listen."

"Why no advocacy for ceiling fans?" He faced me again, lifting a teasing eyebrow, but the effect was ruined by the grim set of his mouth. "Or is this just your binary systems prejudice showing?"

That made me smile, but I persisted. "What if the protections and regulations aren't really about the AI, but more about preserving the essence of what it means to be human?"

That made him pause. "Meaning?"

"We have laws for protecting animals, right? Why not allow cruelty to animals? Where is the scientific evidence that we *need* to protect animals?"

"Animals are alive."

"Yes, but so are trees. And we eat animals, but we have very specific rules about how animals must be treated before we eat them. Why do we do that?

For the record, I agree with protections for animals. But *why* does society have animal protection laws to begin with? Maybe it's a reflection of how we see ourselves. We have protections for animals because we—humans—see ourselves as good, as incapable of injury to those less powerful, or at the very least we see that behavior as evil and unacceptable."

Matt gathered a deep breath, his frown persisting. He glanced away from me, back down the aisle. "There's a kid up there, just a few rows in front of us, and he's traveling with his nanny."

I craned my neck, but it was still no use. I was too short. "How do you know it's his nanny and not his mother? Or an older sister?"

Matt's attention focused on the back of the seat in front of him. "Because his parents are also on the plane. They're in first class. The kid and the nanny are in coach. And I overheard the caretaker ask the parents something as we were waiting to board. The father said, 'We're paying you to take care of it, take care of it.'"

My heart constricted and before I realized I was doing so, I reached out and took Matt's hand. He turned his palm up and lowered his eyes to study our entwined fingers.

"I can't see the value in a set of ethics for the treatment of machines when we, as humans, don't even treat our children ethically." His tone was quiet, but sounded tightly controlled.

"Matt—"

"I truly believe machines can help us become better humans. There's already initiatives to use artificial intelligence to analyze data collected from the body cameras worn by police officers. The AI determines if a cop is likely to use force inappropriately, or is experiencing too much job-related stress, and then intervenes. The officers are taken off duty, provided resources, support, and counseling, before citizens are hurt. Everyone wins. And then there's the justice data initiative, which would take sentencing out of the hands of judges. Some believe an AI would provide fairer decisions about the length of prison sentences than highly trained humans, because research conclusively shows even highly trained humans are riddled with bias and prejudice."

He bit his bottom lip, chewed on it distractedly, and shook his head. "Paying a person to care for you isn't going to work, because people are inherently flawed. Without a paycheck, that kid won't see that nanny ever again. But an AI, one who's entire purpose is to give compassion, I think it would change the world."

The vulnerability in his tone drove me to unbuckle my seatbelt and switch to the middle seat. I wrapped my arms around him and rubbed soothing circles on his back.

"You're a good person, Matt." I pulled away, trying to snag his gaze.

His eyes lifted to mine, brittle with sorrow and determination. "Or, if it doesn't change the world, then at least it might give that little boy up there some consistency. And something of his own to love."

*** 

**ARE YOU SURE** you want to go through with this?"

"Yes."

"But are you sure?"

I heaved a sigh, maybe my hundredth since the plane landed.

We'd already checked into the hotel, but our rooms weren't ready. Leaving our bags with the concierge, we'd grabbed lunch at a nearby café. We sat next to each other in a booth so we could both look out the window.

I couldn't seem to stop giving him hugs. His heartfelt speech on the plane hadn't precisely made me see him, or his struggles, or his research in a new light; but rather it brought everything about Matt Simmons into focus.

And I wanted to hug that Matt Simmons. I wanted to hug all his hurts away.

Matt had dawdled during lunch, accepting my affection cheerfully, and ordering more and more food. Finally, when I'd threatened to leave without him, he paid the check and dragged his feet, walking with the adroit liveliness of a one-hundred-ten-year-old.

My residual feelings of sympathy for my friend began to wear thin as soon as Roger's building came into sight.

Roger being the professional dry humper.

"Matt. I didn't invite you along. You don't need to be here." We caught the door of the building, entering just as someone was exiting and negating the need to buzz Roger's apartment. "If this freaks you out so much, go to the Met and grab a coffee. I'll come find you after."

"No. I'll be moral support." His hand was once again on the small of my back and, though he was walking next to me, it felt like he was hovering.

"Just as long as you're not the morality police." I gave him a stern look.

"Think of me as your bodyguard." He swallowed with effort, looking incredibly tense. "If at any point you feel uncomfortable, just say *Turing test*, and I'll beat the shit out of him."

We stopped at Roger's door and I turned to face Matt; he wouldn't look at me, giving me only his profile. "If you're going to be throwing all this testosterone around in there, you can't come in."

He made a scoffing sound, but I saw the muscle jump at his jaw, like he was grinding his teeth. "I don't know what you're talking about."

"Don't you?"

"No," he said stubbornly, the single word deep and foreboding.

Studying him for a moment, I shook my head and sighed. Again. Deciding that short of asking him to leave, there was nothing I could do about his mood. And if I asked him to leave, I got the sense that we'd end up arguing. And I *really* didn't want to argue in the hallway outside the dry humper's apartment where I was supposed to have been ten minutes ago.

So I knocked.

Matt flinched at the sound, saying nothing.

We waited.

Nothing happened.

I knocked again.

Eventually, I heard a shuffling sound coming from the apartment. I saw that Matt's hands were curled into fists.

Then the door opened and a sick man was revealed. A very, very sick man.

"Can I help you?" he groaned, leaning against the door, looking like death.

Both Matt and I frowned at him, then at each other.

"Uh, Roger?" I asked.

"Yes?" he croaked, his eyes barely open. He was dressed in a bathrobe, flannel pajama pants, and a white T-shirt. And he was shivering.

"I'm Marie, from the—"

"Oh no! I'm so sorry. I didn't call you to cancel." He coughed, and then groaned. "As you can see, I have the flu."

"Yes, I can see that." I winced on his behalf. Truly, he looked like he was ready to pass out and his breathing was labored. "Are you okay?"

"Thank God," Matt muttered next to me and I could physically feel the waves of relief coming off him as he leaned against the doorjamb, apparently unable to support his own weight under the burden of this reprieve.

I had to fight my urge to glare daggers at him. *Stupid dehydrated horse.*

"I'm so terribly sorry," Roger croaked. "You flew all the way out here. I'm so, so sorry." He clutched his forehead, looking dismayed.

"No, no. Don't worry about—" My nurturing instincts kicked in and I glanced over Roger's shoulder to his apartment beyond. "Do you have anyone to help you? Are you by yourself?"

"My boyfriend and I split up last month; he moved out." Roger coughed, weaving a little on his feet. "I'm by myself, but I'll be fine." He only had one eye open, like using both required too much energy.

Matt and I shared another look and I could see that he was just as concerned as I was.

"Let me at least get you some soup," I offered.

Roger shook his head again, his pallor decidedly green, his eyes half blinking.

Before I could think better of it, I turned to Matt. "We can't leave him. Please. Help him. Let him lean on you. Take him to the couch."

Matt nodded at once and jumped into action, immediately stepping forward and encouraging the sick man to use him as a crutch.

Roger made a motion as though to wave us off, but clearly he lacked the physical energy—or mental focus—to do so. As Matt took Roger to the sofa, I crossed to the kitchen and began searching for tea, honey, and lemon.

*What are you doing?* I asked myself as I rifled through Roger's kitchen, this *stranger's* kitchen.

What was I doing?

I only felt a moment's worth of hesitation before I committed fully to helping this man.

*Helping someone in need. That's what.*

I didn't know him. But ostensibly, he was completely alone and terribly ill. And that was unacceptable.

I'd never been very good at witnessing the suffering of others without wanting to do something about it.

\*\*\*

I CHANGED ROGER'S bed, asking Matt to drop the old sheets, plus a pile of dirty clothes, at a laundry down the block. As well, after convincing him that Roger was not a threat to me, especially not in his current weakened condition, I was able to talk Matt into grabbing some supplies while he was out: aloe tissues, chicken soup, chicken broth, bread, applesauce, bananas, medicine, and mint tea.

Roger dozed on the couch fitfully, shivering, and I cleaned, starting with the kitchen then moving on to the rest of the studio apartment, the size of which made my place in Chicago seem palatial in comparison.

Matt returned with the items and we woke Roger to drink the tea and take some medicine for his fever. Half an hour later, Matt helped the man to the bathroom so he could take a tepid bath. Another half hour later, Roger was sitting up on his couch eating chicken soup and looking at us like we'd been sent from God.

"Thank you. I just—" his voice caught, "—thank you so much."

"You're welcome," Matt replied warmly from where he sat on the carpet. His back rested against the wall, his legs were crossed at the ankle and stretched out before him.

"I didn't get the flu shot this year, and I know better. In my line of work, I'm in constant close contact with so many people from all over the city." Roger stopped to cough, covering his mouth with a tissue, then cleared his throat before finishing his thought. "But I was busy and kept forgetting."

"It's easy to have tunnel vision when you live alone," Matt agreed. "Don't you think so, Marie?"

"Hmm?" I was only half listening to their conversation, still moving around the apartment, making sure all the surfaces had been disinfected.

"Marie. Sit down, take a break," Matt said, patting the carpet next to him. "You've already been over everything three times."

"I just want to be sure." I ran the disinfecting wipe over a light switch I was sure I'd missed earlier, catching Matt's pointed look, then glancing at Roger who was watching me with interest.

"Your guy is right, Florence Nightingale." Roger gave me a tired smile. "Take a load off."

Reluctantly, I relented, tossing the wipe in the garbage. Roger watched me as I settled, and I could feel his hazy gaze study us as I sat next to Matt on the carpet. Matt rubbed my back with light circles, his hands moving to my neck and massaging gently along my neck.

"We won't stay long," I assured the sick man. "And you should go to sleep as soon as we leave. Thanks to Matt, you're stocked in chicken soup and essentials for the next three days."

"Thank you, Matt." Roger managed a small grin. I imagined, if the man weren't so ill, the grin would have looked flirtatious.

I peeked at Matt to see if he'd registered what I had. If he did, it didn't seem to bother him.

"You're welcome, Roger," Matt responded easily.

Meanwhile, I still felt uneasy about leaving Roger alone. "Is there anyone at all you can call? Just to check on you and make sure you're okay?"

"Splitting from my partner has made things . . . strained with our mutual friend group." Roger sighed, causing a small coughing fit, and shrugged. "I do have one client I can ask."

"What's his name? Can we call him?" I pushed.

"Her name is Zara." Roger turned his head slowly from side to side, as though searching for something. "Uh, I can call. My phone is around here somewhere."

"I saw it. I disinfected it. It's next to your computer, charging." I stood and crossed to his small desk, finding and then handing him the phone, reclaiming my spot next to Matt.

"You know, I'll ask her if she'd mind talking to you while you're here. I just feel so badly about you traveling all this way and finding me in this state."

"Stop apologizing, you have no control over being sick," I said, hoping to assure him.

"That's a good idea, though. You could talk to his client, then you wouldn't have to actually *do* a session," Matt said in a quiet voice, not quite a whisper, but low enough that only I would hear.

Setting my jaw, I shook my head. "You are relentless."

"So are you." He nudged my shoulder with his, giving me a small, hopeful smile. "Why do you *need* to do this? Consider a different way."

"I don't really have a choice, do I?" I snapped, careful to keep my voice low so as not to stress Roger out.

Annoyance spurred me to stand, picking up Roger's finished bowl of soup and moving to the sink to clean it. I felt Matt's gaze on my back, but I ignored it, and him. His persistence served only to irritate me.

Roger's idea—that I interview his client as a replacement for going through with the session—had merit only because my window of opportunity was so short. I couldn't stay in New York until Roger recovered. And based on my research, I wasn't comfortable with any of the other dry humpers I'd investigated.

That said, there was absolutely nothing amiss about me going through with a professional dry-humping session. I was a journalist. This was for a story. And even if I hadn't been a journalist, it wasn't like I was in a relationship.

Stewing in my aggravation, I decided that Matt's meddling might have been cute at first, but now it was completely inappropriate.

I'd really and truly stopped holding out hope for Matt, that he would change his mind and be open to exploring something lasting with me. I couldn't make the horse drink the water.

I. Could. Not.

Therefore, I was at peace with the nature of our friendship.

*Plus, there's the two small elephants in the room we haven't discussed yet: is he still seeing his lady friend and the fact that he's being pursued by his old employer.*

Eventually, he would have to tell me of his plans to move back to California, if he had such plans.

But a very distinct possibility existed that we would never discuss the woman he'd been snogging in the hallway more than we already had. Because just like me, he could have his opinion about what I did and with whom, but it wouldn't matter. His feelings for me were platonic and therefore his platonic feelings should remain unaffected by any physical intimacy I chose to share with another person.

Right now, I didn't have anyone's feelings to take into consideration other than my own.

\*\*\*

"**WHAT PROMPTED YOU** to try Roger's services?"

Zara, Roger's client, glanced up and to the side, as though consulting her memory. "Dating in New York, at least for a woman, is horrific."

Her frankness made me smile, but I didn't commiserate out loud, wanting to keep her talking.

After Roger had messaged Zara, she came by almost immediately. When she'd seen the state of things—how sick he was and how we'd helped him— she immediately agreed to the interview. Presently, she and I were sitting together at Roger's small kitchen table, talking softly, while he dozed in his bed.

Matt sat on the couch with his laptop open and headphones on, wanting to give us privacy for our conversation, but still not willing to leave me alone with strangers.

"But that wasn't the *thing* that made me seek him out," Zara said, as though making a grave admission.

"What was the *thing?*" I prompted.

"I was assaulted on a date," she said matter-of-factly, but it was clear the incident had—and continued to—affect her deeply. "It happened four years ago. I couldn't bring myself to go out again, not for a long time. Men . . . became these frightening creatures. I saw threats everywhere. Reasonably, I knew I'd been hurt by just one man. I knew that. I *know* that. But knowing and believing are two different things." She gave me a self-deprecating smile that made my heart ache.

I tried to return it with understanding, not pity.

"So . . . when I finally did go on a date, I had a panic attack." Her attention moved to someplace behind me. "My therapist suggested immersion therapy, but it's difficult to be exposed to a date or physical intimacy without *actually* going on a date. One of my therapist's colleagues suggested—informally of course—Roger's services."

"And, if you don't mind my asking, has that worked?"

Zara considered me for a long moment while she thought about my question, finally responding with, "I don't know. I mean, Roger has helped me. He's a beautiful soul."

"Do you think you find him non-threatening because of his sexual orientation? That it's easier to trust him because of it?"

She tilted her head to the side, like she didn't understand the question. "What do you mean?"

"That Roger, being gay, is—"

"Roger isn't gay. He's bisexual."

"Oh." Didn't see that coming.

"You thought he was gay?"

"Yes. My colleague—who recommended Roger to me—implied that he was gay."

Zara shook her head, giving me a warm smile. "No. He's not. And to answer your question, I don't think of Roger as safe because of his sexual orientation. I think of him as safe because of his sexuality."

"Can you expand on that?"

"He's free from shame," she said simply, one of her cheeks showcasing a dimple as she smiled. "It's so refreshing to be around someone—a man—who doesn't feel like he needs to prove his masculinity by being tough or by *not* being vulnerable. I trust him because he is willing to be vulnerable. Roger is loving and patient and truly wants to make others feel good, in the moment and about themselves in the long-term. In a sense, he's a modern day Don Juan. A lover of lovers, and a lover of love. He's shown me that being sexual isn't something to be ashamed of. Not when it comes from a place of mutual respect. Just as important, he's shown me that being sexual doesn't mean *having sex.* It can be wearing a sexy outfit, or holding hands."

"But you said," I glanced at my notes, "you said you felt like Roger had helped you, but you weren't sure if his services had worked."

"That's right." She nodded, taking a deep breath as though preparing herself to speak weighty thoughts, or admit something unpleasant. "I know I should want to have a partner. I know I should want to date someone who I don't have to pay to be intimate with me. But I don't. I don't want to."

"So, you haven't been on any more dates?"

"No. I haven't. Roger has helped me, definitely, but whenever I think about dating someone, I still feel the same crippling anxiety. Except now, now that I have Roger, I have no reason to address that anxiety or clear that hurdle. He gives me everything I need. And so I don't feel like I *need* to date anyone. Ever."

# CHAPTER 19

**FreeHAL**

*A self-learning conversation simulator (chatterbot) which uses semantic nets to organize its knowledge to imitate human behavior within conversations.*

Source: Chatterbox Challenge

**"MARIE?"**

"What?" I blinked, bringing Matt back into focus.

His eyebrows were expectant arches suspended on his forehead as he glanced meaningfully to the side. I followed his gaze and found our waiter had returned.

*Crap.*

We'd left Roger to Zara's gentle care and walked the Village streets until we found a promising-looking and wonderful-smelling bistro. Matt pulled me inside and now here we were.

"I'm sorry," I split my attention between them both, "I still don't know what I want. Can I have a few more minutes?"

"Do you mind if I order an appetizer then? I'm hungry."

"Sure. Go ahead."

"In the mood for anything?" he asked.

"No. Please. Go ahead. Order whatever." I read the menu, hoping something would jump out at me.

"We'll take the beets au gratin and the baked brie tart. Oh! And the chicken liver pâté. And a bottle of wine. Red something. I trust your judgment."

The waiter smirked without looking up, finished writing our order, and left us.

As soon as he was gone, Matt asked, "Are you still thinking about Zara?"

I nodded, setting my elbow on the table and placing my chin in my palm. "I just feel so badly for her."

I'd told Matt the gist of Zara's story as we'd searched for a place to eat. I'd be writing about her anyway, so I didn't feel I was breaking her trust by telling Matt what we'd discussed. Plus, I needed to talk about it. I needed to process it.

"Why? Because her choices don't adhere to traditional ideas of normality? Because she doesn't want a romantic life partner?" Despite the pointed nature of the questions, his tone was gentle.

"No. Not at all. If she'd eschewed traditional ideas of normality because it was her choice to begin with, or because she'd found an innovative solution that brought her true happiness, then I'd applaud her resilience against the pressures of society's dictates. But it's not. She's not happy. This isn't her first choice. She feels . . . trapped."

Matt nudged his silverware until they were all perfectly parallel. "Did she say that?' His voice sounded odd, tight, and he wasn't looking at me.

"She didn't have to. She's found a work-around, and recognizes that it's not what she wants, but fear keeps her from moving forward. She's crippled, but she's not *too* broken, not enough to put the effort in to fix her situation."

He examined me, looking surprised. "Not too broken?"

"Exactly."

"Interesting choices of words."

"Why?"

"Because . . ." An edge of something new entered his voice; was it defensiveness? "Because not everyone wants or needs to be fixed, Marie."

"I know that, Matt. I'm not trying to fix her, and I'm not judging her," *or you, you stupid, stupid dehydrated horse,* "but that doesn't change the fact that I wish . . ."

*Damn.*

"What? What do you wish?" he asked quietly, studying me intently, drawing his bottom lip between his teeth.

Crap.

Crap. Crap. Crap.

*What are you doing?*

I thought I was over wishing for more with Matt, but it continued to rear its ugly head.

*Again, nothing is ever going to happen. You know this. Still wanting him, after seeing with your own eyes that he's sleeping with other women, makes you pathetic. He said he loves sex, didn't he?*

I was so frustrated with myself. I should have known he'd be hooking up with other people. He'd probably been sleeping with other women this whole time. I shouldn't have been surprised when I saw him last Friday.

Let it go. Let it go. *Why can't you just let it go?*

What was it going to take for me to stop wishing?

Zara's words from earlier floated to my forebrain, *knowing and believing are two different things.*

"Never mind." I closed my menu, leaned back, and crossed my arms. "Let's talk about something else."

Surprisingly, he allowed me to change the subject without pushing back. "What are you getting?"

"Matt, you ordered so many appetizers, I don't need to get anything."

"No. You should order something. You know me, I'll probably eat all the appetizers, and my dinner, and part of yours."

He had a point there. Which led me to ask a question I'd been wondering about since he first came to my apartment and ate everything I'd placed in front of him.

"How can you eat so much all the time without gaining any weight?"

Matt took a drink from his water glass, eyeing me over it. "I have a really high metabolism. I was that kid in high school who never got picked for football because I was so weak, but always got picked for dodge ball."

"Why'd you get picked for dodge ball?"

"Because I'd turn sideways and disappear." He returned his glass to the table and seemed to be meditating on its condensation drops.

"Is that why you started working out? To become bigger? Stronger?"

Matt lifted his eyes to mine, the side of his mouth curving into a flirty smile. "Who says I work out?"

Stopping myself just before I snorted, I opened my menu and looked through their pasta dishes again, in the mood for something with a lot of veggies but also meat sauce. I was not in the mood to flirt with Matt the Impervious.

The ache in my chest told me I should never be in the mood to flirt with Matt the Impervious ever again.

He was quiet while I perused the menu, then he said, "I started working out because I wanted to be more attractive to women."

That grabbed my attention, my eyes cutting to his. "Really?"

Matt nodded once. "Yes."

"You didn't think you were attractive before you started working out?"

He shook his head, a hint of vulnerability in his eyes. "No. I wasn't. I know I wasn't."

"Matt—"

"There's nothing wrong with wanting to be admired by the opposite sex, especially when the opposite sex is notorious for not giving guys like me the time of day," he said stubbornly, though he didn't raise his voice.

"Guys like you?"

"Nice guys," he said, sounding defensive, almost defiant, like he dared me to disagree with him.

Before I could catch myself, I asked, "Is that why you still work out?" but then I bit my lip to stop from asking if he'd been working out to impress women.

"No." He shook his head, his attention dropping to the table as much of his defensive posture eased. "That's not why I do it now."

"Why then? For health?"

"No." His eyes moved up and to the side. "Once I did it for a while, I couldn't stop. I like being stronger, faster, more agile. I have a lot of room for improvement and constantly improving myself appeals to me."

"Hmm." I peered at him, absorbing this information.

*I have a lot of room for improvement . . .*

"Do you think," I held my breath for a beat, "do you think you're in a competition?"

"Yes. But not how you mean." His attention was back on his silverware, nudging it with his fingers. "I'm in competition with myself, not with others." He released a breath and it sounded tired, then he leaned forward, placing his elbows on the table, his mouth hitching to one side wryly. "I'd like to think of myself as fine wine, getting better with age, more robust, more complex. But I accept that when I was young, I resembled the simplicity of grape juice."

I exhaled a short, surprised laugh, but then a wave of melancholy crashed over me followed by a spark of anger directed at his parents. Even so, I forced a smile and determined not to allow my emotions to run away from me.

I was not his girlfriend.

I would never be his girlfriend.

His battles were not my battles unless they were suitable for a *friend*.

Just friends. Forever just friends.

Matt returned my smile as I forced myself to think about what he'd said, and I wondered if I felt the same about myself.

*Am I in competition with myself?*

No. Not really.

"What's wrong?" he asked, looking at me with curiosity.

"I think you and I are very different, Matthew Simmons."

"How so?"

"I am not in competition with myself. I'm not in competition with anyone. In fact, I might be the least competitive person I know."

His smile returned, softer than before, coaxing. "That's because you're already great. There's no improving on perfection."

I laughed again, but it was forced. A pang of dissonance and longing had me lowering my eyes, not wanting him to see my turmoil. I wished he wouldn't say such things. How was it that he didn't realize saying such things to me actually hurt?

How was I supposed to keep him in the friend zone when he kept launching verbal sneak attacks against my heart?

*And if I'm so perfect, why doesn't he want to be with me?*

Ugh.

*Just, stop. You're wrecking yourself. Don't twist yourself into knots.*

Recovering quickly, I sent him a mock-suspicious glare, but my accompanying smile felt weird, too big. I made it smaller. "I'm serious. It's why I need to work in an office. It's why I need my friends. It's why I need a . . ."

I stared past Matt, at a spot made blurry by my realization. *It's not just a want. It's not just envy that causes me to feel so inadequate and alone. It's not just that I hate going home to an empty apartment. I need a person. My person. It's why I want to fall in love, and be loved, and love.*

These articles I was writing about solving loneliness, they weren't going to work for *my* loneliness.

For me, they would only ever be Band-Aids, not cures.

*I can't settle for less.*

\*\*\*

WE RETRIEVED OUR bags from the concierge and Matt insisted on carrying mine. I didn't care either way, so I let him, my brain too tired to argue.

"Are you going to work?" he asked, walking into my room as I held the door open for him. "Where do you want the bag?"

"Um, no. I think I'll just veg out for a bit, then go to sleep. And you can put the bag anywhere." I trailed after him inspecting the room. "Do you see the thermostat? It's freezing in here."

Every hotel room in New York is small, at least every hotel room I've ever been in, and this one was no different. The full-sized bed took up most of the main area, with about two feet or less on each side between the mattress and the walls or furniture.

"I don't see it over here." Matt glanced around the diminutive space, setting my bag on a tiny desk. "This room is like a closet. An ice closet."

Searching the wall for the air conditioner control and finding it by the door, I discovered it was set to 62 degrees. I increased the temperature to 70.

"Yes, well, journalists do live glamorous lives. Where do you usually stay when you're in the city?" I smiled tiredly.

He returned my smile, not looking even a little bit tired, and shuffled two paces before lying on the bed. Matt twisted from side to side as though testing the mattress. "I can confirm, this mattress is comfortable."

I didn't miss how he'd neglected to answer my question, but decided to let it go. "I find Marriott beds to always be the most consistently comfortable."

I moved to my bag and pulled out a pair of yoga pants, T-shirt, and my toiletries, wondering how high on the irresponsible scale it would be for me to raid the minibar. Deciding my bruised heart trumped sensible spending—at least for the night—I went to the bathroom to change and wash my face.

When I finished, I found Matt still stretched out on the bed, but now his shoes were off and he'd propped himself up using my pillows. He'd also flipped on the TV.

"What are you in the mood for? *Law and Order* reruns? Or *Law and Order SVU* reruns?"

"Actually, no TV for me." Feeling wearier than I should, I pulled the covers back on the side he wasn't lying on. "But I'm sure your room has its very own TV, should you wish to spend your evening with Lenny."

"Nah. I'd like to spend my evening with you." He immediately flipped off the TV and rolled toward me, clearly missing my hint.

Matt brushed an errant hair from my forehead and I caught his hand before he could place his ice-cold fingers anywhere else.

"Holy crap! Matt, you're like an icicle."

"You said yourself, it's freezing in here." He shrugged, shivering as his gaze traveled over my face. "I think your lips are a little blue."

"Get under the covers if you're cold," I said . . . like an idiot.

And as soon as the words were out of my mouth, I thought to myself, *Self, what the hell is wrong with you?*

Matt didn't need to be told twice, to my infinite vexation, and was under the covers before I'd finished chastising myself.

"Here, turn around. I will spoon you so I can steal your body heat."

I twisted away, sighing loudly and bringing my knees to my chest, deciding that facing away from his handsome face was better than being forced to look at it.

He pressed his front to my back but didn't place his hands on me, a jolt of whoremones—YES, I SAID WHOREMONES—sending a thrill up my spine, making my toes curl.

This was the worst.

I was lying in bed, under the covers, with a mountain of unrequited feelings posing as a man. My heart strummed an aching beat, each contraction a painful *this can never happen, you did this to yourself, this can never happen, you did this to yourself* . . .

"I can't find your legs." He'd lowered his voice to just above a whisper, his lips close to my ear. I felt movement at the bottom half of the bed, as though he was searching for my legs with his.

"I bent them." I gave in to a shiver caused by his hot breath falling over my neck. "I'm all curled up. Where are your hands?"

"My fingers are still too cold."

I hesitated at that, but only for a moment, deciding that if I was in for a penny, I was in for a pound. "It's okay. Here." I reached behind me, grabbing the frigid fingers of one hand, and placed them on my stomach. "I'd prefer if they were warmed quickly, as I don't want to be maimed by these mini-glaciers you call fingertips."

"I'm not going to argue." Matt curled his legs up and snuggled closer. "By the way, speaking of unsavory fingertips . . ."

"Yes?" I rubbed his hand between mine, focusing on warming his chilled bones, which gave me something to think about other than how nice this was. And how unhealthy this was.

Matt had become my crutch.

I'd come to that conclusion sometime after dinner and before this moment. I may not have been paying him to cuddle or dry hump me, but he'd become my crutch nevertheless. Like any crutch, I had two options: keep using the crutch, or get rid of the crutch and learn to stand on my own.

I wasn't ready to make a decision either way. Neither option appealed to both my head and my heart.

"When is your—uh—orgasm thing?"

I stiffened, staring at the wall in front of me, searching my mind for what on earth he could be talking about. "Pardon?"

"Your meditation session, with the guys who . . ." Matt made a jazz fingers movement with his hand still in my grip.

"Oh!" I exhaled a relieved laugh. "That's next month, a month from this Monday."

I felt him hesitate before he asked, "You're actually going to do it?"

"Yeah. I don't see why not."

An odd sound reverberated from the back of his throat, rumbling in his chest. It sounded like part growl, part breath.

"Tell me something," he demanded, his tone now gruff.

"What?"

"Tell me something I don't know about you, something I would find surprising."

He repeated his request from the first night I'd made dinner for him months ago and my first thought was, *I think I'm falling in love with you.*

I closed my eyes, willed the inconvenient realization away just as I willed the concurrent throbbing in my chest to retreat. It didn't work. At least, not as well as I wished. But then, I was lying in bed with him, under the covers; he was spooning me, caressing my arm.

His touch wasn't loving, because he didn't love me, but it certainly felt that way. And knowing the lie of it only made me feel isolated and alone.

It was difficult to dispel these thoughts, especially when they felt intrinsically tied to what we were currently doing. So the reflection, *I think I'm in love with you,* was replaced with, *I'm so lonely.*

Clearing my throat, I eventually managed to say, "I feel like you already know everything there is to know about me."

His fingers stilled. At length, he tugged on my arm, encouraging me to turn and face him. When I did, I was met with his dreamy brown eyes caressing my face, and his now warm, dreamy fingers, also caressing my face.

"Or everything you're willing to share," he said softly.

"Maybe there's such a thing as sharing too much . . . between friends." I caught his hand at my temple, pulling it from where he'd begun pushing his fingers into my hair, and placed it on the bed between us. "Or maybe I don't want to bore you."

Matt plucked my hand from the bed, and massaged my fingers, studying them as he did so. "Nothing about you could ever bore me. You're the most remarkable person I've met."

His earnestness, like so many times before, made me wish anew for things that would never be possible. But the wishing this time felt overwhelming, dangerously unwieldy. I decided to do the only thing I could do.

Leave.

I scootched away, trying to move out of his grip, but Matt's fingers flexed on my hand, holding me in place.

"What are you doing? Where are you going?"

"I have to use the bathroom," I faked a yawn, "and then I think we should go to sleep. We have an early flight."

His fingers tightened for a moment, then relaxed, allowing me to move fully away. I rolled out of the bed and rushed to the bathroom, hoping against hope that he'd take this hint and be gone by the time I returned. I even loitered in the bathroom, brushing my teeth twice, flossing twice, plucking my eyebrows.

When I peeked my head out of the door, Matt was sitting at the foot of the bed. His shoes were on, that was good; but his elbows were on his knees and his hands were in his hair. I didn't know what to make of his posture.

"I'll meet you for breakfast?" I asked lightly, quickly crossing to the bed and jumping under the covers.

"Thank you, Marie."

I waited a beat, waiting for him to explain his gratitude, but he didn't. And he didn't move.

"For what?"

"For all the times you made me dinner. And lunch. And bread."

I shrugged even though he couldn't see me. "I'm happy to do it. I love to cook."

Matt straightened, his hands falling to his thighs. "I don't know if either of my parents know how to cook."

I blinked at that, at the defeated slump of his strong back. "They never cooked for you?"

"No. Never." He didn't need to tell me because I'd already guessed based on Fiona's description of his family. "They didn't eat meals with me ever. I promised myself, if I had kids, I'd eat every meal with them."

"You plan to go to their school and have lunch with them every day?" That was sweet. And it made me feel things I had no business feeling for a friend.

"It doesn't matter." He cleared his throat, his tone thick with something I couldn't define.

My breath caught as my heart did a twisting, painful maneuver in my chest. I had to restrain myself from reaching out to him. I began to wonder if I was just as much a crutch for him as he was for me, but perhaps in a different way. And if that was the case, then perhaps I needed to take Matt's advice and confront the issue head-on, starting with challenging his last statement.

"You don't want kids, Matt?"

"I don't want . . ."

"What?"

"Indifference," he finished solemnly, turning to look at me over his shoulder and giving me a sad smile. "More indifference. My parents are the most indifferent people I know—to me, to each other, to life—and I don't want that for my kids. And I don't want to do that to someone who loves me."

The last of his words rang through the small room and seemed to echo in my head like an accusation, like he *knew* what I felt for him and was giving me a warning shot, reminding me to focus my hopes and dreams elsewhere.

Tears stung my eyes, making me blink furiously, and I had to moderate my breathing in order to maintain control of my reckless emotions. I wanted scream at him, shake him, ask him why it was so easy for him to believe he'd be indifferent toward me, why it was so difficult to believe he might love me in return.

I didn't scream at him. He was the dehydrated horse. He had to drink water himself. He had to *want* it.

Instead, once I'd calmed my racing heart, I asked with forced steadiness, "Have you really never wanted to love anyone?"

"It was easy for me to stop wanting Kerry," he said instead of answering my question, and I got the sense he was speaking to himself more than to me. "It was easy to stop asking about her day. It was easy to let her fight her own battles, to not want to fight them alongside her. It was easy to dedicate myself to my work. I'm good at what I do. It didn't matter that she was intelligent and beautiful. I wasn't . . . attracted to her. I didn't waste time during the day wondering what she was doing, making plans for us, playing hooky from work so we could be together."

"Why do you think you lost interest?"

He made a face and shook his head dismissively. "I didn't lose interest. I married too young, before I knew what I wanted . . . what I needed . . ." Something behind his gaze shifted, heated, as it moved over my forehead, nose, lips, neck, lower.

The air felt suspended between us, as though even the molecules were holding still, and I likewise held my breath. A languid warmth spread through me, traveling the same path as his gaze, followed quickly by the piercing pain of realization.

His thoughts couldn't have been any clearer than if he'd worn a shirt that read, "Marie, I want to fuck you."

I didn't flinch, though it hurt. It hurt horribly to want a whole person and be wanted in return for just a small piece of who I was. It hurt so badly I had to dig my fingernails into my palms to distract myself from the hurt.

Eventually, his eyes lifted, his stare scorching. He took a step forward. "Marie—"

I shook my head, feeling raw and exposed and fatally close to bursting into tears. "I think maybe . . ."

*You should stay.*

No.

He should leave.

*We should have hot sex.*

No!

That's a terrible idea.

*You should tell me what I need to do to make you love me.*

Damn it! What the hell? *Be quiet, heart! I shouldn't have to* do *anything to be loved.*

"I think you should go," I blurted, my brain finally winning the standoff. Tearing my eyes from his, I lay down on the bed and turned away from him. "We have an early flight, so . . ."

I lay perfectly still, my lips rolled between my teeth to keep my chin from wobbling. I listened to him breathe. I listened to my own heart, sluggishly beating. I listened to the air conditioner finally click off.

And eventually, after what felt like an eternity, I heard the door close as he left.

# CHAPTER 20

### ATM

*Automated Teller Machine- an electronic telecommunications device that enables the customers of a financial institution to perform financial transactions, particularly cash withdrawal, without the need for a human cashier, clerk, or bank teller.*

Source: Wikipedia

**I SWITCHED OFF** my phone, completely off, and dialed the front desk for a wakeup call.

And then I cried and drank all the tequila in the minibar.

The next morning, when my scheduled wakeup call informed me that I was alive and had forty minutes to get ready, my eyes were puffy and my mouth tasted like a cactus. But it was also obvious what I must do.

The time had come to relinquish the crutch, to set the crutch free.

Now I just had to decide whether to do it fast, an abrupt and complete cessation, or to take a gentler, more gradual approach.

Powering up my phone, I left it on the bedside table and shuffled to the bathroom, turning on the shower.

Brushing my teeth, I debated both options. Ending things swiftly would be better in the long run, but I knew myself well enough to know I would never be able to summarily cut out him out, I cared about him too much.

As I took my shower, a plan of action began to solidify in my mind. I left the bathroom and marched to my bag, pulling out clothes for the day. By the time I was dressed, hair dry and styled, makeup applied, I was feeling much better. Stronger. More like myself. Empowered by my decision rather than terrified because of it.

Nearly finished packing my things, I picked up my phone, intent on checking in for my flight. And that's when I noticed I had several unread text messages and about a dozen missed calls.

**6:15 p.m. Greg**: *Fiona is in labor, we wanted you to know. Will text when our new imperial highness graces us with his* or *her presence.*

**7:13 p.m. Elizabeth**: *Quinn told me to text you to let you know they're on their way to the hospital. Janie's water broke. I'm meeting them in maternity.*

**8:35 p.m. Elizabeth**: *MARIE! They're both here. OMG!!!!! Fiona is almost done. Please come help me with Quinn. He is completely loco.*

**9:01 p.m. Sandra**: *Where the hell are you? Are Dan and Kat with you?*

**9:17 p.m. Alex**: *I can't trace your cell phone if you turn it off. You better not be dead.*

**10:51 p.m. Greg**: *Baby Archer #3 has arrived. Already screaming at the help and complaining about shoddy service. 7lbs 14oz of perfection.*

**11:07 p.m. Nico**: *Elizabeth could really use your help with Quinn . . . please.*

**11:11 p.m. Ashley (to Dan, Kat, and Marie)**: *Drew is thinking about arranging a search party for y'all.*
**11:14 p.m. Dan (to Ashley, Kat, and Marie)**: *On our way.*
**11:16 p.m. Dan (to Ashley, Kat, and Marie)**: *Marie isn't with us. I don't know where she is.*
**11:18 p.m. Dan (to Ashley, Kat, and Marie)**: *Alex says her phone is off.*
**11:21 p.m. Ashley (to Dan, Kat, and Marie)**: *I'm giving Marie until 8 a.m., then I'm sending Drew after her.*
**11:31 p.m. Dan (to Ashley, Kat, and Marie)**: *Agree. I'll help.*

**4:13 a.m. Elizabeth (to Sandra, Ashley, Marie, Kat)**: *Janie's at 6cm. It's been a long night. Marie is MIA. When you wake up, if someone could come hold Quinn's hand, that'd be great.*

**4:16 a.m. Kat (to Elizabeth, Sandra, Ashley, Marie):** *I'm on my way*

**4:18 a.m. Elizabeth (to Sandra, Ashley, Marie, Kat):** *Thanks, Kat. And, Marie, when you read this—WE LOVE YOU!!!*


I had missed calls from everyone. Quinn, Elizabeth, Nico, Sandra, Alex, Alex, Alex, Ashley, Kat, Dan, Dan, Dan, and Greg. I'd finally finished catching up with the saga from the night before, and was just about to respond to the plethora of texts, when my phone rang. Alex's name flashed on my screen.

I fumbled to answer, bringing it to my ear in a rush. "Hello?"

"You had your phone off."

"Yes. I did. Is everything okay? How's Janie? And Fiona?"

"Janie is still in labor. Fiona had her baby last night. I haven't seen her yet. We have Grace and Jack with us. Are you okay?"

I sat on the bed, rubbing my forehead with my fingertips. "Yes. Sorry. I—"

"You don't need to apologize. Everyone was worried, so I checked the airlines. You're in New York, right?"

"Yes. That's right. I had a trip for work. I feel so badly about not being there. Is Quinn okay?" I began pacing, calculating the time it would take for me to make it back to Chicago.

"He's . . . Quinn." I thought I detected a hint of affection in Alex's tone, but I couldn't be sure. "I told him where you were. He's sending his plane. Can you get to New Jersey in an hour? I already sent your information to Teterboro."

"Teterboro?"

"Executive airport. Easier to fly in and out of than JFK or LaGuardia."

"Uh, yes. I think so. Let me map it." I glanced at the clock by the bed. My commercial flight didn't leave for another three and a half hours. Matt and I had to—

*Matt!*

"Wait. I have someone with me. Matt Simmons."

There was a pause on the other end, then Alex cleared his throat. "Okay. He can text me his passport number or driver's license number—one or the other—or I can just look it up. We'll add him. They'll be expecting you both."

"Okay. But you know, I could have taken my scheduled flight. It's not a huge time difference."

"It's a three-hour difference in arrival time, Marie," he said, like three hours might destroy or save the world. "See you soon."

"See you."

I hung up, needing a moment to catch my breath, then messaged Greg:

**5:05 a.m. Marie:** *Congratulations! So happy for you both. I can't wait to see the baby <3 <3*

**5:07 a.m. Greg:** *Thank you, gorgeous. Here's a snap of Fiona with the babe taken last night. As you can see, the child is perfection, just like her mother.*

**5:10 a.m. Marie:** *Why are you up? Shouldn't you sleep while you can? Is Fiona up?*

**5:11 a.m. Greg:** *Fi is asleep and so is the baby. But I can't sleep when I'm this happy. It would be a waste of the moments that make life worth living.*

His last text made me smile.

And then I sniffed, because it also made me want to cry.

But then I blinked away the tears, straightening my back. A sense of rightness and resolve firming my bones. My person was out there, and I just needed to start looking for him again.

The time had come to surrender my crutch. Because I wanted someone to feel about life with me the way Greg felt about life with Fiona. I didn't want to waste the moments—my moments—that made life worth living.

\*\*\*

I TEXTED MATT and gave him an overview of the events from the prior evening as well as a summary of the modification in our travel plans, informing him that I was on my way down to the concierge to call a taxi. He met me in the lobby just as the taxi pulled up, giving us no time to engage in an awkward greeting.

He didn't kiss me on the cheek, as I gave him no opportunity to do so.

Also helpful, the distraction of my friends' circumstances. The situation provided adequate fodder for discussion all the way to the executive airport and minimal eye contact. I filled him in on what had occurred while I surveyed the city beyond the taxi window.

Everything went smoothly. We arrived, checked in, were escorted to Quinn's plane, buckled in, and we were off. No waiting in lines, no time for idle chit-chat. I opened my laptop, figuring I'd use the flight to type up notes from the day before.

"You're working?" Matt hovered at the end of the aisle, glancing from me to my open laptop.

Without looking up, I nodded. "I should get these notes transcribed while they're still fresh."

I sensed Matt hesitate while I pulled on my headphones and scrolled through my phone for an appropriate playlist. For some reason, I felt like listening to angry girl music.

So I did.

I wrote while Matt sat in the seat across from mine—even though there were twenty-two other seats to choose from—and likewise worked on his laptop. Every so often I sensed his attention on me. I ignored it. I would be strong.

I didn't close my laptop or remove my headphones until after we'd landed, taxied to our hangar, and the flight attendant appeared to tell us we were welcome to depart when ready. With minimal conversation, we got into the car Quinn had sent to pick us up in and it took us straight to the hospital.

Matt's first priority was checking in on Fiona and family. Meanwhile, I hadn't received any new texts about Janie's condition and worried aloud regarding what I might find.

I texted Dan as soon as we arrived to the hospital lot. He was waiting for me just inside the entrance. Other than tossing Matt a *who-the-hell-are-you* glare, he seemed to be singularly focused on getting me checked in.

"What's going on? Is Janie okay? Elizabeth hasn't texted."

Both Matt and I handed our photo IDs to the receptionist so they could make us visitor badges for the day.

"She's still in labor. It's been since seven last night, and Quinn hasn't slept. Janie won't let him in the room, says he's making her nuts. Katherine is in there now. She and Mr. Sullivan arrived after 1:00 AM, then the plane turned around and picked you up once Alex figured out where you were."

I smirked a little because Dan called Quinn's mother by her first name, but could never bring himself to call Quinn's father by anything other than *Mr. Sullivan.*

I knew Quinn's mother, Katherine, rather well as she and I had organized Janie and Quinn's wedding together a few years ago. Neither Janie nor Quinn had expressed any interest in planning the event and I loved that kind of stuff—and I loved to help—so I didn't mind.

Janie had chosen Katherine as her birth coach early on in the pregnancy when it became clear that Quinn's tendencies to want to control everything—

especially where Janie's safety was concerned—wasn't going to work during a vaginal birth.

"Elizabeth says they won't let Janie go past seven tonight, because of something having to do with her water breaking yesterday and after twenty-four hours there's an increase in infection problems, or something like that. I don't know." Dan tugged his fingers through his hair, looking truly stressed.

Matt and I accepted our visitor badges, placing the stickers on our shirts. I then placed a comforting hand on Dan's shoulder.

The three of us walked to the elevators while I smoothed gentle circles on Dan's back. "Hey. Everything is going to be fine. Elizabeth won't let anything happen to either of them."

Dan sighed, jabbing at the call button for the elevator and then rubbing at the swirly neck tattoos peeking out of his T-shirt collar. "I'm just glad you're here. Kat's exhausted. She's been sitting with Quinn since early this morning. I want her to go rest, but she won't listen to me. Mr. Sullivan is also there, but he's mostly quiet other than telling Quinn to calm the fuck down and reminding him that women do this every goddamn day. In fact, it almost looks like he's enjoying Quinn's anxiousness, which I think is pissing Quinn off. And I can't tell Quinn he's overreacting because, what the hell do I know?"

We boarded the elevator and Dan pressed the button for the fourth floor.

"His pacing is driving me nuts. I asked Elizabeth if we can sedate him, and she said *no*." Dan snorted, rolling his eyes. "But the good thing is they have Janie in this special room, bigger than the others, with its own waiting room outside. So he can pace all he likes without tripping over doctors and nurses trying to do their job. It's the VIP suite, where I'm guessing the acronym stands for Very Irritating Patients' Husbands."

"That would be VIPH," Matt chimed in good-naturedly, saying something for the first time since we arrived.

Dan's eyes cut to Matt's. "You think I don't fucking know that? Who the fuck are you?"

I had to struggle to keep from laughing at Dan's surge of aggression; clearly, he'd reached the end of his patience.

"This is Matt Simmons, Fiona and Greg's next-door neighbor. He's here to see them."

"Oh." Dan continued to inspect Matt with suspicion. "Well, Fiona crossed the finish line last night. Three-hour labor, bing bang boom. I saw her and Greg this morning; it's like night and day with those two and what Janie and Quinn are dealing with. Greg was whistling. *Whistling*! And giving their little gnome a bath. Cutest fucking baby I've ever seen. Meanwhile, Fiona is sitting up in bed, knitting. *Knitting*! She looks like she's been on vacation, all well-rested, smiling and shit." He shook his head again, like he couldn't believe two pregnancies and deliveries could be so entirely different.

The doors opened and we departed, Dan turning and pointing down the hall. "So that's where Greg and Fiona are. They'll scan your badge again and double-check whether you're allowed in, if they want to see you before they open the security door."

"Thank you." Matt nodded at Dan, then to me he asked, "Where will you be? I'll call you after I'm done."

Dan's glare of distrust returned and he answered before I could. "She'll be here all day, taking care of her people. If you want to help, bring the woman some food, her knitting, or give her a back massage. Come on."

Dan took me by the arm and began leading me away, but Matt stopped our momentum by grabbing my wrist.

Tugging me forward, he slipped his hand around my waist and captured my mouth with a kiss.

It happened so fast, I didn't have a moment to respond or react or enjoy the feel of his warm, soft lips moving over mine. Or the abrupt spike of aching pleasure that flooded my chest, spurring my heart into a reckless rhythm, and cinching my throat with emotion.

*What . . . what . . . WHAT?*

I'd just placed my hand on his torso to steady myself when he ended the kiss by brushing his lips over mine once more, and then stepped away. Our gazes locked and I blinked at the intensity I found there, especially since the remainder of his features appeared studiously devoid of emotion.

"I'll see you soon," he said, making his words sound like an order.

I nodded, certain my face betrayed how confused I was, and allowed myself to be pulled in the opposite direction by Dan.

My friend glanced over his shoulder and back at Matt twice as we walked. Or rather, Dan walked, I stumbled, still caught in the moment Matt's lips had captured mine.

*What was that?*

I lifted my fingertips to my mouth, wondering if I'd just imagined the last two minutes. I had no idea how to feel about it. I couldn't even believe it had happened.

*What the hell was that?*

Once we were out of earshot, I sensed Dan's gaze flicker over my profile.

"Is that guy your boyfriend?"

"No."

*No. He's not.*

*He's not.*

*He's not.*

"You like that guy, though."

Inspecting my friend, his pointed gaze targeting mine, I released a perplexed breath. "It doesn't matter. He's not interested in me that way."

Dan snort-laughed. "Oh, he's interested in you *that* way. That kiss and the look he was sending me when I took your arm, I know that look."

I struggled how best to summarize the situation with Matt, just like I was struggling to wrap my mind around the kiss. "We're friends. I think. I think we're friends. I don't know. I think he'd like to be friends with benefits. But that kind of arrangement doesn't interest me."

Dan grunted noncommittally at that, apparently in deep thought, and we walked quietly for a while. He helped me navigate the security checkpoint that would lead us into the VIP labor and delivery suite, but pulled me to a stop just outside the door to the waiting room.

"I'm gonna give you some unsolicited advice, okay?" Dan peered at me, as though making sure I knew to take his words seriously. "But it's good advice, even though I'm tired as hell, so it might not make much sense."

"Sure. Go for it." Even in my muddled state, I couldn't help but smile at my friend.

"You like that guy, you tell him flat out. You just lay what you want and everything out there. Don't waste time not saying things that need to be said. He'll always be in your mind, wrecking the possibility of things with other people, because your heart can't move on until it knows for sure a door is closed."

I managed a reassuring smile. "Thanks for the ad—"

"But then, if the door opens, make sure it's the right door, not a different door. Because then you'll be in the room, but it's not the right room. And then you're stuck in the room, you've committed to the room, and you'd be an asshole for trying a new door in the same house when you're already *in* a room. And then your fucking heart won't stop looking for a window." He lifted his hand between us face up, shaking his head, clearly irritated about something, then let his palm fall to his leg with a smack.

I stared at him, waiting patiently until he'd finished his tirade.

Dan was right, he was tired. His words were slightly slurred with lack of sleep, but I thought I understood his meaning well enough.

His peering persisted, like he wanted to make sure I understood his point, then he added, "I'm serious. Hearts are bastards that way, always looking for a goddamn window."

# CHAPTER 21

**Synthetic Environment for Analysis and Simulations (SEAS)**

*A model of the real world used by Homeland Security and the United States Department of Defense that uses simulation and AI to predict and evaluate future events and courses of action*

Source: United States Department of Defense

DAN'S SUMMARY WAS entirely correct.

Kat was exhausted.

Desmond—Quinn's dad—was amused by his son's out-of-control worry.

And Quinn was out of control with worry.

As soon as Quinn saw me, he crossed to me in three steps and engulfed my body in a squeezing hug, catching me completely by surprise. We'd never hugged before. In fact, I'd never seen him hug or touch anyone but Janie.

Peripherally, I heard Dan say to Kat, "Okay. Marie is here. I found a bed for you, come with me."

Two sets of footsteps sounded behind me and a small hand covered my shoulder. I turned as Quinn relaxed his arms and found Kat, giving me a grateful smile. "I'll be back in an hour."

"She'll be back in a few hours," Dan corrected, tugging on her hand and pulling her out of the room.

I chuckled at his bossiness. Something had changed, but I was given no opportunity to figure out what the deal was because Desmond had stood and was waiting for a hug.

"Good to see you." Desmond gave me his version of a smile, which was similar to Quinn's version of a smile, his hawkish blue eyes scrutinizing me as we separated.

"You too." My gaze cut to Quinn, and I grinned. "Ready to be a father?"

He was *not* smiling. "She's been in labor for almost twenty-four hours."

"I know." I smoothed a hand up and then down his arm, smiling at the uncharacteristic wrinkles of worry on his forehead. "From what I understand, it's not unusual for labor to take longer with the first baby."

"First?" he scoffed, shaking his head vehemently. "No. Last. We're not doing this again."

Desmond's lips twitched and he sent me a tired yet thoroughly amused look.

Quinn gritted his teeth, his hands on his hips, clearly needing someone to rant to. "There's no way in—"

Quinn's tirade was interrupted by the far door opening suddenly and Elizabeth poking her head out. "Okay, Daddy. It's time. You have three minutes to suit up if you want to catch a baby." She moved to close the door, paused, and grinned at me. "You're here."

"I'm here."

"Yay," she exclaimed with feeling, then shut the door.

Quinn's eyes swung to me, large and panicked. "What do I do?"

I couldn't help it, I laughed. So did Desmond.

But I also gave him another quick hug, pulling back and holding his face in my palms like my father held mine when I was a girl. "You're going to go in there and meet your child. And then you're going to kiss your wife and tell her how amazing she is. And then you're going to thank the doctors and nurses for doing such an excellent job. And then you're not going to worry, because you're just going to enjoy your family. Got it?"

He nodded, swallowing, committing my instruction to memory.

I scanned the room, dropping my hands from his face, looking for what Elizabeth meant when she said suit up, and found a folded pile of blue hospital garments on a chair by the door. Picking it up, I helped Quinn into the gown, giving up on the buttons in the back. He was simply too big, so I did my best with the ties at the top and waist.

"Bend down," I ordered, stretching the elastic of the hair covering wide so I could fit it over his head. He did as instructed, his face a stunned mask of disbelief and wonder.

Not three seconds later, Elizabeth appeared again and motioned for Quinn to enter. "Come on, come on. She's got three pushes left."

Quinn nodded numbly as he moved to the door, his usually steely blues now wide and rimmed with a plethora of emotions that looked completely alien to his typically stoic façade. Anxiety, excitement, wonder, fear, and the anticipation of joy.

Folding my hands under my chin, I had to roll my lips between my teeth to keep from crying, not quite understanding the impulse. Desmond put his arm around my shoulders as we watched him go. And just as the door closed behind him, the other door burst open, Kat and Dan swiftly walking through it.

"We got the text and we hurried back. Is it over?" Dan came to a stop next to me, looking and sounding hopeful.

"No." I shook my head, a happy tear spilling onto my cheek. "It's just beginning."

***

"IT'S TRUE. SHE planned the entire wedding." Greg stood in the corner of Fiona's hospital room, rocking from side to side, patting the bottom of his third child in a gentle rhythm. He was telling Matt the story of Janie's wedding. Everyone was.

We—Greg, Fiona, their new baby, Dan, Kat, Katherine, Desmond, Matt, and I—were all crowded together in Fiona's room. It wasn't huge, but it was surprisingly large, with plenty of places to sit. When I'd remarked on its size, Greg told me it was the second of the two VIP postpartum maternity rooms. Quinn had arranged it, wanting Janie to have Fiona close by.

Janie, Quinn, and Desmond Sullivan III—their new son, named after both Quinn's father and Quinn's deceased brother—were next door, getting to know each other. Fiona, who looked more refreshed than anyone who'd just had a baby had a right to look, had invited everyone into her room for lunch.

The woman was a super ninja.

I swear.

Super. Ninja.

I was sitting in the chair next to Fiona's bed. Dan, Kat, Desmond, and Katherine were sitting on the long couch under the window, and Matt was standing next to Greg, arms crossed, sneaking glances at the baby as though it were the ultimate curiosity. Or about to explode. One or the other.

Every time it moved or made a noise, Matt would ask, "Is it okay? What's wrong?"

To which Greg would reply, "She can smell your fear."

"How long did you have to plan that wedding, Marie? Two months? Something like that. A huge Boston wedding. Insanity." Fiona shook her head at me.

"Hey. Katherine did a lot of the work," I pointed out, avoiding Matt's gaze. My feelings in chaos, I was barely treading water. I'd been avoiding him—his gaze, and just him in general—since I'd entered the room. "And Quinn's ex-girlfriend helped find Janie's dress."

Dan snorted, shaking his head. "That lady wasn't his girlfriend, they just used to fu—"

Fiona cleared her throat loudly, lifting her eyebrows meaningfully at Dan.

"Sorry. Sorry." He held a hand up as though he surrendered and peeked sheepishly at Katherine.

Quinn's mother smiled at Dan; Dan and Quinn had grown up together, therefore Katherine had known Dan his entire life. "It's okay, Daniel. I think Des and I are ready for a nap. Come on."

As she stood, she pulled her husband up as well. They made their rounds to each of us: Katherine handing out hugs—even to Matt, I noticed—and Desmond shaking hands with everyone but Fiona, Kat, and me.

After Quinn's parents shut the door behind them, Dan said, "They were acquaintances. At best. I don't think he even remembered her name."

Kat was looking at him like he was hilarious, shaking her head.

His eyes slid to hers. "What?"

"Nothing." She shrugged.

"Didn't you ladies used to call Quinn's ladies slamps or something? I think I remember that."

"That was Elizabeth's shorthand for describing the dynamic between men and women who have lots of sexual partners. And she called Quinn a Wendell. She reads a lot of Urban Dictionary entries, I think." Fiona, who was knitting, said all of this without glancing up.

Kat's smile slipped and she glanced at her fingers, then pulled her left hand through her hair, something glinting off her third finger. "Where is Elizabeth, anyway?"

I squinted at Kat, my attention dropping to her left hand where it rested on her lap, and I had to suppress a gasp.

"Hopefully taking a nap." Greg switched the babe from one shoulder to the other. "She worked a full shift yesterday and was up all night checking on us and Janie. I was going to have Matt take a look at her."

"Why?" Kat asked.

"I suspect she's a robot."

"You think everyone is a robot." Fiona shook her head at her husband.

"Matt should create a robot test," Greg persisted. "You all have to take the test before you can hold the baby."

"Is anyone thirsty?" Kat stood, picking up her empty soda can. "I'm going to go get another drink."

Dan stood too. "I'll help."

"No." I stood, walked to Kat and looped our arms together as I pulled her out of the room. "I'll help."

She gave me a startled look, but didn't argue or ask why she needed help buying another soda. As soon as the door shut behind us, I spun on her.

"Kat."

"Yes?" Her eyes were wide, bracing, even though she was smiling.

"Why are you wearing a wedding ring?"

She stiffened, her smile growing similarly hard, less natural. Sighing, her smile completely dissolved, leaving her eyes anxious and the corners of her mouth pinched.

"I had to," she whispered.

"You *had* to?"

She nodded, swallowing. "I had to."

I attempted to parse through what *I had to* might mean. "Did your family make you marry someone?"

She shook her head, but said, "Yes. But it's not like you think."

Giving her a hard stare, I stepped closer, holding her shoulders, and tried to keep the worry out of my voice. "What's it like, then? And why didn't you come to me for help? Or if not me, then Fiona? Or Sandra and Alex? Or—"

"I went to Dan for help," she admitted on a rushed whisper, closing her eyes and releasing a shaky breath. "Dan helped me."

"Dan?" I searched her face, looking for a clue as to what she could possibly mean. "Helped you how?"

Kat opened her eyes, ripe with tension and guilt, and said, "He married me."

\*\*\*

KAT FILLED ME in on her predicament. The story had been . . . concerning. I was concerned for her *and* Dan. I'd also pledged to help however I could. What she needed was my support, and that's what I would give her.

Selfishly, I appreciated the distraction from my own worries, which felt small and silly in comparison.

I left the hospital around 3:00 PM, feeling worn out. Matt left with me, giving me the impression he'd been waiting until I was ready to depart. We found one of Quinn's SUVs ready to take us home, our luggage in the back.

Matt said nothing until we were in the car and on our way. Then he pressed the button for the privacy window, closing the barrier between the driver and us, and drawing my attention to him.

"Why do women give men blowjobs?" he asked, staring forward, his tone curious and conversational.

I blinked at him, my lips parting in surprise. "Excuse me?"

"Hear me out." He glanced at me. "Answer the question. I have a point."

"Uh, I guess . . . maybe some women like it."

"Do you like it?"

A rush of feeling masked as heat flared over my cheeks, making my neck hot. "Matt."

"Humor me." He turned more completely in his seat. "Do you like it?"

"I mean, I guess. It's not my favorite thing, but I guess I like doing it." I crossed my arms, realizing that this was the kind of conversation we used to have all the time. And I never felt uncomfortable about it until I'd seen him kissing someone else.

"I like going down on women."

I huffed, closing my eyes. "Good for you?" *And good for the women you deem fuckable.*

Yeah, yeah, yeah, my internal thought process was bitter and snide. So sue me.

"Why do you think that is?"

"Because you're hungry all the time?" My voice was carefully deadpan. I couldn't do this with him. Not anymore.

"Be serious."

"Fine." I clenched my teeth. "Because you like that it's sexual."

"Yes, that's part of it. But it's not the main reason. I think women like giving head and men like cunnilingus because of the *giving* part."

"That's an interesting theory." My heart was beating erratically, and I was unsure how I was feeling. I was leaning toward mad, but that wasn't quite right.

"You know, Elon Musk thinks life is a simulation. That humanity is really just a computer simulation controlled by an advanced society."

"Elon Musk thinks too much."

"What is life?" Matt asked quietly.

"I'm going to assume that's a rhetorical question."

"Life is a struggle for relevancy." Emotion poured from his words—emotion that had been absent up until now—and had me opening my eyes to peek at him. His stare was on me, trapping mine, making it impossible for me to look away as he continued. "And you can't be relevant, you absolutely cannot be relevant, if you contribute nothing. If you take without giving. What is a relationship if not a microcosm of life?"

"You think being relevant is an essential part of a relationship?" I didn't like how that sounded.

"Yes. But I can tell from how you asked the question you're misunderstanding my meaning." He moved like he was going to reach for my hand, but then pulled back, setting his teeth. "Theoretically, for the sake of this discussion, let's say—as an example—you and I were in a relationship. I would be concerned about my relevancy to you. But rarely, if ever, would I be concerned about *your* relevancy to me. I wouldn't be thinking, *what has Marie done for me lately?* I think good people struggle more with their own relevancy—am I contributing, am I important, am I needed—than they do with the world, or with their partner."

"So how do you make a person relevant to a robot?" Most of my earlier anger had dissipated, replaced with sincere interest in the topic of discussion. This was a gift of his, distracting me by being fascinating.

"Unless the robot is sentient," his attention moved over my shoulder, growing hazy, "capable of making its own decisions and possessing free will, I don't think you can. No human will ever look at a robot and think, *It needs me, it wants me because of who I am.* And even if it did, so what?" His gaze moved back to mine. "What is the value of being needed by an artificial intelligence?"

I swallowed, caught by the animated intelligence in his gaze. "What is the value of being needed by another person?" I asked quietly.

"Pride."

"Pride?"

"Yes." His breathing changed, taking larger and larger breaths. "Admitting that you need another person is relinquishing pride. What if that person rejects you? What if they don't need you? It's a big risk for a person, but for an AI? Where's the risk? With no risk, no true sacrifice or vulnerability, there is no value."

"What are you saying? You're giving up on your Compassion AI?"

"No . . ." He bit his lip, his eyes dropping to my mouth. "No. I'm not giving up. I'm changing my aims, though."

"Because you think people need to be needed?"

"I know it." He swallowed, the corners of his mouth tugging upward, his eyes darting over my face, and then he blurted, "Have I ruined our friendship?"

I stiffened, wincing at the vulnerability behind the question. This was one of the times where he looked so earnest, I wanted to wrap him in a hug and kiss any trace of hurt from his memory.

I considered asking him about the kiss back at the hospital, about what it meant or why he did it, because I *hoped* it meant he'd changed his mind about long-term relationships. But then I reminded myself that my hopes were responsible for the current state of my heart. It was time for me to be pragmatic instead of hopeful.

I already *knew* the answer, it was time for me to *believe* him. Hadn't he said over dinner the night before, "Some people don't want to be fixed"?

*He's attracted to you, that's why he kissed you, that's why he made a pass at you in New York, and that's why he's wondering if he's ruined our friendship now.*

Asking about the kiss wouldn't help make things any clearer. Things between us were already clear, *I'd* been blind. I didn't need him to say it. My heart could not handle another rejection of my hopes. Nor did I think our friendship would survive if I laid myself bare and told him I wanted a forever with him.

I knew what he'd do and what he'd say. He'd let me down gently and try to salvage some sort of friendship. Or he'd try. He'd *try* to love me. And how devastating would that be? I didn't want someone to *try* to love me.

*No. Nothing of our friendship will survive if I ask him about the kiss.* So instead, with a lump in my throat, I said, "No. Of course not." And gave him a reassuring smile that felt both too big and too small. It was and wasn't a lie. I was the one who'd ruined our friendship. *I ruined it by wanting much more of him than he'd ever be willing to give.*

As awful as that was, I had to own it.

He inspected me, as though endeavoring to read my thoughts, and the weight of his gorgeous dark eyes felt unbearable. "Don't lie to me. Please."

Dropping my gaze to the seat between us, I gathered a steadying breath. I had to. His words, his voice, and his watchful glare made me feel unsteady.

"I'm not lying, Matt. I think what's between us isn't really a friendship. Not anymore. It's grown into an anomalous dependency, one that I believe is not what either of us want. Or deserve. And it's not something you've ruined. It just is."

Lifting my gaze, I found him staring at my neck. His features were devoid of all expression, but eventually he nodded.

I swallowed past a thickening lump in my throat, adding, "I care about you, Matt. I always will."

He closed his eyes, turning away from me, giving me his profile. Yet I could tell his features were still blank.

Compelled, I continued, "But I also think we both need to return to our own lives and stop using each other as a crutch."

Matt's eyelids opened, but he kept his gaze studiously forward. "Am I going to see you again? After today? Or are you planning on avoiding me?"

A sharp, cutting pain originated in my chest and sliced outward, up my neck, down to my stomach, and along my arms.

Gripping my forehead, I struggled to speak coherently. "We're supposed to see each other next week. When your friends are in town. I'm still planning on being there, as long as I'm still invited."

"Yes. Of course you're still invited." He nodded slowly, clearing his throat.

I turned my attention to the window at my side, not looking at my reflection or the streets of Chicago, but rather turning my deliberations inward. The day had been a crazy one—crazy happy, crazy worrying, crazy concerning, and now crazy sad—and I wished I could live it all over again. I didn't know if I would have done anything differently, but so many of the moments were worth treasuring and holding on to.

"I want you to know," his deep voice, roughened with emotion, broke the silence and drew my eyes back to his profile, "that any part of yourself you're willing to share with me—any time, any energy, any thought—I exist as a ready audience."

A genuine—albeit small and wobbly—smile tugged at the corner of my mouth. "This also goes for food? You'll also be open to accepting food?" I tried to tease, infuse some lightness into this bleak moment.

His answering smile was just as genuine, but it was also desolate. So terribly, terribly sad. "Of course, Marie. That's a given. Food always goes without saying."

# CHAPTER 22

**Relay**

*A robot that can be used by hotels (such as The M Social Singapore hotel) to deliver room service to guests. It navigates using 3D cameras, can negotiate elevators, and maneuver around people wandering down the corridors.*

Source: Savioke

MATT DIDN'T TEXT me over the next five days.

The lack of communication made life seem somehow both louder and muted. I zoned out frequently, staring out windows, at random objects. I also went on a lot of walks, all over the city, at all times of the day.

I felt . . . mournful. Like I'd lost something essential.

*Someone* essential.

But he'd never really been mine, so I struggled to push those thoughts away and buried myself in work.

Losing myself in a story was one of my favorite things about my job. The act of researching for writing was usually a minefield of rabbit holes for me, where I'd misplace hours of my life chasing the threads of interconnected topics. I loved it, but it was hard to *stop*. However, now I gave in to it; the time spent researching felt like a reprieve, the only time I wasn't thinking about him.

Staring into space. Researching. Having no appetite. Going to bed early.

Basically, if you add political activism and woodworking to that list, I was becoming my grandfather.

Presently, it was Thursday afternoon, and I was staring at the nonexistence of particles in my water glass, wondering for the first time in over a week if I should message him. I'd wanted to message him many times, but didn't, because I knew it wasn't a good idea.

However, this was different. We were supposed to meet this weekend. I'd made a list of potential activities, and even though he'd said I was still invited last week, I had to wonder if he'd changed his mind.

"Knock, knock."

I blinked away from my water glass, startled, and saw Camille standing just outside my office.

"Oh my gosh, you're back!" I stood immediately and rushed to my friend, opening my arms for a hug.

"Yes. I'm back." She sounded tired.

I pulled away, examining her. "Are you okay? I got your letter."

She smiled, also tiredly, and walked past me into my office, sitting in one of the chairs across from my desk. "Yes. I'm good."

I followed, opting for the second chair rather than walking back around my desk. "You're good?"

"Actually, I'm great," she huffed, shaking her head, then lifted her left hand to show me.

For the second time in less than a week, I was staring at an unexpected wedding ring.

My hands flew to my mouth. "Oh my God."

"I know." A huge smile claimed her features and she shook her head like she couldn't believe it. "I know. We're married. I'm married. To a baker in Germany."

"Holy cow. What are you going to do? Are you moving to Germany?"

She shook her head. "No."

"Is he moving here?"

"No."

"No?"

"No. We're just . . ." she shrugged, laughing, "we're going to make it work."

Camille and I traded awestruck smiles, with me finally breaking the silence. "I'm so happy for you."

"Thank you," she said on a rush, grabbing my hand. "Thank you for saying that. My family thinks I'm crazy. I think I'm crazy. But I love him. I feel like I've found my soulmate. I couldn't just walk away."

I nodded, my eyes stinging, my throat tight as I rasped. "I get that."

"Oh, sweet Marie," she pulled me into a sitting hug over the arms of the chairs, "your guy is out there. Believe me, he is. He might be in Germany baking bread, or South America making music, or Ethiopia acting as a tour guide, but he's somewhere."

*Or in Chicago, building robots.*

I smiled against the onslaught of threatening tears; God, how I *hated* it when people said those words to me. Saying, *your guy is out there* to someone without his or her person is like telling an *X-Files* fan that you have proof of aliens, but you can't share it.

*Thanks for nothing.*

"Yeah, maybe."

"No," she pulled away, ensnaring my gaze with hers, "he is. I promise. And when you find him, be open to it. Don't use obstacles as a reason to walk the other way. Open that door when he knocks. Be brave."

I sniffled, pressing my lips together and shaking my head. "What if it isn't bravery? What if it's recklessness? How will I know the difference?"

Her mouth hitched to the side and she laughed lightly. "When you figure out the answer to that, let me know."

***

I WAS WORKING from home Friday afternoon, submerged in a research rabbit hole, when I glanced absentmindedly at my phone. I did a double take.

Matt had texted me.

**Matt**: *Dinner tonight? Kerry and Marcus are here.*

I stared at the text, reading it over and over. Finding no hidden message, no secret confession of longing.

My heart deflated.

*Whomp, whomp.*

Nevertheless, I responded.

**Marie:** *Sure, sounds good. What time? And where?*
**Matt:** *7:30, Alinea, Lincoln Park*

*Fancy.*

Alinea was quite the swanky destination restaurant and even boasted a celebrity chef. Reservations were notoriously difficult to come by.

Glancing down at my leggings and tunic, I knew I'd have to change. And probably shower. And wear a bra.

I stared at his last text for a full minute, debating whether or not I should return his message. I also thought about typing crazy things like, *I miss you.*

But I wouldn't, and I didn't.

Instead, I closed my laptop and went to take a shower. My track record being what it was, I knew it would take me several hours of trying on clothes before I finally gave up and settled on the least of all evils.

It turned out the least of all evils was a dress I'd completely forgotten about. I'd bought it for $50—a Donna Karan originally worth over $500—at a rack sale, but it was one size too small at the time. Slipping it on, I discovered I'd lost weight. I guess a few weeks of chaotic feelings and grief can do that.

The dress was sky-blue silk, sleeveless with a scoop neck. It had a round, flowy skirt that ended mid-thigh and was slightly longer in the back than in the front. Typically, I'd never wear anything this short for no other reason than I usually didn't like short skirts on myself. However, when I paired it with red silk heels, I really liked how I looked in it.

I left my hair wavy around my shoulders and makeup-ed the hell out of my face. I loved makeup. I'd always loved makeup. But I rarely took the time to really do it right. Tonight was one of those nights. Full-on mask: lip stain, eyeliner, doing everything but false eyelashes. I even painted my nails red to match my shoes and lips.

The late summer evening was warm enough that I didn't think I'd need a sweater, so I didn't bring one. Grabbing my clutch, I left my apartment ten minutes late and decided to take a taxi instead of the L to make up the time.

The closer the cab got to the restaurant the more tension gathered in my stomach. By the time I pulled up and paid the driver, I was feeling markedly jittery. So when the car door opened without me opening it, I sucked in a startled breath as my eyes shot to the person standing on the curb.

Matt bent and peeked his head inside, his eyes ensnaring mine, sending spiky, prickly hot sensations all through my body. His hair was—as usual—askew, so I knew he'd been shoving his fingers into it all day.

He also wore a suit and a small, happy smile.

He was so handsome.

I held my breath because I was afraid my feelings were going to fall out of me, tumble all over the inside of the cab, and make a mess of my makeup.

"Valkyrie," he said, his smile spreading as he offered me his hand.

"Professor," I said on an exhale, lost in his warm gaze. I took his hand, and a spark raced up my arm at the contact.

"Thank you for coming." Helping me out of the cab, he closed the door behind me but didn't release my hand.

"Thanks for inviting me."

"You're always invited. To everything," came Matt's quick reply, said with his trademark sincerity, the kind that made my heart flip.

*Unfair.*

*So unfair.*

His gaze made no detour from mine as he led me to the restaurant. "I was waiting for you. They're inside already and ordered drinks, but I didn't know if you'd want a margarita or a lemon drop so they ordered you both."

"Oh," I said, suddenly nervous at the thought of meeting his ex. I hadn't been nervous about it until just that moment, given my focus had been on seeing Matt again. "Am I dressed okay? I've never been here before."

Matt blinked, tearing his gaze from mine for the first time since I arrived, as though not yet having noticed what I was wearing. Then he blinked again and his lips parted as his gaze traveled over me.

"Yes," he finally said, turning his attention to the approaching maître d'. "You look fine."

"Fine?" I asked, glancing down at myself, doubting the dress for the first time since slipping it on earlier.

"You see," the muscle at his jaw ticked, "I'm not allowed to say you look delicious, or hot, or enticing, or sexy, or fucking gorgeous, or any of the other thoughts I'm currently having. So, yes. You look fine."

*Well.*

That stunned me speechless, as if I wasn't already contending with a riot of feelings.

Gaping at his profile as he placed my hand into the crook of his elbow, I allowed him to lead me through the restaurant, following the maître d'. My heart was racing and I was having . . . too many thoughts.

Some of my thoughts were about his suit. It was a damn fine suit. Damn. Fine.

But most of my thoughts were about not acting like a crazy person.

*Pull it together, Marie. He's attracted to you. This is not news. He did want to sleep with you in New York, remember?*

He didn't look at me again, but I did notice he scowled at a few tables as we passed, eventually placing his arm around my waist and tucking me against his side. I tried not to let myself notice how much I missed this, his touch, his closeness.

*Him.*

So I forced myself to focus on the interior of the restaurant. It was atypical in design. Instead of one big open room, it had multiple floors with smaller rooms. Each table was like the perfect table at my coffee shop; set off to the side, allowing for privacy and encouraging conversation. The walls, screens, and tablecloths were lavender and beige, which shouldn't have worked, but it did. Giving the small rooms an unobtrusive, open feeling without being stark.

We approached a table by the window on the second floor, where a man and woman sat holding hands and sipping cocktails. Upon spotting Matt, the woman stood, her lively eyes moving to mine as a smile split her face.

"You're Marie," she announced, coming around the table to shake my hand.

I nodded, returning her grin and finding that—even though Matt's earlier words had thrown me for a loop—smiling at this woman felt easy. "Kerry."

"Yes." Her plush, purple painted lips widened over large, straight white teeth; her light brown, almost golden eyes were wide and rimmed with striking black lashes. Her skin held a smooth tan with a hint of rose, like she loved spending time in the sun, and she had a sprinkling of freckles on her nose and cheeks. Her hair matched her lips, dark purple, straight and glossy, cut into a stylish bob. "It's so great to finally meet you," she said warmly. Her other hand came up so she was cradling mine in both of hers as her gaze moved over my face with open interest.

"You too," I said, meaning it. Maybe I hadn't consciously thought as much, but seeing her now, I realized I'd been enormously curious about this woman.

Who could be indifferent to the sexiness that was Matt? Who wouldn't want to have hot sex with this man? How was that possible? His brain made me want to strip naked half the time, and his goodness made me want to strip naked the other half of the time.

So, naked with Matt all the time was basically want I wanted.

*Missionary once a week? Was she crazy?*

"Hi, I'm Marcus," came a male voice to my right. I turned and accepted the handshake he offered. The first thing I noticed about him was his height. He was tall. Really, really tall and lanky. His hair was dyed fire-engine red, styled in a curly, lopsided Mohawk. His eyes were dark brown, his face was remarkably attractive in a classical that's-a-handsome-man kind of way.

"Nice to meet you. I'm Marie."

"Yes. We know." Marcus let my hand go and sent his wife a furtive glance. "Matt hasn't stopped talking about you since we landed."

"Let's sit." Matt had moved around me and pulled out my chair.

"Oh, thank you." I sat, noticing after he pushed it in that he was sitting across from me. Marcus and Kerry were on my right and left respectively.

The maître d' laid a napkin in my lap and then left us.

Kerry placed her hand near my plate to draw my attention. "Matt told us how you two met. I think that's the best first-date story I've ever heard."

My attention flickered to Matt. His eyes were on me as he took a sip from his drink. I assumed it was tequila, neat, because that's what he always drank.

"You mean where he gave me a fake name? That wasn't technically a date."

A guilty, but remarkably unapologetic smile spread over his features, his eyes twinkling back at me. "It was a date. And you were doing some light reading, as I recall."

I chuckled. "That's right. Reading is a hobby of mine."

Matt laughed at that and so did our tablemates, which clued me in to the fact that he must've already shared the name of the book I'd had with me.

"Our first date was boring in comparison." Kerry gestured to her husband. "We went to an art gallery, then made out on the beach."

"You call that boring?" Marcus asked, sounding amused and offended.

"Well, in comparison to Marquis de Sade and a social behavioral deception study, I'd say the evening was pretty tame." Kerry gave Marcus a saucy grin.

"How did you two meet?" I spotted two cocktails by my plate—a lemon drop and margarita Matt had alluded to earlier—and selected the lemon drop, deciding the fortifying warmth of vodka was preferable to the loose-limbed spiciness of tequila.

"Matt set us up." Marcus sent Matt a grin.

I almost choked on my cocktail, but swallowed just in time, rasping, "Matt set you up?"

"Marcus worked at the Starbucks near my office. He and I got to talking one day about automation." Matt's eyes were on his drink.

"You know, how robots will be doing the jobs of all humans in a few years?" Marcus shot me a teasing grin. "The subject turned to creativity and whether art is unique to the human experience. He said something about an AI that can compose original music. I told him I was a painter, and we talked about how difficult it was to teach an artificial intelligence about art appreciation, or humor, or other qualities that are inherently human."

But I was still stuck on the *Matt set up his ex-wife with her current husband* part, so I repeated, "Matt set you up?"

"Yeah, and we were still married at the time. Separated, but still married." Kerry nodded, giving me a funny look, which was when I realized I'd allowed the full extent of my surprise to show on my face.

Swallowing, I glanced down at my plate to gather my composure, and laughed lightly.

"So, Matt brings Kerry into the Starbucks one day . . ." Marcus continued to tell his story, and I gave him my attention, but I was only half listening.

I mean . . . *what?*

That's weird, right?

Matt hadn't followed through setting me up with Dr. Merek—and we were only friends—but he set up his *wife at the time* with another man? While they were still married?

I glanced at Matt and found him watching me with a thoughtful but peculiar expression, which I imagined mirrored mine.

The fact was, I thought I knew him. I thought he'd shared so much of himself with me over the last few months. But at times like these I wondered if I would ever truly know him.

One thing was for certain; I doubted I would ever understand him.

# CHAPTER 23

**BenevolentAI**

*A machine learning AI that can draw inferences about what it has learned. In particular, it can process natural language and formulate new ideas from what it reads. Its job is to sift through vast chemical libraries, medical databases and conventionally presented scientific papers, looking for potential drug molecules.*

Source: BenevolentBio

**THE SERVER TOOK** our dinner orders while we shared easy and friendly conversation.

Over dinner, Kerry told a few bizarre and uncomfortably funny stories about working with AI engineers. For example, she had a female colleague who'd named her AI "Bitch" and would say things like: "Bitch, what time is it?" and "Bitch, I asked you a question." And she had a male colleague who'd named his AI "Disappointment."

While laughing at one of Marcus's stories about purposefully getting people's names wrong on their Starbucks cups, I realized that I really liked both of these people.

Kerry reminded me of Matt. A lot. She had a naïveté about her that was exactly him. For example, the way she asked questions, which often felt like overly personal non sequiturs. Also, like Matt, I got the sense she didn't realize some of her questions were inappropriate for having known me less than two hours.

*Where do you buy your bras? Do you want to get married? Why do you think men like doggy style? Do you like doggy style? Is that your real hair color?*

Once I made the connection—that she and Matt shared this peculiarity—her questions didn't catch me off guard quite as much.

Whereas Marcus reminded me of my brother, Abram. They were both artists—Abram was a musician, Marcus was a painter—and I could sense the tender heart beneath the sardonic façade, especially in the way he looked at his wife.

The server had just removed our dinner plates and brought me my fourth lemon drop when the conversation turned to Matt's decision to move to Chicago last December.

"Matt hated working for corporate. He'd prefer to be a hero and take a huge pay cut, which I call the do-gooder tax." Kerry sneered at Matt, like he or his decisions smelled bad.

"Why do you hate corporate? The politics?" I guessed. The haze of alcohol made looking at him easier.

He shook his head, glancing from his tequila to me. "Politics are just as bad in academia. Maybe even worse."

"Then why?"

"Because of the, what's that phrase you use all the time?" Kerry poked at Matt. "Not broken enough culture?"

My eyes locked on Matt's and he nodded once, holding my gaze captive. "That's right. I call it not broken enough."

I knew he was thinking back on our dinner in New York, when I'd referred to Zara's lack of motivation to change her circumstances as "not broken enough." I hadn't said it at the time, but I viewed Matt the same way, choosing the safety of crutches and Band-Aids rather than the risk of actually loving someone.

"Broken? Referring to what?" I questioned, ignoring the wake of goosebumps tickling my skin.

Matt returned his attention to the table. "It's their mentality, the 'It's not broken enough' mentality of for-profit companies."

"What do you mean?" Marcus asked.

"It means he's a snob," Kerry grumbled. "A nerd purist."

I licked the sugar off the rim of my lemon drop, glancing between the three of them.

"It means, in corporate America," Matt's gaze darted to my mouth, then away, then to his friend, "there is no benefit to solving a problem or finding the best solution to a problem. There is only benefit—monetary benefit—in making a problem less irritating, or less pressing. This is because if a company actually solves a problem, or solves it with the best solution, the company will ultimately lose money."

"Give me an example," I asked, taking another sip of my drink.

"I can give you hundreds. Take dating websites for example. Every time they successfully pair a couple, they've lost two customers. Therefore, it's in their best interest to find the sweet spot of maximizing profit—by not pairing too many couples successfully too quickly—and being just slightly better than their competitors. Dr. Merek and I theorize, though we cannot prove it because we haven't been given access to this data set, that these dating websites are using the same psychology that's used by casinos to keep people coming back. Meaning, they match people even if they're not *actually* a match, with random actual matches thrown in so customers have some good experiences, but not too many to actually pair someone."

"It's like that experiment with those pigeons and the button, where pressing the button would randomly give the pigeons food." I made the comparison to Skinner's famous experiment in the 1960s, noting that my words were starting to slur.

"Yes. Exactly. Casinos use that psychology with great success, as do most other for-profit companies, if they're smart. Facebook's algorithms don't show you what you want to see; they don't show you what you've explicitly *told* them you want to see. They show you what will keep you on their site for the longest period of time, so they can display as many ads as possible. For every one post you're interested in, you're shown thirty shitty updates. We're all the pigeon, scrolling through our newsfeed for a random nugget of food."

"Ugh. That's depressing. You're depressing. Boo."

Kerry sent me a big grin. "Did you just *boo* Matt?"

"Yes, I did."

She giggled.

Matt's gaze warmed as it moved over me and he bit his bottom lip briefly before continuing. "It makes us good consumers, and suspicious of solutions that actually work. Think about it. Drug companies make billions selling products that manage symptoms. But how many actual cures or preventative agents come from Big Pharma? Whereas, how many cures or preventative agents have come from government-funded research or through non-profit patient-advocacy groups?"

"The March of Dimes funded the polio vaccine research, right?" Marcus asked.

"That's right," I confirmed. "I've been researching the origins of vaccines for a series I'm working on."

"So this is why Matt left his cushy corner office in sunny Palo Alto for his cramped office in windy Chicago." Marcus grinned at his friend.

"And cheerfully pays the do-gooder tax," Kerry added, tossing back the last of her margarita with flourish.

Matt smiled at his ex, rolling his eyes at her good-naturedly. "We all pay eventually. I'd prefer to pay with cash now rather than my soul later."

"Ouch." She gripped her chest, mock-wincing. "Be careful, Matt. You might force me to leave and cry on my big pile of money."

"So you're not taking the job offer with Gamble?" I asked before I thought too carefully about the question.

Matt's gaze cut to mine, surprise flashed behind his eyes, and he frowned.

"Who told you about the job offer?" He sounded irritated.

"Um, Fiona did."

"When?" he demanded, his eyes somehow both wide and narrowed.

"Three weeks ago, I guess." I shrugged, waving away the topic because—even with the numbing cushion of alcohol sustaining my spirits—I still felt a pang of hurt that he hadn't told me about it himself.

His attention dropped to the table and he looked like he was doing calculations in his head, or trying to solve a puzzle, or sifting through memories.

"Let's go dancing." Kerry tapped the table with her fingertips. "Is that possible? Can we do that? Is there a place to go?"

"Yes. There are lots of places." I pushed the remainder of my drink aside, deciding it was best if I cut myself off from the teat of liquid recklessness. "What do you like? Club music or what?"

"How about eighties? Do you know a place like that?" she asked excitedly.

"Yes. I do." I licked my lips of the residual sugar, deciding to take them to Club Outrageous, a club that switched themes every season. I remembered my friend telling me that the summer theme was yuppie chic of the eighties.

"Cool. Let me run to the restroom and we'll take our car. It's a limo, so there's room for all of us," Kerry whispered as she stood. "Do you need to go?"

I shook my head. "No, thank you."

Marcus stood. "I'll go with you."

My mind was still on the logistics of dancing as Kerry and Marcus departed. Quinn's company handled the security of Club Outrageous. All I'd need to do to gain entrance was drop Quinn's name.

I glanced at Matt, again finding him watching me.

Maybe it was all the sugar and vodka and good food flowing through my system, or maybe it was the dark, intent look in his eyes. Or maybe it was all the pent-up emotional, intellectual, and sexual frustration I'd been carrying around, hiding from him for weeks.

Who can say what inspired my recklessness?

All I knew was, I wasn't feeling cautious as I leaned forward, slowly licked my lips, and found his foot under the table with mine. I then slid the pointed toe of my shoe up the back of his calf.

His eyes flared, his eyebrows hitching subtly with surprise.

"Do you like to dance?" I asked, sounding husky to my ears. If I'd been totally sober, I would have had a hard time keeping a straight face.

But, I wasn't.

Inhibitions were lowered.

And he was in a suit.

And I was in a dress.

"I'd like to dance with *you*," he responded, lowering his hand beneath the table and catching my ankle, his hot palm cutting through the warm fog of inebriation.

He'd touched me before, but this was different. This touch felt intentional in a new way, like the difference between a high five and a caress.

"Do you know how?" I teased, feeling breathless as his fingers lightly skimmed halfway up my calf. "Or will I have to show you?"

"I know how," he said easily with dark confidence. "But I'd also like you to show me."

\*\*\*

MATT HELD MY hand as we left the restaurant, both of us making a pit stop at the restrooms prior to leaving, which earned a reprimand from Kerry.

"We could have all gone together and saved time. It would have been more efficient," she said, earning her a quizzical smile from her husband, like he thought she was cute.

I gave directions to the driver, although he indicated he knew where it was.

Once in the limo, Matt and I sat next to each other, his arm resting along the back of the bench seat behind me. Kerry and Marcus sat across from us in a mirrored position and we spoke of random topics—movies, books, advances in AI technology—during the short drive.

As I suspected, gaining entrance to Club Outrageous wasn't a problem. In fact, I recognized the bouncer as one of Quinn's security team, Stan Willis. He was a nice guy who'd done his best to provide unobtrusive security to Janie and all her friends during Janie's bachelorette party in Vegas.

Things hadn't gone as planned, but that's a different story.

However, the shenanigans in Vegas did mean Stan remembered me. As soon as he saw me, I smiled and he stiffened.

"Marie." I saw his mouth form my name. He stood, stepping away from the other bouncer as I approached.

"Hey, Stan." Waving, I gave him my biggest smile, seeing that the line to enter was wrapped around the block. "Do you think you can get us in?" I asked as soon as I was within earshot, a club mix of "Funkytown" booming from the building behind him.

"Yeah, yeah. Absolutely." He backed up a few steps, opening the latch for the velvet ropes. "How many people you got?"

"Four." I turned, planning on motioning my companions forward, but Matt was standing directly behind me.

"Okay, I need wrists." Stan's eyes moved over Matt, then he reached behind the podium, extracting four armbands. "And I'll radio the guys inside, have them open up a VIP booth for you."

"Hey, thanks."

"No problem. Tell Mrs. Sullivan I say hi."

Matt stepped to the side, allowing Kerry to go after me, then Marcus, and then he extended his own wrist, and we were good to go.

I still felt a little hazy from my four lemon drops, and also from the way Matt continued to either hold my hand or pull me close to his side, so I didn't take much note of our surroundings. To my mind, it looked like any other high-end dance club, with flashing lights, loud music, and a lot of bodies.

But Kerry and Marcus seemed to be pleased, grinning and dancing their way over to the bar area. Matt and I followed, and I made a mental note to drink only water from this point forward.

A server dressed in hot-pink leggings and an off-the-shoulder sweater approached us just as we reached the bar. "Are you Marie Harris, party of four?"

"That's right." I nodded.

"Okay, come with me." She waved us forward and began walking toward an area blocked off from the rest of the club with another velvet rope.

Beyond the rope was a half flight of stairs that led to a corridor with doors on one side and the wall at the back of the club on the other. We walked past several doors until we reached the very last one.

"Here, this one is for you. Your party is the first to use this room as it was just finished being redecorated this week. And please accept the champagne on the house." She smiled brightly and handed me a slip of paper. "Here's your access code. You can enter directly from the dance floor, but you have to type in the code. If you want drinks, just press the red button on the side of the table. Enjoy."

The server motioned for us to enter and we dutifully did so, trading perplexed but pleased glances. Inside was a small-ish room with dark velvet thickly cushioned couches lining the walls. Tables were on either end and another table was in the middle of the space. On top of the table was a champagne bucket, bottle, and four glasses. Just as she'd said, a red button was in the center of the table.

"This place is awesome." Kerry turned to me abruptly once we drew even with the table.

I noticed another door on the wall facing out toward the dance floor. Both the wall and door appeared to be made of reflective glass or high quality Plexiglass, which allowed the room's inhabitants to look out over the dance floor, but which—I guessed—obscured the room from the partygoers outside of it.

I glanced at the access code, then passed it to Matt, who read it and passed it to Marcus. Kerry was opening the champagne while checking out the lay of the club beyond the room. The music was muted, not nearly as loud as it had been in the main club, but Marcus found a switch on the wall that increased the volume or lowered it.

"It's dark in here," Kerry remarked, lifting her chin toward me. "Do you want some champagne?"

"No. I'm good. I think I might go find some water."

"Should I press the button?" Matt asked, like the button was magic. *Blarg! Must he be so cute? Must he?*

I realized my sobriety was returning faster than I'd expected, and with my sobriety came awareness of how close he was standing to me. "No, it's fine. I'll go grab it from the bar."

"Let me go," Matt offered, leading me to one of the velvet couches and encouraging me to sit. He bent and brushed a kiss at the corner of my mouth, holding my gaze as he stood and untangled our fingers. "I'll be right back with waters for everyone."

Kerry deposited her champagne on the table, "I'll go with you. I'm supposed to convince you to take that job."

"It's not going to happen." Matt shook his head at her, opening the door for his ex, loud music from the club spilling into our little room.

I didn't catch what she said as they left, but I thought it sounded like, "I don't expect it to." Or something like that.

Once the door shut, the sound from beyond once again muted, leaving me alone with Marcus and the poured glasses of champagne.

He was wandering around the room, as though looking for more switches. "Do you think there's a light switch?"

"I think there must be. Why? Is it too dark?" Some of my earlier unease was reemerging now that the alcohol was leaving my system.

Had I really played footsie with Matt at the restaurant?

And why did I feel *mostly* obstinately pleased about it, rather than concerned?

"Nah." He turned from his search and reclined on the couch across from mine. "Just curious. This is comfortable. I want one of these."

I examined him, thinking, *he doesn't look like the kind of guy who's going to be happy with once-a-week missionary.*

Yeah, it was a weird thought.

But it was also true.

Marcus seemed laid-back, but he was clearly smitten with his wife.

And before I could stop myself, I said, "I can't believe how cool you are about Kerry and Matt spending time together."

Marcus shrugged. "Why wouldn't I be?"

"Aren't you concerned about residual feelings? They were married for a while, right?"

"Six years I think. Maybe seven."

"Exactly."

"The answer is, no. I'm not worried. Not at all. They still care about each other, I know they do, but it's purely platonic. Like, waaaay platonic. He's not hot for her and I *guarantee*, she's not hot for him."

"How do you know?" I agreed with him based on what I'd witnessed thus far, but perversely, I wanted his perspective. *Needed his perspective.*

"Dudes know."

That made me chuckle. "Sorry. That's not going to cut it."

Marcus inspected me as though debating whether or not I was trustworthy. Seemingly making his decision, he sat up on the couch and leaned forward, elbows on his knees. "Okay. So, you didn't hear this from me, but Kerry told me, during the last few years of their marriage, they didn't have sex. And before that, they only did the deed—like—once a month."

I blinked once, slowly. "That's it?"

Matt had said they were indifferent to each other, and watching them over the course of the evening I saw mutual respect and admiration, but I hadn't seen any signs of longing. So I didn't know why I was pushing this issue now.

Other than maybe . . . I was trying to understand Matt better. And here was a rare opportunity with someone who had access to the inside scoop.

"Yeah. That's it."

"No, I mean, that's why you think their feelings are platonic? Matt said they were both too busy, they never saw each other. Of course they weren't humping like rabbits, they didn't get a chance."

Marcus was already shaking his head before I finished. "Her schedule isn't any different now than it was then, and we've been together going on three years. I see her every night. Sure, she might get home late or work most weekends, but if she's in town, I see her every day. And whenever we see each other, we're humping like rabbits."

I caught myself mid-eye-roll, instead closing my eyes and sighing.

"I'm telling you," he continued unprompted, "neither of them wanted to do it with *each other*. Neither could relinquish control. The way she tells it, he's a boss in the bedroom, and so is she—which is *fine by me*. But it didn't work for them. It's no fun fucking a control freak if you're a control freak. What he needs is someone who'll lie back and enjoy the ride," he finished with a suggestive grin, though it wasn't pointed at me. Clearly, he was thinking of himself and his wife.

Embarrassingly, my muscles had tightened when Marcus said, "he's a boss in the bedroom," and my mouth had grown inexplicably dry.

I lifted my eyes and found Marcus giving me a speculative look. "You two never . . . ?"

In comparison to Kerry's earlier questions about doing it doggy style, I considered Marcus's indirect question now relatively tame.

Yet I still felt a measure of embarrassment when I shook my head. "We're just friends."

He looked not exactly surprised, more like I'd revealed something critical about myself. "Huh."

"What?"

"You dig him, right?"

"Am I that obvious?"

"No. You're not, actually." He chuckled. "That was a blind guess. Matt said you're the kindest person he's ever met. Friendly with everyone. I can't get a read on you one way or the other." He shook his head, then added under his breath, "But he is."

That had me sitting straighter in my seat. "Matt? Is what?"

"Nah-ah. I'm not selling him out."

"Matt? Selling Matt out?"

Marcus pressed his lips together, crossing his arms and shaking his head.

I was about to threaten him with a champagne bottle-related injury when I spotted Kerry walking up the stairs to the room, Matt trailing behind her; they both held four water bottles.

Marcus stood to open the door, giving me a teasing look and shaking his head, mouthing, "I'm not telling."

"Oh man, we have to go dance. I demand we dance for the next two hours!" Kerry dumped the bottles on the couch where Marcus had been sitting, then grabbed his hand and pulled him out of the room.

Meanwhile, Matt strolled in after her, moved to the side as she tugged Marcus out, and then crossed to one of the tables next to where I was sitting. He deposited three bottles on the table and uncapped the fourth, handing it to me.

"Thank you." I stood, accepted it, and took several long gulps.

Matt turned and pulled off his jacket, discarding it to the cushion behind me. He then loosened his tie, which drew my attention.

"Oh, that's the tie I got you." I glanced between him and it, shocked I hadn't noticed it before now.

He nodded and laid it reverently on top of his jacket, undoing the top two buttons of his shirt. "You said to wear it when I needed good luck."

Nothing about his comment sounded offhanded, and my stomach fluttered accordingly.

I took another drink from the bottle, eyeing him. "Did you need luck tonight?" I cursed the slight tremor in my voice.

He nodded, shoving his hands in his pockets, considering me for a beat before admitting quietly, "I'm glad you came."

"Me too," I agreed quickly, bringing the bottle back to my lips and scowling at it when no water emerged. I studied its contents, realizing it was empty, then laughed at myself. "I guess I was thirsty."

Matt's smile was small and his nod was subtle. Despite the mass of bodies clearly visible beyond the wall of glass, or perhaps because of them, their frenzied movement in comparison to the stillness between us, the moment felt loud with significance and tension.

My anxiety returned, mostly because I didn't truly regret playing footsie with Matt. And therefore, since I didn't regret it, I felt anxious about what I might do next.

Setting the empty bottle on the table, I turned and gazed at the huge dance floor. The lights had just dimmed beyond the glass, leaving our little room darker.

Thoughts like, *maybe you can have one night together, where is the harm in that?* kept floating through my mind, seducing me with the fantasy and provocative flashes of images. My lungs had difficulty drawing in enough air.

"Marie?" Matt asked from directly behind me, and I couldn't help but think, *this would be a great place to have hot sex. We should totally do that.*

A short intro on drums followed by a solo saxophone playing a familiar melody reverberated over the speakers. I recognized the song, but couldn't immediately place it, as I was too busy talking myself into making a move on him.

"Yes?" My skin felt too tight, so when I felt Matt's fingers in my hair, pushing it to the side, I released a surprised—yet not surprised—breath.

He bent to my ear, whispering, "We have to dance to this. Come on."

"What?" I glanced over my shoulder and tracked him with my eyes as he came around me, grabbing my hand. Perplexed and disappointed, I let him lead me out the door, to the dance floor, where the music was much louder and George Michael had just begun crooning.

Matt pulled me through the throng of bodies, then stopped near the center of the crowd. He encouraged my arms around his neck and placed his hands on my waist, pasting our bodies together.

We swayed to the music and I tilted my head back, watching with wonder as the nut began lip-syncing along with George Michael. Not only did he lip-sync, he lip-synced *with feeling* to "Careless Whisper" by Wham!

I giggled at his theatrics and his face split with a giant grin. I'd forgotten how funny he was. I loved this about him. My heart squeezed.

Spinning me out to one side, then twisting me toward him, my back connected with his front. His arms wrapped around my middle, his nose and lips nuzzling my neck and ear, his hips leading mine in an expert, sensual sway.

And that's when I realized that Matt Simmons actually knew how to dance.

Like, *really* knew how to dance.

He had fantastic rhythm.

His feet weren't guilty.

And moves. He had impressively good moves.

He was such a good dancer that he didn't even appear to be thinking about it, like it was second nature. His hands smoothed from my shoulders down my arms, his fingers threading with my hands and lifting them, encouraging me to face him again as he returned them to his neck. All the while, still mouthing the words and moving his body as though it was an extension of the music, and therefore so was I.

Damn.

He was sexy.

The first iteration of the chorus drew to a close and the saxophone took over. Matt's smile slowly waned as we gazed at each other, his hands sliding deliberately from my sides to my lower back. His dark eyes dropped to my mouth, heated, his lips parted, and he inclined his head just an inch closer.

I could only stare at him, feeling both paralyzed and caught by the thrilling yet terrifying current of his intent.

Terrifying because this was Matt. My crutch. My crush. My mountain of unrequited feelings. My friend who wasn't really my friend, who I had non-friendly thoughts about.

All.

The.

Time.

I thought of him, of cuddling with him, of how he felt beneath my fingers, behind me, his lips on my neck . . .

*He's going to kiss me,* the flare of panic only serving to intensify the sensations thickening my blood, sending me head-first into a spiral of confusion and desire.

If I gave in to this, surrendered to this thing between us, it wouldn't be bravery.

It would be recklessness.

# CHAPTER 24

### Iamus

*A bio-inspired technology for music composition and synthetization of music, where computers do not mimic musicians, but develop their own style (with no human intervention).*

Source: Melomics Media

**HIS LIPS BRUSHED** mine. Just a soft whisper. It felt like a test.

It also felt like torture. He was torturing me.

Unable to endure his gentleness, I lifted my chin and dug my nails into the back of his neck, fusing our mouths together.

With feeling.

And that seemed to be all the encouragement he needed.

Abruptly, everything about him turned fierce, with biting teeth and devouring tongue. His strong arms wrapped around my body, as though to trap me, as he plundered my mouth in the most exquisite of all kisses.

Holy crap.

HOLY CRAP.

He was a great kisser.

I was dizzy with how great this felt, how necessary. Or maybe it was the lack of air. I didn't know. All I knew was that we were just going to have to keep kissing for the rest of our lives and that was that.

And *plunder* was exactly the right word. He lifted his head, sucking on my lip, tasting me anew, groaning when I responded with enthusiasm, tightening his hold when I shifted against him, licking and stroking the inside of my mouth. The twisting ache in my abdomen became overwhelming.

And yet . . . I wanted to be sure he was enjoying himself. I wanted to make sure he was feeling the same fireworks of arousal and wonder that were igniting in my chest. So I endeavored to give, and give, and give.

And then the tempo changed. Both the music and the rhythm of his kiss. The bass kicked up, strumming and thumping, long, savoring beats, reverberating through my chest, steady and intoxicating.

We were moving. Matt moved me backward, still kissing, his mouth on my neck, my jaw, biting and tasting and sucking my skin with impatience and hunger. His fingers dug into my shoulders and backside, his hold on the brink of painful. Likewise, I tried to mirror his movements, kissing his neck, wanting him to feel as desperately out of control as I did.

He steered us while we consumed each other, expertly weaving through the crowd, which seemed to instinctively recognize that this was a crisis.

At the stairs, he separated from me and I moaned my discontent, reaching for him. But then he bent, hoisting me over his shoulder, and I gasped.

He climbed the stairs and punched in the four-digit code. Then I heard him curse. "What the fuck is the code?"

"3-4-5-7," I said, laughing with desire-induced hysteria, my arms wrapping around his waist to keep myself steady.

"Thank you," came his short reply, punching in the numbers again, and we were through the door.

I didn't spare a thought for how obvious we were being, not one single thought. Because . . . *whoremones*.

Instead I began frantically pulling his shirt from his pants. And when he set me on the ground, I frantically undid the buckle of his belt. His hands were at the back of my dress, searching for the zipper while our mouths mated.

"Damn it," he breathed against my lips just as I released his buckle, winning the getting-the-other-person-more-naked race.

Unbuttoning his pants, I shoved my hand down the front of his boxers.

"Marie, fuck." Hissing, Matt pushed himself into my palm, a reflexive movement. Momentarily paralyzed, his forehead met mine and I saw him struggle, battling for control.

He felt so good, so right, so thick and hard and long and big and smooth and hot. The want in me clawed, demanding, obliterating caution, silencing what was left of reason, yet the desire to please him was just as strong, if not stronger.

I . . . worried.

Although I'd never felt so certain I would perish without satisfaction, I fretted that *I* wouldn't be able to provide what he needed in return. And so I rubbed my body against his, impetuously seeking friction and sensation and touch, hoping to communicate to him that I wanted to be an instrument of his satisfaction as well.

But then in the next moment, he yanked my hand away, holding my wrists hostage at my sides, and walked me backward, his mouth once again capturing mine for a starving kiss. Like I was the answer. Like all his hunger would end if he'd just kiss me long enough.

My calves hit the couch and the strength of his advancing momentum sent me downward, my bottom hitting the velvet sofa, jarring me. He followed, kneeling on the floor, placing my arms around his neck while in the next moment his fingers slid under my dress. His thumbs gliding along the interior of my thighs, he parted my legs, making me tremble.

"Let me touch you," I begged, spreading myself wider for him as I moved to the edge of the couch. His fingertips inched higher. I gasped, the throbbing want built within me, becoming brutal and demanding. "I want to make you feel good."

"Lie back," he instructed, brushing his knuckles against my center, rubbing me teasingly through the lace of my panties.

I shuddered, unable to comply. My nails were anchored to his shoulders. I whimpered, "Please, Matt. Please. I need you to feel good, too."

A tremor overtook him, followed by a desperate growl as he hooked his fingers into my underwear and tugged them down my legs. His movements were urgent, lacking finesse.

But it was perfect, the sign I craved. His frenetic desire was perfect as it heightened mine.

"Take off your dress," he demanded, removing his outer shirt, leaving him in his white tee.

I had to lean forward, clumsily reaching for, then finding the pull of my zipper under my arm. Once it was undone, his hands were there, pushing it over my head and tossing it to where his jacket and tie were, discarded ages ago.

He pulled me forward by wrapping one strong arm around my waist, nipping and suckling my breasts through my bra. Laying me back on the couch atop his dress shirt, he tugged one strap of my bra down my shoulder, exposing me, sliding his hand around to unhook it as his mouth both worshipped and tortured my body with decadent kisses and bites.

"Take this off." He tugged at the loose bra.

Matt's large hands squeezed and massaged and fondled while I pulled the offending garment down my arms, then lifted his T-shirt, needing the feel of him, wanting his skin flush against mine.

He leaned back, evading me, his eyes blazing a trail over my bare skin as I instinctively covered myself. He pulled my arms away from my body, his unapologetic gaze moving from my breasts to my stomach, then lower, licking his lips.

"Matt," I pleaded.

His eyes lifted to mine abruptly, hooded and sharp, as if gripped by a sudden thought, an acute obsession. He leaned forward, his hand moving between my legs, parting me, stroking me.

I cried out at the contact I craved, rolling my hips, gripping his strong shoulders for purchase as he demanded on a growl, "This will not be the only time."

I nodded, panting, feeling empty, needing more. I wanted to touch him, stroke him, and drive him mad like he was so expertly doing to me. And the worry persisted, that maybe I couldn't. That somehow the pleasure I could give to him would fall short of his expectations.

"Tell me how badly you want me inside you," he ordered, bending to bite my neck, then soothed the sting with his tongue, adding, "How badly you want me to fuck you."

*Whoa . . . !*

All the air left my lungs in a whoosh at his unexpected sexy talk, my head lolling to the side, offering more of myself. I'd never been a dirty talker, maybe I never had the confidence to do so. But something about it sounded so essential in that moment. So perfect. I *needed* his rough voice. I *needed* the brazen harshness of his words. They calmed the voices of doubt in my head.

"Do you want me, Marie? Because I want you. You're so wet, is that for me?"

I couldn't speak, so I nodded, a keening sound slipping past my lips. His fingers at my center were a gentle contradiction to the ravenous kisses he lavished on my breasts, then stomach, then hip, then lower.

"Do you want my mouth on you? On your pussy? I can't wait to taste you."

*God, yes!* The affirmation of his words, of his want, they both soothed and excited me. I couldn't breathe, I could barely see, and my heart galloped between my ears. Every filthy word out of his mouth drove me mad with desire.

Holy shit.

*Who was this guy?*

And who was I?

I watched his progress, the sight of his head moving between my legs, kissing my inner thigh, skimming his lips along the sensitive skin until he parted me with his thumbs.

My toes curled, then pointed, every muscle in my body tense. Usually, I wanted to give head first, to make sure my partner was feeling good.

But as Matt licked me, groaning, his sounds effectively silenced my concerns about his arousal and renewed thoughts of perishing. I might die from pleasure. The flat of his tongue lapped leisurely, tasting, savoring. I moaned. Loudly. I couldn't help it. Convinced I was on the brink of madness, I ached. I hurt. The carnal sounds of his mouth comingling with my hedonistic sighs made me restless.

"I want you," I panted, my fingers in his hair, grabbing and pulling and pushing.

He groaned, slipping two fingers inside me, stroking me in tempo with his tongue.

"Not this way," I implored, reaching for him, clawing at his shirt, determined to take it off this time.

I wanted him face to face, I wanted his body moving against mine, I wanted his grunts and sighs, the tense and release of his muscles.

"Please, please." I was so close, so close. I panicked. I didn't want to be selfish, and coming now felt unfair to him. I wanted *his* pleasure.

He lifted his mouth from me and placed a wet, suckling kiss on the inside of my thigh, trailing his tongue along the skin and breathing on my center.

"Tell me what you want."

He was torturing me again. But damn. It hurt so good.

"I want you inside me." I reached for him.

He evaded me, increasing the tempo of his finger. "I am inside you."

"Please, Matt. Please. Let me—" I groaned, frustrated but wildly aroused by his wickedness.

"You're amazing, so beautiful. Touch yourself." His voice shook slightly as he positioned my hands, one kneading my breast, encouraging me to roll and pinch my nipple, the other replacing his fingers at my center.

I moaned in protest as he moved to stand, so he leaned forward, and whispered in my ear, hot breath and an exorbitant amount of masculine confidence scorching my skin, "Don't stop. Will you let me watch you touch your perfect body? You're so sexy."

Then he stood.

With his eyes on me, and his encouraging words ringing in my ears, I didn't know how much longer I would last. I felt vulnerable, but oddly empowered by my vulnerability. Matt's gaze held mine as he pulled his wallet from his pocket, pulling his shirt from his torso, and then finally shoving down his pants and boxers.

I bit back another moan at the sight of him, my sex clenching, because every inch of him—from his long legs to his mad-scientist hair to his seductive mahogany eyes—was perfect to me.

Deftly, he removed a condom from his wallet and ripped it open, discarding the wrapper and rolling it down his hard length. Then he was on me again, but this time he removed my hands from my body without a word, encouraging me to stand and hold on to his shoulders. His mouth crashed down to mine and he picked me up. My legs bracketed his waist as he turned, sitting on the couch with me straddling him.

Instinctively, I rocked against him, needing the friction, needing the feel of him, and shuddered when I felt his erection nudge against my entrance.

He hissed, grabbed my hips, and held me still. His teeth were clenched as he commanded, "Do you want to ride me? Would that make you feel good?"

I nodded, moaning, shifting restlessly as I used him to stroke myself. Matt released his hold on my hips. With one swift movement he positioned me over him and thrust upward, filling me. I gasped, my nails digging into his skin. He felt so good, so right, so necessary. I wanted this to last; I wanted the feel of him beneath me to last forever.

But then he encouraged me to move, to ride him, splaying his hands on my body as he thrust upward with sinuous deliberateness.

"Oh, God."

"Mmm . . . Do you like that?" He nuzzled my breasts, loving them with soft bites and licks, watching them move and sway with hunger in his gaze as I rolled my hips in time with his.

I liked it. I loved it. Yet I couldn't turn my mind off. I wanted to know it was good for him, too.

"Matt, please—"

"I could spend all day between your legs." His hands grew covetous, massaging, cupping my breasts and tugging at my nipples. His words of praise sent spikes of white-hot heat to my core.

I wanted it to last, to last for him. But it was too late.

I splintered with a fierce cry as he thrust into my body faster and faster as I came, making me bounce on his lap. I bowed toward him, holding on as I tensed and tightened and released and pulsed. My eyes were closed against the overwhelming reality of sensation, riding the wave of pure ecstasy until it became an abyss.

But he was there, catching me before I could fall, wrapping me in his arms and holding me close. Matt laid me back on the cushion, his agile form still moving over mine, still moving inside me.

"You're so lovely," he said.

My eyelashes fluttered open, our eyes mating along with our bodies.

And then he said, "God, Marie. I'm so in love with you."

And I stiffened beneath him. My mouth fell open. I stared at him and his words, spoken so earnestly on an anguished exhale.

Too many thoughts.

Too many feelings.

Too big.

Too much.

A rush, a wave, a tsunami.

The earth moved, at least for me it did, it shifted on its axis and left me feeling unsteady. Dizzy. Euphoric. Terrified.

Meanwhile, Matt also stiffened, his movements abruptly ceasing as he blinked, his eyes flaring with panic, clearly just realizing what he'd said.

And what was just as clear? He'd never meant to say it.

"Fuck." His wide stare moved over my face. I felt him tense, as though he was planning to withdraw.

So I reached for him, I wrapped my legs around his back and held fast to his arms. "No, don't. Please."

I lifted my head, kissing his parted lips, smoothing my hands up his arms to knead his shoulders until I felt his body relax. He groaned into my mouth as I rolled my hips, then he angled his chin away until his forehead met mine, separating our lips. His breathing was erratic and, though he once again moved within me, and my body lifted to meet his rhythm, I could tell he was still fighting the surge of panic.

"You feel amazing," I said, honest in my mindlessness.

The answering tremor in his body told me he liked my words.

The tension at my core built once more. I pushed my fingers into his hair and he answered with an agonized growl. Suddenly, his thrusts became harder, longer, less fluid, and I marveled as his control slipped and then snapped.

A thrill of wonder twisted in my lower belly, spreading to my heart and tightening my throat with emotion as he came, chanting, "I love you."

# CHAPTER 25

### Smart Tissue Autonomous Robot (STAR)

*A robotic arm with an articulated suturing tool and a force sensor to detect the tension in the surgical thread during operation. The arm is equipped with cameras that create a three-dimensional image, to guide the robot as it deploys the tool, and also a thermal-imaging device to help distinguish between similar-looking tissues. The robotic arm is controlled by a computer program with a repertoire of stitches, knots and maneuvers that permits the arm to plan and carry out a procedure, known as anastomosis, which involves sewing together two parts of a bodily tube.*

Source: Children's National Health System

MATT COLLAPSED ON me, yet he still had the mindfulness to support himself on his elbows, depressing the cushion on either side of my face.

But our bodies were pressed together. That was the crucial point.

Meanwhile, I wrapped my arms around his shoulders and my legs around his narrow hips, encouraging him to give me more of his weight.

His labored breathing at my neck sent sparks along my skin, reigniting the embers still so close to the surface.

He loved me.

*He loves you.*

…

…

…

*God, universe, if there's anyone out there, please don't let me fuck this up.*

It wasn't that I considered myself a fuck-up. It's just that I wanted this, him, us, so badly. I wanted *him* to be my person, because he felt so right. He didn't feel perfect, but that just made him feel even more right.

I squeezed him tighter, not wanting the moment to end. I was equal parts thrilled and terrified by the possibility of what would happen next.

"Marie," he whispered against my hair.

"Yes?" I closed my eyes, bracing.

"You're holding me too tight."

"Oh, sorry." I loosened my arms, having to use a mental crowbar in the process.

Taking a deep breath, Matt lifted his head and immediately kissed my mouth, encouraging me to lift my torso so he could slide his arms beneath me.

We kissed. For a long time. We kissed for so long, I became aware of our surroundings again. The dark room, the velvet couch, the still-sparkling glasses of champagne, the glass wall overlooking the dance floor, and the sounds of Cyndi Lauper over the speakers telling me that girls just want to have fun.

I must've been mad. Just a glass wall separated us from hundreds of people, a mere four-digit code separated us from Kerry and Marcus. But I couldn't bring myself to care. Because he was still kissing me, and he loved me, and everything about him felt like the perfect combination of heavenly and sinful.

When he pulled away, his gaze lowered to my mouth, and the look in his eyes was decidedly smug. With impressive fluidness, he lifted himself and turned to the side. Immediately, I felt the loss of his body. I mourned it even though my muscles, especially in my legs and hips, were beginning to cramp.

"Your lips are swollen," he said, discarding the condom, then returning to lie next to me on his side. Matt smoothed his palm from my thigh, over my hip to my chest. Pausing in its upward trajectory, he fondled my breast. His eyes watched his hand, and the possessiveness in his gaze felt more intoxicating than the four cocktails with dinner. "That's why I stopped kissing you," he muttered.

"What?"

"I stopped kissing you because your lips are swollen. They must hurt."

I breathed out an incredulous breath. "Who are you?"

His eyes cut to mine. "You know me."

"Do I? Because, I have to be honest, I wasn't expecting . . . that."

"What were you expecting?" he asked carefully.

"I don't know. But the dirty talk was a surprise," I admitted, tracing his collarbone with my finger, deciding I'd start with the dirty talk rather than jumping straight to, *YOU'RE IN LOVE WITH ME????*

*Since when?*

*Tell me everything.*

*Leave nothing out.*

The side of his mouth hitched, again smugly, and his eyes returned to his hand on my breast. "You said yourself, I'm full of surprises."

"Yes, you are."

"You didn't seem to mind." More smugness.

"I didn't. I don't. I approve." The words tumbled from my mouth because I couldn't say them fast enough.

That made him smile, just briefly, then he swallowed. I watched his profile as the smile melted away and the lines of his face grew stark. He seemed . . . distant. Or rather, reluctantly present but ready to leave. Enigmatic. Like he couldn't decide what to do next and not knowing what to do next was a foreign state for him.

I covered his hand on my breast with mine.

"Matt," I whispered.

"Hmm?" He didn't look at me, his eyes were still perusing my body. It was as if he was trying to memorize the sight of me.

I reached up with my free hand and cupped his jaw, tears stinging my eyes as I admitted, "I'm so in love with you."

Matt's gaze darted back to mine and he blinked, breathing the word, "What?"

"I love you." I also blinked, because my eyes were overflowing with tears. "I love you so, so much."

*Why are you crying, Marie?*

I didn't know.

I honestly had no idea.

Feelings? Whoremones? Maybe a nearby, but as of yet unseen onion?

"You do?" he asked, sounding so entirely stunned, I physically ached for him.

From what I could see through the blurriness of my tears, Matt appeared to be overwhelmed by both thoughts and emotions. Eventually, he released a sudden breath and gathered me in his arms, burying his head in my neck.

I huffed a laugh, returning his embrace, giving in to the euphoria of loving him, and knowing he loved me in return. What that meant, what came next, would have to wait. I was having difficulty breathing. He was holding me too tight.

But, honestly, I didn't mind.

*** 

**WE DRESSED. WE** left. We went back to my place. Matt did two things on the way.

He texted Marcus and Kerry, letting them know we'd left and that they would have to find their own way around tomorrow.

He kissed me. A lot. On my neck, face, shoulders, arms, hands, wrists, fingertips, and sometimes mouth. But he did so gently, like he was still concerned about my lips.

We were kissing as we entered my apartment, as he reached for the light switch and turned it on, as I reached for it immediately after and turned it off.

"Marie—"

I slid my hands under his shirt, whispering, "Let's make love in every room."

He made a grunting noise. Actually, it was more of a groan-grunt of helplessness. "Yes. We definitely will. Multiple times. But first," he caught my wrists and held them between us, "first I want assurances."

"Assurances?"

"Promises. Or oaths. Vows will also do." Though his words struck me as silly, his expression was stern.

"About what?" I tried to twist out of his grip, to touch him. He wouldn't let me.

"I need to know." His breathing changed as he stared at me. "When? When did it happen?" Matt loosened his hold on my wrists, bringing my hands to his neck. I was beginning to suspect he liked it when I touched him there. "What did I do to make you love me?"

I grinned, pressing a quick kiss to his mouth, loving that I could now do that whenever I wanted.

"You were yourself."

His eyes told me he didn't understand. "Meaning?"

"No. That's it. I love you, for being you."

He stood straighter. "Then when did it happen? What triggered it?"

Studying him, his furrowed brow, the displeased turn of his mouth, I felt perplexed. A prickle of concern tickled the back of my neck.

"Matt, love doesn't work that way. It's not a binary system of on or off. It's not a 0 or 1." I smoothed my hands to his shoulders and then his arms, gripping him tightly should he try to abruptly move away. "It can be sudden, or so I've heard. But the love I have for you, what I feel for you, wasn't 'triggered' by any one thing. I love you . . ." I paused, because he flinched a little at the words *I love you*, making my heart rate tick up. So I repeated, "I love you, because of who you are. Because of the man I've come to know. I love you."

He was shaking his head before I'd finished speaking. "How many people do you love, Marie?"

I searched his eyes for a clue as to where he was going with this. "I don't know. I've never counted."

"Do you love Fiona?"

"Yes."

"How about Quinn?"

"Yes . . ." I was glaring at him now, my fingers having relaxed on his arms.

"How many more?"

"What's your point?"

"I love one person. And she's standing in front of me." This statement sounded accusatory, belligerent.

"Are you—" I dropped my hands, stepping out of his grip, "—are you saying my love is worth less because I love many people?"

"I'm saying you are exceptionally gifted at loving people, even when they're undeserving of it."

*. . . What?*

*WHAT?*

Okay, that?

That made me mad.

"Wow." I backed away from him, feeling like I'd been slapped, like my lungs were suddenly on fire. Looking everywhere but at Matt, I tried to find the lid to my temper. It had suddenly blown off. "Okay. Wow. Wow."

"It's not an insult."

"The *fuck* it's not." Placing my hands on my hips, I angled my chin and met his eyes. "But you're not insulting me. You're insulting yourself. And if you wanted to make me angry, that was the fastest way to do it."

He glared at me, his head turned slightly to one side like he was bracing for a blow. "You're too generous." His voice was deep, quiet, just above a whisper.

"No. I'm not. *You* have self-worth issues." I punctuated the word *you* by pointing my finger at his heart.

He swallowed, wincing, but said nothing, and I knew I was right. I was so right. I was the rightest I'd ever been about anything.

And my rightness made me feel like screaming. It made me want to grab him and shake him until he understood how remarkable he was. How kind, good, clever, thoughtful, intelligent, sexy, wonderful—just everything.

"You. Jerk." I shook my head, pissed off beyond reason. "You think you're not amazing, but you are. And, sure, I could stand here and make a list of all the reasons I love you, of all the ways you are special and awesome, so hilarious and witty, and brilliant, and—" I cut myself off, shaking my head faster. "Nope. I'm not going to do that. Because if you don't believe these things about yourself, nothing I say is going to change your mind. I'm not going to force you to drink the water, Matt. Even though you should DRINK THE DAMN WATER!"

He swallowed with effort, like something was stuck in his throat. A long moment passed, my shouted words seeming to echo in the apartment, between us. The silence wasn't deafening, it was remarkably quiet and still.

Eventually, he cleared his throat. "I know I'm smart," he said, like it was a concession, like he was willing to admit one positive thing about himself, but no more.

My chin wobbled and I had to hold my breath for several seconds to keep myself from crying.

Staring at him—staring at his exceptional and expressive eyes, so stubbornly skeptical about his own value—I realized that loving someone who doesn't love himself was like being stabbed, and having no way to stem the flow of blood. I was helpless in the face of his own indifference.

Only he had the power, and my powerlessness increased my frustration.

*Stupid, fucking dehydrated horse!*

He took a step toward me. "Marie—"

"Do you think I'm stupid?" I asked.

"No. Of course not. I don't think you're stupid." He reached for me and I let him slide his hands around my waist.

"Do you think I have poor judgment?"

He hesitated.

I opened my mouth, prepared to yell at him again.

"You were going to let a stranger dry hump you."

I heaved an aggravated laugh. "A man I'd carefully vetted, with multiple sources, and had spoken to over the phone several times, and who'd been vouched for by more than one personal friend. Do you know there are dry humpers in Chicago? There are lots. I didn't feel willing to meet *any* of them. This guy was the only guy. The *only* guy."

Matt furrowed his brow. "I didn't have all that information."

"So you don't trust my judgment?"

"I do. I do trust your judgment."

"Do you think I'm a liar?"

"No. I don't," he answered right away.

"So when I tell you that you are amazing, that you are exceptional, do you believe me?"

He hesitated, and I saw a fierce debate war within him.

"Fine. Here's the thing, you need therapy."

He lifted his chin, the sudden flash in his eyes told me he was about to argue.

I rushed to add, "You need to love yourself. Because, if you can't love yourself, then I can't count on your love for me."

"Wait a minute, no." His tone was hard, edged with resentment, as though he resented that I was questioning his love for me. "You cannot possibly believe that I don't love you. I'm—"

"You said yourself that people need to be needed. And pride, the fear of rejection, makes the love offered meaningful. If you don't love yourself, if you don't see your own worth, then what are you risking by loving me?"

Matt snapped his mouth shut.

"My love—" I paused and took a deep breath to calm down, because I realized I was still yelling. Forcing composure into my voice, I started again. "My love is worth a lot. A. Lot. Because I know I'm awesome."

The side of his mouth hitched reluctantly, his eyes warming as they moved over my face. "True. You are."

"I. Love. You. I love you, Matt. I'm in love with you. I'm desperate for you. I think about you all the time. Did you know I have a crush on your chin? I love your chin. And your brain gives me lady-boners. I've been walking around with a serious case of blue bean for months."

He huffed a laugh, his eyes turning glassy as he again swallowed with effort.

"But," I gathered his face between my hands, holding him with reverence, hoping he'd witness and accept the admiration and adoration in my eyes, "I refuse to have you question your value. In doing so, you insult me. If you want to be with me, you're going to have to find a way to accept that you're not just worthy of great love, and you don't just deserve great love . . ." I pressed a kiss to his mouth, and then whispered against his lips, "You must demand it."

I didn't miss how he'd fisted his hands into the fabric of my dress as I spoke, or how his gaze grew agitated with anxiety, or how he leaned closer, hovering, anxious.

"So . . . " he cleared his throat, visibly hesitating; I got the sense he was afraid to speak his next thought.

"Nothing you say is going to make me stop loving you."

"What if I told you I was a Slytherin?"

"I would still love you."

"What if I—"

"Matt. Say it. Ask it. Speak. Trust me, but also trust yourself. Trust you're worth me fighting for."

His eyes shone with emotion. "I want us to be together. I want to be with you, all the time, from now on."

"Good. Me too." I couldn't have stopped my smile or my sudden happy tears even if I wanted to. I had to press my lips together—again—to fight the wobble of my chin.

"What if I don't go to therapy?" he blurted, swallowing. "What if I don't want to? Will you . . ." he tugged me closer using the fabric of my dress, "do I have a choice?"

"Yes. Of course. It has to be *your* choice. If you don't want it, I can't force you."

"But you could." Matt's signature sincerity usually made my heart melt, but this time it broke my heart instead. His voice was thick, roughened with anguish and a hint of resentment. "If you told me I had to, in order for us to be together, I would."

I was shaking my head before he'd finished, whispering because I didn't trust my voice. "Please don't. Don't do that to me." I lifted my chin to give him a kiss. "Don't shift your responsibility to me. That's not fair, and that's not who you are."

Matt studied me, his eyes moving between mine. Eventually, he nodded, releasing his fistfuls of my skirt and sliding his arms around me. As he pulled me to him and we embraced, I felt the tension drain from his body.

"Thank you," he said, the words muffled as his mouth was pressed to my shoulder.

"For what?" I smoothed my hand up and down his back, needing this, needing to hold him. Loving that I could.

"For being you." He placed a kiss on my neck, adding roughly, "For loving me."

# CHAPTER 26

**Falcon Heavy and the Dragon Space Capsule**

*The rocket and the capsule (respectively) that will be used to take the first two space tourists around the moon. Projected launch 2018.*

Source: SpaceX

WE DIDN'T MAKE love in every room on Friday night. Instead we stripped naked and cuddled in my bed. I had so many questions. I wanted to know *everything*, what he'd been thinking over the last few months, when he'd realized he loved me.

But we didn't talk. We held each other with touches meant to comfort rather than arouse.

However, on Saturday, we made love in every room. All day. I didn't have many surfaces in my apartment, so each was christened a few times by Sunday morning and with wild, abandoned enthusiasm—which left me speechless. I hadn't expected him to be so . . . so . . . talented at making me come. Every. Single. Time.

Marcus had been right. Matt was a boss in the bedroom. He was precise and verged on domineering, frequently making me wait until I begged for relief. But his bossiness was an aphrodisiac, as was his dirty talk. Both demolished my brain's predisposition to worry. He told me how much I pleased him. And since he demanded control, I happily surrendered to his enthusiasm for worshiping my body.

But, again, we didn't talk, not about anything substantive. And that was fine with me, because we used the time to settle into the idea of us as an *us*. It felt necessary, and I got the sense we were both protective of the newness, of the wonder of finally having admitted the truth to each other.

Early Monday morning, when he left me, Matt pledged to contact me in the afternoon about dinner and plans for the rest of the week. We hadn't touched on the topic of therapy again after our talk on Friday, so I was surprised to receive a text mid-afternoon Monday.

**Matt**: *I have an appointment this Wednesday with Thomas. Sandra recommended him.*

I knew of Thomas. Sandra claimed he was a gifted adult psychotherapist and had spoken very highly of him many times. She even had the image of his face on two of her custom-printed T-shirts. Don't ask.

I frowned at Matt's message for several minutes, sorting through my feelings on this announcement—the surprise, then happiness, then apprehension—before messaging him back.

**Marie**: *I hope you're doing this for yourself.*

**Matt**: *I am doing this for myself, because myself wants to have more sex with yourself.*

Despite the faulty reasoning of his text, I laughed. As I was typing to tell him he needed to revaluate his priorities, he texted again.

**Matt**: *And I'm doing this because I suspect you are as wise as you are beautiful.*

**Matt**: *I want to deserve you.*

My heart twisted and I pressed the phone to my chest, sighing. I could almost see him, the heartfelt intensity in his eyes.

**Marie**: *You *do* deserve me. And I will keep reminding you until you believe me.*

**Matt**: *I look forward to being reminded.*

**Matt**: *Dinner tonight?*

**Matt**: *I'll cook.*

After I recovered from my shock, I quickly typed,

**Marie:** *Matt? Cook? Does not compute!*

**Matt:** *I anticipate conducting a system-wide diagnostic on you tonight, AF 709.*

AF 709?

*. . . Hmm.*

That sent me to *Wikipedia*, which had me looking at a picture of Julie Newmar playing the role of AF 709—Rhoda the Robot—a very, very sexy life-sized android in the short-lived TV show *My Living Doll.*

*Ahh, the 1960s. So astonishingly sexist.*

And yet, overflowing with splendid role-playing ideas.

***

"IS THIS A joke?"

"No."

"Marie . . ." Matt shook his head, his mouth moving with no sound emerging, his expression one of extreme confusion and disbelief. "You *friend-zoned* me."

He said *friend-zoned* like I'd reported him to the IRS for a tax audit.

"Matt. Come on." I shook my head, rolling my eyes before taking a sip of my wine. "I invited you over here to cuddle. On. My. Bed."

It was Monday night. Matt was standing in my kitchen, chopping vegetables for homemade tomato sauce. He claimed he only knew how to make three dinners: lasagna, meatloaf, and grilled anything.

I was sitting at the countertop, enjoying the view, and had finally broached the topic of why it had taken him so long to make a move.

"What was I supposed to do? Force my lascivious attentions upon you? Send dick pics? Hope the sight of my cock would bring you to your senses?" With each question his irritation eased into good-natured teasing. "And, as data collection for future seducing efforts, will that work?"

I had to take a deep breath before responding, because Matt said the word *cock* so easily. He didn't say it often. In fact, this was the first time he'd said it outside of sexy times, but I hadn't yet grown accustomed to it coming from his mouth.

I hadn't grown accustomed to his dirty talk during sex either. Though I hadn't yet told him how much I enjoyed his skill in this area, I got the impression he knew anyway.

"How much more obvious should I have been?" I challenged.

"No, no, no. There is no *obvious*. Not after a friend-zone maneuver. A friend-zone maneuver is the end of a book, not the end of a chapter. It's the nuclear weapon of maneuvers. Short of flat-out telling me you wanted to change the nature of things between us, or stripping naked and ordering me to pleasure you, I wasn't ever going to catch on to any hints."

"You seriously had no idea? How is that possible?"

"Friend zone. Friend. Zone. Otherwise known as The Scoreless End Zone."

"I only did that because you said you weren't interested in long-term relationships."

He gave me another look of incredulity. "What?"

"You said you were finished with long-term relationships. You said you'd read that book, blah, blah, blah. In fact, when I asked you if you ever wanted to get married again, you said *hell no*."

"*That's* the reason? That's why you friend-zoned me?"

"Yes. I even told you that, if you recall, that night I saw you at Sandra and Alex's and you walked me to the hospital so I could visit Quinn."

He blinked at me. "I thought that was just an excuse."

"What? Why?"

"Because. You weren't that into me. I thought you were lying to spare my feelings."

I choked on air. "Is *that* a joke?"

"No. Not a joke." His attention moved back to the mushrooms he was chopping, and he laughed.

"Matt, you said you didn't want anything long-term with anyone."

"We're now stuck in a recursive loop. I am the chicken, you are the egg." He scooped up the mushrooms and added them to the big stockpot, stirring a few times with a wooden spoon, then replacing the lid, letting the contents simmer.

I huffed, feeling enormously frustrated by my inadvertent—though well-meaning—self-sabotage. "Do you mean to tell me, you've been open to a relationship with me all this time?"

He hesitated, coming around the counter and standing next to me, stealing a sip of my wine. "Define relationship."

"Falling in love. Being together. Long-term."

"No." He shook his head once. "You are correct. I wasn't open to that. Not when we met."

"Oh. Really." I crossed my arms, lifting my chin. "So what did you have in mind when we first met?"

"So many things." He wagged his eyebrows, grinning wickedly around another sip of wine, then added more seriously, "To be honest, I thought you were a long shot. I wasn't open to a relationship with anyone and I couldn't imagine a scenario—even before you friend-zoned me—where you would want something like that with me."

"Why? What made you think I was a long shot?"

His head reared back. "Have you met yourself? You're . . . intimidating."

"What? No I'm not."

"You are. Your confidence is intimidating, because it's entirely valid. And your goodness. And," his gaze blazed over my body, "the rest of you."

That had me smiling, so I forgave him for stealing my wine. "When did you change your mind?"

He didn't respond right away. Instead, he finished my glass while he shifted his eyes up and to the left. Abruptly, his gaze cut back to mine and I got the sense he was bracing himself for my reaction.

"I changed my mind when I came home and found you and Jack in the hallway. Last month."

I stiffened, my heart giving a twinge of protest at the memory, and I dropped my eyes.

*Crap.*

"Marie."

I really didn't want to talk about this. I didn't want to be reminded of him with another woman, not when my feelings for him had been so strong, even then. It felt like he'd cheated on me, on us. Rationally, I knew he hadn't, but once again, believing and knowing were two different things.

"I don't want to talk about this." I shook my head.

"Too bad." His hands came to my shoulders, pulling me up from my stool. "Look at me."

I didn't look at him. "I was so mad. And hurt." My heart gave another painful lurch.

"I love you."

"Sorry." I shook my head, more resolutely. "I don't think I can talk about this."

"We have to."

"Why?" I glared at him. "Why do I have to talk about the night I found out you'd been sleeping with other women?"

"Because I don't need therapy to know *not* discussing things that bother you is a terrible idea." The set of his jaw struck me as remarkably stubborn.

*Damn his pushing! Why can't he just let me be the dehydrated horse this time?*

"We can discuss it later." I shrugged out of his hold and walked the pithy distance to my living room.

"Or we can discuss it now, and have make-up sex after."

That earned him another glare.

He glared back, not looking contrite.

"Fine. I'm angry that you slept with someone else when we were spending so much time together."

*Aaaand* I was yelling. But once I started, I couldn't stop.

"I rented a car and drove to my parents' house three hours away," I pointed in the general direction of where they lived, "and cried on my mother's shoulder for fifteen minutes. Do you know how much that pissed me off? I haven't cried to my mother about anything since I was in elementary school and Rhena Davis said I smelled like a dumpster."

Matt twisted his lips to the side. "That bitch. Rhena Davis is the one that smells like a dumpster."

"I'm serious," I raged. I was then unable to keep the hurt out of my voice as I added, "You slept with someone else and it hurt. A lot. Exorbitant hurt. Don't make a joke out of this."

"I didn't."

"That wasn't a joke?"

"No, I mean—" he crossed to me and lifted his hands to touch me but I flinched away, causing him to release a frustrated sigh and pull his fingers through his hair, "I mean, I didn't have sex with her. We kissed, but that's it. I haven't been with anyone since the crazy lady two years ago. There's been no one until you."

Startled, my mouth fell open and I blinked at him for several seconds as this information permeated my brain. "You didn't?"

"No. I didn't. But," he reached for me again and I let him hold my arms, "yes. That was my plan. I'm not going to lie. Being with you all the time and not being able to . . ." He ground his teeth. "Not being able to touch you, be close to you, not in the way I wanted, was extremely frustrating. As much as I loved being with you, I hated how I felt after we spent time together."

"How did you feel?" I asked numbly, trying to keep up.

"Not good." He released a humorless laugh. "Like I wasn't good enough, for you to—"

I cut him off with a kiss, unable to bear the rest of his words, and wrapped him in a tight hug. His hands came around me, immediately sliding to my bottom and squeezing, pressing my hips to his. But then in the next moment he'd ended the kiss, cradling my jaw in his palms.

"I'm not finished."

"This is difficult to hear." My stomach hurt, thinking that I'd caused him misery simply by being with him. "I want to make it up to you."

"Then listen."

I nodded, covering his hands with mine, bracing myself. "Okay. Okay. Tell me."

"When I spotted you in the hall, I was happy to see you, as always. But then, you looked upset. Really upset. And surprised. And that confused me. But it also gave me hope."

"Oh." I blinked some more, processing his words and trying to figure out how I felt about them.

"You were who I wanted, and you were also unobtainable, off limits. But when I saw how upset you were, I made her coffee, apologized for wasting her time—admitted I was hung up on someone else—and sent her home. I texted you about coming over. You told me not to."

"That's what made you change your mind about long-term commitment? Seeing me hurt?"

"No. Not just seeing you hurt. I considered what it would feel like to see you with someone else." Matt released another harsh laugh. "And, I have to tell you, it made me feel like shit. I hypothesized there existed a possibility that you were thinking about me the same way I'd been thinking about you, given the way you reacted. And if that was the case, if you were even a modicum as infatuated with me as I was with you—"

"Infatuated?"

"Besotted."

"Besotted is better." I nodded encouragingly.

"If you were besotted with me, even a very little, or were willing to give me a chance at something real, then I'd be an idiot not to try." Tilting my chin up, he brushed a soft kiss against my lips, his tongue darting out at the last moment to taste me. "I had to do everything in my power to convince you to love me back."

"Oh, Matt." My fingers slid to his wrists, my heart fluttering. "Why didn't you say something? When we went for coffee that Monday? Why not tell me all this then?"

He gathered a deep breath, his hands falling from my face, responding flatly, "You asked me to set you up with Dr. Merek."

I winced. "Oh. Yeah. I forgot about that."

He shook his head at me, giving me a look of teasing disgust. "How could you?"

"What? He's cute. I like his beard," I teased back.

Matt's mouth fell open with more teasing disgust. "He's a *psychologist*, Marie." Then, whispering loudly, he added accusingly, "It's one of the soft sciences."

I scoff-snorted. "Kerry was right. You are a snob."

He smiled, I smiled, we smiled at each other, and then I released a sigh. Even though I hadn't realized I'd been carrying around this burden of frozen feelings, with the exhaled breath I felt myself thaw.

"See? Aren't you glad we talked about it?"

"Yes. You were right. I'm glad we . . . resolved that."

"Is it resolved?" he asked imploringly, his expression turning stern. "We have to do things in order. I don't want to have make-up sex until all the arguments are done."

"But if we save some arguments for later, we get to make up more than once." I reached for the waist of his jeans, widening my grin.

Still frowning down at me, although now it looked more like a suppressed smile than a frown, Matt's hands lowered to my thighs, skimming his fingertips up the back of my legs. "You're brilliant."

"I know."

He placed a featherlight kiss on my neck. "I love you."

"I know that, too."

"Talk to me, Marie." His arms came around me once more, squeezing. "You have to talk to me, even when it hurts. Nothing will be right between us if you don't."

I nodded, returning his embrace. "I will," I said, knowing that not every argument would have a happy ending. Yet, I trusted his goodness. I trusted he'd never knowingly hurt me, and I hoped he likewise knew I would never knowingly hurt him. That trust meant we had to give each other every opportunity to prove the other right.

\*\*\*

"I DON'T UNDERSTAND why you didn't take Quinn up on his offer to hire a cleaning service." Greg was holding his youngest daughter, now eleven days old, while helping his son sort through the materials list for middle school and order the items online.

"Because, Mr. Fiona, it's more meaningful if we clean the apartment, because we do so with love. And Quinn and Janie will have to suffer through our love tomorrow." Sandra was at the kitchen sink, washing the refrigerator's crisper drawers. All the perishables were on the counter and Alex had bagged up the spoiled or old food for the trash.

Meanwhile, I was wiping out the inside of the fridge, scowling at a very stubborn, crystalized bit of goo. "What is this? I'm going to need a jackhammer."

It was Tuesday evening and we'd all convened for our usual knit night gathering. But instead of knitting, we were cleaning Fiona and Greg's apartment, making them dinner, and doing their laundry. Quinn and Janie were the only ones absent, but we'd made plans to clean their penthouse tomorrow.

Drew and Ashley had driven up from Tennessee. They were only staying for three days, but it was wonderful to have them even for a short period of time.

"The second bathroom is finished." Kat walked in, wiping her brow with the back of her hand. "I think we only have vacuuming left, but I want to wait until Fiona wakes up."

"Is Dan still re-organizing Grace's toys?" Sandra tossed over her shoulder. "Who knew he'd be so into color-coding Barbie doll shoes and arranging dream house furniture."

Greg made a discontented face, but said nothing. I knew he didn't like the fact that Grace owned Barbie dolls; he felt they perpetuated unrealistic and unhealthy ideas about female beauty.

"He was helping me in the bathroom." Kat reached for the solo cup with her name on it and filled it with the filtered water from the door of the fridge. "But, yes. Now I think he's with Grace in her room, helping organize the toy bins. Elizabeth and Nico are in there, too."

Sandra and I shared a look, but said nothing. She'd also noticed the ring on Kat's finger. We'd all noticed at this point, but neither Dan nor Kat were ready to fully discuss the situation.

"Where is Drew?" Alex finished tying the two trash bags, addressing this question to Greg. "Is he back from the hardware store yet?"

"Yes, now he and Ashley are in Jack's room folding the laundry." Kat refilled her cup.

"Has anyone seen our neighbor?" Greg asked the room. "Or have you seen my phone?"

"Who? The weirdo that tricked Marie into a date?" Sandra wrinkled her nose.

I paused my work, my neck heating and my heart doing the twist and shout. I hadn't yet told anyone about Matt and me. Everything was very new. And everyone was very busy. And it hadn't come up.

"Professor Simmons is a weirdo?" Jack glanced between his dad and Sandra.

"Everyone in this room—you included—is a weirdo." Greg shifted his infant daughter from one shoulder to the other. "He said something about stopping by today when I saw him yesterday morning, but I was too delirious to remember you were all coming over."

"Well then. I'll just go over there and *un*-invite him." Sandra placed a washed drawer on a towel next to the sink.

Bracing myself, I faced the kitchen. "Don't do that—"

"Be nice." Alex sent his wife a look as he hefted the two trash bags over his shoulder. "He's cool."

Kat made a scoffing sound, crossing her arms. "I'm with Sandra. I still don't like how he treated Marie."

I shut the fridge. "He didn't—"

"What did he do?" Jack's eyes were now rounded with the interest of a nine-year-old finally allowed to take part in adult discussions.

"It's a long story." Greg's voice was grumbly and tired as he scratched his chin. "Why don't you pick a backpack? How about this Madame Curie one?"

I moved to the middle of the kitchen and summoned my courage. *Why do I feel so nervous about this?*

"I want Minecraft." Jack turned his attention back to the laptop.

"Ada Lovelace, you say?" Greg closed the computer. "Minecraft wouldn't even be possible without the mother of computer science. Take this into the other room and pick out a backpack that will make you proud twenty years from now. Go."

Jack dutifully grabbed the computer and left the kitchen.

Twisting the rag I'd been using to clean the fridge, I gathered a deep breath and said, "Matt—Professor Simmons—and I are together."

Sandra and Kat stiffened, their eyes swinging to me, stunned shock written all over their features.

"What?" Sandra breathed, turning off the water.

"Oh?" Alex shared a look with Greg; if I wasn't mistaken, they were both hiding smiles. "What a surprise."

Sandra's gaze cut to her husband. "You knew?"

He shrugged, glancing at Greg again.

"*You* knew?" This came from Kat and was directed to Greg.

"Who knew what?" Dan strolled into the kitchen and walked straight to Kat, stealing her solo cup and taking a long drink.

"Marie and Matt—Fiona and Greg's next-door neighbor, the guy at the hospital last week—are dating. They're together." Sandra sounded incredulous and wiped her hands on a towel with exaggerated movements.

"Oh. Yeah. I knew that." Dan nodded. "Nico told me."

"What?" Kat, Sandra, and I asked in unison.

"How did Nico find out?" Sandra swung her eyes to me. "Did you tell Elizabeth?"

I shook my head, but before I could answer, Dan said, "I think Drew told Nico."

"Oh my God." I shook my head, so confused. "How did Drew find out?"

"From Quinn," Alex said as he strolled out of the kitchen. "Quinn told me, too."

"Well then, who told Quinn?" Kat rubbed her forehead.

"I did." Greg patted his daughter lightly on the bottom, soothing her.

"Then who told you?" Sandra placed her hands on her hips.

Greg kissed his daughter's forehead. "Matt."

"Matt told you?" I stood straighter, feeling surprised and . . . touched. "When did he tell you?" I kinda liked that he'd told Greg. It made me feel warm and fuzzy.

"Yes. Matt told me, yesterday morning after I remarked on his gleeful walk of shame."

"Walk of shame?" Sandra's eyes darted to me, amusement and question written all over her features.

"Yeah, he was wearing the same suit he'd been in Friday night."

"Go, Marie!" Dan stepped forward and offered me a high five, which I returned numbly, amazed at how quickly these men shared information with each other.

And, by the way, why would any of them be interested in who I was dating? It didn't make sense.

Greg picked a piece of lint off his jeans, looking smug. "But I knew before he told me."

Kat glanced at me, then back to Greg. "How?"

Greg smirked at Kat, then at Sandra. "It was written all over his face last week, for anyone who was looking. Fiona called it, too." Then to me he said, "We've been gossiping about you two all week."

"You and Fiona?" I smiled, relieved that Fiona knew. I hadn't been looking forward to telling her, not after she'd warned me away from him weeks ago.

"She's thrilled." Greg returned my smile with a soft one of his own, seemingly reading my mind. "She had her reservations, but seeing you two together at the hospital was all the assurance needed. We couldn't be happier for you both."

Standing in front of the kitchen sink, Sandra was shaking her head, her eyes unfocused. "Okay. I'm so confused. About so many things. First of all," she pointed at me, "I need the whole story. When did this happen? I didn't even know you liked him. And secondly," she turned to Greg, "what is the deal with you guys and the efficiency of your man-gossip phone tree?"

Greg gave her a droll look. "Don't be a hater, Sandra. You ladies need to learn how to communicate more effectively."

Kat laughed, shaking her head. "This is nuts."

"What I don't understand is why you told Quinn to begin with." I turned back to the fridge, allowing my face to show how perplexed I was about Matt and me being a topic of conversation.

"Are you kidding?" Greg stood and began swaying back and forth, shaking his head at me. "Marie. You saved my life last spring. You saved both Fiona *and* me. You organized Quinn and Janie's entire wedding. If memory serves, you also threw a tequila bottle at those Boston guys who showed up to grab Janie a few years ago, spurring everyone into action and effectively saving every woman in this room. Of course Quinn wants to know. And Alex, and Drew, and Nico, and—"

"And me." Dan moved to refill Kat's solo cup, adding simply, "You're a hero, Marie. We want to make sure this guy is good enough."

Inexplicably, emotion clogged my throat, robbing me of my ability to do anything but swallow for a few moments before I managed, "You'd do the same for me. You all would."

"Exactly." Greg nodded once, sending me a soft smile that looked foreign on his typically sardonic features. "Which is why I told Quinn as soon as I found out. We're looking out for you, kid. And don't you forget it." But then added, "And now you and Fiona have more in common."

I sniffled, prompting Kat to cross to me and place her arm around my shoulders. "How so?"

"Now you've both seen Matt's penis."

# CHAPTER 27

### Retrieval Robot

*A robot that is swallowed and used to collect dangerous objects ingested accidentally. The device is based on foldable robot technology, where the robots fold up, a bit like origami, into small structures less than a few millimeters in diameter so that they can be swallowed like tablets. Then, once inside the body, the capsules enclosing the robots dissolve, allowing the devices to unfold, and reconfigure themselves to retrieve the object.*

Source: Massachusetts Institute of Technology (MIT)

AN OPPORTUNITY FOR Matt and me to prove our trust in—and good intentions for—each other arrived earlier than I'd anticipated.

Once again, we were at my apartment. He said he liked it because it felt like a home. Whereas, other than a few of Grace and Jack's drawings hanging on his walls, his place felt like a pit stop.

Presently, he was sitting at the kitchen table, his hands in his hair as his mouth moved wordlessly, as though reading to himself from the computer screen. I was sitting on the floor by the couch, using the cushions as a surface for my storyboarding notes and biting on the end of my pen.

The cuddling story was done and sent, as was the dry-humping piece. The OM appointment was set for two days from now.

"You know, they have programs for that."

I glanced up from my papers. "For what?"

"Storyboarding."

"Oh. Yeah. I know. But I like this better. I can see my notes, what I've written, and it reminds me of what I was thinking at the time." I frowned at the paper in my hand. It was from a phone call a few weeks ago—just before my trip to New York—with my writing partner.

Tommy had attended an OM session in San Francisco and had already sent me his notes. However, we'd decided to split up the last two paid services. He took the life coach and I was supposed to hire an escort.

But, again, that was weeks ago, before everything had changed.

"You look troubled."

I didn't look up this time. "I'm . . . debating."

"Anything I can help with?" I heard his laptop close and the scrape of the kitchen chair on the floor as he stood.

Taking a deep breath, I let the phone call notes fall to the floor and leveled Matt with a bracing stare. "I'm supposed to hire an escort to take me to David's engagement party."

He stopped, mid-movement, his eyes widening to maximum diameter as he stared at me. "Come again?"

"For my story about paid services. I'm supposed to hire a male escort." Rubbing my eyes, I sat back on the carpet and sighed.

"Well . . . okay. That's interesting."

That made me laugh and I lifted my eyes to his, finding him smiling at me. "So, what am I going to do? I agreed to do this before things changed between us."

"Do you want to do this?"

"No. Yes. I mean, I don't know. I *want* to finish what I started. I want to finish writing these pieces. This whole series was my idea and it's getting a lot of great feedback. I'm really proud of it."

He nodded all through this. "Okay. Then, you should do it."

"Really?"

"Yeah." He shrugged. "As long as you feel comfortable, then—if you're asking about my feelings—I'm fine with it."

I gaped at him. "I can't believe you're okay with this."

"Why not?"

"Because, honestly, if the roles were reversed, I would *not* be okay with it. I would absolutely not want you to hire a female escort for work, or research, or anything else."

Matt smirked at me. "Jealous?"

"Hell. Yes. I don't want anyone touching you but me. And if that makes me possessive, then so be it."

His smile widened. "You know you can trust me."

"I know. But it would still piss me off." Recognizing this about myself, and being able to communicate as much to Matt without having to worry about upsetting him was . . . amazing. Truly revolutionary for me. I'd never had that with anyone. And I appreciated him so much for it. The trust between us was a gift.

And so, I decided I wouldn't hire an escort. If I couldn't handle seeing him with a female escort—even for work—I felt it was unfair to ask that of him.

He was laughing at me, at my freely admitted covetousness, crossing to where I sat, and lowered himself to the floor. "I have no plans to hire an escort."

"And no female companion robots, either." I lifted my index finger and pointed at him. "None of that."

"Don't worry. We're going in a different direction. At least, I am. I'm focusing on a Compassion AI for foster kids. One that will be assigned to them as soon as they enter the system and stays with them through to adulthood."

I straightened, blinking at him, my heart emitting a burst of heat that traveled down my arms and up my neck. "Oh."

He met my gaze evenly, a small smile on his mouth. "I think that's where I can do the most good." He'd drawn his legs up, his elbows resting on his knees.

"I'm sure you will." Cupping his jaw, I kissed him on the mouth, then on his cheek. "I'm so proud of you. You are amazing."

"Oh? Tell me more." He caught my hand before I pulled it away, holding it against his face. "Leave nothing out."

"Well, not many men would be cool with their girlfriends hiring an escort for research. But, it doesn't matter, because I won't be—"

"I think it'll be interesting. Besides, I have questions, too."

I stiffened. "Um, what?"

"Yeah. Once Quinn and Alex thoroughly vet him, the three of us can go. We'll just update our RSVP numbers with your ex."

A burst of laughter escaped my throat. "You want the *three* of us to go? To David's engagement party?"

"Yep." He nodded once, his tone still even but a glint of devilry lit behind his eyes.

"Matt."

"Oh wait." His mouth fell open in a cartoonish movement. "You thought I'd be okay with you hiring a male escort and going out on your own?"

I pushed his shoulder, wrinkling my nose at him.

He caught my wrist. "Oh, no. No. That's not going to happen. No way. Not unless you take one of my terminator robots."

Laughing again, I tackled him to the ground. He could have resisted, but he totally let me. "Listen to me! I will not be hiring a male escort. Not now, not ever." I kissed him, nibbling on his delectable bottom lip, then lifting my head. "If I can't handle the thought of you hiring a female escort for research, then I can't ask you to be okay with it for me. That's not fair, and that's not right."

"Thank you. I appreciate that." I was lying atop him now. He pushed a hand into my hair and used his other arm as a pillow. "So what are you going to do?"

I rested my elbow on his chest and my chin on the palm of my hand, considering him. "I'll have one of the other staff writers do it. It wouldn't kill me to have another contributing writer. And I can re-interview the guy I was going to use—over the phone—and maybe a few of his colleagues."

He nodded, his eyes on where his fingers combed through my hair. "If this compromise bothered you, you would tell me. Right?"

"Right. But this doesn't bother me. This feels right."

"Good." He took a deep breath, and when he exhaled, it sounded relieved. "I'm glad you changed your mind about that other thing."

"What other thing?" I kissed him again. I couldn't help it. His lips were addictive, so close to that chin I loved.

"The orgasm thing."

I stared at him, my body tensing. "What?"

His eyes cut back to mine. "The orgasm meditation place."

"Um . . . " I tilted my head to the side. "No. I'm definitely doing that."

"Excuse me?" His hand stilled in my hair and the wrinkle I found so adorable appeared between his eyebrows. "You're not."

"Yes. I am."

After a protracted pause, he rolled me to the side, his fingers digging into my hip. "Marie. I'm definitely not okay with you going to an orgasm meditation place and getting fingered by some stranger."

"Matt—"

"No. If you do this I will be really fucking pissed off." His voice lifted with each word, and the way he was moving his jaw told me he was serious.

Really fucking serious.

I tried not to smile, but it was impossible. I loved how angry this made him. And what did that say about me? Clearly, I was still crazy Marie. Sick-in-the-head Marie. Loony Marie. The wearing-a-sweater-dress-in-mid-May, and running-after-my-hopes Marie.

His eyes moved over my face and he clenched his teeth. "Is this funny?"

"Listen, just listen to me—"

Abruptly, he sat up, shaking his head. A flush had appeared high on his cheeks.

*Jeez, he's really pissed.*

*. . . Yay!*

"Matt."

He shoved his fingers into his hair, causing an accidental and haphazard Mohawk. "I can't look at you right now."

I reached for his arm. "There's no touching, Matt. No one is going to touch me. It's all instructional. No one was ever going to touch me."

He stilled, moving just his eyes to mine. Several seconds passed. Then a few more.

"What?"

I sat up and straddled his lap, wrapping my arms around his neck. "They don't allow people who arrive without a partner to stay for the actual meditation. I was always going to go just for the instructional sessions. No one was ever going to touch me. That was never going to happen." I finished by rubbing my nose back and forth against his.

He released a huge breath, wrapping his arms around me and squeezing tightly. "You're going to pay for that."

I tried not to laugh, but it was difficult. Rolling my lips between my teeth, I snuggled closer, whispering in his ear, "I love you, Matthew Simmons. And I don't want anyone but you to power on my CPU."

***

"I'LL START." MATT lifted his hand.

I glanced at my boyfriend askance.

"Okay, Matthew, why are you here?" The OM instructor turned to Matt, her smile looked gently encouraging.

I shook my head subtly, disbelieving of . . . well, everything that had happened since I woke up.

The day had begun like any Monday. Matt had slept over and awoken early—as usual—to make coffee and get ready for the day. Except, after making coffee, he'd rejoined me in bed. And that's when he'd informed me that he'd contacted the OM studio and added his name to the roster. As my partner.

I don't think I actually believed him until we walked into the building and he'd given the receptionist our names. But, here we were, sitting on the floor in a large, spacious room that reminded me of a tastefully decorated high-end yoga studio. And Matt had just volunteered to go first, sharing his reasons for attending the session.

"I'm here because I'm invested in self-improvement, and strengthening my relationship with my partner," he said with his trademark honesty and lack of embellishment.

I kept my eyes studiously forward, trying to mask my smile and the warm blush staining my cheeks. He was the best. The absolute best.

"Thank you, Matthew. Anyone else?"

We went around the room, each person taking a moment to say something about themselves, and explain what had prompted them try orgasm meditation.

One woman shared that her ex-partner had wanted only intercourse, and she'd had a difficult time encouraging him to engage in foreplay, that he would rush or make her feel guilty for wanting it. She said it had affected her relationship with her current partner—who was with her—and that she needed to re-learn how to experience and trust playful touch.

Her partner said he wanted to be supportive and encourage her journey of self-discovery.

One man spoke up to say he couldn't achieve orgasm unless he masturbated and, even though he grew hard with a partner, he could never finish inside someone. He hoped orgasm meditation would help him relax, focus more outwardly, and truly engage with another person.

A few women said they wanted to become more in tune with their own bodies, what brought them pleasure, what they liked.

Another of our group said he was there because he wanted to improve his technique, which drew a few amused chuckles.

One of the couples explained that they'd been in marriage counseling for the last few months, wanting to save their thirteen-year marriage, and realized they'd never really talked about sex, what the other person wanted or expected, so they thought OM would be a good place to start the dialogue.

I swallowed, my throat suddenly dry. I hadn't expected everyone to be so open, candid. I hadn't expected . . . well, *normal,* everyday people.

Part of me had expected exhibitionists and hedonists, horny people looking for a cheap thrill, or damaged people looking for an escape.

Shame on me.

Finally, the instructor turned to me. "Marie?"

I managed a smile, but it felt too big. "I'm here because I want to know more about orgasm meditation," I said, swallowing stiffly. My heart beat strangely in my chest, somehow both racing and sluggish. I felt everyone's eyes on me, as though they expected more. More of a reason for my presence. More sharing. More.

Or maybe I expected more.

From myself.

And maybe that was *my* problem.

"And because," I blurted, bracing but unable to stop myself, "when I'm intimate with someone, I can't seem to stop thinking about whether he's having a good time. I can't . . ." I glanced at Matt, finding him studying me with surprise, but also concern and reassurance. "I worry that I'm being too selfish. And I have trouble getting out of my own head to fully enjoy myself."

As I continued to speak, the surprise dissipated from Matt's brow, leaving a small smile, his eyes infinitely accepting. Compelled by his compassion, I returned his smile with a hesitant one of my own.

"Thank you, Marie." Our instructor gave a small bow, turning her attention to the rest of the class. "You are not alone, and your feelings and worries are not atypical. But the goal here is to feel, without shame or judgment. This isn't about gratification. There is no finish. There is no climax. There is only feeling, trusting, listening to your body, and meditating on the lessons you learn."

\*\*\*

AS I'D TOLD MATT, only the people who'd brought their partner were able to stay for the guided meditation. What I didn't tell Matt was that I was dreading the guided meditation.

Seriously, seriously dreading it.

Those who'd arrived on their own participated in the sharing session, the lectures, and the discussions, but had to leave once the last theory portion was over, which had been my plan. I'd wanted to learn all about the practice, but hadn't wanted to actually *do* it. Not in a room full of strangers.

I didn't want to share that part of our intimacy. I was selfish of him, of us.

So as the day wore on, I grew more tense. I knew he sensed it, but how could I tell him that I didn't want to go through with it? He'd taken a day off work and I was going to, what? Turn his generosity into a waste of his time?

No.

*I can deal.*

*I can power through.*

These were the thoughts on repeat in my head when our instructor warned us that we had five more minutes until the last break was over. That meant everyone who'd arrived alone would be leaving. Matt found me chatting with one of the other couples, doing my best to wear my journalist hat.

He'd excused us both and pulled me away from the group, into the OM studio, to the main room where we'd be doing the guided meditation in a few minutes.

*Gack!*

"I've been doing some reconnaissance." Matt leaned close, whispering in my ear.

It was becoming very real now. Pretty soon I'd be lying on my back with my underwear off, my legs spread and Matt's fingers on me while I did my absolute best to meditate on what my body was telling me . . . I was pretty sure my body was telling me to take my sexy boyfriend and flee.

I glanced around the empty space. "Why are you whispering? We're completely alone. Everyone else is outside in the courtyard."

"It's more exciting if I whisper." He rubbed my back, smoothing his hand from my shoulder to just above my bottom. I'd noticed, since I'd made my confession earlier regarding my fears about being too selfish, he'd been especially handsy. I wasn't complaining.

"Fine," I whispered, playing along. "What kind of reconnaissance?"

"Turns out, some of the people who arrived alone are planning on meeting up later to try out OM without the benefit of the guide."

"Hmm."

"Interesting, right?"

It was interesting. It was *very* interesting, and would definitely make it into my article. "Good job, partner. That's excellent information. Thank you."

His gaze grew intense, as though he was trying to impart his thoughts without speaking them.

"What?"

He sighed, clearly irritated that I couldn't yet read his mind. "Marie. Do you have anything you'd like to say?"

I felt my eyes grow wide and I held my breath, but said nothing.

"Say it." He dipped his chin, his hand caressing me lower, over my backside, sending lovely tendrils of desire unfurling in my belly despite the anxiety churning there.

"I don't want to disappoint you," I blurted.

"And?"

My forehead fell to his chest and I spoke to his feet. "I don't want to stay. I wasn't planning on staying. I want us to leave. I don't want our intimacy to be clinical, not that this would make it clinical, but I'm not ready to do this kind of thing in a room full of strangers. I want hot sex."

His hand had come to my face, cupping my jaw, and he tilted my chin backward when I'd finished.

Gazing at me, a whisper of a smile on his lips, he kissed me once. "Then let's go."

"You took off work."

"To be with you. No judgment for the couples here, but I'd prefer not to digit-tize you in front of people we don't know."

"Digit-tize. Nice."

"I know, right? I'm going to use that one again."

He lowered his head, covering my lips with his, giving me a soft, sensual kiss. He tasted me with a slide of his tongue, moaning into my mouth when I encouraged him to deepen the kiss, pressing my body against him. I melted, becoming more liquid than solid, and twisted my hands in the fabric of his shirt.

Abruptly, tugging on my hair, he broke away with one last biting nip. "I love you, Marie. And I want you to be selfish with me."

Giving in to my smile, I nodded. "Okay. Then, when we get home, I want you to make dinner."

"Sounds good."

"Naked."

He paused, one eyebrow lifting in surprise. "Sounds good."

"And then, after dinner, I want you to talk dirty to me."

Matt's gaze grew hooded and he entwined our hands together. "Why wait until after dinner?"

*** 

LATER, CLOSE TO midnight, while we were lying in bed together—cuddling, naked—I traced the outline of his handsome face with my fingertip, feeling amazement.

Here. Now. Touching him as I pleased. My heart swelled with the sweetness of it, with gratitude. I hoped I would never take these moments for granted, never take him for granted.

"You like my face." He sounded certain.

"No. I love your face."

"I love your face, too. And your bosoms."

That made me laugh, and I dropped my hand to his cheek, "Look at me."

He complied, his eyelashes fluttering open until his gaze focused on mine.

"Beautiful," he said, the single word full of wonder. Abruptly, his hand began stroking my hip and bottom, as though the sight of me made the action compulsory.

"Thank you."

"No. Thank you." His eyes followed the progress of his fingers as they slid to my lower belly, then up to the valley between my breasts. "Tell me something."

"What?"

"Tell me what you want me to do to you."

"How about you finally administer that questionnaire?" I teased.

His hand paused and his gaze jumped to mine. "Ah. Yeah. About that."

"What? Don't tell me you don't want my data."

"Oh, I do. But I can't have it."

"Why not?"

"Because we were explicitly forbidden from becoming involved with anyone who signed a consent form for the study."

It took a while, but the full weight and meaning of this revelation finally sunk in. "You mean, you didn't consent me or administer the questionnaire, all this time, because you wanted—"

"To impregnate you. Yes."

I smacked his shoulder lightly and chuckled at his silliness. "Because you wanted to be with me."

He ducked his head, also smiling. "Exactly."

"You are something else." I was unable to stifle my grin or the delighted heat coursing through my veins.

"I kept putting it off. At first I told myself it was because I wanted you to feel comfortable with me, so you'd give me honest answers. I also told myself I was being so nice to you, hanging out with you so much, for the same reason. But then," his gaze moved back to my body and he lowered his head, placing an achingly tender kiss between my breasts, "then I stopped lying to myself and admitted the truth. I wanted you, all of you, all the time."

"Even more than you wanted to work?" I teased.

"Yes." He nodded somberly, his focus still on my body, and I threaded my fingers into his messy hair.

"It's funny." He placed another kiss on the side of my breast, saying absentmindedly, "People, when they're connected to the cloud—the Internet—they zone out on real life. But an AI can only function when it's connected to the cloud, because they have no real life. They are more real to us than they are to themselves."

"That's deep, Professor." I tugged on his hair, forcing his eyes upward.

"It's seductive, to live in a virtual space, especially when the real world isn't what you want it to be." His gaze moved over my face, and I got the sense he was speaking mostly to himself as he said, "You—being with you—was the first time I wanted real life over a virtual existence. You distracted me. I'd never been distracted before."

"You distracted me, too."

His stare sharpened, finally focused on mine as he positioned himself above me, an imposingly masculine presence, making my heart quicken. My legs fell open to cradle him as he lowered his strong body to mine and gave me a playful kiss.

"I want vacations with you," he nuzzled my nose, "with no Internet connection."

I mock-gasped. "Are you sure we're ready for that kind of step?"

He licked my bottom lip and rubbed his growing erection against my center. "I want candlelit walks on the beach and sunset dinners."

"There's something wrong with your user interface," I said on a pant, instinctively tilting my hips, chasing the feel of him. I was going to correct him, tell him it was candlelit dinners and sunset walks on the beach, but speech suddenly failed me.

He grinned. "Oh?"

"Yes. You need to input the device."

"Why?" His eyes danced as he moved above me, making me crazy.

The need was building within me. I couldn't focus on words when he rolled his hips like that. Nevertheless, I tried to tease, "I need more RAM."

Matt barked a surprised laugh and then devoured my mouth with a hungry kiss just before sliding into me, filling the empty ache between my thighs. I gasped for real this time, tilting my pelvis to take more of him as he pulled away and planked above me.

"You want this firmware?" His voice deepened to a reprimanding growl as he stroked me unhurriedly, making me crazy.

"Yes, please. Hard drive, hot sync, boot disk, computery words." I arched my back, my eyes closing. I could take no more of the sight of him above me, it was too much.

"You are so fucking sexy." His movements were slow, deliberate, rhythmic. It was the best kind of torture.

"Harder. Please," I begged, my breath hitching.

He didn't comply, instead demanding, "Tell me you love me."

"I love you."

He increased his tempo, but kept his thrusts gentle. I whimpered.

"Tell me there is no end to us."

"There is no end."

Matt rewarded me with a rough roll of his hips, making me cry out.

"Tell me this is forever." His voice was tight with restraint and emotion, causing me to open my eyes.

Immediately, I was arrested by his expressive, gorgeous gaze, equal parts possessive and vulnerable. Reaching for him, I guided his mouth to mine and kissed him once, my hands sliding down his back.

"I'm yours. Forever."

"And I'm yours." He swallowed, so earnest, so sincere.

"You are my person," I whispered, feeling the rightness and inevitability of the words.

He huffed a laugh, made complex with unspoken desires and hopes, and nodded. "Yes, Marie. I am your person."

I felt emotion prickle behind my eyes and my mouth curved into a beaming smile. Goodness, how I loved this man. This funny, sweet, amazing, remarkable man. I loved how he made me feel, like I was the most beautiful woman he'd ever known, both inside and out.

He not only felt right, he felt like he'd been made especially for me. And I for him.

For the first time in my life, I was encouraging my hopes. I allowed them to run and fly. To the sky. To the stars. Because that's what my life was going to be from now on.

Matt, me, and perpetually soaring hopes.

# EPILOGUE

### Mind-Reading Robot

*MIT's Computer Science and Artificial Intelligence Laboratory made a robot that responds to a human's brain signals. The robot can sort various objects, making choices based on the brainwaves of a person wearing an EEG (electroencephalogram) cap who is watching the robot work.*

Source: Massachusetts Institute for Technology (MIT)

### *Meet Matthew Simmons*

INVENTION IS THE fruit of desire and/or disinterest. Most people don't realize, but desire and disinterest are closely related.

Desire as a motivator is obvious—think rocket ships and porn. Disinterest as a motivator is less obvious, but might be the more powerful of the two. We humans *hate* to be inconvenienced.

As an example, I've always been disinterested in clothes. The quality of, trends of, price of.

Winter, I needed to be warm.

Summer, I needed to be *not* naked, yet still clothed. Because of laws.

But now, shopping for clothes is one of my favorite things to do.

"I like this tie on you." Marie held up a strip of silk against me, her knuckles brushing along the fabric of my shirt, and tilted her head to the right side. "The color brings out your eyes."

"Does it?" I captured her hand, holding it in place against my chest, and stole a kiss. She tasted like cherries because she was wearing something cherry flavored that made her lips shiny.

"Yes. It does." Marie smiled, her face close to mine.

She did this. When we shopped, she looked at me for a prolonged period of time. She touched me, often. She stood close, sometimes she whispered in my ear.

Thus, I didn't shop for clothes, I shopped for the process of shopping for clothes.

I remain disinterested in clothes. Except for suits.

The buying of the suits months ago was done with one goal: make Marie think of me in suits, which—according to her own admission—were synonymous with non-platonic thoughts.

I now know—now that we'd discussed everything after the friend-zoning in great detail—that she'd been having non-platonic thoughts about me well before I'd worn my first suit, and that the suits hadn't been the catalyst for her feelings.

But I still wore them.

Because Marie liked me in suits. She looked at me differently. She looked longer. And showing her she's worth the effort is important. *She* is important to *me*.

"Do you even need a new tie?" She stepped away, regarding me with suspicion. "Didn't we just buy you four last month?"

"I don't recall." Obviously, that was a lie. "We have the faculty dinner next week and I need something for that."

"None of the other ones will suffice?"

"I should make a good impression. Most of them still think I'm an undergrad."

I've come to understand clothes matter to most people because society decrees how a person is 'packaged' reflects the internal values, abilities, and personality of that person. This packaging is often called 'personal expression.' Since deciphering this, I've resented the concept of personal expression.

As a child, what did my clothes say about me?

They said: I'm irritated that you people want to judge me by what I'm wearing and therefore I think you're really fucking lazy.

But they also said: My housekeeper does my laundry; she irons everything, including my jeans and T-shirts. My gardener likes grunge bands and always brings me concert tees. My driver thinks I should wear belts with shorts. And my nanny picks out my clothes.

However, when I became a teenager, I realized actually not giving a shit and wanting to look like I didn't give a shit were two very different style choices.

Funny how that happens. Funny how, in order to project to the world who you are, you're often required to behave in an opposite way. But I digress.

My disinterest in clothing was the catalyst for my first AI. Instead of allowing myself to be forced into spending precious minutes (daily) to ensure the clothes I wore reflected my internal values, abilities, and personality, I developed an algorithm to do it for me.

Using data available via image search and defined parameters regarding individuals whose style I wished to mimic, the program created a virtual closet of clothes. I sent the closet to my mother's personal shopper and had her purchase the items in my size. The housekeeper then arranged the purchased goods (complete outfits) on hangers in my actual closet. Instead of thinking about what I should wear, I outsourced that decision based on coded procedures.

Because I was disinterested, because I desired to save time.

The unintended consequence of this little time saver was a big cash payout. I showed it to the computer science mentor my senior year of high school. He showed it to a friend. That friend showed it to a group of angel investors. They wanted it, but not a teenager as a CEO.

So I sold the program upon my eighteenth birthday, thereby allowing me to sever all connection to my parents. I haven't spoken to either of them in twelve years. I'm not sure they've noticed.

Thomas—my shrink—told me their disinterest in me had everything to do with their own psychosis and nothing to do with my value as a person. I believe him, primarily because he's the expert. He has a Ph.D. And even though I still think of behavioral science as a soft science, the guy knows his shit.

Secondarily, I believe him because I respect him, because he is both intelligent and good. All data indicates he is to be believed.

But, again, I digress.

I pushed my fingers into my pockets, a trick I'd learned early on when in close proximity to Marie. It helped me keep my hands to myself. I made a mental note to never again shop on a Saturday. The store was busy and I couldn't touch her where and how I wanted. Because of laws.

My left hand connected with a small velvet box within my pocket. I fiddled with it, twisting it, running my finger along the seam.

The box.

It had been in the pocket of whatever pants I was wearing since the weekend after Kerry and Marcus had visited. Since Marie told me she loved me. Not wanting to plan something cheesy and elaborate, I'd been waiting for the right moment.

She shook her head and returned the tie to the table. "I think you have a tie habit."

I shrugged, not denying it, instead allowing a slow meaningful smile to claim my mouth. I did have a tie habit and we both knew it. Ties were versatile in their applied uses. As an example, I had more ties in her nightstand drawer than I had in my closet.

"You're bad." Her smile mirrored mine, though her cheeks were now pink.

"You like me bad." I bent forward to brush my lips against hers.

She gave a wistful sigh. "Come on, let's go."

"Where are we going?" I let her tug my hand from my pocket and pull me towards the exit.

"You're taking me to lunch, and then home. Fiona gave me a new cake recipe and I've been wanting to try it."

That had me standing straighter and my mouth watering. When it came to Marie's cooking, I was a Pavlovian dog. "What kind of cake?"

"You'll see."

I rearranged our hands so that our fingers were woven together. "If it's her coconut cake, we should definitely buy a new tie."

"Why?"

"I'll have to tie you up until you agree to marry me."

She laughed and time stopped, just a little.

Pragmatically, I knew it was impossible for time to stop *just a little*. Time is relative, and can be slowed—theoretically—but cannot be halted. Not outside of a particle collider experiment gone horribly wrong and/or a black hole.

But when Marie laughed, when her mouth curved in a perfect arch, when her eyes became the combined colors of hydrogen on the visible light spectrum, when the manifestation of happiness as perfect music passed her lips, then time stopped.

Just a little.

I've never been a funny guy, not purposefully. Not until Marie. Not until I heard her laugh for the first time. Everything about it was addictive. You have to *want* to talk to people in order to have an occasion to be funny, and there were only two things I enjoyed as much as talking to Marie.

One involved her cooking, the other involved her body, and both involved eating.

***

"I KNOW WHAT I like." I shrugged, licking my lips, poised to pounce as soon as she finished pressing the white shavings to the frosting.

I have no shame when it comes to—

"Coconut." Her tone was flat but also teasing, and she lifted an eyebrow at me.

"Yes." I was hovering, but no aspersions ought to be cast on account of my hovering. She knew how I felt about coconut before she made the cake. Nothing about my hovering should have been surprising.

"You're coconut crazy. For your birthday, I'm going to get one of those coconut bras."

I blinked and then stared at the most amazing woman on the planet (not a controversial claim). "That would be so awesome."

She chuckled, wiping her hands on a towel.

I was already reaching behind her for the plates. "Are you finished? Can we eat—"

"Na-ah," she pushed at my chest, backing me out of the kitchen. "Not yet."

"What?" I sounded panicked because I was panicked. I'd been forced to watch her bake for the last three hours, the alluring aroma of toasted coconut and baked coconut permeating the air.

And now we weren't going to eat it? Perhaps she was a closet sadist.

*I can work with that.*

Marie steered me into the bedroom. "I want you to take off your clothes."

I immediately removed my shirt and then unbuckled my belt, not needing to be told twice. "Please tell me we're going to eat that cake naked," I bent to her ear and whispered while I unzipped my pants, "off each other."

"No." She shivered, then she added, "Maybe. I don't know. Possibly."

I kissed and then bit her neck.

She shivered again. "Okay, yes. We can do that. But first," she braced her hands on my shoulders and held me away, "first you need to lie on the bed."

I lifted an eyebrow at her command and the nervous tremor in her tone. "Marie . . ."

"Please?" She was biting her lip now and had dropped her hands from my arms, twisting her fingers. "I need to do something and I need you to lie down."

I inspected her. She was definitely nervous. "Okay. Fine."

Stepping out of my pants, I lay on the bed as instructed, tracking her every movement as she reached into her nightstand with lightly shaking fingers and pulled out a length of rope.

She reached for one of my hands and I stiffened. "What's the rope for?" She'd never tied me up before.

"It's not rope, see?" Marie trailed the edge of it over my abdomen, placing her knee on the mattress next to me. "It's knit, and made of silk and bamboo."

"It's fancy rope."

"Now we won't have to ruin your ties."

"I don't consider them ruined."

She huffed. "It's very soft."

"It's soft, fancy rope."

Marie set her teeth and glared at me. "You've tied me up. Why can't I tie you up?"

"After months of being regulated to the friend zone, I don't like the idea of my movements being restricted."

The side of her mouth lifted, but her glare persisted. "Listen, just give me five minutes, okay?"

I examined her, the stubborn set of her jaw, and her appearance of anxiety. "Why are you nervous?"

She huffed again. "You'll find out once I tie you up."

"You'll release me if I ask?"

"Of course." She touched my wrist again and this time I allowed her to secure me to the headboard. Once that was done, she reached for my other wrist and tied it as she straddled my waist, her breasts—sadly still encased in her dress and bra—were in my face.

Testing the knot twice, she jumped from the bed and searched the second drawer of the nightstand. Apparently finding what she was after, she straightened and faced me, her hands behind her back, looking very serious.

"Matt."

"Valkyrie."

A hint of a smile relaxed her features as she sucked in a large breath. "So, we've been dating for a while."

"Not long enough."

"And I—I—what?" Her face fell. "What do you mean not long enough?"

"Just that we should have started dating sooner."

"Oh." She nodded, the movements of her eyebrows telling me that my words had disconcerted her.

I crossed my ankles. "Why aren't you naked?"

She shook herself. "Oh. No reason."

"Then why am I naked?"

"Because I didn't want you to be suspicious."

That made my eyes widen and made me suspicious. "Suspicious? About what?"

"Stop rushing me. Let me say my thing." Marie stood straighter and lifted her chin, her eyes darting over my body. "And stop doing that."

"Doing what?"

"Flexing your . . . muscles."

"I can't help that muscle. It sees you and flexes all on its own."

She slid her teeth to the side and cleared her throat, her eyes now studiously focused on mine. "So, as I was saying, we've been dating for a while now and I think things between us are going very well."

That made me frown. "That's a severe understatement of fact and is therefore an imprecise ascribing of value."

She must've liked my argument because she grinned. "I'm glad you feel that way."

"It's not a feeling, it's a fact."

Marie laughed. The sight and sound had me relaxing further on the bed.

"Okay, so it's a fact. And given the *facts*, I think it's time we moved—or at least we considered moving—on to the next step . . ." her smile dwindled until it left her eyes absent of humor and full of hopeful anxiety, ". . . in our relationship."

Before I could question her meaning, she placed one knee, then the other on the bed and knelt next to me, withdrawing a blue velvet box from behind her back. I stared at her, not masking my confusion, as she opened the box and revealed a set of gold square cufflinks with engraved wavy lines.

"One is sine, the other is cosine. One is you, and one is me." Her typically melodic cadence was now tight with nerves. "Marry me?"

I stared at her—at her spectacular eyes, presently both gray and green—my mouth embarrassingly agape, finally managing to say, "You . . . ?"

"Want to marry you." Her voice broke, wavered, but she nodded with certainty. "I love you, Matt. I love you completely. I want to spend the rest of my life with you and I hope that you—"

"Stop." I shook my head, closing my eyes, squeezing them shut. "Damn."

This wasn't how it was supposed to happen.

Seven months.

I'd been carrying that ring around for *seven fucking months*.

And she distracts me with coconut, gets me naked, ties me to a bed, and proposes.

"Damn."

I felt her shift on the bed, heard her breathing change, and my eyes flew open. To my everlasting regret, the hopeful anxiety in her expression had been replaced with confused hurt. Thus, my growl of frustration couldn't be helped.

"No, Marie. No. Don't make that face. Don't have those thoughts. You don't know—listen, stop. Grah!" I pulled against the bindings, wanting, needing to reach for her.

But I couldn't.

Because she'd tied me up with soft, fancy rope.

Taking a deep breath and releasing it carefully, I lifted my chin towards my pants where they lay discarded on the floor. "Can you bring me my pants?"

"Of course." She nodded jerkily, closing the box on the cufflinks and shoving them back in her drawer, then darted to my jeans.

I watched her rushed movements, having to grit my teeth to keep from spewing profanities. She placed the jeans over my middle, as though to hide my nakedness, and the action drove a frustrated laugh from my lungs.

Great.

Just . . . *great*.

With still shaking fingers, she untied my right wrist. "I'm sorry. I should have gone with my original plan."

"Original plan?"

"I was going to bake the cufflinks in the cake." She sighed, shaking her head. "But, see, well, Janie and Quinn got engaged after he tied her up, and you said that thing about tying me up until I agreed to marry you and I just thought—I thought—I guess I don't know what I thought."

With my right hand free, I shoved it into the left pocket of my pants while she worked on the other wrist.

"And if you need time to think about it, I completely understand. I know it was sudden. But I saw the cufflinks and it felt like—I don't know—a sign? So I got them and—"

Now that both of my hands were free, I caught her around the waist and pulled her down, laying her back on the bed and rolling over her.

"Marie," I kissed her quickly. "You never cease to surprise me."

She nodded, her brow still knit with worry. I kissed her again, deeper, because she tasted *awesome* and it felt like the right thing to do in the moment.

But before things could get out of hand, I lifted my head, placed the box— *the box*—on her chest, popped it open, and showed her the ring inside.

And improvised.

"Marie Harris, I don't want to think about my life without you. You are the sine to my cosine, and those cufflinks are perfection. So is your cooking, everything you make is perfection. And delicious. And you're delicious. I love how you taste. I want to taste you now. But first, I have to finish saying this. I love how you feel. I love your bravery and honesty, I love how fucking smart you are—sorry for cussing while proposing, but you are so fucking smart— and how good, how deeply, deeply good. And sexy. Petabytes of sexiness."

Unable to restrain myself, I kissed her again, noting that her mouth was open and it took her a few seconds to respond because—clearly—I'd shocked the hell out of her.

Leaning away, I pushed my fingers into her hair and looked straight into her eyes. "To put that quantity into perspective, one petabyte is one million gigabytes."

"Oh," she said, the word more breath than sound.

I sucked in air, suddenly nervous for reasons I couldn't presently comprehend, and prepared to ask the question I'd been wanting to ask, but hadn't because I'd wanted to wait for the right moment.

"Marie, will *you* marry *me*?"

She released a short exhale, her eyes darting between me and the ring, her smile growing massive, and nodded. "Yes. Yes. Of course!"

In the next moment she reached for my face and brought my lips to hers. We kissed while I surreptitiously removed the ring from the box and slid it on her finger. I wanted her wearing that ring as soon as possible. I'd waited long enough. But now I understood, I shouldn't have waited.

Because every moment with Marie might not be perfect, but it would always be the *right* moment.

### -The End-

# About the Author

Penny Reid lives in Seattle, Washington with her husband, three kids, and an inordinate amount of yarn. She used to spend her days writing federal grant proposals as a biomedical researcher, but now she writes books.

Published in 2017, 'Dating-ish' is Penny's 14th novel.

**Come find me-**

**Mailing list signup**: http://pennyreid.ninja/newsletter/

(get exclusive stories, sneak peeks, and pictures of cats knitting hats)

**Facebook**: http://www.facebook.com/PennyReidWriter

**Instagram**: https://www.instagram.com/reidromance/

**Goodreads**: http://www.goodreads.com/ReidRomance

**Email**: pennreid@gmail.com …hey, you! Email me ;-)

**Blog**: http://pennyreid.ninja

**Twitter**: https://twitter.com/ReidRomance

**Ravelry**: http://www.ravelry.com/people/ReidRomance

(if you crochet or knit…!)

## Read on for:

Penny Reid's **Booklist** (current and planned publications)

Acknowledgements, links, and resources

# Other books by Penny Reid

<u>Knitting in the City Series</u>
(Contemporary Romantic Comedy)
*Neanderthal Seeks Human: A Smart Romance* (#1)
*Neanderthal Marries Human: A Smarter Romance* (#1.5)
*Friends without Benefits: An Unrequited Romance* (#2)
*Love Hacked: A Reluctant Romance* (#3)
*Beauty and the Mustache: A Philosophical Romance* (#4)
*Ninja at First Sight* (#4.75)
*Happily Ever Ninja: A Married Romance* (#5)
*Dating-ish: A Humanoid Romance* (#6)
*Marriage of Inconvenience* (#7, coming 2017/2018)

<u>Winston Brothers Series</u>
(Contemporary Romantic Comedy, spinoff of *Beauty and the Mustache*)
*Truth or Beard* (#1)
*Grin and Beard It* (#2)
*Beard Science* (#3)
*Beard in Mind* (#4, coming 2017)
*Dr. Strange Beard* (#5, coming 2018)
*Beard Necessities* (#6, coming 2018)

<u>Hypothesis Series</u>
(New Adult Romantic Comedy)
*Elements of Chemistry*: ATTRACTION, HEAT, and CAPTURE (#1)
*Laws of Physics*: MOTION, SPACE, and TIME (#2, coming 2018)
*Fundamentals of Biology*: STRUCTURE, EVOLUTION, and GROWTH
(#3, coming 2019)

<u>Irish Players (Rugby) Series – by L.H. Cosway and Penny Reid</u>
(Contemporary Sports Romance)
*The Hooker and the Hermit* (#1)
*The Pixie and the Player* (#2)
*The Cad and the Co-ed* (#3)

# Acknowledgements, links, and resources

## A Note from the Author

If you've read any of my books, you know I enjoy weaving current events, unresolved ethical issues/questions, and shenanigans into the stories. My characters are always different people at the beginning of the story than they are at the end of it, because I take them (and you) on a journey of discovery.

The idea for this book was borne out of discussions with my single female friends, who have often lamented the quality of single men they've encountered. One of my recently married friends, when she was single, would frequently argue, "It took me seven years to find a car I actually like driving. What makes me think I'll find a life partner in less than that?"

One evening I posed the question: if you could replace a human companion with something else, would you? The responses I received were as varied as the women themselves.

I hope you enjoyed Marie and Matt's adventure. ♡

## Links and Resources

Orgasm Meditation
As far as I know, there is no company called *Single Sense* that teaches OM. But there is a company named *One Taste* that trains people how to conduct OM (orgasm meditation). I used the text from their website—word for word—to describe the procedure/act/purpose of OM in chapter 6.
http://www.womenshealthmag.com/sex-and-love/orgasmic-meditation
http://onetaste.us/

Cuddling
*The Cuddle Sutra* is a real book (proper title: *The Cuddle Sutra: An Unabashed Celebration of the Ultimate Intimacy*). I bought it for research (for *Dating-ish*) and my husband and I tried out several of the poses. We found it to be really sweet. I recommend it to try with your partner (or companion robot). However, the website and studio described in *Dating-ish* (CuddleBuddies.com) were both fictional. Sadly, my husband didn't want me to visit a real cuddle salon and I respected his wishes.
There are a few companies that do offer to pair clients with professional cuddlers, which are below:
http://thesnugglebuddies.com/
https://www.cuddlecomfort.com/

ROBOTS!!

All the other robots and AI mentioned in this book (the Japanese nurse robot, etc.) other than Matt's prototype are all real. None of them were made up. DeepMind (Google) was—for me—the most fascinating of the AI projects I researched. Specifically, this article:

http://uk.businessinsider.com/google-deepmind-aggressive-gameplay-2017-2?r=US&IR=T

I could likely spend the next 30 or so pages waxing on and on about AI, robotics, and the ethical issues surrounding automation, but I won't. I like you all too much.

'Til next time.

−Penny Reid